The Bad Neighbour

The Bad Neighbour

The Bad Neighbour

Jennie Ensor

This edition produced in Great Britain in 2023

by Hobeck Books Limited, 24 Brookside Business Park, Stone, Staffordshire
ST15 0RZ

www.hobeck.net

Copyright © Jennie Ensor 2023

This book is entirely a work of fiction. The names, characters and incidents portrayed in this novel are the work of the author's imagination. Any resemblance to actual persons (living or dead), events or localities is entirely coincidental.

Jennie Ensor has asserted her right under the Copyright, Design and Patents Act 1988 to be identified as the author of this work.

All rights reserved. No parts of this book may be used or reproduced by any means, graphic, electronic, or mechanical, including photocopying, recording, taping or by any information storage retrieval system without the written permission of the copyright holder.

A CIP catalogue for this book is available from the British Library.

ISBN 978-1-915-817-09-9 (ebook)

ISBN 978-1-915-817-10-5 (pbk)

Cover design by Jayne Mapp Design

https://jaynemapp.wixsite.com

Are you a thriller seeker?

Hobeck Books is an independent publisher of crime, thrillers and suspense fiction and we have one aim – to bring you the books you want to read.

For more details about our books, our authors and our plans, plus the chance to download free novellas, sign up for our newsletter at **www.hobeck.net**.

You can also find us on Twitter **@hobeckbooks** or on Facebook **www.facebook.com/hobeckbooks10**.

Are you a thriller seeker?

Bookouture is an independent publisher of crime, thrillers and suspense fiction and we have one aim – to bring you the books you want to read.

For more details about our books, our authors and our plans, plus the chance to download free novellas, sign up for our newsletter at www.bookouture.net.

You can also find us on Twitter @bookouture or on Facebook www.facebook.com/bobooks810

For my step-children, John and Lauren

Part One
2020

Chapter 1
Bird Woman
3 March

A strange thing happened a few minutes ago. I was coming out of the shed when a bird – possibly a magpie, it was hard to tell in the fading light – flew over from the woods, circled once above the cottage then dropped out of the sky like a stone. In all the years I have watched them, no bird has ever done such a thing.

Some might consider it an omen. This sunset sky is suitably ominous, aglow with intense yellow-green strands as if it was wired with neon.

I must turn in soon. The family of thrushes woke me before dawn, clamouring for a place at my bedroom windowsill.

The blackbirds and parakeets have visited again, and the sparrows are still building a nest in the eaves. They took away fragments of my leftover timber. This afternoon I spotted long-tailed tits and a red kite through my binoculars.

The highlight of my day happened while I was putting grains out on the tray, now strapped to the buddleia. A robin flew down and brushed her feathers gently against my cheek, as if to say thank you.

I don't know what I'd do without my birds. People think it is strange for a human to be so close to them, but I'd rather be with birds than most humans.

As usual, I've been repairing the cottage, nailing a piece of wood into the bathroom floor and replacing some rotten window frames. It is a good thing I am a practical woman. The cottage won't have long left, though, unless it gets proper attention. The roof has started leaking again despite all my attempts to patch it. I fear the council might declare it unsuitable for habitation, if they ever come to inspect – and I can't imagine living anywhere else.

My little shack suits me perfectly, tucked into a corner of the woods where people don't go except for occasional ramblers and the postman with increasingly rare letters. I have no neighbours. No one knocks on my door wanting anything from me. I do not have to pretend to have heard of whoever is currently famous or what is on the TV or what the villagers are up to.

Brampton is as good a location as any in which to live, I suppose. The rich perch on their hilltop overlooking the poorer ones like me, scattered about reclaimed marshland among pylons and midges.

All is quiet now, except for a buzzing from the power lines. They are almost obscured by young hazels and alders, which have shot up in recent years. The reduced view from the balcony means I no longer catch glimpses of the river. I do miss watching the water birds. However, there are many excellent observation sites nearby that I must explore further, especially the lake and the hilltop. I expect it will do me good to come out of my hidey-hole for a while.

Chapter 2
Ashley
17 March

Ashley picked up her backpack and opened the front door. Outside, the neat curve of semi-detached houses basked in sunshine. Bay windows and car bonnets gleamed. In front gardens, early blossoms puffed up branches – spring, thankfully, was still carrying on as normal.

Next door, a note was attached to Tara's front gate.

Meeting moved to the green. Please bring your own chair and refreshments.

She glanced across the road to the grassy area that formed the centrepiece of Wilton Close. Damn, the others had already arrived. She heaved a sigh. It was too late to go back and fetch anything; she didn't want to draw attention to herself by being late for the group's first meeting.

Ashley crossed the road and was about to step onto the green when a metallic red mobility scooter whizzed along the pavement towards her. On it was seated a solidly built man with ripples of greying hair. He was hunched forward, his face bearing a resolute expression. She stepped out of the way quickly in case he didn't stop in time. But he veered onto the grass and brought the scooter to a halt a short distance from another man and three women, forming an uneven circle.

She took in the disparate group. Tara was sitting in a stylish wicker chair. A pashmina in a patchwork of startling oranges and pinks was draped over her ample frame. Beside her, a middle-aged, jauntily dressed man in an olive-green waistcoat over a butter yellow jumper was settling into a low-slung picnic chair. He opened the lid of the takeaway coffee cup nestled inside the arm of the chair and scooped off froth with a plastic spoon. Beside him, Scooter Man, seated higher than everyone else. Then a bespectacled, sixtyish woman fidgeting on a stool and a long-limbed young woman in leggings and trainers with a sweat-band around her head, sitting cross-legged on a yoga mat.

With a flutter of trepidation, Ashley approached the circle. She felt less substantial than usual and even shorter than her five feet four inches. Before, she had enjoyed meeting new people. Since moving to this village though, she would feel her body tense as she waited for a sign of acceptance. Some people became awkward or showed hostility when they found out she was married to a man with a different skin colour and religion. Tara, for example.

Soon after Ashley's family arrived in Brampton last year, Tara had invited the four of them over for tea and home-made brownies. The woman had offered up a spate of advice about all aspects of the village before enquiring about the family she was going to be living beside. Ashley couldn't forget Tara's shocked expression as Zac explained he was a Muslim, albeit a 'relaxed' one; a white woman married to a second-generation Pakistani Muslim and their mixed-race children were clearly not her ideal neighbours. From time to time as they bit into impossible-to-resist chocolate brownies, Tara's curiosity had slipped onto her face, as if she was thinking, *What are you doing with him?*

Ashley put down her backpack and prepared to sit down.

6

Immediately, the young woman sprang up, the flat of her hand raised.

'Sorry, you need to sit there!' Sporty Woman pointed to a snip of wool on the grass. Her name was something plant-like, Frond or Fern... 'We all need to be as far apart as possible.'

With a sigh, hopefully inaudible, Ashley shifted her position to the spot indicated, half a metre along. Scooter Man gave her a sympathetic look. He was wrapped inside a rug, his jaw set and his light blue eyes alert, tapping a finger against the Thermos mug on his lap.

'Ashley, so glad you could make it.' Tara's bright voice contained a hint of sarcasm. 'We've run out of agendas unfortunately, but I'm sure you'll be able to follow.' Despite her intention to ignore her neighbour's less-than-likeable traits, Ashley bristled. 'I think most of us know each other already. But for Ashley's benefit, could we run through our names?'

'Hello, Ashley. I'm John.' Scooter Man nodded.

'Hi, I'm Ferne.' Sporty Woman waved, smiling.

Jaunty Man wiped froth off his moustache. 'Greg, pleased to meet you. And this is Ursula.'

'Hello, there.' The older woman sounded stern. She carried on trying to get her stool level.

'Lovely to see everyone, thank you all for responding to my call for volunteers.' Tara opened the notepad on her lap and swept the five with a full-beam smile. Her voice carried effortlessly, probably reaching the dog walker throwing sticks on the opposite side of the green. 'I called this meeting to discuss how we can best support our most vulnerable residents at this time of national crisis. As you all know, from Saturday the over-seventies have been advised to stay inside their homes to stop them catching Covid. We have a lot of elderly residents in the Wiltons, and many need help getting their food and medical supplies. I suggest we start compiling a list of who they are and visit them ASAP.'

'We could bring them some toilet rolls while we're at it,'

Jaunty Man suggested. He had a nasal voice with an American twang.

'Let's not get sidetracked, people.' Tara sounded irritated. 'As I was saying...'

Ashley watched Jaunty Man place some biscuits onto a plate and offer them to John, who helped himself, then lay the plate in the centre of the circle.

'Help yourselves, everyone,' Jaunty Man said as Tara paused for breath. 'Tony made them yesterday – with scrupulously washed hands, of course.'

'Should we be sharing food, Greg?' Tara stared at the biscuits. 'We could be spreading the virus.'

'Before we go any further, Tara,' Stern Woman began, 'I think we should consider the practicalities of meeting like this. As I understand from the government's guidelines, we're supposed to be staying in our homes if at all possible, and having no physical contact with each other.'

Tara's gaze flicked skywards.

'I'm well aware of that, Ursula. That's why we're taking the trouble of meeting here on the green where there's plenty of fresh air, keeping well apart from each other.' Tara looked pointedly at John. 'As you know, some members of the group would prefer not to take part in online meetings.'

'I'm sorry.' Stern Woman – Ursula – looked less than sorry. 'But given we're meeting in order to help the community, we don't want to be accused of going against government guidelines, do we? I suggest we help those members get online, so we can all meet safely.'

John dragged his fingertips down his jaw, showing several days' growth. 'I spend enough time at my computer already, reading emails – and like me, my computer isn't the most reliable of machines.' He gave a rueful smile. 'But in the circumstances...'

'I'll help set you up, John,' Sporty Woman offered.

'Thank you, Ferne.' Tara carried on stroking her pashmina.

After a flurry of exchanges re how the group's next meeting would be conducted, Tara interrupted.

'That's settled then. Our next meeting will be held on Zoom. Ferne will send everyone the link and password. Please put your names and email addresses down on this piece of paper.' She brought out a sheet of A4 paper from her bag.

'Should we be passing pieces of paper around?' Greg asked – mischievously, Ashley guessed. 'We might be passing on Covid. We should write on our own paper.'

Ursula frowned. 'I haven't any spare paper with me and I don't want to tear a page out of my notebook.'

Ashley caught Ferne's conspiratorial smile at Greg. She looked away, unable to shake the nagging fear that she would always be an outsider in this place.

'We should get on.' Tara turned to the next page of her notebook. 'Item two – the area we will cover. Do we want the group to support only residents of the Wiltons? Personally, I think we should extend our remit to those elsewhere in the village—'

'Brampton has two WhatsApp groups already,' Ursula pointed out. 'Do we want to step on their toes?'

'Lots of older people don't do WhatsApp. Besides, most of the messages on there won't help anyone through the Covid crisis, as far as I can see. When I went on one group this morning there was precious little support, just people wanting a chit-chat—'

'Support can take different forms, Tara.' A terse note entered Ursula's voice. 'People are stunned by what's going on, don't let's forget.'

'My mum is so scared of the virus she only goes out at night now,' Ferne pointed out. 'With a sign saying "Keep Away".'

'My husband won't even leave the house,' Greg added. 'He's a little overweight but he's healthy and only forty-two—'

Everyone started speaking at once. Ashley stretched out her legs, resisting the temptation to lie back on the grass. It looked so green and springy... She did her best to maintain an alert veneer while her thoughts turned to her teenage children – Sam's sudden interest in Arabic and all things Muslim, and Layla's long silences of late. Sam was now insisting on being called Samir, as he had been named. Layla had at first welcomed the move away from her London school and had made friends at her sixth-form college, a few miles outside the village, but now seemed troubled again.

'What else is on the agenda?' John rubbed his hands briskly up and down his thighs, bringing her back to the meeting. 'I'm turning to ice. I don't think I can last much longer.'

Laughter rippled around the circle. All agenda items had been covered and all tasks on Tara's list had been allocated. Ashley's job was to design leaflets calling for the vulnerable and the over-seventies to make themselves known, which others would print and put through letterboxes.

'Goodbye, all.' John reversed his vehicle towards the pavement.

Tara waved. 'Bye, John. Keep safe – and no breaking the speed limit!'

The scooter sped away. Tara glanced around the ragged circle.

'We've made excellent progress. See you all next week on Zoom. Look after yourselves.'

'It's getting chilly, isn't it?'

Ferne had turned to Ursula, who was dislodging herself from her stool. Ashley put away her pencil and notepad, watching as Greg joined the two women, and the three walked slowly down-hill together.

'You've been quiet, Ashley.' Tara appeared behind her. 'Is everything all right?' Sympathy flooded her voice.

'I'm fine, thank you,' she replied, irritation welling up. 'I didn't have much to say, that's all.'

'Is Zac going to be working from home?' Tara's large hazel eyes glowed with curiosity. Ashley suddenly felt vulnerable, a field mouse being assessed by a bird of prey.

'We don't know yet.'

'It would be difficult for him, I should think. He's used to getting out and about.' Tara smiled pleasantly.

She said nothing. Conversations with Tara often made her feel clumsy, as if she was under attack. What was the woman trying to insinuate? She liked the idea of Zac being at home on weekdays as well as the weekends. He always worked such long hours. Without his daily commute to the office, they would have time to talk – in theory, anyway.

'At least you and I can get out of the house.' Tara looked towards their houses. 'I feel sorry for people who'll have to be stuck at home shielding, especially those like Elspeth who live by themselves.' She lowered her voice as if Elspeth might be listening. 'You've met her, haven't you?'

Ashley nodded. She'd been invited in to Elspeth's for a glass of wine soon after visiting Tara, and had taken to the elderly woman immediately. In contrast to Tara, with Elspeth one knew where exactly one stood.

'I was at her seventy-eighth birthday party last year,' Tara went on swiftly. 'About sixty people turned up, would you believe? She's impressive for her age – she still dances in the garden every day before breakfast.' Tara frowned. 'I have a feeling she isn't taking this shielding business seriously, though. She told me she's been meeting up with friends while she still can.'

'It must be hard being suddenly cut off from everyone you know,' Ashley said. She checked her watch, feeling a strong impulse to extricate herself from Tara. 'I'm sorry, I have to go. Layla hasn't been well and I have to get some things from the supermarket.'

'I hope she feels better soon. You'd better go and look after that family of yours. Take care, now.'

Ashley turned away. She couldn't help thinking, the less she said to Tara about her family, the better.

11

Chapter 3
Elspeth
18 March

E lspeth pulled her front door shut, checked her tote bag once
more and prepared to make her escape.

Oh no, Tara again. Her neighbour was standing in the
adjoining garden by the dustbins, half hidden by the tower of
cartons, bottles and squashed cardboard boxes balanced precari-
ously in her arms. With admirable deftness, Tara tipped the load
into the green bin.

Elspeth eased open her front gate. At the hinge's loud protest,
Tara stepped up to the fence that divided their front gardens.

'Hello, love.' Tara wore a smart outfit that showed off her
generous cleavage. Clearly, she wasn't staying in today – a
meeting with one of her clients, perhaps. 'How are you today?'

She considered. So far, as days went, this one was decidedly
lacking. Her left ear, judging by the buzzing and whining inside
it, had become home to a particularly stubborn wasp. Her right
foot – bunion and now heel – hurt more than usual, she'd chipped
her favourite mug while washing up and had mislaid her address
book. On top of all that, the world was grinding to a halt.

'Not the best,' she replied.

'This situation is awful, isn't it?' Tara opened her mouth to say more but Elspeth got there first. She didn't want to be the last one to arrive at Mira's, today of all days.

'Sorry, Tara, I can't stop. I'm off to my book group and I'm running late.'

Tara's eyes widened. 'Haven't you heard the news? Boris wants all the over-seventies to stay at home from now on. You're not supposed to be going anywhere.'

'It hasn't started yet!' Flaming Nora. Tara had become a friend as well as a neighbour – but the woman could be so meddlesome, as if she was Brampton's judge and jury. 'We're going to meet up once more to say goodbye.'

'Are you sure that's a good idea? What if one of you has Covid and passes it on to the rest?'

'None of us have any symptoms. We're going to meet in Mira's garden. I hardly think anyone is going to begrudge four old women getting together one last time before we're shut away. Boris isn't going to find out, is he?'

She strode off before Tara could reply. Blasted Boris. What were things coming to, that the over-seventies were being treated like lepers?

Halfway down the hill, she slowed to rest and take in the gloriously green countryside spreading out to a distant horizon. Wilton Close, circling the hilltop, offered the best views in Brampton. What would the village be like now, with Covid on the loose? She wondered what she might find. Setting off again, she wondered if she should have taken the Triumph instead. But getting the old Spitfire going was such an effort lately, and given the state of her hearing it might be safer to walk.

Down on the main road, far fewer cars passed than usual. She carried on, past an unattended bus stop and the strip of shops, nearly empty. Where was everyone? It was disconcerting, like being in a film set.

The High Street was deserted except for a long line of people straggling towards Waitrose. A few wore masks over their noses and mouths. She didn't recognise anyone. Passing the entrance, she nearly collided with an elderly masked woman carrying bulging shopping bags emerging from the automatic doors. The lower part of her face looked like a puffin's beak.

Elspeth hurried on. Everyday life had become surreal.

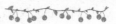

The meeting with her friends was briefer than expected.

After awkward hellos – no one had wanted to hug or stand too close to each other – the four of them set up with cups of tea, sandwiches and blankets in a sheltered spot in the garden and discussed how they would all cope with The Edict, as Lou called the government's shielding advice. Mira could rely on her son and two daughters – they had organised Ocado deliveries for her and set up a rota to collect her medication. Lou had a younger sister who'd promised to pop by every few days with everything needed to sustain life. Alice had her step-daughter and a niece within easy reach.

Mira turned to Elspeth. 'What about you, Else?'

'Oh, I'll manage. I'll order food online from Morrison's.'

Elspeth felt a little anxious. The Green Goddess, where she bought most of her supplies these days, didn't deliver, so she'd have to rely on the supermarket. As an only child without children, she didn't have kindly younger relatives to do things for her – the closest to a relative was her godson, who'd recently moved to New Zealand after years of being a shortish drive away.

When they'd done with tea, Lou, who'd had pneumonia, complained she was going to freeze to death if they stayed outside any longer. They moved into the conservatory, keeping the door open for ventilation until someone complained about a draught.

'So, chaps. It looks like this is it.' Mira poured a small measure of brandy into everyone's glass. 'See you all on the other side.'

Lou knocked back her drink in one. 'You make it sound like we're going into battle.'

'Aren't we?' Alice sounded gloomy. 'Who knows when we'll see each other again? Unless we did a Skype call or something.'

'I'm not sure about video calls,' Elspeth began. Since her hearing loss had started, she had problems with phone calls, whether landline or video.

'That's a good idea,' Mira interrupted. 'Why don't we do a Zoom session? I'll look into it. You'll have to go to the doctor, Else, and get your hearing tested,' she added, louder than necessary.

Elspeth didn't reply. According to her friends at least, her current bout of tinnitus and accompanying hearing difficulties probably meant she was going deaf. She knew she should talk to her doctor about it and see an audiologist. But the thought of having to wear an ungainly plastic lump behind her ears for the rest of her days...

At Mira's front door, another round of hesitant hugging ensued. Elspeth wiped the corners of her eyes and set off for home. She would miss these good-natured chats. One more strand of normality had been severed – for how long?

Elspeth was in the back garden attempting to cut back a mass of dead forsythia stems when Tara waved from the other side of the fence.

'Hello, Elspeth! Did you manage to get a home delivery slot with Morrisons?'

'They didn't have any left.'

'Surely, they could find you a slot. Did you tell them you're over seventy and shielding?'

Elspeth considered telling Tara the whole saga. How her broadband connection had kept breaking off, so by the time she'd filled in the supermarket's online form a message had popped up to inform her: *Sorry, we have no home delivery slots available.* She'd phoned customer support but couldn't get through for fifty minutes. Finally, she'd phoned Waitrose. The man on the other end said he would be able to set up a delivery slot over the phone. Just then, the whining in her left ear started up again and she couldn't hear much of what the man was saying. After asking him to repeat his question several times – 'Which cabbage do you want?' it sounded like – she'd ended the call, tossing the handset across the floor.

She released a long breath.

'I've spent all afternoon trying and got nowhere.'

Tara stepped closer to the fence.

'I'm more than happy to help out. I can pop into the supermarket and the health-food shop once or twice a week and pick up whatever you want.'

Elspeth frowned. She was feeling more ancient and incapable by the minute, but was reluctant to have any sense of obligation towards Tara. Although the two had become friends over the years, this was more out of necessity than desire, in Elspeth's view at least. Tara could be good company but had a tendency to over-react to things, like the year Elspeth had forgotten Tara's birthday, and had overlooked inviting Tara to her impromptu summer party. Tara had sulked for days afterwards. It was more like the behaviour of a neglected child than a fifty-something woman. Also, it was rather disconcerting how from time to time she would stand on her terrace, surreptitiously watching Elspeth while she worked or exercised in the back garden.

'I appreciate the offer, but—'

'Right, that's settled. I'll pick up your meds from the chemist, too.'

Tara clasped her hands together with an expression of triumph and something else, indecipherable. Her eyes gleamed in the early evening light. A region at the back of Elspeth's scalp tingled, as if she'd noticed a huge daddy-long-legs waiting in a corner of her bath.

'Really, Tara, I don't want you to go to any trouble. My prescription is quite complicated—'

'It's no trouble.' Tara smiled and put her sunglasses back on. 'We're neighbours, aren't we?'

Chapter 4
Tara
23 March

O n the TV Boris Johnson was announcing important news, his voice deadly serious. From midnight, people would have to stay at home except for 'shopping for basic necessities, exercise, medical need and key workers travelling to and from work'.

With a groan, Tara turned Boris off. All this sounded draconian, to say the least. How could this tiny 'coronavirus' wreak such havoc? Where would the country end up – and, more importantly, where would she? She poured herself a glass of red wine and popped the last gyoza into her mouth.

She was going to do her bit, as the Prime Minister had requested. She would help the vulnerable in the community in their hour of need. The residents of Brampton would appreciate her more as a result. This fledgling group could be the perfect way to make herself known further afield... As possibilities flowered, a tingle of excitement grew. What else might it lead to?

First though, she'd have to deal with Elspeth. Tara sighed, reached for her notebook and began to write.

This morning I spent half an hour queueing outside Linda's Pharmacy while one person at a time was let in, then another half an hour on Elspeth's doorstep (she stayed in the hall with the door ajar) trying to sort out what she should and shouldn't have received from her five prescriptions. I got extremely irritated when she informed me that the large paper bag I'd collected was missing the Omeprazole for her digestion, which she had specifically requested. Yet another visit to the pharmacy is needed.

She's managed (with my help shouting instructions over the phone) to get food deliveries set up from Ocado, though she's still dubious about the concept of ordering online. To give her credit, she's texted to say how grateful she is for my help. I'm a wonderful friend and neighbour and she's sorry she was short with me.

Feeling calmer, she put down her pen. Starting a journal had been one of the few helpful suggestions the therapist had made during the years she had consulted him. Noting down troublesome feelings did indeed help to diffuse them – and was considerately cheaper than a therapist.

She finished her wine. Maybe she would venture outside for a stroll, while one could still do such things.

As she passed Ashley's gate, Zac bounded out. She managed to step aside just in time.

'Sorry, Tara! Didn't see you there.'

'Zac.' She took in his trainers, T-shirt and thigh-hugging leggings. 'Did you see the announcement on TV?'

Zac nodded. 'Looks like we're all in for a rough ride.' He sounded distracted. Ahead, Bulldog Man crossed the road onto the green, led by his eager dog.

'Have you stopped going into the office?'

'Yeah, it'll be Teams meetings from now on and no more sessions at the gym.' Zac pressed a button on the electronic device on his wrist. The man was in good shape for his age, she couldn't

19

help noticing. He always wore designer suits, too – the hedge fund he managed must be doing well.

'I'm already working from home,' she said, picturing with a twinge of regret the spacious office off the High Street where once she had met her clients. 'And now I'm in charge of our local Covid support group, I have a lot to keep me busy.'

She gave him a friendly smile with a smidgeon of flirtation. Plenty of women would enjoy spending time with Mr Khan – not just talking, either. Ashley was lucky to have him.

A young man stepped out of number 32's front door to drop a pizza box into the recycling bin – the Khan son. He had obviously stopped shaving, though one could hardly call that mass of facial hair a beard.

'Dinner in half an hour!' Ashley yelled from the hall. Zac shuffled from one foot to the other and pressed his electronic device again.

'I must get on,' he said, stepping away from her.

'Nice to chat with you, Zac.' Tara smiled again. She was about to say something else but her neighbour had sped off with a curt nod. Deflated, she imagined him tripping on a paving stone. How rude!

She shouldn't be bothering with Zac, she knew. Of course he was unavailable, thanks to that non-entity of a wife. Ashley scuttled around the village like a dormouse, too scared to open her mouth.

Tara went back inside and lay on the sofa, ruminating. She didn't feel like going for a walk any more. What did Zac see in Ashley? And why was a woman like that surrounded by family, when Tara had no-one? The other day, while dropping a load into the recycling bin, she'd caught a glimpse of the pair hugging in their living room. The curtains had been wide open and the lights on, so of course people were going to see in... Clearly, Ashley wasn't averse to taunting her less fortunate neighbours.

She let her eyes close, imagining Ashley preparing a meal in the kitchen this very moment, eagerly chopping onions for one of those spice-fests of which the Asian family were so fond – a little too impatiently, given her culinary competence and the sharpness of the knife in her hand. An accident was waiting to happen, surely. She couldn't help smiling as Ashley, with a scream and a gush of blood, brought the knife down hard onto her finger and sliced it cleanly in half.

Alas, it was only make-believe.

The therapist would have had something to say about this, no doubt. *You need to come back and work with me to defuse your violent impulses*, or some such thing.

The memory came swiftly. She felt it tugging, forcing itself on her, and the usual dry mouth and sensation of swaying, being about to fall.

She's standing on a rocky outcrop high up a cliff, peering at the strip of indigo blue sea below. Wind froths the waves, blows her hair across her eyes. The sun is warm on her arms and legs. Noisy birds soar beside the cliffs. A sick feeling in the pit of her stomach. Something bad has happened...

Then she's running uphill, as fast as she can. But her legs are heavy, she can't get enough breath. It's too late. In her ears, a shrill sound, a clamour of wind and shrieks of gulls.

Chapter 5
Bird Woman
30 March

The birds of Brampton were quiet this morning; little of note to report. Humans, however, are showing unusual behaviour.

Few depart in their cars between 7am and 8.30am any more, even on weekdays. By 10am this grassy oval on the top of the hill is churning with people 'exercising': walking around while scrolling their phone screens or lost in the spell of their headphones, stopping to tuck into sandwiches or take in the view. The activity continues until sunset. Fortunately when I arrive, half an hour before dawn, this bench is always empty.

I am getting to know the residents of Wilton Close, the loop of houses surrounding my observation post.

10.00am

The woman from number 33 has come out of her front door. She adjusts the position of the green bin in her front garden, stoops to pick up a fallen plastic wrapper, which she drops into the black bin, then has a long look up at the house next door down the hill, number 32.

Ten minutes later the brown-skinned man and the wiry woman with wayward auburn hair return to number 32 on their bicycles, looking like they need to sit down. (The young male left from the house shortly after 9am, head down and headphones on, and set off at a fast pace. I haven't sighted the young female for two or three days.)

The dancing lady at number 34 has come out with a watering can and a mug to tend to her hanging baskets. As usual, she waves at me.

10.30am

The scraggy-jawed American who likes brightly-coloured waist-coats has emerged like a scarlet macaw from his nesting place, carrying two metal cans. His moustached mate follows, carrying two fold-up chairs, which he places under the cherry tree in their front garden.

The young female who always wears silver trainers and a pink strip around her forehead is shouting instructions from her living room at people on her computer screen.

A woman with short grey hair and heavy-framed spectacles has just hurried past, humming.

The sturdy little man with the bulldog bends down and peers at the base of the lamppost, the dog's lead in one hand and a dog-waste bag in the other.

11.30am

The woman at number 33 has emerged again. Now she is strutting about the oval with a sour face. She has just asked a group of adolescent girls who were sitting on the grass, sharing a packet of chips, to move further apart. Once her back was turned, one of them put up two fingers at her.

Now she is heading over to two young men doing press-ups.

As usual, she ignores me. She is not alone in that respect. I am invisible to most of them, apart from the dancing lady and the man at the butcher's. They are not invisible to me, however. When there are no birds to draw, I have plenty of interesting human material nearby. My sketch pad is filling up, though I still find hands difficult.

The man who lives down the hill has not yet sped past on his electric vehicle, scattering any elderly people who happen to be on the pavement. I expect he will appear soon.

Chapter 6
Ashley
31 March

On the Zoom screen in front of Ashley a distorted close-up of a face appeared, skin tones bleached and thick wavy hair surrounding it like a helmet. She glared at herself. In a good light her appearance was capable of pleasing her, even now she was past fifty. It certainly didn't today.

'We can't hear you, Ashley,' someone said as face-filled squares hopped about on the screen. 'Have you muted yourself?'

Ashley swore under her breath and tapped again at the buttons at the bottom of the screen. Her sound had got stuck.

Tara came into view, combing her fingertips through her highlights.

'Good to see everyone again – our second Zoom meeting!' Tara's smile showed a lipstick-smudged incisor. 'Ashley, are you with us? Hopefully, we'll have fewer technical issues this time.' Tara screen-shared the meeting's agenda. 'First up on the agenda, our shielding residents – who is helping them and who is being helped. Ferne, you were looking at this, weren't you?'

A furry white tail whipped back and forth in Sporty Woman's square, hiding the young woman's face.

'Ferne?'

Ferne reappeared, hair pulled back in a pony-tail.

'Sorry, Pearl is exploring. What were you saying?'

Tara's brow creased.

'Helpers and helpees. You've got the list of shielding residents and helpers, haven't you?'

'I've got the six of us down as helpers along with twelve other residents of the Wiltons,' Ferne reported. 'But there's an over-supply of helpers – most haven't managed to help anyone yet. A lot of shielders seem reluctant to seek help, leaving some helpers annoyed at having no one to help...' She sighed, rolling her eyes. 'Olive in Wilton Road has complained that our group has snaffled all the shielders in the Wiltons, and there aren't enough left for the other residents.'

Tara tsked. 'I hope you told her not to be so picky! I'm sure there are plenty of others in the Wiltons who could do with help, but they're too proud to ask.'

Ashley unwound a paperclip left on Zac's desk. What would become of this group? There was little to show for their efforts so far – and it was frustrating that the flyer she'd spent hours creating hadn't elicited a bigger response.

'I know someone in Wilton Park Road,' Ursula said. 'He's just turned ninety and doesn't have relatives or friends nearby. I'll knock on his door this afternoon.'

'What about the birdwatching woman?' Belatedly, Ashley remembered to raise her hand. 'I don't know her name, I'm afraid.'

'The one always wandering about in second-hand clothes with binoculars?' Tara frowned. 'That's Bird Woman. She keeps to herself – I doubt she'd want our help.'

'She lives in a tiny run-down cottage beside the woods,' Ursula explained. 'I used to see her working in her vegetable patch on my way to rehearsals. She tries to be self-sufficient, I gather. Anyway, she's about my age, nowhere near seventy.'

The discussion was interrupted by technical issues. John had to have help restoring his video after his square went black, and a ghostly whine dogged the meeting even when all were temporarily muted. Ashley tried to concentrate. She was extra tired today; she hadn't been able to fall asleep till nearly three worrying about her daughter. Layla had been glued to her phone again, peering at Instagram posts.

'Some ought to be shielding but aren't,' Tara was saying.

'We could keep a watch on all the oldies' houses to see when they come out,' John said, his face deadpan. 'Then ask to see evidence of their age and full details of their situation.'

Ashley couldn't help smiling. John didn't care how popular or unpopular he was, she sensed, or what Tara thought of him – not much, clearly. Tara glared at the bottom corner of her screen.

'I'm a bit pressed for time, guys,' Ferne announced, pulling on her sweat band. 'I have to give my Zoom Zumba class at twelve. If we could end on time, it would be appreciated.'

'On to the last item on the agenda, the proposed Brampton Food Initiative.' A scowl flickered across Tara's face. 'It's clear that many residents of the village are struggling as a result of the Covid situation. Given there's no food bank in Brampton and the nearest one is twelve miles away, I propose that our group steps in. We could start a food bank for the village – on a much smaller scale, of course. Does anyone have any spare food they can donate to the less fortunate? Tins in your food cupboards that have been left languishing, extra items from your weekly shop that would otherwise go off?'

'I've got five bunches of bananas,' John said. 'Ocado delivered them yesterday. I meant to tick six individual bananas, not six bunches.'

'I grow veg in my allotment,' Ferne offered. 'I had a ton of carrots last summer... I ended up giving most to friends.'

Greg raised his hand. Ashley squinted at his textured green shirt, which was creating a moiré pattern on her screen.

'What about baked goods? Tony can make his courgette and walnut loaf – it always goes down well at gatherings—'

27

'Nuts aren't a good idea,' Ursula cut in. 'Too many issues with allergies.'

Ferne waved enthusiastically. 'I'll help with baking, Tara. Are cakes OK?'

'Thanks, love,' Tara replied. 'That would be marvellous. I'll bake some cupcakes myself.' She paused. 'Though maybe we should concentrate on savoury, as it's going to people in need.'

'For heaven's sake, everyone likes cake!' John's eyebrows met in the middle. 'Especially,' – he made air quotes – 'the "needy".'

Ashley banished her smile.

'I could bake something too. Though it might not be up to M&S standards.' She scarcely baked any more. But it was something tangible she could contribute, at least.

John nodded. 'None of us are Michelin chefs.'

'Speak for yourself,' Greg countered. 'I reckon Tony's lavender shortbread would give Mary Berry a run for her money.'

'I hate to be a fly in the ointment.' Ursula blinked through her thick-lensed spectacles. 'But if we're going to supply home-sourced produce to the public, doesn't it have to be of a certain standard? Someone could sue us. What if one of us accidentally includes a nut fragment and someone dies of an allergic reaction? Or they might accidentally pass on Covid if they haven't washed their hands properly.'

'I think we're all aware that we have to wash our hands thoroughly before preparing food, Ursula.' There was an edge to Tara's voice. 'Perhaps you could approach that woman you know on the council and see if we need permission to set up a food donation scheme. I'm sure in these perilous times, they'll waive any red tape.'

'Who are we going to give the food to?' Greg fingered a button on his shirt.

'Whoever turns up and is in need,' John suggested. 'That's what they do at the Elven food bank. We could ask them to

28

register first, and to bring proof of their address so we know they're local.'

'Good idea, John.' Tara beamed.

'We could use the community hall,' Ferne added, 'or put up a trestle table on the green.'

'We might have to start off outside,' Tara replied. 'I've already checked the community hall and it's closed at the moment due to Covid. On the other side of the river might be best – most of our takers will be from that side, I should think.'

'But anyone could pretend they were in need. How would we police it?' Ursula clearly wasn't convinced.

'People won't take our food unless they can't afford to buy it themselves, will they?'

'But what about the shielding and those who can't get out of their houses easily?'

'We could take it in turns to deliver...'

Ashley felt her attention wander. Sam's vow to stop drinking alcohol had held. That in itself was no bad thing, but she worried that he was spending too much time with his new friend, a strict Muslim. And what on earth would they do for Layla's seventeenth birthday, now that no one was allowed to go out of their homes unless for an essential purpose? The party had been arranged down to the nth detail. It would have to be cancelled...

A deep sigh escaped her. She closed her eyes, imagining herself as a slender but resilient tree, bending in gusts of wind but carrying on despite the challenges that came her way. A silver birch perhaps, or a graceful, thirty-metre-high ash. She had never minded her slight build with not much in the way of breasts or hips, but had always yearned to be tall instead of an underwhelming five foot four.

'Ashley? You're not falling asleep on us, are you?'

She opened her eyes and sat up straight. Damn, she'd forgotten to mute her microphone.

'Sorry, Tara. I'm a bit distracted today. Family life, you know how it is.' Then she remembered. All Tara's relatives were either no longer in touch, or no longer alive.

Tara didn't respond.

'I take it the meeting is closed?' Ursula frowned. 'I've got to tend to choir business, I'm afraid. The committee has to rethink our rehearsals for this term. Goodness knows how we're going to manage singing on Zoom.'

'Yes, of course.' Tara sounded distracted. 'Ferne, did you take everything down?'

'Ferne's left,' John replied. 'And I'm off to potter in my shed.'

Ashley clicked the Leave button quickly. She didn't want to be left alone with Tara, even online.

That afternoon she did small jobs in the house, weighed down by unease. Had it been a mistake to volunteer for this group? She wasn't looking forward to spending further time with Tara, virtually or otherwise. But she would have to try to put her dislike of Tara aside. She'd wanted to help those around her during this global crisis, hadn't she? Besides, getting more involved in local life might help her to feel more at home in this village.

Her thoughts turned to this evening. What was she going to cook that would please everyone, and would they all be able to have a conversation that didn't turn into an argument? So much for thinking that this enforced period at home would be a chance for her family to grow closer. She had planned activities from weekly family film nights, with titles chosen by everyone in rotation, to a table-tennis competition. But no one had shown enthusiasm. Her offspring had other things to do – even Zac preferred to sit on his own, reading or staring into space. She thought sadly of the graphic design job she'd given up soon after Sam was born. Oh, to have a career again...

'No one's forcing you to drink alcohol, are they?' Zac's raised voice from the kitchen interrupted her thoughts – another argument with Sam. 'Your mother and I like a glass of wine occasionally! While you're living under our roof, you'll have to put up with how we do things.'

Ashley hurried upstairs. Layla was still in her bedroom on her phone to her best friend. Her voice was loud enough to hear through the closed door.

'God's sake, Anna! Of course I'm upset. My sodding birthday party has been ripped to shreds!'

Needing to escape, Ashley changed into her walking boots and went outside. She passed Tara's house and stopped outside the house further up the hill. Elspeth was in her front garden watering her hanging baskets, chock-full of plants in vibrant colours. As usual, she had enviably sleek, fashionably styled blonde hair. She was around eighty at a guess but could easily pass for ten or fifteen years younger.

'Hello there!' Ashley called loudly.

'Hello, Ashley.' Elspeth turned around, her face brightening several notches.

Ashley leaned over the gate.

'I love your wildflowers,' she said, pointing to the hanging basket as Elspeth walked towards the gate, with a dancer's upright posture and a springy energy, as if any moment she might leap into the air for the heck of it.

'Sorry, dear.' Elspeth cupped her hand around her ear. 'I'm finding it hard to hear people lately, especially when they're wearing masks.'

'I love your wildflowers!'

A smile transformed Elspeth's face, which was striking, with her green eyes and sculpted cheekbones, despite its wrinkles and age spots. Not so long ago, this woman would have been beautiful. She dressed beautifully, too.

'Thank you, dear. I'll give you some seeds...' Elspeth seemed pleased for the chance to talk. They discussed Ashley's ill-fated attempts at gardening, then moved on to matters relating to the pandemic and the changes to their ways of life they had been forced to make.

'I used to be so busy doing things and seeing people...' Elspeth was interrupted by a loud cough from behind. Ashley, startled, spun around. Tara stood there, her face shiny from exertion, a bulging shopping bag hanging off each shoulder. For Elspeth, presumably.

'Oh, hello, Tara.' Tara didn't reply, looking at her with an expression that conveyed intense dislike, as if Ashley was doing something she shouldn't.

'I suppose I'd better be going,' she said to Elspeth.

'Bye, Ashley.' Elspeth waved cheerfully. 'See you another time.'

Tara stepped past Ashley, blanking her, then pushed open the gate and addressed Elspeth.

'I've brought your things, love. I'll leave them in the porch as usual.'

Ashley turned away, a shiver creeping down her neck. That was weird. Tara was reacting more like a possessive lover than Elspeth's neighbour... She took the path off the cul-de-sac that would take her into open countryside. Thank goodness, the village of Brampton and its inhabitants would disappear for a while.

Chapter 7
Tara
2 April

'Elspeth! Are you there?'

Tara rang again on the doorbell, then brought the knocker down with force.

No response.

With a flare of irritation, she wiped the perspiration off her brow with a tissue. What was the woman doing? Why couldn't she get her hearing sorted? She pushed open the letterbox and shouted through it.

'Elspeth, it's Tara! I've got your prescription!'

The sound of running feet. Elspeth approached the door, breathing heavily.

'Sorry, I fell asleep in the garden. Have you been there long?'

'Nearly five minutes! I phoned your mobile but you didn't pick up.'

'I'm sorry. I did put the ring tone on maximum volume... Did you manage to get everything?'

Tara's irritation mounted.

'I couldn't get any Ritinadine, whatever it's called. Apparently, it's been discontinued due to problems with supply. The

33

pharmacist said you need to ask for a replacement medication from your GP.'

'But I need it today! I've run out. I thought I had another packet but I couldn't find it when I looked in the cabinet—'

'Let's stay calm, shall we? The pharmacy said you need to ask the doctor to issue a new prescription with a replacement medication.' She couldn't get her head around the intricacies of how the prescription service worked – or didn't, as often as not. 'I'll get it tomorrow.'

A long pause while Elspeth fidgeted, looking uncomfortable.

'Would you mind very much going back this afternoon to get it, Tara? I'll get onto the surgery right now. I need to take those pills every day for my oesophagal condition – acid reflux can cause cancer. My throat has been sore since I ran out yesterday.'

Christ. She was hot and tired and needed a long sit-down. Queuing again outside the pharmacy was the last thing she wanted to do. But she couldn't let Elspeth down.

'All right then. Text me when you've got it sorted.'

'Thanks, darling, you're an angel! If you could get a few things from the health-food shop too, while you're at it... I'll text you a list.'

Half an hour later, Tara settled onto the sun-lounger in the shade with a Mint Julep and a pile of paperbacks. A message flashed onto her mobile.

Prescription all sorted and here's what I need from The Green Goddess x

Tara scrolled through the long list of items from the health-food shop, along with several items that Ocado had omitted to deliver the day before. She let out a long breath.

'Tara, are you there?' Elspeth's head and shoulders bobbed up from behind the sprawl of shrubs at the fence. 'Did you get my message? The surgery has sent over another prescription to the chemist with the replacement pills. If you could collect it before they close, I'd be eternally grateful.'

'Of course. Let me finish my drink and I'll drive over.'

She took a sip of Mint Julep. Elspeth didn't move, a worried expression settling over her face. 'It's five past five now. I'm not sure what time they close...'

'Six thirty. Don't worry, there's plenty of time.'

'Sorry, Tara – but do you think you should be driving after drinking alcohol? I wouldn't want anything to happen.'

Tara plonked her glass down. 'For God's sake, Elspeth, stop being so neurotic! I'm only having one drink – which I bloody well deserve, thank you very much!'

The queue outside Linda's Pharmacy was even longer than before. Tara shuffled forward, keeping her distance from the woman in front. The shop was understaffed again today, the flustered assistant had announced to everyone in line, presumably as an excuse for the shoddy service.

'Excuse me, are you in the queue?'

The woman behind her glared. Tara glared back. She shuffled forward each time another person was allowed into the shop. There was still the stuff to get from The Green Goddess too.

By some miracle, the pharmacy managed to deliver the medication on Elspeth's new prescription within ten minutes without a quibble.

'Anything else, madam?'

'No, thank you.' As she said it, she regretted not buying something extra for herself, such as a new lipstick to help distract herself from the wrinkles showing on her face during these Zoom meetings. Even with the filter on, being confronted by oneself for hours at a time was not an enjoyable experience.

Thankfully, the health-food shop was pleasantly cool, given the long list of items she had to get – seaweed-flavoured miso soup, gluten-free ginger loaf, artichoke paste and other such curiosities. They were expensive, too, £5.95 for a carton of prune juice! How did Elspeth afford all this on her widow's pension? But of course, Elspeth had been earning good money as a dancer for years.

She headed upstairs for the final items on the list, a bottle of ridiculously overpriced arnica-infused massage oil and a hair-colouring kit in Soft Natural Blonde. Elspeth always had her locks exquisitely cut and highlighted courtesy of Curl Up and Dye, Brampton's premier salon; she must be desperate to risk colouring her own hair.

Tara turned to go back downstairs. As she passed along the aisle, several rows of lipsticks tugged at her attention, their colours displayed irresistibly above gleaming metal cases. A brilliant coral shade drew her eye; she couldn't resist picking up the tube. £12.99. How did anyone afford to pay so much for a lipstick? Without thinking, she dropped the lipstick into her basket.

The whole lot including the lipstick came to ninety pounds. As usual, she slipped Elspeth's Halifax card into the card reader and tapped in the PIN – 8181, nice and easy to remember. She tucked the lipstick into her makeup pouch, picked up her shopping bags and left the shop.

While walking back to Wilton Close, she felt a flutter of indecision. She ought to give Elspeth the money for the additional purchase. What if Elspeth noticed the lipstick listed on the receipt? That wasn't likely, though. Elspeth's kitchen was cluttered with ancient phone bills and garden centre receipts that had probably never been looked at. If Elspeth did happen to notice the extra item, Tara could say she meant to pay her back but forgot in the stress of going back to the pharmacy in the heat. It was true enough. Besides, she deserved a small recompense for the effort she'd put in to help out her neighbour, didn't she? Elspeth could afford one measly lipstick.

She left the bags on the doorstep, rang the doorbell and stepped back as usual. Seconds later, the door opened and Elspeth appeared, her face steeped in concern.

'Thanks for going to all that trouble. I felt bad at making you go out again when it's so hot.'

Why did you then? she wanted to spit back. She was fond of Elspeth, more than she was prepared to let on. But sometimes she hated the woman for her bluntness and lack of gratitude. Elspeth didn't seem to appreciate any of the effort that Tara was making to be a good neighbour.

'Don't worry about it, love,' she said. 'If you need anything else, let me know.' Her ankles had swollen in this unusual heat and she could murder another Mint Julep.

'What's this?' Elspeth was picking items out of a shopping bag. She held up a two-pack of dairy-free chocolate mousse.

'I thought you might like it for dessert.' Tara pushed her fingernail into the flesh of her thumb. She had to keep calm, despite the hot waves of anger now seeping through her body, and an urge to open a mousse and push it into Elspeth's face. If Elspeth had the gall to say *It's not what I usually eat* or *I'm on a diet...*

But Elspeth was showing off her dimples and slightly protruding front teeth.

'Thank you, Tara, that's kind. Now go home and put your feet up.'

Chapter 8
Ashley
4 April

Ashley dug her hands deeper into her jacket pocket. It was early on a Saturday morning and cold. Beside her, Tara and John were seated behind three laden trestle tables, waiting for their first customer.

Most members of the group had been baking solidly all week, judging from the number of tarts, loaves and cakes displayed. There was also fresh fruit and veg, tins and packets, and a new-looking teddy-bear. Tara had set up a collection point at Ursula's house for residents' donations. The local bakery had donated sandwiches approaching their sell-by date, and Ferne's friend had contributed three large boxes of eggs, laid by her chickens.

The three of them had set up the food stall at 9am, on an unused patch of grass between a mobile phone tower and the railway line, where, according to Ursula, who'd suggested the spot, kids usually played on their bikes or sold weed. It was definitely in 'the poorer part of the village', as Tara referred to it.

'Do you think there's something happening today?' Tara asked from behind an eye-catching floral-print face mask.

'Saturday morning is happening,' John replied, rubbing a stubbly jaw. 'Everyone's tucked up in bed.'

'Maybe our sign is too small.' Ashley turned to the banner strung up between two trees behind them: Delicious nutritious home-made food – FREE to those in need. 'People are driving straight past.'

'It's only half past nine.' John sat on his scooter under a beanie, thick woollen jumper and blanket. 'The sun's out, it will warm up soon. We need to be patient; we've done all we can. Ferne's put notices up around the village and I've told Mrs Gale in the post office. Word will spread.'

A car approached, slowly. A woman stared out from the driver's side. Three children stared too.

'Hello!' Tara called out. 'You can park over there.' She pointed to a large sign saying PARK HERE in front of their cars. The car kept on going.

Ashley bit off another piece of chocolate. This was going to be a long morning.

'Someone's coming!' Ashley pointed to a bearded young man with a rucksack over his shoulder ambling towards them.

'Good morning,' Tara greeted him. 'Welcome to the Brampton Food Initiative.'

The man's eyes remained on the pile of Sheba tins donated by Ursula, whose elderly cat had just died.

'How much?'

'It's free,' Tara replied. 'This is a new service to help Brampton residents who are struggling with the lockdown measures and can't afford their usual groceries.'

'That would be me.' The man rubbed his jaw. 'All my work has dried up, I've had to get by on gardening jobs. I'll take this lot off you for starters.'

'We're providing essential cupboard items such as pasta along with delicious home-made food. We're going to be here every Saturday morning.'

He started transferring the cat food into his rucksack, then held up a rectangular object wrapped in clingfilm.

'What's this?'

'Courgette and feta loaf,' John replied. 'It's home-made and absolutely scrumptious.'

The man transferred the item to his rucksack.

'And this?'

'That's lemon drizzle cake,' Ashley replied. 'I made it.'

'Brill, I'll have that for my tea.'

He scooped up the cake and she felt a surge of gratification.

'Ah, here's someone else. It's the woman from the pet shop.' Tara leapt into action. 'Hello... Belinda, isn't it? How are you this morning?'

By 1.30pm, all that was left on the trestle tables was a mass of squashed cupcakes wrapped in clingfilm, a tin of chickpeas and a tub of Vanish! verruca powder.

The mood was jubilant as they packed the stall and its contents back into Ursula's station wagon, on loan to Tara. Ashley was as surprised as the others that practically everything had gone.

John looked up from his notebook. 'Thirty-seven people came to the stall and thirty-one took something away with them – whatever was left to take, anyway. I must admit, I didn't think there'd be so many takers.'

'Next time we could restrict each person to a maximum of five items, say,' Ashley suggested, 'so the early ones don't get the lion's share.'

'Excellent idea, love. We'll start to fine-tune our process now we know the scheme has legs.' Tara smiled at Ashley. Although she probably didn't mean to sound condescending, her reply felt somewhat so. 'I'd invite you all back to my place to celebrate our success. But given Covid guidelines...'

John raised an eyebrow.

'See you on Zoom,' he said to Ashley, then waved briskly to Tara and scooted off.

Back at Wilton Close, Ashley helped Tara move the trestle tables from Ursula's station wagon into Ashley's garage. When they'd finished, the two women stood on the pavement outside their houses.

'Thanks so much for your help today, Ashley.'

'Any time, Tara. It was a pleasure.'

It had been, she thought, an unexpected one. Perhaps she should give this village – and Tara – another chance.

'Look over there,' Tara said suddenly, in a disapproving tone.

Ashley looked to where Tara was pointing, on the green opposite. Three women were sitting on the bench, shoulder to shoulder. Groups of young people sat or lay on the grass, without face masks and with little attempt at social distancing. Children ran about shouting.

'Don't they realise they could be spreading this vile disease?'

Unsure how to reply, Ashley said nothing.

'We have to do something. People are flouting the rules.'

She watched as Tara strode across the road. A minute later, her neighbour hurried back, cheeks flushed.

'They won't budge! And you wouldn't believe what one of those women said to me. I'm tempted to call the police.'

'Do you think that's wise?'

But Tara had vanished indoors, Ashley realised, as Bulldog

Man appeared on the pavement a few feet away. He gave Ashley a hard look from under the peak of his cap.

'Morning.' Ashley nodded at him and glanced at his dog, now lifting its leg beside the wheel of their car.

The man grunted, tugging on the dog's lead. 'Ernie, get off.'

'Is anything the matter?' she asked. Though she had no wish to get into conversation with this man, it did no one any harm to be polite.

'My dog's ill.' He jerked his head towards the dog. 'Got a kidney infection, the vet says. We might have to put him down.'

'Sorry to hear that.' Even though the man had an unpleasant demeanour, she did feel for him. It was awful to lose a pet. At ten years old, Sam had fed his hamster something that had disagreed with her, leading to Dilly's rapid decline.

'How's Tara's new scheme going, then? She's giving food away, I hear.'

She bristled at his disparaging tone.

'Very well, thanks. We give out free food every Saturday to those in need of extra help.'

'I might be over myself to get a few tins, the way my work's going. This blasted lockdown...' Bulldog Man glared at her, as if the state of the nation was her fault, then glanced at Zac's car and its urine-streaked rear wheel. 'Your husband's still got his cushy job, I bet. Everyone wants the darkies, these days. Too scared to let 'em go in case—'

'Excuse me.'

She strode to her front door, not wanting to spend another second listening to the foul words of this man, though his remarks were mild by the standard of some she and Zac had received. In London there had been occasional unpleasant remarks aimed at Zac, herself and/or their children, but since moving to Brampton she'd heard 'Paki' and worse, disturbingly often.

While she fumbled for her keys, Zac appeared on the other

side of the front door and opened it. He turned away without saying hello.

'What's the matter?' she called to his retreating back.

'Sam's stormed off,' he said. 'He wouldn't say where he's going – God knows when he'll be back. Layla's crying in her room and won't let me in. I think she's had a fight with Anna.'

Oh, no. Why couldn't her family be happy for just one day? She hurried upstairs to try to comfort her daughter.

Chapter 9
Elspeth
6 April

A bee hovered about the camellia bush. Elspeth stepped closer, watching its purposeful activity. The humming was fainter than normal. Her hearing really was going, she thought with a stab of gloom. It was set to be another glorious day in Brampton, unlike the usual unremarkable April fare. But while she appreciated the decent weather of late, and there were endless jobs in the house and garden that needed tackling, she was starting to feel like a prisoner. Most of all, she missed her book group friends. Over the years, they'd become like the siblings she'd never had.

Mira had invited them all to another Zoom session to 'catch up' and discuss the latest book. But Elspeth would rather wait until they could all meet up again in person. The last session had made her feel like an unwilling witness to her body's deterioration. She hadn't caught about half the conversation owing to the whistling sounds in her ear and intermittent internet drop-outs.

The others had been kind and considerate about her hearing difficulties, repeating phrases in loud, slow voices, recapping what had been discussed and giving her extra time to reply. Lou had offered to record the session so that Elspeth could replay it later and catch any parts of the conversation she'd missed. That had made it even worse, somehow – her affliction was now a real, undeniable Thing. Leaving Lou mid-sentence, she'd run upstairs and flung herself on the bed, sobbing.

She shook her head at the memory. What a drama queen! At least she still had her faculties – that was the most important thing. She could still recognise her friends and remember her own name. What did a little hearing loss matter in the grand scheme of things?

'Elspeth, is that you?' Tara's voice came from the other side of the fence.

No, it's Doctor Who! Of course it was her, who else would it be? A burglar coming to pilfer some plant pots? She let out a long breath and climbed onto the small platform of bricks she'd erected beside the fence.

Tara's face was made up, her lips coated in a glossy shade of coral.

'Hello, Tara. How did the food stall go?'

Judging by the length of Tara's reply, the event had been a success. She nodded along to Tara's gush of words, offering occasional interested-sounding interjections while trying to keep an appropriate distance from her neighbour. In her enthusiasm, Tara was talking extra loudly. Hopefully, no malignant viruses would hop over the fence.

'Did you hear what I said, Elspeth?' Tara was frowning.

'I don't know. What was it you said?'

'I just said, someone should—' Tara stopped abruptly, her frown deepening. 'Look, Elspeth. I'm saying this as a concerned friend, so don't take it the wrong way. You need to get your hearing sorted. I looked it up on the internet: tinnitus is usually due to hearing loss. These days you can get all sorts of hearing aids. Some are so tiny you hardly know they're there—'

'I've already told you, don't you remember? I had an appointment with the audiologist at the hospital but they postponed it due to Covid.' She lowered her voice, realising that she was shouting too. 'It's not until August now.'

Tara tutted, moving her head from side to side.

'That's months away. Why don't you go private?'

'I'm not insured, Tara. It would cost a lot of money.' There were the repairs to the gutter to pay for, the overdue lopping of her lime tree, the worsening damp problem in the kitchen...

'But you can afford it, can't you? It would be worth it surely, to be able to hear properly and join in with the world around you.'

Another trickle of irritation coursed through Elspeth, becoming a deluge. Tara was right, to an extent, but from the way she spoke you'd think Elspeth was living in Buckingham Palace.

'To be honest, Tara, I could do without you bossing me around, trying to tell me what to do all the time. And always harping on about what everyone else is doing wrong, never noticing your own faults!'

That felt better. Elspeth dismounted the platform of bricks and hurried inside.

The latest government coronavirus briefing, with its unrelentingly grim statistics, left Elspeth too miserable to do anything much. As of yesterday, a total of 5,373 people in the UK had died in hospital after being infected with the virus, or 'the rona', as young people now seemed to call it. The number of deaths was up by 439 from 4,934 the day before. Just over half of those who had died were over eighty.

She switched off the TV and went up to her bedroom. It was her favourite spot in the house, with a terrace overlooking the back garden and distant rolling hills. A framed photo on the wall caught her eye; herself on stage in the outfit she had worn for her first professional performance as a contemporary dancer in 1965, a year after graduating. Beside it, a large photo of the dance troupe she had choreographed thirty years later. What fun her life had been in those days, living for months in hotels and minibuses, the camaraderie and the backstage chatter... Such a contrast to her life now, interred in this house with nothing to look forward to but the resumption of life on the other side of this plague, and seeing her friends again – if they or she didn't croak it in the meantime.

What a gloom-fest, Elspeth! She gave herself a mental kick. Get a grip, old girl. You're not dead yet.

She settled into the armchair. Through the window, a patch of amber light glowed in the western sky. Underneath, the landscape was magnificent. She picked up the Kate Morton paperback she was meant to be reading for the book group and opened it at the bookmark. The story was enjoyable, but her concentration wasn't good of late.

Minutes later, she looked up, realising she'd been reading the same sentence over and over, each time its syntax tangling into a tighter knot. Oh, dear. Was that a sign of dementia, or just fatigue induced by the state of the world and her own reduced status within it?

Elspeth put the book down, wondering if Tara would re-appear tomorrow. There'd been no sign of her since their hot words this morning. She'd probably upset Tara by her plain speaking. Her neighbour liked to dish out home truths but obviously wasn't so keen on getting them back. The woman could be a pain in the backside, there was no denying. If they hadn't been neighbours she doubted they would be friends, given Tara's intermittent angry outbursts, unreasonable demands and general over-the-top-ness.

Many years ago, not very long after Elspeth had moved into the house next to Tara, Tara had asked Elspeth to help her 'sort out her loft', which was full of unopened boxes. When Elspeth said no, she had a friend staying with her, and anyway, being a hoarder herself she was hardly the best person to ask, Tara had launched into a tirade. Why was Elspeth being so selfish, couldn't she do this one thing for Tara? Then there was the time that Tara's printer packed up and Elspeth had been expected to step in and print sixty letters to put through nearby letterboxes asking for residents to oppose something or other the council was planning. Elspeth had only agreed because Tara had started to raise her voice and become tearful, signs of an imminent temper tantrum.

But she was loath to disrupt their friendship. Whatever happened, they'd have to keep on living next door to each other – and she had a feeling Tara would be a formidable foe.

The ringing mobile phone cut off her thoughts. *Oliver* flashed onto the WhatsApp screen. She accepted the call. Her godson! She felt a flutter of excitement. They had exchanged texts since his move to New Zealand but not yet spoken.

'Hello, Oliver?'

'Of course!' He had a slight accent already. 'Hello, Elspeth.'

'It's lovely to hear from you, dear. How are you getting on in your new job? You've been on my mind a lot.'

'I've been working all hours on the project, as usual. I'm having a few days off to recharge, thought I'd give you a bell. How are you? What's happening over there?'

'Life is a challenge, that's for sure.' She told him about her hearing loss, reminded him to speak loudly and filled him in on the latest situation in the UK. The casualties of the pandemic were growing day by day. As one of those deemed vulnerable, she'd been told to stay home and shield herself from Covid-19.

'You're not going outside the house at all?'

'Only into my garden. It's government advice for oldies like me. I haven't seen anyone except a couple of neighbours for nearly a month.'

'It sounds as bad as it is here. Jacinda is keeping all of New Zealand in isolation. How are you managing with food and so on?'

'My neighbour Tara has been helping me out. She often

stands too close though, and doesn't always wear a mask... Then there's the risk of picking up the virus from a tin of soup or something. It's such a bind, wiping down all your groceries.' She hadn't gone as far as Mira, who now disinfected everything that came into her house.

'You shouldn't believe everything you hear, Elspeth.'

'What do you mean?'

'The government has its own agenda, didn't you know? They're trying to control you. All this crap about people needing to hide inside their own homes – it's out of the Middle Ages! Your civil liberties are being trampled over.'

A fervent note had slid into his voice. She felt uneasy.

'But it's backed up by science, isn't it?' she said. 'The lockdown, I mean. They need to stop infection spreading—'

'Science!' He spat the word as if it was poisonous. 'That lot can't be trusted. Scientists are biased – medical research is the worst. It's all driven by big pharma, these days.'

A sense of disbelief washed over her. Was it really Oliver she was talking to? He'd become more right-wing in the past few years, banging on about 'evil Hilary' and other wacky stuff. But he'd not sounded like this before.

'I heard someone on the BBC the other day talking about research,' she began. Oliver pounced.

'The mainstream media are just a mouthpiece for the government! They're trying to brainwash everyone into doing the government's bidding. Why should you have to cower indoors like a mouse just because you're old?'

'I'm only seventy-eight,' she shot back. 'Not that old!'

'You haven't got any immune conditions, have you?'

'No...'

'Then why obsess about getting Covid? It's a coronavirus like flu, no big deal. And as for wiping everything down with disinfectant... Honestly, Elspeth, you need to start thinking for yourself.'

Indignation flushed through her. She swallowed her hasty

reply and waited until she was composed enough to speak normally.

'Thank you, Oliver, I'll definitely have a think about everything you've said.'

'Get out and see your friends, do something normal, that's my advice. Do you want to spend the rest of your days sat around indoors, moping?'

She didn't reply. Honestly, this was the limit.

'Sorry, I didn't mean to come over so strident.' Oliver's voice had quietened so much she could hardly hear him. 'I'm concerned about you, that's all.'

'I know what you're saying is coming from a good place. I do happen to have my own views, though.' He started to interrupt again. She cut him off before the conversation descended into an argument. 'I'm sorry, I've got to go.' She cast around for an excuse. 'I promised to call Mira before ten.'

'No worries, Elspeth. Good to talk, we must have a longer chat next time. Don't forget what I said, will you?'

After saying goodbye, Elspeth cradled her head in her hands. She wanted to howl. Where had her good-natured, intelligent, funny godson disappeared to? She heartily wished he hadn't phoned. Not only were they on opposite sides of the world, they were on opposite sides of an ideological divide every bit as far apart. Thank God they hadn't got onto discussing Trump.

A few seconds later, the phone rang again. This time, it was the landline.

'Hello?'

'Elspeth, it's Miranda. Can you hear me OK?' Her friend's voice crashed into her ears; it was so loud it was distorting.

'Hi, Mira. I can hear you, yes! You don't need to talk so loudly.'

'I've got bad news, I'm afraid. About Lou.' Mira's voice became worryingly gentle.

'What's happened?' Lou had caught pneumonia again, Mira had informed Elspeth just last week.

'Her sister phoned me this afternoon. Lou's passed away.'

'She's dead?' It couldn't be... But of course, they were all in their seventies and eighties now. Death was poised to strike at any moment.

'I'm sorry, Else. I know you were close to her.'

'From pneumonia?'

'She had Covid apparently, not pneumonia – or the two together, possibly. The doctor didn't know it was Covid at first. He told her to stay in bed; she'd be safer at home than in hospital with all the Covid patients. Then she went downhill suddenly. They did another test and it was positive.'

She couldn't speak.

'Are you OK, dear? Do you want me to come over?'

'No, I'll be all right,' Elspeth finally replied. 'She seemed so full of beans the last time we were all together.'

'I know, it's hard to believe she's gone. Alice doesn't know yet. I'm going to phone her next—'

'Was her family with her?'

'Her sister was, and the kids came in to say goodbye. Thank goodness, she wasn't in hospital.' Mira's tone lifted. 'Do you remember, she complained about a fart?'

'She complained about a fart?'

'No, silly! She complained about a DRAUGHT.'

Elspeth's laughter escaped in a vigorous hoot.

'Poor Lou,' she said. 'I'll miss her.'

'So will I. But it was a good way to go, I suppose. She went quickly – and at home, with her family...' Mira trailed to a halt.

Elspeth pondered. Would her own end be quick? Would she have a loved one by her side? She pushed the thought away.

'When's the funeral?'

'She can only have a small one. Covid restrictions... I think it's family only.' Mira sounded apologetic. 'But her sister said she might organise something on Zoom. I'll send you the link when I get it.'

Elspeth sat on the terrace watching the hills fade into darkness, and thought about not having said goodbye to Lou or being able to go to her funeral. One by one, memories came of their times together. Happy, funny, downright annoying... She found herself alternately chuckling and wiping away tears.

As she prepared for bed, her godson's idiocy came back. It was probably just as well he hadn't called after she'd had news of Lou's death, or she would have given him both barrels... This was the start of a war. Victims of the coronavirus now included one of her closest friends – even the Prime Minister was in hospital with it. Oliver could stick that up his arse. Who might the virus fell next – Mira or Alice, perhaps – or Elspeth herself?

Getting dressed next morning, she glimpsed Tara watering plants on the roof terrace adjoining hers. Elspeth put a top on and stepped out.

'Morning, Tara. Sorry for being so ratty yesterday. All this being confined to barracks must be taking its toll.'

Tara put down the watering can and came up to the low, creeper-covered divider.

'I should apologise too. For being so bossy.' Tara's face clouded. 'It comes from having two sisters, maybe.'

'Are you the eldest, then?' Tara never talked about her parents and siblings, avoiding the subject if it ever came up.

'No, I was the youngest. I had to keep my wits about me – they could be merciless. But they're both dead now.'

'Oh, I'm sorry. I didn't realise.' She was momentarily stumped for something to say. Tara sounded oddly emotionless about her sisters being dead.

'Don't worry, it was a long time ago.' Tara inspected her nails.

'What happened to them?'

'Zoe had an accident in our garden when she was thirteen. Evie drowned six months later.' Tara picked a long blonde hair off her sleeve. She didn't meet Elspeth's eye.

'It must have been awful. I wish I'd known.' Elspeth reached over the railing to touch Tara's arm.

'It was a long time ago, as I said.' Tara's voice was brisker, back to normal. 'Enough about me. I thought I heard you crying last night – you sounded so upset. I nearly came over to see if I could do anything, but after our little quarrel...'

Elspeth explained about Lou's death. She'd known Lou for nearly forty years. Today, the loss of her friend seemed bigger, less unreal.

'Oh love, I'm so sorry.' Tara sounded ready to cry herself. 'And you can't even go to a funeral to pay your respects. Can I help cheer you up? If only we didn't have to keep our distance, I'd ask you over for lunch. I can't even give you a hug.' Her face brightened. 'I know! It's a lovely day, why don't I bring up some salad and we can eat lunch together, keeping our distance. We can each bring our own plates and cutlery.'

Elspeth nodded, uncertain.

Tara carried on. 'If you could push your table level with mine...'

She did as Tara suggested so that their two tables adjoined the low, creeper-strewn railing.

'That's about two metres between us, isn't it? We should be safe from the virus.'

Elspeth refilled her glass as well as Tara's, on the other side of the railing, with the expensive French white she'd been keeping for a special occasion. Lunch with her neighbour after weeks of hermit-like existence was enough of an occasion, surely.

'This is divine,' she said, taking another mouthful of chicken and avocado salad. 'You're a whizz in the kitchen.'

'Thanks, love. It's nice to have someone to prepare food for, to be honest.'

Elspeth nodded. A lifelong feminist, she had never hankered after having someone to prepare food for, let alone an ungrateful husband. Sadly, her days of grateful lovers were over.

'How are things with your PR business?'

'I haven't got much work at the moment.' Tara looked glum. 'Not since lockdown started. That's why I'm putting so much into this support group. Doing things for the elderly gives me something to focus on—' Tara stopped herself. 'I'm sorry, Elspeth, I didn't mean it like that. I don't see you as elderly.'

'I don't mind being called elderly,' she countered. 'I'll be eighty soon, after all – I might not have long left.'

'You're going to last a long time yet, I'm sure.' Tara pierced a chunk of avocado. 'Have you heard the latest about Boris, by the way? He's been taken to hospital with Covid – he's in intensive care!'

'I did hear something about it. I hope he'll be all right.'

'He's so overweight, he could easily die.' Tara didn't look at all concerned about the PM's fate.

Elspeth felt uneasy, though she wasn't sure why. A silence settled between them, somewhere between companionable and awkward.

'Back in a minute.' Tara pushed back her chair.

Her neighbour returned with a plate of home-made carrot cake. Their conversation resumed.

'I think you need cheering up, Elspeth.' Tara was studying her with those large blue eyes of hers. 'How about we do a routine from your garden workouts?'

'If you really want to...' She wasn't in the mood for dancing, especially after a meal. But Tara sounded so enthusiastic.

'Great, I'll get some music.' Tara hurried away, this time returning with a portable stereo. 'Show me some steps and I'll try to follow.'

They each cleared a space on their own roof terrace. Elspeth began with simple steps, which Tara had no trouble copying. Soon she forgot herself, leaping and twirling with abandon. This was more fun than she'd imagined it would be.

'Oh, fuck.' Tara was trying to do a pirouette. Her standing leg wobbled before she crashed onto the decking.

'Tara? Are you all right?' Elspeth leapt over the dividing rail and bent over Tara's sweaty, inert body. Then Tara moved and started laughing.

'Else, you're a devil! That was impossible!'

'I'm sorry, I got carried away.' Elspeth started to laugh, too.

'You were back to being a prima ballerina,' Tara said, hauling herself onto a chair, 'and I was desperately trying to follow... I haven't laughed so much in ages.'

'Nor me.'

'Let's do it again soon. On the grass, next time.'

'Maybe Ashley could join us,' Elspeth suggested. 'She's a bit lonely, I think—'

'I'd rather you didn't ask *her*, if you don't mind.' Tara wrinkled her nose as if referring to a slug. 'She's not a good friend like you are.'

Elspeth said no more.

Later, weeding around the rose bushes, she reflected on Tara's reaction to her suggestion to invite Ashley. Given Tara and Ashley both belonged to the local Covid community thingie, she had imagined that the pair got on reasonably well. But Tara had let slip several catty comments about her other neighbour recently. *Ashley's a cold fish* and the like.

Elspeth angled the hoe beneath another weed and pushed to dislodge it from the soil. It was worrying that Tara had taken a dislike to her newest neighbour. She wondered how things would turn out. Few people, certainly not Ashley, would choose to be on the wrong side of Tara.

Chapter 10
Tara
9 April

Tara brushed a cobweb from the window in the kitchen. The house badly needed a clean; Marina hadn't been able to come since lockdown started. She ought to get out the vacuum cleaner and the mop.

She settled onto the sofa. There were other tasks to do too, most importantly the monthly accounts. But they would only make her depressed. She knew from a cursory glance at the figures that her business was struggling. Enquiries had fallen off a cliff and there had been little client income since an overdue payment for her work on *Spot That Bird!*, a guide to birdwatching for unobservant, tone-deaf idiots in suburbia, or something similar.

The sensible thing to do would be to swallow her pride and apply for one of the government's Covid handouts. It didn't mean she was a profligate or a failure.

Undoubtedly though, if she had managed to put aside a reasonable amount of money from her inheritance and done something sensible with it, she wouldn't be in this situation. She'd have been able to spend her days in comfort, living off rented property income and investments. Instead, she had ended up in a characterless house in a charmless backwater. She'd squandered tens of thousands of pounds on fleeting pleasures. Luxury cruises, West End shows, spa days, cosmetic enhancements, overpriced drinks... What did she have to show for it all? Only a few spangly dresses that she no longer had the chance to wear.

It wasn't just the money. The dozens of friends who'd once eagerly accompanied her to theatres and restaurants had leached away as her bank balance declined. Even her fiancé had deserted her, the man who'd followed her around like a little dog and declared he would do anything to make her happy.

She went into the kitchen and set about preparing to bake a fruit loaf containing candied orange peel. Baking always made her feel better. She'd wanted to try the recipe for ages; it would put Greg's husband's efforts in the shade.

The rhythmic kneading, somewhat more forceful than warranted, began to lift her spirits. Loaf tin on the shelf, Tara slammed the oven door and washed her hands yet again. The government's cajolings for everyone to wash their hands frequently were turning her into a hygiene freak.

Task over, the empty hours stretched ahead. There was no peace or comfort in being alone – she couldn't potter contentedly as some did, distracted by happy memories. It was as if her inner self had been hollowed out and replaced by a gaping hole.

Before the restrictions began, there had always been someone willing to listen, or to pretend to. But with visits to the hairdresser and the beauty salon now impossible, and the smallest of human interactions thwarted by having to stand two metres apart, there was no one to moan to about absent cleaners and life plans gone astray, even to discuss the five o'clock Boris Briefings with.

She peered through the kitchen window. Once again, the sun was blazing in a blue sky and the grassy area enclosed by Wilton Close crawled with bodies, as had become the norm now practically everyone was home twenty-four/seven.

The green was her favourite spot for people-watching. A steady supply of targets was guaranteed: young people snogging or smoking marijuana, dog-walkers cursing wayward dogs, mothers shouting at wayward children... If anyone noticed her scrutinising them, she could pretend to be absently looking out of the window while chopping vegetables. But today, seeing people together relaxing and enjoying each other's company, she felt even more alone.

She bit her lip. Apart from Elspeth, she had no real friends left. No children to help her out either, or grandchildren to dote on...

Thank goodness for Elspeth. She felt a surge of gratitude towards her neighbour. The woman was an inspiration, the way she kept on battling to make the most of life, keeping herself nimble in body and brain. What fun it had been to dance with her – or at least try. Who'd have thought she was seventy-eight?

Outside, Bird Woman went past in her mismatched clothes, binoculars strung around her neck and a brimmed hat perched on her head. She crossed over onto the green and walked towards the bench. Noticing a white smear on the window, Tara went out and rubbed at the glass on the garden side with a kitchen towel and bottle of cleaning fluid. Birds, what were they good for?

Her thoughts returned to the crisis gripping the land. More people than ever were being struck down with this virus, dying in their droves in care homes and gasping for breath in hospital. This pandemic could be exactly what she needed. It could help to lift her out of the ordinary. People might not like her, but as long as they didn't ignore her... She could become a local personage, whom people noticed and consulted about things of importance.

This latest project would be the start, she decided. The *Elven Herald* – the web version, at least – might put her picture in the local paper with an article about her. She imagined the caption below her smiling face: *Tara Sanderson, Founder of the Brampton Food Initiative*. Yes, the food bank would be the key to her future success. She hadn't given herself enough credit. She was just the sort of person journalists loved, a local resident helping others in challenging times. The publicity would be a boon to the PR business, too. Played right, it could lead to bigger, more lucrative opportunities.

Tara stood back and examined the window. It was squeaky clean again. Energised, she poured herself a glass of water, put on her trainers and set off to find the vacuum cleaner. If she was to become Queen of Brampton, she needed to get her house tidied and looking less like an alcoholics' convention. A journalist might be sent over to do an interview; she didn't want readers of the *Elven Herald* to see all these empty wine bottles and unwashed glasses lying around and get the wrong impression.

To start with, she would clear out the loft. There were far too many boxes of old things up there that were of no use now. The task had been put off for years and had to be tackled sooner or later.

After tossing another outdated item of clothing into the rubbish pile – a halter neck dress last worn in her twenties – she tore open the first of the sealed boxes. They had lain there since she'd moved into this house. She pulled out a photo album, flicked through the images of herself and her sisters, and quickly put it down, her stomach fluttering. That was going in the bin, first chance. Next, a cheap glass ring that a boy at school had given her... Why had she kept all this?

In the next box, among old CDs and other items of no interest, she found a Timex watch with a battered strap. Dad had given it her the year before he died. She held it up, her heart constricting. She'd forgotten this was here. All the other things he'd given her were carefully put away. She turned her attention to the last box, tossing most of its contents onto the rubbish heap, and lifted out the last item: a white, leather-bound book – no, a diary. *Diary 1982* was embossed in gold-coloured letters on the front. It was locked shut with a fake metal clasp.

Memories rushed back. Hours of writing in secret, alone in her room, when her sisters were busy or out of the house. The need to get something out of her and down on paper, and with it the nagging fear that Zoe and Evie would read what she was writing about them.

She hesitated. Did she really want to look at anything that would remind her of those days with her mother and sisters?

On the other hand, it would be fascinating to have a peek into her eleven-year-old thoughts. She'd forgotten so much from those years after Dad died, when her mother had stopped noticing Tara, and her sisters had started ganging up on her... Especially from 1982, the year both her sisters had died, and she had been left alone with her mother's icy silence and obvious regret that Tara hadn't died instead of Zoe or Evie.

Most of her memories – all the happy ones – were from before Dad died, before Zoe fell and cut her cheek, before Zoe and Evie grew close and started to exclude Tara. On holiday, feeding the donkeys, watching films at Christmas, cooking Mexican chicken together... The five of them had been a real family. Ivy, her mother, had been there, looking out for them all. Dad a gentle, amiable presence, showing Tara how to ride a bicycle and make popcorn, describing inventions his company was looking at and how things worked around the house. Her sisters had been nice to her back then, how big sisters should be.

She remembered Evie brushing her hair for her, letting Tara share her chips and taking her ice-skating on Saturdays. Paddling with Evie in the foamy waves then racing each other along the beach. Games of hide and seek with Zoe. Clinging to the rope swing in the garden, shrieking with delight as Zoe pushed her, each time sending her higher. The three of them together, giggling as they jumped on a bouncy castle, hair strewn over their faces. She had felt safe, loved, the certainty that she belonged. Then Dad collapsed from a stroke and she didn't see him again.

Everything changed. Ivy was usually absent, either cooking, working or 'seeing a friend', and Tara and her two sisters would be left to their own devices. She would watch Zoe and Evie with their heads together, whispering excitedly. When their mother was out of the house they played tricks on her, like suddenly leaping up while the three of them were watching TV, turning off the lights and slamming the door. This period was vague in her mind now, though she vividly recalled being lost and alone on a long unfamiliar street close to dark, having no idea which direction to take because her sisters had run off, and the sense of bewilderment she'd felt. Why were her sisters doing this to her? She wished they could love her like they used to.

From time to time other memories came, out of the blue, with jarring sounds and distorted images that made the hairs on the back of her neck rise. Similar to dreams, only not dreams. More like snatches of video, so short and jumbled up you couldn't grasp exactly what they showed or when they were taken. It was like peering into a foggy landscape, desperate for a landmark to pinpoint where you were but seeing only a whitish-grey blur.

The therapist had accused her of locking up memories from childhood because they would be too painful to remember. But he hadn't realised how frustrating it was to be in the dark about your own past. Maybe it was time to unlock those memories.

The key was nowhere to be seen, though. Finally, Tara took the diary down into the kitchen, found a pair of scissors and rammed the blade underneath the clasp. It sprang apart.

On the diary's first page she had written in large letters in dark green felt-tip pen: *Diary of Tara Sanderson* Heart thudding, she turned the page. The handwriting was weirdly small, as if she hadn't wanted anyone to read it.

January 13th 1982

I can't take this any more. I hate my bloody sister, I wish she was dead.

It's Zoe again. She's come up with a better way to torment me, with things she knows she can't be blamed for. Yesterday she borrowed the earrings I bought with my birthday money and broke them – it was an accident, she says. Today she 'accidentally' slammed the kitchen drawer shut on my finger and wouldn't say sorry. Mum says my finger will heal, not to make a fuss.

She skipped through for the next entry about Zoe.

February 8th 1982

I thought things couldn't get any worse, but they have. My pendant went missing from my chest of drawers, the one from Dad. I went into Zoe's room and asked if she'd seen it. She was standing at the mirror, taking off her make-up – now she's even wearing make-up to school.

She told me to stop pestering her and called me Metal Mouth again.

I went round the house searching. Mum said it will turn up. I wanted to yell, Zoe's taken it! But what's the point? Zoe can never do anything wrong in Mum's eyes, nor can Evie. They're her darlings.

After going to bed I couldn't sleep so I got up and looked again. I found my pendant on the kitchen floor in pieces too tiny to glue together. Even so, I got a dust pan and brush and swept them into an envelope. My sister has destroyed the most precious thing I own. She must have taken it from my room, bashed it with the hammer and left it on the floor so it would look like it fell off my neck and someone stepped on it by accident.

I know why she did it. Zoe knows I'll be prettier than her once my brace is gone. She wants to hurt me like I hurt her. She's always blamed me for what happened because I was running after her when she fell, though that was her fault because she and Evie wouldn't stop laughing at me for putting everything Dad ever gave me into the suitcase under my bed and locking it. But I was only eight. How was I to know my sister would trip on a paving stone and rip her cheek open?

It's almost four now. I can't stop thinking of bad things happening to
Zoe. They go through my mind, one after the other. She falls over while
running across a busy road and a lorry runs over her leg. She falls off a
ladder and dislocates her arm...

Tara put the diary down, leaned against the sink and tried to
make sense of what she had read. Her legs were trembling.

No, it couldn't be. Zoe had died in an accident, a tragic accident. That was what the inquest had said... But what if Zoe's
death hadn't been an accident? What if something else had
happened to her?

Chapter 11
Ashley
14 April

The Zoom meeting was progressing in fits and starts.

'There are far too many people on the green these days,' Tara said. 'I think we can all agree on that. On a typical day, there are people doing yoga, people working out, people picnicking—'

'It has lovely views over the countryside,' Ursula broke in. 'Of course it's going to attract visitors from outside the Wiltons – especially people who live in flats and are stuck inside most of the day.'

'But they don't need to come here to exercise and have picnics, do they?' Tara carried on in an increasingly strident tone. 'It's our space, for local residents...'

John muted himself, reached behind to a shelf in what looked like a garden shed and moved partly off camera. He appeared to be getting on with a repair job while the 'Covid Committee' meeting proceeded.

For the first time in the meeting, Ashley put her hand up. This felt like being in infants' class again.

'Yes, Ashley.'

'Surely, the point isn't who is and isn't allowed onto the green, but whether the people on it are safely following the guidelines?' She failed to keep the note of exasperation out of her voice. 'If they aren't, are we within our remit to ask them to change their behaviour? Maybe we could ask the council to put up signs reminding people to keep their distance.'

'Or report them to the police,' Ferne said, 'as Tara suggests—'

'We could all rush over *en masse* to anyone exercising or picnicking, brandishing water pistols,' John couldn't resist.

'Thank you, Ashley and Ferne. Excellent points, both. John, your input isn't helpful. Actually, it's not the people on the green I'm most concerned about, it's the behaviour of people when they're at home – or not at home, as is often the case.'

Ashley's headache was worsening. As the weeks went by, Tara's Nazi tendencies were becoming more apparent.

'Aren't we meant to be a source of support for local people, not an enforcer of government Covid guidelines?' Ursula asked, without a question in her voice. 'It's the police's job to enforce them, surely? Not this group's.'

'But the police aren't enforcing them, Ursula,' Tara replied. 'It's our community that will suffer if the green becomes a Covid hotspot.'

John moved back into view. He didn't bother raising his hand.

'Why can't you report people to the police yourself if you're so concerned?'

Tara glared back at him.

'Yes, Ferne? Is your arm up to say something or are you just stretching it?'

Ferne lowered her arm.

'I support you on this, Tara. My mum's immuno-compromised, so I understand why it's important to keep to the rules. There's a couple near us still having dinner parties – Mum's livid but she doesn't want to grass up the neighbours. If we as a group reported people breaking the rules, we'd have more impact than as individuals. It wouldn't be so difficult to do, either.'

'That's a good point. We all know people who flout the rules, but we're afraid to say anything in case they retaliate. Several residents on Wilton Close, for example, seem to think they're above the law—'

'No one among us, I hope, Tara?' Greg said with a wink.

'I won't name any names, but a couple just down the road from me goes out in their car on day-trips three or four times a week. And last week I saw five men go into Bulldog Man's house, all carrying six-packs of beer.'

Ashley watched John reach down and tug hard at something – a stray nettle, perhaps. From his expression, he wished he could do the same to Tara.

'Excuse me.' John slapped a surface loudly. 'I've had enough. For the record, I strongly oppose the group getting involved with matters outside its remit. I don't agree with naming and shaming rule-breakers. I joined hoping to be of service to others, not to snitch on my neighbours!'

Tara's nostrils flared. 'I think we'd all like to conclude this meeting soon. I propose that the group reports anyone flouting lockdown rules to the police. Can we vote on it? Everyone who can keep a civil tongue in their head, that is.'

John's square went black.

Ashley lingered at the low wall separating Elspeth's front garden from the pavement. Elspeth stood outside her sunny porch, watering can in hand, among the collection of pots sprouting herbs and wildflowers. A wide-brimmed lilac hat hid her eyes. Ashley fastened her mask over her nose and mouth, and gave a small wave.

Since moving to this village, she had grown used to waiting for the other person to make the first move. Certain people smiled and talked pleasantly to her face, she realised, yet would say less pleasant things behind her back. The other day in the post office queue, she'd overheard snatches of conversation about *the Asian family in the Wiltons*. Overtly racist, they had made her stomach curdle. To her dismay, she recognised one of the two women as Belinda at the library, who had advised Ashley about local activities she might participate in soon after the family moved to Brampton. But Elspeth wasn't one of those people, she reminded herself.

'Elspeth!' she called out.

'Hello, Ashley.' Elspeth put down her watering can.

'Such pretty flowers,' Ashley ventured as Elspeth put her mask on and came over. 'You seem to have a knack for gardening. Most of what I plant withers or gets eaten by pests.'

'They make a sort of bower, don't they? If that's the right word. How are you, dear?'

Ashley shrugged and reached for the right tone, which hinted of her problems without being gloomy or over-confiding.

'It's been a bit of a challenge lately, with everyone at home. Zac finds it difficult not being in the office.' After an all-too-short period of enjoying the togetherness, everyone was snapping at each other and tempers would flare at the smallest of things. Sometimes, she would imagine going for a long walk and not coming back.

'I can't remember if you told me his job.'

'He manages...'

Elspeth tapped her ear.

'Sorry, my hearing has been dreadful lately. Could you stand a bit more to that side?'

Ashley raised her voice. 'He's a manager at an investment firm. It's a good job, but demanding.' Her husband was frustrated with working from home, she knew – being surrounded by two irascible teenagers wasn't the ideal environment for Skype chats with High Net Worth clients.

'How are your children getting on?'

'They miss their old lives, too. Sam is in his second year at uni – his lectures are online now and he can't see his uni friends. Layla is miserable because her seventeenth birthday party had to be cancelled... and some of the girls at college are giving her a tough time.' From the messages she'd glimpsed on Layla's Snapchat recently, she suspected her daughter was being bullied. They hadn't gone back into the classroom since the lockdown started, yet her classmates seemed to be messaging each other even more than before.

'Layla's in sixth form, isn't she?'

'St Hilda's College, yes. She started last September, just after we moved here. It has a good reputation. That's why we came, partly.' Ashley hesitated. Quite a few villagers had asked her why she and her family had moved to Brampton, as if it was something she needed to justify. *Why come all this way when you were settled in London?*, a woman had asked her at a St Hilda's event last term. She decided to trust Elspeth. 'She was having trouble at her school in north London, where we used to live. Her close friend died in a car accident. Layla found it hard to cope. We thought it would help her to move away.'

Elspeth nodded, her eyes dampening. 'I hope she'll be all right.'

Ashley glanced up at the top window of the adjacent house, number 33. Had there been a flicker of movement behind it?

'It's tough moving to a new place,' Elspeth added. 'Especially with so many intolerant people around.'

She nodded, recalling the words she'd spotted on Layla's Snapchat. *How's your jihadi brother today?* Sam had mentioned a variety of slurs and insults addressed to him, more noticeably since he let his facial hair grow. Days after returning home when his university switched to online tuition, a youth lobbed a stone at him, hitting him in the shoulder.

'Zac has to put up with all sorts,' she said. Racial and religious insults were a part of his life, her husband had told her. He was sure that his chances of becoming a partner at his firm had been sabotaged by colleagues with racist views.

Before they moved to Brampton, he warned her and the kids that *the haters won't disappear*, but that bigotry came from only a small minority, and they should do their best to ignore it. 'His family accepts me far more than mine do him.'

She explained that before he died of his heart condition, her father had come around to having Zac as a son-in-law. Her mother, however, from a nice part of Surrey, had found it hard to accept the prospect of Ashley being married to a Muslim of Pakistani heritage. She hadn't spurned him outright, but had turned down most invitations to visit and had only once invited them to visit her in Thursley.

'What a sad state of affairs. You wonder why some people have children.'

Ashley smiled at Elspeth's frank response. Relations between herself and her mother had been sliding downhill for years. They hadn't seen each other in person for ages and communicated via text messages.

'Zac's parents have been good to me, though. They made me feel part of their family from the start.' This was despite one of Zac's uncles declaring Ashley an unbeliever who wanted to make Zac betray his faith. In part to make things easier for Zac, she'd organised a family trip to Pakistan and done everything she could to embrace Zac's heritage without becoming a Muslim herself. 'They adore Sam and Layla. And, unlike my mother, they never forget their grandchildren's birthdays... How about you, Elspeth? Sorry, I didn't mean to hog the conversation. How are you coping? It must be difficult having to keep isolated all the time.'

Elspeth let out a sigh.

'I'm used to having all my friends over and going to see them. And I miss doing things in town. I used to be so busy. But now...' She glanced down at the rosemary growing behind the wall, pulled off a short stem, put it to her nose and sniffed. 'I'm lucky, though. I still have my garden.' Behind her mask, Elspeth smiled – a resigned one, Ashley guessed.

'I hope I'm not treading on any toes – I know Tara has been helping you out. But do you need a hand with anything?'

'It's kind of you to ask, dear. I don't think so, at the moment... Tara has been getting things for me from the village.' Elspeth took off her hat and ran her fingers through her short blonde hair. 'A chat every so often would be lovely, though. Outside, of course. I miss having ordinary conversations.'

'I'd be glad to. I'll pop over tomorrow morning, if that's OK?'

'Excellent,' Elspeth replied.

Bulldog Man, as Tara called him, approached Elspeth's gate on his way to the green, giving both women an interrogatory look.

'Bloody masks,' he remarked loudly as his dog stopped to piddle at the base of a nearby lamppost. 'They're worse than bloody burqas.'

Elspeth rolled her eyes. Ashley smiled and checked her watch.

'It's been lovely to have a real conversation.' The corners of Elspeth's eyes creased. 'I've hardly spoken to anyone for days, apart from the postman – through the letterbox, that is. And Tara, of course.'

'How do you get on with her?' She hoped her question didn't sound gossipy. Elspeth glanced over at Tara's porch.

'Tara's been such a help. Sometimes she's gone out two or three times in a week for me. But she can be sensitive, to say the least... especially given how she can be to other people. I often have to bite my tongue.'

Ashley couldn't help laughing.

'I know what you mean,' she said. 'I'm on the local Covid Committee with her, and have to see her every week on Zoom. At the Saturday food stall too, sometimes. If anyone doesn't agree with her, she can be difficult. I don't usually say much in case I

71

upset her.' She ought to stand up to Tara, she reminded herself; she needed to become more assertive.

'That's just it! She can be lovely and generous but also a pain in the backside, to put it bluntly. Worse than that, sometimes. So be careful what you say to her.' Elspeth glanced upwards.

Ashley followed her gaze. From behind one of the upper windows in Tara's house, something moved. All of a sudden she felt anxious.

'Thanks for the heads up,' she said. 'See you tomorrow.'

Chapter 12
Elspeth
15 May

E lspeth woke with a stab of pain from her heel, yawned and reluctantly hauled herself into a more upright position. Her body was as stiff as a mannequin this morning. She made herself a cup of tea then did her morning exercises: rotations of her neck, wrists and ankles, stretches in front of the mirror then some cat-cows and downward dogs. Excepting her foot injuries, a casualty of years of dance, such daily movements had kept her body in good nick. She sat back down. She didn't feel up to a vigorous workout today.

At midday, she limped into the back garden with a mug of green tea. Despite it being another gorgeous day, she felt grumpier than usual.

'Elspeth! Would you like me to cut back some of those brambles?' Tara's head popped up from behind the fence. A gloved hand indicated the further reaches of Elspeth's garden. 'It's like a jungle down there.'

She couldn't catch the rest. She heaved a sigh, put down her mug and walked over to where Tara was pointing. Though the shrubs were overgrown in places and there were indeed a few

73

brambles, to her eyes this end of her garden was perfectly lovely. The butterflies and bees liked it too.

'Hello, Tara?'

'I'm over here! I can't see you. Can you stand on your bricks?'

'Not easily,' she replied. 'My foot is bad today. You want to come over and cut down the brambles?'

'Not just the brambles. There's a mass of ivy growing up from your side. It's suffocating my honeysuckle.'

For goodness sake.

'I'm not blaming you,' Tara carried on. 'I know your gardener can't come now, and you haven't been up to much gardening yourself lately. But it really is a mess down there, Elspeth. We need to tackle it before it gets any worse.'

The use of 'we' was particularly galling. Tara wasn't going to give way, clearly.

'When do you want to do it?'

'Right now would be good. I'm already dressed for gardening. I'll use my own gloves, to be safe. You can never tell with Covid, can you?'

'You'd better come over, then. I'll open the side gate.'

Elspeth watched Tara emerge from the shed and attack the excess greenery. She couldn't help feeling annoyed by the interruption to her peaceful afternoon, just as she was about to settle down in the sunshine. She went inside to read.

'Elspeth! I've been calling for ages!'

Tara stood at the kitchen window, her face red with exertion.

'I'm coming. I was reading, I didn't hear you.' She'd been making progress with *The Lake House* – the characters were gelling and time had flown by.

She pulled a mask over her nose and mouth and went into the back garden. It was open. Tara waited on the step outside, sweat dappling her T-shirt. She wasn't wearing a mask again, Elspeth noticed with a stab of annoyance.

'I've done most of the pruning.'

'Thanks so much, dear. I'll come and have a look.'

She followed Tara down the garden path. Halfway down, a heap of brambles and ivy lay on the grass. The fence looked bare now and offered less privacy than before. She felt a pang of sadness. She'd have to plant something else to cover the fence, hopefully less intrusively.

'What do you think?'

'It's...' She struggled for something that wouldn't antagonise Tara, then gave up. 'You've done a lot of work. To be honest though, it's looking a little... bare.'

A scowl crossed her neighbour's face. Tara was going to be upset now.

'I'll come back tomorrow to finish up and move all this mess.'

'You won't cut back any more, will you? I quite like those tendrils of ivy growing on the fence.'

Tara scowled again then gestured to the path. 'These weeds need clearing.' She turned her attention to the top half of the garden, gazing into the border. 'And these ferns are going to spread everywhere, if you're not careful.'

'I know.' She wished Tara would stop meddling and leave her in peace. 'I'm going to plant some climbing roses there instead.'

'That one?' Tara pointed to Elspeth's new rose plant, sitting on the wall in its pot.

'Yes, Ashley gave it to me – she bought it for me the other day. Isn't it lovely?'

Tara looked at her blankly, then frowned.

'I thought the garden centres were shut.'

Oh, dear. Tara's oversensitivity was becoming ridiculous of

late. Any mention of Ashley was liable to bring on either a barbed remark or a chilly silence.

'They opened again the other day. I thought I might get some more to go along the fence here.'

'What sort do you want? I'm happy to go to the garden centre for you.'

No, thank you. It was on the tip of her tongue. She didn't want Tara buying garden items on top of all the other things. But if Elspeth said no, Tara would get the hump.

'Thank you. I'll text the names of the ones I want.'

They stood near the house watching a blue tit nibble at the bird-feeder. Tara was showing no signs of leaving. Elspeth gave in.

'Would you like a cup of tea?'

'Thanks, that would be nice.'

Elspeth set down two cups of tea on the wrought iron table and arranged the chairs a good distance apart. Tara wanted to discuss the difficulties that many in the village were having as a result of the pandemic restrictions.

'Sandy at the flower shop is worried she'll have to close for good,' Tara was saying. 'And I heard that the hair salon is struggling too. I'm finding the restrictions quite difficult myself, actually.'

'Really?'

'Not having any family around makes it harder, I think, and I haven't got many friends left in the village, truth be told.' Tara gazed into her empty cup then looked up at Elspeth. 'Except for you, of course. I'm glad we're still friends, Elspeth.'

Elspeth felt another flare of irritation. At times, Tara could be so needy.

'I've plenty of friends nearby,' she said, 'though lately I've hardly seen any of them.' That didn't come out quite right, Elspeth thought. It sounded as if she didn't consider Tara a friend. 'Apart from you, that is.'

Another chilly silence.

'And Ashley.' Tara was studying her intently. 'She's been over here quite a lot, I've noticed. Don't you worry she might infect you with the virus?'

For a few moments, Elspeth was too taken aback to speak. She tried to think of how to say what she wanted politely, but couldn't.

'For goodness sake, Tara! Ashley is helping me get through this dreadful situation, just as you are!' Though unlike you she always wears a mask, she thought. A ball of frustration inside her began to unwork itself. Before she could think better of it, she added, 'You're acting like a jealous child! Why can't you think of someone else's well-being before your own, for a change? Were you like this with your sisters?'

Tara got to her feet abruptly, her face stony, and marched away.

Oh, what a blunderpuss. 'I'm sorry, Tara! I didn't mean that—'

No reply was audible, to Elspeth at least. But she had no problem hearing the slam of her front door.

Chapter 13
Tara
16 May

S he placed the five climbing roses in the trolley and joined the
long queue for the till. They were a glorious 'ballet shoe
pink', top of the range, £39.99 each. The garden centre had only
recently re-opened and was crammed with people desperate to
catch up on the arrival of spring, pushing trolleys heaped with
plants and bags of potting mix. Just her luck to be behind this
man, who was buying what appeared to be a significant fraction of
the centre's produce. She heaved a small sigh as he plonked two
garden gnomes and a portable picnic set onto the conveyor belt.
No doubt he intended to join the throng of outdoor enthusiasts in
local grassy spaces, now people were allowed to sunbathe in
public again and go out to exercise willynilly.

Tara packed her purchases into the boot of her Mini and
drove towards the village to pick up the latest version of Elspeth's
prescription. As she started the ignition, the usual rattle from
whatever was wrong inside the engine greeted her. This latest
issue might be the death knell for her dear old Mini. Its MOT was
coming up soon. How was she going to afford to get it fixed along
with the transmission and everything else that needed repairing?
Then there was the cost of petrol, and the outrageous price

charged by the council simply to be allowed to park outside your own house. But the thought of going on public transport was too depressing to contemplate. At the lights, she leaned forward and picked up a browning apple core from the Mini's passenger footwell. There was no denying, sometimes life could be a bitch.

The queue outside the pharmacy was shorter than usual, but the wait was longer. She shuffled along, her impatience growing. How much longer would it take to get inside the pharmacy? And why was she giving up her precious time for an old woman who didn't appreciate her? She was a fool to wait on Elspeth like this. The woman didn't deserve her help – all she did was criticise and belittle. Accusing her of being selfish and *acting like a jealous child*, indeed! And how dare Elspeth insinuate that Tara was jealous of Ashley? Tara had gone out of her way to be a good friend and neighbour, and Elspeth had repaid her by insulting her.

It was now painfully clear that Elspeth, the woman whom Tara had grown so fond of over the past two decades, now preferred Ashley's company to Tara's. Elspeth was extra chirpy whenever Ashley was visiting – practically every day, now – as they sat together in Elspeth's back garden. With a twinge of envy, Tara remembered how loudly and long Elspeth and Ashley had laughed together the last time, apparently not caring whether anyone else might notice.

The pair had been laughing at her, most likely, discussing her behind her back and picking over her faults. They found her an object of amusement. She had caught their furtive glances towards her house. She had been too far away to see properly, but could imagine the glee in Elspeth's eyes as she'd made that joyous snort.

Tara *was* jealous of Ashley, Elspeth was right.

Back at Wilton Close, Tara parked outside, took out two of the five rose pots from the Mini's boot and put them on Elspeth's doorstep with the bag of pharmacy items. Then she went back to the car to get two more pots. After lifting the last pot, she put it back down. Frustration and anger surged inside her. She'd take this rose as a small payment for her generosity in helping out her neighbour all this time. Elspeth wouldn't miss it, would she?

Tara stabbed Elspeth's doorbell with her finger to announce her arrival and went home to change into her gardening clothes. She might as well finish the job now. This was absolutely the last time she would do anything to help Elspeth.

On her return to Elspeth's house, she saw that the side gate was now open. Anger ripped through her. What did Elspeth think Tara was, a servant expected to use the side entrance?

It took over an hour for her to clear the remaining brambles, ivy and an assortment of other weeds, then dump them all into Elspeth's garden waste bin. Tara wiped her face and stood back to admire her handiwork. Elspeth might not be overly pleased with what Tara had done. But the garden looked like a garden now, not an aspiring wilderness.

Elspeth stepped away from the kitchen window as Tara knocked on the back door, opened it a few inches and put her head into the room.

'All done.' Tara smiled. 'The garden looks much neater now.'

'You haven't taken away all the buddleia, have you?'

'Not all of it. It's a weed, it grows wild everywhere.'

Elspeth frowned and folded her arms.

'Did you get a receipt from the garden centre?'

Her voice remained frosty, her expression glacial. Tara had a strong impulse to stomp as hard as she could on the woman's foot. What sort of friend was Elspeth? Not even a *Thank you for all your hard work* was forthcoming.

'It's somewhere,' she replied. 'Did you look in the carrier bag with your medication?'

But Elspeth had already left the kitchen and didn't reply.

Before leaving, Tara went back into the garden. She scanned the border along the fence for Ashley's climbing rose. She stared at the imposter, bile burning her throat. It looked larger and further advanced than the climbers that Tara had just bought for Elspeth, a picture of glorious vitality.

With a glance at the house to check that Elspeth wasn't in sight, she hurried to the shed and retrieved the secateurs. Breathing heavily, she leaned over Ashley's rose. One quick thrust of secateurs and a stem was severed. Its cargo of small, perfectly formed flowers fell to the soil.

A surge of adrenalin-charged satisfaction went through her. She squeezed the blades against another thick, rose-laden stem, imagining it was Ashley's arm. How dare that woman take Elspeth away from her? She tried to stop herself from removing a third stem, but in the end had to give in.

Chapter 14
Elspeth

As soon as she saw Tara leave the house, Elspeth locked the side gate, went into the kitchen and searched for the receipt from Sunshine Garden Centre. She found it at the bottom of the pharmacy bag, screwed up into a tiny ball.

She smoothed out the receipt and stared at it. How odd. Tara had bought five roses but only four plants were lined up on her kitchen worktop. There was one missing. She sat down at the table, uneasy. Surely, Tara hadn't taken the fifth plant for herself? She wouldn't do something like that, would she?

But suddenly it seemed quite possible. Tara could easily have taken the missing plant from her Mini into her own house rather than delivering it to Elspeth's porch. And Tara had made excuses about receipts being unavailable several times; she'd lost the receipt or she'd forgotten to ask for one at the shop.

Thoughts churning, Elspeth went upstairs to the computer and performed the protracted sequence of tasks needed to access her bank account. Scrolling through the statement, she made a note of the amounts charged to her account on the days that Tara had gone shopping for her. One or two of the amounts seemed somewhat high. Without the receipts, it was impossible to know whether there was anything untoward. She ought to have been firmer about asking for them, so she could see exactly what Tara had bought. But that had seemed untrusting.

She made another mug of tea, a knot of anxiety forming in her gut at the thought of the state in which Tara had left the garden. Maybe she shouldn't look just yet... Elspeth walked towards the end of the garden, where Tara had been working, and stood blinking in disbelief. The small area of wilderness, which had provided a home for butterflies and bees, was gone. Not only that, the cluster of intense purple buddleia that had grown by the fence had been virtually removed... She felt a spurt of anger. Had Tara had done this on purpose, to upset Elspeth?

Surely not.

Around her, amid faint strains of birdsong, daylight slowly faded. Elspeth wiped the dampness from her eyes and walked towards the border, cleared to make room for her new roses. She had plenty already but no white ones or climbers. Anyway, one could never have too many roses... She would plant the new ones that Tara had bought alongside Ashley's rose. That might be therapeutic.

Her breath caught. No, surely not...

Beside the new rose plant lay a stem studded with unfurling buds. It had been cut clean off. A second stem lay on top, at an angle. A third stem fell limply from the plant, almost severed.

Her legs felt too weak to hold her weight. Elspeth slid down to her knees on the grass, her heart thumping. How had this happened? Who would have done such a thing? Despite the warmth, she shivered. This was a wanton act of vandalism.

Tara had to be responsible. She had been in this garden only a few hours ago; no one else had been here. She had been here alone when Elspeth went back inside the house, so she'd had the opportunity... But why?

The answer came in no time. Ashley had given the rose to Elspeth; that was why.

For the second time Elspeth brought the knocker down on the door of number 33, this time with as much force as she could, then took several steps back onto the path. Tara had to hear that, surely... The door opened and Tara appeared in a dressing gown, a towel wrapped around piled-up hair, face moist, red and unpleasantly scrunched. No face mask, of course.

'What is it, Elspeth? I'm in the middle of washing my hair. Has something happened?'

'Yes, something *has* happened.' The dressing gown's sleeves were badly frayed, she noticed, and one tie holder was missing from the waist, causing the gown to sag and expose a section of Tara's large, plump breast. She frowned. 'Perhaps you could come over when you're dressed.'

'Tell me now, can't you?' Tara adjusted her gown.

Elspeth wondered where to start. The missing buddleia? The missing receipts? The missing plant? The vandalised rose?

'I found this receipt from the garden centre.' She held it up. 'For some reason it was screwed up into a ball. There appears to be a plant missing. You bought five roses but only delivered four.'

'Really? How odd.' Tara's eyes had taken on a strangely bright hue. 'I'm sure I put five plants into my trolley. I must have forgotten to take one from the checkout.' Tara tucked a strand of dripping hair under the towel. 'Oh, I remember now. There was a man in front of me unloading a stack of awful gnomes, along with about twenty plants. He might have taken it by mistake.'

The excuse was uncheckable. Tara shifted her weight from one foot to the other.

'Is there anything else?'

'Yes, there is.' Elspeth took a breath. 'One of my rose plants has been damaged. The one Ashley gave me.'

Tara's eyes widened. 'What damage do you mean?'

'Two stems have been deliberately hacked off. And another is hanging by a thread.' She fought to keep the emotion from her voice. 'The plant might not survive.'

'I'm so sorry to hear that, love. How on earth could something so terrible have happened?' Tara sounded mystified as well as horrified; either she was telling the truth or her acting skills were first-rate.

'You were in my garden just this afternoon—' She stopped abruptly. To accuse her neighbour outright of wanton vandalism could be tricky.

'It might have been a fox.' Tara rubbed her chin as if contemplating. 'I noticed bits of rubbish and empty cartons on your lawn earlier and put them in the dustbin.'

'Foxes don't bite through rose stems, Tara.'

'It may have been extra hungry. Or it was a cub, practising its chewing—'

'Don't be ridiculous!'

Elspeth tried to imagine a fox cub chewing through her rose. Tara removed the towel from her head and draped it over her shoulders. Her expression darkened.

'Are you accusing me of lying?'

'I honestly don't know what to think.'

'When did you notice the damage?'

'About ten minutes ago. So?'

'The damage could have been done by some creature after I left, couldn't it? There's a fox that comes into my garden sometimes, so it can probably find a way into yours. Especially in the early evening, when it's getting dark. There's a hedgehog that visits, too. They can nibble through goodness knows what.'

Elspeth breathed hard, unable to summon any words.

'I suppose it's not absolutely impossible,' she said finally.

Tara beamed. 'There you go, I knew there'd be an explanation.'

An explanation? The woman was unbelievable. Tara went back inside, leaving Elspeth on the doorstep.

After sitting for a long time on the sofa in fading light, Elspeth dialled Mira's number.

'Hello, Elspeth. How are you?'

'Things are a little difficult, actually—'

'Sorry, my dear, but I'll have to cut you off. My granddaughter is over – we're having a socially distanced chat in the garden. Would you mind if I called you back tomorrow?'

'Of course.' She tried not to sound despondent. 'Speak soon.'

She phoned Alice. She was about to ring off when her friend said 'Hello' in a suspicious tone.

'Alice, thank goodness you're in.'

'Elspeth, lovely to hear from you! Only I can't talk now, I'm trying to get this Zoom connection working – it's a right pain. It's my wine society meeting, we're having a quiz. I'm meant to be adjudicating.'

She bid Alice goodbye and ended the call, mentally trawling through the list of her surviving friends. A dozen, at least. Since the pandemic, she'd not seen any of them. The only contact had been unsatisfactory snatches of conversation over the phone, which began with her apologising for not being able to hear as well as she used to, and ended with promises on either side to meet up 'when things get back to normal'. Whenever that would be.

She phoned Ashley.

'Hello, dear, sorry to call so late. I'm not interrupting anything, am I?'

'Not at all, I'm just watching the news.'

'Would you be able to pop over for a few minutes?'

'What is it, Elspeth?'

'Tara has...' A surge of emotion stole her words. Tara might have convinced someone else more forgetful, in a more advanced state of decline. But the performance hadn't worked. Elspeth still had her wits about her, if not her mobility or her hearing.

'I'll be over in two minutes,' Ashley said.

Her next-door-neighbour-but-one stood a good two metres from the front door, as usual a mask covering much of her face.

'What's happened?' Ashley's voice was concerned. 'Are you OK?'

'Come through. I'll show you. I'll open the side gate.' Elspeth switched on the outdoor light and led the way to the border along the fence. 'Look.' She pointed to the damaged plant, looking away quickly.

'Oh my God.' Ashley breathed in sharply, brought her hand up to her face. 'Who did that? Not... It wasn't...?'

She nodded.

'Bloody hell, Elspeth. Tara did that?'

'Unless it really was a fox, as she tried to make me believe. I'm going to sit down. I don't feel so good.'

She sat down at the table on the side of the garden farthest from Tara's house. A large, bushy shrub provided a screen from prying eyes. Ashley leaned forward.

'Tell me what's going on.'

'This may sound crazy. I can hardly believe it myself.' She motioned to Ashley's face mask. 'You don't need to bother with that now, dear. I think I'm safe enough out here. Besides, Tara has been standing next to me without one often enough.'

She explained all that had happened, including the over-gardened garden, the missing rose and her suspicions that Tara had been stealing from her.

'That's horrendous.' Ashley put her hand on the top of Elspeth's arm. She seemed lost for words.

'It's only small things she's taken, as far as I can see... But that isn't the important thing.' Her words came out in a rush, a tremble catching her voice. 'I've known her for so long. I thought she was a friend, I thought I could trust her. And all along... She stole from me and attacked your rose, then lied about them both.'

Ashley glanced behind her shoulder towards Tara's house, and lowered her voice.

'I know we don't know each other all that well, yet. But honestly, Elspeth, I'm concerned about Tara. I really think it's best that you stay clear of her for a while.'

Elspeth fought back the tears. She didn't want Tara to come over any more, to help in any way whatsoever.

'Maybe you should, too,' she replied. 'She's been acting weirdly ever since you started coming over... She's put out that I spend more time with you than with her, I think.'

'She's jealous of me?' Ashley raised her eyebrows, mulling it over. 'I can understand in a way – you've been her friend for such a long time, then I come along... Why would she be stealing from you, though?'

'I'm not sure. She seems to think I'm rolling in money... She's always been funny about my family having an aristocratic connection. Nothing amazing – my great-grandfather was an Earl, that's all. But I inherited some things because of it. Furniture, clocks that don't work, antique jewellery...' Her thoughts turned back to practicalities. 'I hope you don't mind me asking, but would you mind getting me some shopping occasionally? It would be once a week at most. The pharmacy has started delivering my medication, thank God, so it's really only a few bits from the health-food shop.'

'Of course I wouldn't mind. I'd be only too happy—' Ashley broke off. She was staring at something in the distance, above their heads.

'What is it?'

'I just saw a blind move upstairs. The light has just gone off.' Ashley sounded fearful. 'I think she's watching us.'

'Oh, flaming Nora. I can't believe this.' Trying not to be obvious, Elspeth rotated her neck towards her neighbour's house. The blinds were half closed, unmoving. She had an urge to laugh. But Ashley was looking pale. 'Let's go in the kitchen. She won't be able to see us there.'

'No, we shouldn't, you're still meant to be shielding. If anything happened to you because of me, I'd never forgive myself.'

'Well, I need a drink. Will you join me in a whisky? Or something more ladylike?'

Ashley smiled. 'No, whisky's fine. I'm not very ladylike.'

'Nor me.'

Elspeth returned with two shot glasses of Teacher's.

'I don't think she'll see much of us behind this,' Ashley said, glancing up at the window again. She had shifted her chair so both it and her were engulfed by foliage.

'I can't see much of you either,' Elspeth replied, smiling. 'But we can't be too careful, can we? She might have a pair of those infra-red binoculars or something.'

Ashley tittered. Soon they were both laughing, louder than seemed wise in the circumstances.

'Elspeth!' Ashley stage whispered across the table. 'Not so loudly! She might hear.'

Elspeth tried to stop laughing but couldn't. She grabbed her cardigan and held its sleeve over her mouth, which resulted in a noise like someone being smothered.

'That's exactly what I needed,' she said when she'd recovered her composure. 'If Tara overheard, I don't care.'

'Bollocks to Tara!' Ashley replied. 'It's sad though, that anyone would react as she did. Worrying, too. What must be going through her head?'

'I really don't know.' Elspeth didn't want to know, either.

Instantly, she felt guilty. She had been slightly insensitive to her neighbour's needs – and perhaps a little selfish. Tara had done such a lot for her over the past couple of months, there was no denying. At one time, Tara had been dropping supplies onto Elspeth's doorstep two or three times a week. 'I've been thinking... I might give her a gift to say thank you for helping me out.'

'Good idea. What do you have in mind?'

'She likes earrings – she often compliments me on mine. There aren't any jewellers open, though.'

After Ashley had left, a thought struck her. She did already have some earrings – unworn, inside a gift box, the ones she'd bought months ago, intending to give to Lou for her birthday. But now Lou was no longer around... She couldn't keep the gift for herself; it would always be a reminder of her friend's death. Why not offer it to Tara? The earrings would only go to waste otherwise. With any luck, she thought with a twinge of unease, the gift would soften the blow when she told Tara about the end of their arrangement.

Chapter 15
Tara
17 May

As Elspeth's front door opened, Tara saw that Elspeth had dressed up. She was wearing a stylish ensemble of the sort she'd routinely worn before lockdown. No mask, today. A pair of simple but striking emerald earrings graced her ear lobes.

Tara shot a smile at her neighbour.

'What a lovely day it is. How are you keeping, Elspeth?'

Elspeth returned Tara's smile with a twitch of her thin lips, ignoring Tara's question.

'Let's go into the garden, shall we?'

From the formal, slightly chilly tone, it was clear that this request to 'pop over' wasn't to partake in a chat over morning coffee. Tara followed her neighbour through the hall and kitchen into the back garden.

Elspeth motioned to the bench on the patio, under a large sunshade.

'Sit down, I'll be back in one minute,' Elspeth said suddenly and rushed away.

Tara took off her mask, which squashed her nose and made it drip, and wandered towards the table on the opposite side of the garden. The table bore two telltale rings; it hadn't been cleaned

91

since Elspeth and Ashley had sat there last night. She had witnessed the last few minutes of their nocturnal tryst from her bedroom. Recalling their laughter, a distant memory tugged at Tara's mind.

Tarantula, Tarantula!

She pushed it away, strolled back to where she was meant to be and lowered herself onto the cushion-less bench, avoiding what looked like a dried-up splodge of bird shit.

Elspeth returned with two glasses of water and a fancy gift bag, which she placed on the patio table. Placing her foot on top of an upturned flowerpot, she sat down in the adjacent chair.

'I wanted to let you know how much I've appreciated your help all these weeks. You've been so kind – I don't know what I'd have done without you.' Elspeth seemed distinctly ill at ease. Her fingers pressed nervously into her neck.

Tara said nothing. With a smidgeon of envy, she noticed the large, strikingly set emerald on Elspeth's middle finger sparkling in the sunshine. One of Elspeth's family heirlooms? Elspeth probably had a matching necklace too, going by the size of the jewellery box on her dressing table. Tara had glimpsed the magnificent wooden box at one of Elspeth's birthday parties, while admiring Elspeth's bedroom furnishings en route to the ensuite bathroom – there'd been a queue at the one downstairs. Her own jewellery collection now consisted mostly of the sort of insubstantial tat enjoyed by teenagers. She hadn't bought anything nice for herself in ages; even her newer clothes were looking worn, or out of date.

'This is to say thank you,' Elspeth said, pushing the bag across the table towards Tara.

Tara loosened the gaudy ribbon. There was a small, hinged velvet box inside. She took out the box and lifted the lid.

Earrings. She picked one up. It looked fragile. Little beads of red hung from a dull blue central stone.

'That's coral,' Elspeth gushed. 'And turquoise, of course. I hope you like them. I thought they looked so pretty – and a little bohemian.'

Bohemian? Tara held the earring closer. It was cheap rubbish. Elspeth could easily have afforded a more substantial gift, something as striking as her own jewellery. Instead, she'd given her this... junk.

'Thank you, Elspeth.' Tara smiled, trying to control her swirling emotions.

Was this Elspeth's way of getting rid of her? Her neighbour was clearly on edge. 'Did you have something to tell me?'

Elspeth fidgeted, looking as if she had a passionfruit stuck up her bottom.

'Actually, I wanted to say... As it looks like the restrictions will be ending soon... I should be able to manage on my own, from now on.'

'But the restrictions aren't over yet, Elspeth. The current advice for the over-seventies is to stay shielding.'

Elspeth's brow creased. Her lips squeezed into a thin line. The emerald on her ear flashed in the sunshine.

'It's kind of you to be so concerned, Tara, but I'll manage. I'm going to start going to the shops myself soon, whatever Boris tells us to do. I don't want to burden you any longer.'

'I see.' She did see, very well. Her help was no longer required, plain and simple. Cold anger spread through her body.

'If this is about the rose plant I mislaid in the garden centre... I'm sorry, really I am. And as I said, I was very sorry to hear about the damage to Ashley's rose.'

Elspeth frowned again.

'Look, Tara. I really have appreciated all your help with my shopping and sorting things out at the chemist and what have you. I know it's not been easy for you – I'm fussy about my food and I've got grumpy at times. Now, though, I feel it's better for the burden to be shared, as it were. There are plenty of others who'd be willing to do a bit now and then.'

'Like Ashley?'

Elspeth's cheeks reddened. She pulled her fingers through her hair, growing out of its once-immaculate cut.

'Ashley is a possibility, yes.'

'I see.' Tara put the earring back in the box and checked her watch. She knew it; Ashley was taking over. 'I'd better not keep you any longer, I've got Saturday's food stall to organise – we're doing a roaring trade, did you know?'

Elspeth got to her feet with a small smile. She looked relieved.

'You're doing a great job, dear. Keep up the good work. Brampton needs you. Now, forgive me but I'm expecting a call soon from my godson in New Zealand.'

Tara stood too, reluctantly scooping up the little box. Clearly, Elspeth wanted to cut their conversation short. Perhaps, though, she might have a speck of interest in hearing Tara's big news before they parted.

'Did you know I'm going to be on the Alan Garfield show in a couple of weeks?' The interview had just been scheduled, after her endless emails to the programme's producer.

Elspeth looked blank. Maybe she didn't listen to the radio much now her hearing wasn't so good.

'It's the most-listened-to programme on the local radio station,' Tara explained. 'Thousands of people listen in.'

'That's wonderful, Tara. I'm glad you've found your niche.'

'It's not about me!' she snapped. 'It's about spreading the word that we have a community in Brampton.' She followed Elspeth through the miscellany of objects cluttering the passage at the side of the house. Several watering cans, a sack of compost, toy ducks... A thought struck her. 'I must say, I'm impressed you managed to find some jewellery when only the essential shops are open. The hardware shop doesn't sell jewellery now, does it?'

Elspeth stopped midway through opening the gate and turned, a worried look on her face.

'I bought them earlier, before the restrictions started.'

'Oh. So not with me in mind, then?'

'Actually, they were going to be a birthday present for a friend.' Elspeth sounded apprehensive.

'You decided not to give them to her?' She was genuinely curious.

'I didn't get the chance to, unfortunately. She died, quite suddenly.' Elspeth shoved the gate open, standing against the fence to make room for Tara to pass. 'Good luck with the interview. I'll try to listen in... I'd better be getting on. I've got to get my audiologist appointment sorted with the hospital.'

'After you've talked with your godson?' Tara gave a parting wave. The woman's subterfuge was only too obvious. 'Goodbye, then. Thanks again for the lovely gift.'

At home, Tara got out the earrings, laced the hooks through her ear lobes and stood in front of her dressing-table mirror. The blue of the stones jarred with the unsubtle red beads. The earrings looked distinctly vulgar, not the sort of thing she would ever wear. A wave of anger reared up.

'That mean-hearted, spore-ridden old chimpmunk! Who the hell does she think she is?'

This meagre offering was meant to show Elspeth's appreciation of the long hours she'd put in week after week to tend to her neighbour's needs? After all that effort, all she got was a shoddy pair of earrings originally intended for Elspeth's dead friend?

She pulled out an earring and tossed it to the floor. A horde of tiny beads scurried across the floorboards.

Fuck's sake, the sodding things were so flimsy they couldn't even withstand a gentle toss to the floor! What had she done to deserve such a feeble gift? She pulled off the other earring and flung it away from her as hard as she could. It hit the wall with a satisfying crack. Finally she strode out of the house, slamming the front door.

Outside, it was as hot as a summer's day. Across the road, the green was packed. As she passed Ashley and Zac's house, she noticed the daughter – Layla? – strolling towards her. The girl was pretty, it had to be said, with Ashley's slight frame and Zac's near-black eyes and high cheekbones. Beside her, a young woman with greasy bottle-blonde hair and a tattoo on her upper arm. Both were preoccupied with their conversation, not noticing where they were going. Tara girded her arm to jolt them, and carried on.

She knew she ought to stay away from other people when she felt like this. Anger simmered off her, renewing every time it abated. What a mean woman Elspeth was. How disingenuous, foisting a present meant for a dead person onto her...

After a while she found herself at the poor end of the village, where people were badly dressed in low-quality leisure wear exposing sagging rears and flabby thighs. She got that some people had very little money, but did they have to dress so tastelessly?

'Afternoon, Tara!'

She turned to the speaker, a large-bodied woman in a floral print dress and plimsolls, pushing a toddler in a chariot laden with Lidl bags.

'Hello, Mrs...' She knew the woman, but from where?

'It's Janine, from the council. I was at the Zoom meeting about your food initiative.'

'Ah yes, I remember you! Mrs Dowdy.' The woman hadn't been particularly helpful at the meeting. It had been called by the council during the early stages of the food initiative, supposedly to ensure that the food being offered met 'minimum standards'.

'Mrs Doughty.' A scowl passed over the woman's face. 'How is it all going, then? I've heard your name all over the place, lately. Your Saturday stall certainly seems popular.'

'Yes, we've had to restrict people to one box each... We're doing all we can to source extra food. We have a baking rota now, and garden produce is coming in.'

'Very good.' Mrs Doughty coughed. 'I hesitated to say anything, but as you're here... There have been complaints to us recently about the standard of the food on offer.'

'Oh? What's wrong with it?'

'Nothing terrible. Over-salty bread, cakes with soggy middles, that sort thing.' Mrs Doughty gave an embarrassed titter. 'Several residents have sent in photos of tins beyond their use-by dates. As this venture has been helping the local community, we haven't taken any action – we don't want to jeopardise an operation that benefits so many. But if things don't improve...'

Another thin smile. With an effort, Tara smiled back. She longed to ram a cake with a 'soggy middle' into this woman's face and watch the smile disappear.

'How many people have complained, may I ask? Four? Five? Ten?'

'I'd rather not discuss the details, if you don't mind. I'm telling you in the spirit of friendly cooperation. Well, enjoy the rest of your day.'

Mrs Doughty turned away. Tara continued her walk.

She knew exactly what this was all about. It was a week since the group had reported a cluster of local infringements of lockdown rules to the police: Bulldog Man for serving beer to at least twelve people one evening in his back garden; Mrs Smythe for impromptu social afternoons at the Bowling Club; and the arts and crafts shop for getting around the restrictions by selling hammers. Then there were those rampant exercisers and picnickers on the green... Belatedly, the council had put up notices forbidding picnics and barbeques, and a pair of constables had strolled around asking people to disperse.

These complaints were from disgruntled rule-breakers trying to pay her back, surely, nothing to do with the food's quality. This wasn't France, where people cared deeply about what they put into their mouths. In rural England, no one cared about the occasional salty sourdough loaf or slightly undercooked Victoria sponge, for heaven's sake. She spat a globule of phlegm, imagining Mrs Doughty's pudgy face on the receiving end. How dare they try to undermine her project?

Splat.

'What the fuck?' It was the lycra-shorted grandmother who cycled everywhere, one of the food initiative's most loyal customers, carting off a dozen tins of cat food every week. The woman wiped slime off her cheek, her eyes round with surprise. Under her indignant stare, warmth climbed Tara's neck.

'I'm so sorry! It wasn't meant for you! I mean, it wasn't meant for anyone, I just had a frog in my throat.'

The woman walked on, shaking her head and muttering.

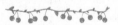

Tara gazed down at the back gardens of her neighbours. On warm evenings like this, the back terrace was perfect for watching what was going on.

Uphill, Elspeth was nowhere to be seen. Downhill at Ashley and Zac's, Layla and the same female friend as before were laid out on their terrace on reclining chairs. The pair sat very close, talking in low voices. Neither wore masks. They were definitely from different households, though. Where were Ashley and Zac?

Didn't they care that their daughter was breaking Covid rules –
and what about their Muslim values?

She sighed and went back to her fledgling *Mention to Alan*
list.

1. The Wiltons Covid Community Support Group –
   still supporting elderly and vulnerable residents in
   local streets and beyond, through the selfless actions
   of its members.
2. Brampton Food Initiative – from humble beginnings,
   the BFI now offers food and household goods every
   week to hundreds of residents and local families in
   need of assistance

She started to feel apprehensive. The interview, scheduled for
early June, would be live. What if the show's host mentioned
anything negative or potentially embarrassing?

But that was unlikely. Alan Garfield wasn't one of those quarrelsome sorts who sought out controversy. Besides, Alan's show
had more listeners than any other local radio station. This was her
chance to shine in front of thousands. No longer would she simply
be a woman trying to survive the pandemic like everyone else –
she was poised to become a person of distinction. A minor
celebrity, even. In a relatively small, local sense, of course.

She pushed the list away. No need to overthink things.

Oh God, what was going on next door? Layla was crying and
the friend was offering a tissue. There was a bottle of wine
between them, and two glasses.

Suddenly the friend looked up and saw Tara. Tara looked
away quickly. What Ashley's daughter got up to wasn't any of her
business, was it?

She lay in bed in the dark, in turn excited and worried about
the interview. From next door, the girls' voices drifted through her

bedroom window, loud enough to hear distinct words between the intermittent crying.

'Don't be like this, hun. They're not worth getting worked up over.'

Another bout of tears.

'Fuck them! They're just jealous cos you're so pretty and the boys like you. You're the nicest, kindest friend I've ever had...'

It went on for hours. The night was warm, her open window admitting a much-needed breeze – she was damned if she was going to close it because of the noise from next door. Several times she fell asleep only to be woken by loud giggling or sobbing. She woke again at 5am, once again hearing the girls' voices.

Damn those two! She put on her dressing gown and went to the kitchen to make a mug of tea, deep in thought.

Ashley's daughter's friend had spent the night at the house. Two young women from different households without any social distancing, sharing a bottle of wine together and talking into the early hours and beyond... That was a blatant breach of the rules, by the daughter of someone who ought to be setting an example to the community. This clearly *was* her business – and other people's, too.

Who are you to judge, with all that you've done?

Tara tried to ignore the small voice. She shouldn't have taken that damned diary out of the box; it was messing with her head. Yet it was hard to resist the urge to look at it again, to find out more. Since reading those two early entries, she was starting to remember more about life with her mother, Zoe and Evie. But she still couldn't recall much from the year that her sisters had died, both in terrible circumstances.

Zoe had fallen from a rope that was attached to a tree in their back garden, on that day in March during the party for her thirteenth birthday. Tara had been there along with Zoe's friends when the rope snapped in two. Evie had drowned six months later. Tara had been with her earlier but they had become separated. It had been warm, at the end of summer, just before school started again. The two of them had swum at Myers Beach then decided to go on, heading along the rock-pooled path at the bottom of the cliffs towards Black's Beach. She had gone on ahead, as far as she could remember, impatient to swim at her favourite beach, which she didn't get to do often. But they never got there. The tide had come in faster than either of them had realised.

Despite the inquests finding both deaths to be accidental, her mother had expressed doubt that the rope Zoe had been swinging on had simply snapped without human intervention. Furthermore, for weeks Ivy had questioned Tara about the day of Evie's death, as if she imagined Tara had somehow played a part in her sister drowning, despite the fact that Tara had tried to save Evie by running for help.

Frustratingly, Tara's recollections of both days had always been hazy, as if a small part of her brain had gone to sleep. As the years went on, her childhood became even hazier. There were few distinct memories and many jumbled impressions. She'd gone to the therapist to get some control over her angry impulses, also wondering if he might be able to help salvage some of her lost memories. He hadn't. Instead, he had told her she couldn't expect to remember events that were profoundly disturbing. *The mind forgets what it can't assimilate.*

Tara finished her tea and put down her mug.

She went into her office and pulled open the desk drawer, where she'd placed the diary after taking it down from the loft. What harm could it do to look at the diary one more time? Then she would burn it. She couldn't wait any longer. Knowing the truth would be better than sensing the ghost of something unreachable inside you. It was a bit like needing to watch the next scene in a horror film. You had to know what happened next, even though you knew it might give you nightmares.

She opened the diary.

After the two entries she'd already read, there was a spate of entries describing ordinary things: a trip to the cinema, what went on at school, the kids in her class, punishments meted out by teachers, a boy she'd kissed... Nothing whatsoever about life at home or how her sisters had died.

Then something different.

February 27th 1982

Mum is staying with her friend whose house was flooded, leaving my sisters to 'look after me', haha. All day yesterday they kept to themselves, whispering whenever I came close – nothing new there. I got ready for bed, relieved they had left me alone.

I was fast sleep when something brushed against my hair. I opened my eyes and saw a gigantic spider right in front of my face. It was just hanging there, legs twitching – the most horrific thing I have seen in my life. I screamed and tried to get out of bed but I couldn't move. The spider batted into my face.

A tarantula, it looked like.

Then I heard someone ran out of my room and the light came on. The spider collapsed onto the duvet. It was a fake one made out of black plastic. The middle was attached to a long black cord that went to the end of a stick.

I heard Zoe and Evie laughing from Zoe's room. I've never heard them laugh so hard. They kept on for ages, making creepy howling noises.

I hate Zoe. I know the spider was her idea because she knows how much I hate spiders and she once put a dead one in my shoe. Anyway, every trick my sisters play on me is always her idea.

I've had my own idea. What if Zoe had to go to away for a while? To hospital maybe. Something could happen to her that looks like an accident. Even if Mum and Evie suspect it was me who hurt her, they'll never know for sure.

I'm going to think up the perfect thing.

Tara skipped forward through the pages, scanning the entries for dates. March 5th, March 18th, March 22nd, March 27th... Fear made her hands cold and clammy. March 28th was coming up, the date of Zoe's death. The entry for the 28th was in particularly tiny handwriting. It took up the full page and continued over the next page, whose date she had crossed out.

March 28th 1982

The rope was in the back garden when we moved in. It was old and already fraying, high up where it rubs against the pear tree when you swing on it. I just helped it along. Last week I went outside with a knife from the kitchen drawer and cut a bit more away, until there was scarcely any rope left in that one place. No one saw the damage because it was so high up, I suppose. Anyway, Mum is too busy to notice things like that.

Zoe always used to be swinging from the branch. But sod's law, she didn't go on the rope any more after I cut it, as if she guessed what might happen if she did. Today though it was Zoe's thirteenth birthday party.

All her friends came. Before I could do anything to stop them, they all decided to go and play in the garden.

They took turns to swing on the rope. Mum told me to join them so I watched from near the pear tree. I was frightened in case someone else had an accident instead of Zoe.

Should I suddenly pretend to notice that the rope was literally hanging by a thread? I was about to yell Get off! to Lydia, Zoe's best friend, when she climbed down and Zoe took her turn.

Zoe climbed up higher than the others and swung out as far as she could. She started doing tricks, holding out one leg to the side and hanging upside down. Mum wasn't looking. I saw her through the dining room window, head down, setting the table for the birthday tea.

I didn't see Zoe fall. I heard the thump when she hit the ground though. Someone screamed, then they all were screaming. No one moved except me. I went up to where my sister was sprawled on the grass.

Zoe lay there with one arm squashed under her body and her neck pushed up at a strange angle. Hair was draped over one eye, the other eye was wide open. A long piece of rope had fallen on the grass near her hand. I could see the frayed section at one end where it had snapped.

My hands started to tremble. I felt so cold, I couldn't get my breath. I hadn't meant to kill her, I just wanted to hurt her enough that she'd have to go to hospital for a while. But now she's dead.

An ambulance came and took Zoe away. Then the police came and asked everyone questions. Evie told them she was in her room with her boyfriend when it happened. Mum told them she ran out of the house when she heard screaming. I told them it was an accident. Zoe had been swinging on the rope one second and was lying on the ground the next.

The police spent a long time in the garden looking around and taking photos. After they left, I went into the dining room and helped myself to a piece of birthday cake. I didn't think about it. By then it was late and I was really hungry and it seemed a shame to let the cake go to waste.

Mum came in and called me a 'heartless devil'.

Later Evie came into my room and said she knew it was my fault Zoe
was dead. I told her it was an accident, how could it be my fault?

Tara stared at the page. The writing blurred. She could hardly
take in the words – her own words. Somehow, what that girl had
done had been excised from Tara's mind.

After a long time she read on, scanning the pages for
anything else about Zoe's death. There was only one short
entry:

April 5th 1982

Evie has stopped talking to me and doesn't seem to like me being near
her. I catch her staring at me sometimes like she's trying to work something out. Mum is even colder to me than before. I don't mind though,
because no one laughs at me any more or does nasty things.

Tara buried her head in her hands. She was going to be sick.
How could she have done such a thing to Zoe, her own sister?
What sort of person was she?

But the truth was there in her own words, in black and white.
Tara had caused Zoe's death. She must have known it all along.
Her brain must have let go of it because the truth would be too
painful. She shut her eyes tight. A horrible realisation was
dawning.

What about Evie? What if Evie's drowning six months later
hadn't been a freak accident, either? Could she have forgotten
something important, so as not to get into trouble? Was Evie's
death her fault, too?

Tara reached out to turn the page and stopped, her heart
thudding. She closed the diary. No, not yet. She needed to stop
reading.

Her brain didn't stop, though.

The memory swooped in from that long-ago day, the clearest it had ever been.

She's striding between rockpools, trainers in her hands, warm sunlight on her arms. Her legs golden brown against the white of her costume.

Then she's standing on the rocky outcrop, peering down at the green sea below. Wind buffeting her hair, her body. There's something in the water... No, not something, someone. It's Evie. Her sister is floundering, her arms moving ineffectually, her little head bobbing in the foamy waves.

Tara runs up the steep cliff path to get help, as fast as she can. Only her feet seem weighed down, her windpipe hurts and her heart thumps painfully against her chest. Her lungs can't take another breath. She knows she has done something bad, so bad that the world has broken into tiny pieces and will never be the same again... In her ears, that shrill sound. But it isn't the wind or the gulls, part of her realises. It's her own scream.

Chapter 16
Ashley
2 June

After another night of worrying, Ashley woke late. She checked the calendar on her phone and groaned.

Oh no, Tuesday – another group meeting. Her daughter was sliding into depression and neither Zac nor she knew how to deal with it, and her son seemed to be falling under the influence of his fundamentalist friend. The last thing she needed was two hours on Zoom listening to the up-and-coming saviour of Brampton boast about her blasted radio interview.

She joined the meeting ten minutes late, apologising to the array of faces on her computer screen. As expected, Tara was basking in post-interview glow. She was heavily made up as usual, with a dazzling shade of lipstick and a matching top.

'I must say, I was surprised at just how sweet Alan was. He put me at my ease straight away – and he was so charming! Just before we went on air, he winked at me and said I had a natural radio voice, beautiful and deep. And he'd heard my cupcakes were to die for.' Tara winked. Titters from the others. 'Alan's assistant took a photo of me and him together afterwards, with his arm around me... Did everyone tune in yesterday?'

'Of course.' Greg jumped in. He sported a paisley scarf

around his neck. 'You were a star, Tara. What was it Alan said at the end? Our group is a wonderful example of local people joining together in a time of crisis to look after their most vulnerable...'

'...and restoring community spirit,' Ursula finished off. 'Well done, Tara.'

Tara beamed. 'Now everyone knows who we are, anyway.'

'Everyone knows who you are, might be more accurate.' John's eyes fixed on a point in front of his screen, presumably containing Tara. 'You implied that you were the driving force behind everything – and I noticed you mentioned your business at least twice—'

Greg raised his hand. 'I think we can forgive a little self-promotion in the circumstances. Tara *has* been the driving force behind this group, hasn't she?'

'We've all worked hard,' John countered. 'Finding helpers for the vulnerable, manning the stall and organising this, that and the other so that the group can make a difference. It's been a joint effort.'

'I think we should *all* be proud of ourselves,' Tara broke in. 'I know we've had our differences, John. But we can rise above them, I hope. Perhaps a celebration is in order, now the restrictions have lifted a little? Outside, of course.'

'Excellent idea.' Greg sounded pleased. 'I'll provide the rum punch. Tony has perfected his recipe.'

A deep crease appeared between Tara's eyebrows.

'Moving on... I'm afraid I have something rather worrying to report. I had an impromptu meeting recently with a member of the town council. Apparently there have been complaints about the quality of food that we're handing out.'

Ursula put up her hand. 'One of the choir told me her neighbour found a squashed fly in a sourdough loaf, which he got from our Saturday stall. Fortunately, he spotted it before taking a bite.'

'Was it one of our loaves?'

'No one here made it. I think it came from someone in the Wiltons, but I'm not sure if it was bought or home-made.'

'Thanks for that information, Ursula. Sadly, I think there's a certain element of the village that is trying to undermine our efforts. I wouldn't be surprised if Bulldog Man found out that we reported him to the police—'

'*We* didn't report him, Tara, *you* did.' John broke in. 'I made my objection clear at the time. And I hope you're not insinuating that one of us is responsible for him finding out?'

Tara cleared her throat and examined the papers in her hand.

'Of course I'm not insinuating anything, don't be ridiculous! But we did vote on it, John, if I can I remind you. There was a consensus that the group should take a stand on people flagrantly breaching the rules, for the benefit of the community.'

Ashley's frustration mounted. She spoke for the first time, surprising herself.

'Can I suggest we move on to the next item on the agenda? I'm sure we all have things to be getting on with. This bickering isn't helping anything.'

'Hear, hear!' Greg responded. 'Well said, Ash.'

'Finishing up on food quality,' Tara went on, 'I think we can all agree that we need to put a stop to anyone who might be donating substandard food. We're already checking the use-by date on pre-made food. Can I propose that someone volunteers to randomly sample home-baked produce?'

'That's all very well, Tara,' Ursula began, 'but how is random sampling going to find a fly inside a loaf?'

Everyone started talking at once. Ashley felt her mind drifting and her eyelids drooping. This room was hot in the sunshine and she had slept badly again...

Tara coughed over the melee of voices.

'Everyone, if I could have your attention, please. Something has come to my attention concerning a member of this group.'

Ashley stopped doodling. Tara continued.

'I have reason to believe that this person hasn't been adhering to the Covid rules. In particular, the one about people not being allowed to visit the homes of others outside of their own household unless it's in a caring role, such as someone who delivers shopping to an elderly person.'

Silence.

'I don't want to name any names. I'm sure the person concerned knows who they are.'

Ashley realised she was holding her breath. She let it out and tried to resume her previous expression of mild frustration and boredom. There was no doubt in her mind who Tara was referring to.

'Excuse me for jumping in.' John raised an electronic hand. 'But is it appropriate for us to be discussing what members of the group may or may not be doing outside of these meetings?'

Tara gave an exaggerated sigh. 'I'm not naming anyone, John, I'm merely addressing the wider issue of standards and how they are upheld within this group. As I see it, given our special role in the community, each of us should take extra care to stick to the government guidelines—'

Ferne, rosy-cheeked and sweaty-browed, her hair up, stopped doing neck and shoulder rolls.

'What is it exactly that they're meant to have done? Are we talking about something small like – I dunno, going for a walk with a friend and popping into their place for five minutes to use the loo, or something more like—'

'Having everyone over for a massive party?' Greg suggested.

'I'm sure we'd all agree that each of us should be upholding the guidelines,' Ursula said in a prickly voice. 'But isn't it a matter for our own consciences rather than discussion within the group – unless Tara's saying that one of us has been holding large parties?'

'I wouldn't say it is quite on that scale, Ursula.' Tara wiped perspiration from her brow. 'Nevertheless, there have been quite serious breaches of the guidelines – such as making social visits to a vulnerable elderly person.'

Ashley's heart thudded. *It wasn't like that at all!* The words died before they reached her lips. Tara was twisting everything.

'Unfortunately,' Tara continued, 'it isn't just the person themselves who is breaking the rules, but one of their family, too—'

'This feels like a witch hunt to me.' John's eyes narrowed. He tapped the end of his pen on his desk, the sound clanging through Ashley's speakers. 'It goes without saying that we should all follow the rules as well as we're able. But we all slip up sometimes. None of us deserve to have our misdemeanours raked over here.'

'I agree with John,' Ursula said. 'If you're concerned about someone in this group, Tara, you should tackle them in private.'

Ashley felt her throat dry up. Tara was staring into the screen, her jaw clamped tight. She looked ready to disembowel both John and Ursula – not to mention Ashley herself.

Her post-meeting walk took longer than usual. She set off at top speed, keen to get away from this house, this street, this village. She felt queasy and light headed – and she could kick herself for not responding to Tara's verbal assault during the meeting. The woman was a hypocrite and a vindictive bully, more concerned about getting publicity than genuinely helping anyone.

Uneasiness pooled inside her gut. What had Tara meant by 'one of their family' breaking the rules? Surely, Tara wasn't talking about Anna's visit to Layla? Maybe, technically, it had broken the rules. But Layla had been distraught over some Snapchat messages that afternoon and badly in need of her best friend. The two had spent most of the time out on the terrace in the fresh air, well away from anyone else.

She recalled the empty bottle of wine she'd found on the terrace next morning. Had they been too loud and disturbed her neighbour?

Oh, shit. She'd have to speak to Tara. Her heart sank at the thought. The last thing she wanted was to confront that quarrelsome, interfering, bigoted woman. Besides, what if it escalated the situation and ended up making things worse for Layla? Weeks ago, Ashley had reported the social media bullying of Layla to the head of the Academy, and Zac had instructed their daughter to stop using Snapchat and Instagram – as if that was going to happen. Since then, things seemed to have calmed down.

She powered herself on, trying to focus on her surroundings rather than the thoughts rampaging inside her mind. If she'd known what Tara was like, she'd never have moved next door. But it was too late now.

Chapter 17
Elspeth
5 June

Elspeth woke early to chirping sparrows, which appeared to be building a nest in the wall. Despite the unsettled weather, much cooler than earlier in the week, there was no sign of rain. Her spirits soared. At last, she was going to be out of this house for a short while – away from Tara! For a few hours, she could forget about her increasingly sore right foot and the growing number of words she could no longer summon at will, not to mention the fact that she was going deaf and living next to a spiteful bizum.

She showered, dressed, ate a light breakfast – she would save herself for the cake this afternoon – placed her outfit on the bed and went outside with a bucket of hot soapy water. The Triumph stood on the road outside her front door, patiently awaiting an outing and looking rather sorry for itself. The bonnet and windscreen were dark with dust and grime, and a cobweb decorated a wing mirror.

Forty minutes later Elspeth stood back and admired the now-shining soft-top, in a fit state to be driven. She lowered herself into the driver's seat and turned the ignition key. Three times the engine spluttered feebly. The fourth time, nothing.

'Hell and damnation!'

She let go of the steering wheel and sank back into the leather seat. Anger fused into disappointment.

This was her own fault. Since the start of lockdown, she'd stopped using the car regularly and had only intermittently remembered to turn the engine over every few days to keep the battery charged. She'd have to walk to Mira's – or the old Raleigh would get her there, if she could find the bicycle amid the clutter. That would be safer for other road users. An old woman slowly going lame, deaf and losing her marbles was hardly the ideal driver of a feisty sports car, was she?

Her eyes began to well up.

Face it, Elspeth. You've already driven for the last time. Before she knew it, tears were slipping down her cheeks.

Sensing she was being watched, she looked around and met Tara's searching stare. Tara was watching Elspeth through her kitchen window. Her expression was a mixture of curiosity and disapproval – and something else. At once, Elspeth patted her cheeks dry and climbed out of the car. A shivery sensation lingered at the top of her head, as if she'd seen something repugnant.

The three of them took turns to light the tea lights set out on a table in Mira's garden around a large, framed photo of Lou. Then, standing two metres apart from each other, keeping their masks on, each in turn read out the tribute they had written for their friend.

Alice read a poem Lou had written a few years before, not a particularly good one. It brought tears to all their eyes, though.

Elspeth blew her nose. Momentarily forgetting herself, she

gave Alice a hug. Soon they were all hugging, long and hard. It was like finding water after weeks in a desert, Elspeth thought. You'd never imagine something as ordinary as water could taste so sweet.

'We aren't supposed to be hugging, are we?' Alice said.

'Oh, sod that,' Elspeth replied. 'A few hugs can't hurt, can they?'

'Not if we've been keeping ourselves to ourselves,' Mira replied. 'Let's not get hung up about a few hugs.'

'I've seen my grandson in the garden a few times.' Alice sounded worried. 'But we've kept our two metres.'

'I've been careful, too,' Elspeth added. 'Now, who else is for cake?'

Thankfully, the sad mood changed into one of celebration.

Now more than two people were allowed to meet outdoors, she had suggested a small gathering to remember Lou.

'Another glass of Prosecco, Elspeth?' Mira poised the bottle above Elspeth's fluted glass.

'Go on then. A small one as I'm cycling. I don't want to end up squished in the road.' She helped herself to a second slice of cake.

'How have you been?' Mira asked extra loudly, pulling her chair closer to Elspeth's. 'We've been worried about you. You haven't been to any of our Zoom meetings.'

Elspeth explained about her ongoing communication issues. But at least she could report that her audiologist appointment had finally been arranged.

'How are you managing without any family around? I don't know how I'd cope without mine nearby.'

'I do my best. That's all anyone can do, isn't it?' She didn't mention the long hours feeling simultaneously trapped and anxious about going out, and wondering how soon it would be before she lost her hearing – and her mind, for that matter.

She stayed longer than planned. The Prosecco slipped down

easily, as did the little snacks that Mira kept bringing out. The company of her friends became more enjoyable by the minute as the thought of going home to an empty house became less and less appealing.

At last, Elspeth put down her glass and got to her feet. The shadows were lengthening, but it would be light for an hour or so yet. She looked around Mira's garden at the flowers and shrubs in bloom, at the height of their beauty.

Maybe, she mused, it would be all right if she didn't stay around too much longer. She'd had a glorious time, hadn't she? She'd laughed and loved, and in her own small way had made her mark on the world.

Chapter 18
Tara

Elspeth paused her loving ministrations and stepped back, rag in hand, to admire her car. It was low-slung and shapely, a gorgeous shade of blue-green. Tara felt her hands clench into fists, her nails digging into her palms. This was too much. Clearly, despite the crisis facing the country, Elspeth could afford to keep her shiny jewel of a sports car. But did she have to flaunt the fact in front of her car-less neighbours?

Tara stepped away from the kitchen window. She imagined scratching the lovely paintwork with a nail. But she must try to keep her anger in check. If she didn't, bad things would happen again.

She pictured her Mini on the garage forecourt, sold for way less than its rightful price, and felt a tug of bitterness. Her life had been turned upside down by this godawful pandemic. All the money she'd spent last year upgrading her home office had been for nothing. Without clients, what was the point of a nice office? She could no longer afford to run a car, even.

She thumped the worktop. No-one had been willing to lend her any more money to tide her over this rough patch, and Zac pointedly ignored all her hints that her business had good invest-ment potential. Now she had to survive on government handouts.

But all was not lost. The radio interview had produced a rash of enquiries from potential clients. There was a pompous-sounding author seeking media coverage for his debut novel, with clearly more cash than sense, and others on the non-fiction side... She would be a fool not to use her increasing profile to her own benefit – who knew how famous she might end up? She wasn't just appearing on the radio; the county's lifestyle magazine had agreed to a piece about her efforts to help the local community and the village podcast had asked if they could devote an episode to her. And she still had this house. She would never have been able to afford this place without the inheritance. Her mother would have loved it, too.

At the cough of an engine trying to start, she darted back to the kitchen window. Elspeth was sitting inside her car, one hand on the steering wheel, no longer in casual clothes. Her lips were now red and a row of jewels glinted above her low-cut top...

Well, well, well. She'd assumed Elspeth was doing one of her occasional battery charging sessions, not actually going some-where. Where was the woman gadding off to, all dolled up like that? Some kind of gathering, to be sure.

But there was no time to dwell on Elspeth's affairs – she needed to start getting ready for the food stall tomorrow morning. Given that everyone in the group had become unavailable for one reason or another – could they begrudge her success? – she would have to man it alone.

Chapter 19
Ashley

'**M**ind yourself, I'm right behind you!'

Ashley looked up to see the small vehicle scoot soundlessly past and abruptly halt. John's face crinkled into a mischievous smile. He was older than her, in his late fifties or early sixties.

'Oh, hello, Ashley! I didn't realise it was you.'

'Hello, John. Sorry, I was miles away.' She'd left the house after the family's evening meal to take advantage of the long light evenings, hoping to walk her troubles into insignificance.

'No, I'm the one who should apologise. I was probably going a little fast, truth be told.' He patted the mobility scooter's frame. 'A friend fixed the motor to put some life into this thing.' Although his tone remained serious, his lips twitched as if holding back a smile. 'I'm afraid I sometimes use this contraption to relieve my frustration at life. Woe betide anyone who gets in my way.'

'I understand. I'm glad you weren't going any faster, though.'

'I do my best to only mow down those who've treated me poorly, or people I don't like. Talking of which...' John maneuvered the scooter towards the edge of the pavement to make room for a stout man in a tweed cap, a dog straining on a short leash at his side. Bulldog Man passed briskly by, glowering at the pavement. Suddenly he stopped and turned.

'Oi, you two!' His glower deepened as it fixed on them. He pulled his cap higher up his sweating brow. 'I know it was your band of do-gooders who reported me to the police – all because I dared have some mates over for a few jars to celebrate my son's first kid coming into the world. You can tell that evil cow in charge she's not getting away with it!' He walked off without waiting for a reply.

John gripped the scooter's handle, his cheeks slightly flushed, staring at the departing figure.

'I have some sympathy with him,' he said. 'Tara's stepped over the mark, this time, reporting people to the police. And all that guff in the meeting about someone in the group breaching Covid guidelines. Singling someone out for criticism like that...' He saw her discomfort. 'What's the matter?'

She had to tell him.

'It was me. I was visiting the old lady who lives next door but one from me. She asked me to come and chat to her. I didn't think there was any harm in it. We both had masks on and it was outside...'

She trailed off. John was frowning.

'Tara was complaining about you visiting an elderly woman who needed someone to talk to?'

'Yes, Elspeth.' It was a relief to admit the truth and not be judged. Since her arrival in this village, she'd been anxious in case she said or did anything to upset anyone, and her family suffered as a result. 'She's Tara's next-door neighbour – they've been friends for years. Tara's helped her out a lot the past few months, collecting prescriptions and so forth. Now they've have fallen out. Tara is jealous of me, Elspeth thinks.'

John didn't seem surprised.

'She had a run-in with Bryony once, over some petty thing. They were both in the WI. Tara invited someone she knew to give a talk on motivation and overcoming obstacles etc., but attendance wasn't great. Everyone was far more interested in the female chef who turned up the following month – my wife's suggestion. Bryony said Tara gave her the cold shoulder for months afterwards.'

Oh, great. Unease washed over her. What else would she discover about this woman? She and her family had to live next door to Tara for the foreseeable future.

'Have you known Tara long?' she asked.

'She's been living in the village almost as long as I have.' John's brow furrowed. 'When she first turned up, she was a young woman. Bryony and I wondered where she'd got the money to buy a house in one of the most desirable streets in Brampton... She didn't seem to work much and she was always out spending money.'

It would be nosey to ask, she thought. But suddenly she wanted to know.

'How did she get the money to buy the house?'

'After her mother died Tara inherited the estate, so Bryony gathered. Apparently Tara's two sisters both died as children. She moved here from Somerset or Devon, I think. That's all I know.' He licked his finger and began rubbing at a mark on the front of the scooter.

'It's all very mysterious, isn't it?' She was keen to know more. But it didn't seem right to be prying into someone's past for no reason apart from a vague sense that all was not as it should be with Tara. 'I wonder what she gets out of running the food stall? The Brampton Food Initiative, I mean.' She smiled. 'Apart from fame and extra clients, of course.'

'Ah, we think alike.' John gave a throaty chuckle. 'I'm sure she gets pleasure from helping others, as most of us do. But I imagine other things come into it too.'

Ashley glanced up and down Wilton Close. What if Tara knew that she and John had been talking about her, behind her back? Fortunately, unless the woman possessed a drone with surveillance capabilities, this end of Wilton Close was beyond even Tara's range of hearing.

'See you next week,' she said as John prepared to continue on his way.

'Lovely to talk with you, Ashley. See you at the next install-ment of the Covid Committee. What joys will be in store for us at the next meeting, I wonder?'

She waved goodbye, feeling happier than she had in a long time. Not only had the conversation lifted her spirits, John had become a friend and fellow bulwark against Tara.

Chapter 20
Tara
6 June

W here was everyone? This was ridiculous. It was 10am, an hour after she'd set up the stall, and only three customers had shown up.

She surveyed the area around the trestle tables: a neglected patch of grass backing onto the river, giving onto a minor road, behind which was a small hill and an ugly pylon. A cloud of midges was erupting from the algae-strewn river. The hot weather had vanished; the morning was cloudy and the breeze cool – maybe that explained the lack of customers.

Tara zipped up her jacket and went back to her audiobook, *Strategies for Financial Success*. The author had made a mint by various unconventional methods, from which he had put together a plan for lesser mortals to follow. So far, she'd not been impressed. Her own less-than-conventional methods had yielded plenty of fruit over the years.

Minutes later, a tall slim young woman strolled towards the collection of fold-up tables. She wore a tatty leather jacket over a red cotton skirt and matching wellingtons.

'Good morning!' Tara put on her brightest smile. She didn't

bother to ask if the girl had registered with the Brampton Food Initiative. 'We have plenty of produce today, take your time.'

The girl gave a hesitant smile, loitered for a while and left with a cranberry and almond loaf, a carton of oatmeal milk, a collection of tins and packets and two boxes of tampons. This was more than the eight items maximum per household, but that hardly mattered on a quiet day. Anyway, none of the volunteers consistently enforced the rule.

Tara settled back again with her book. Surely, the usuals would turn up soon. Dogfood Man always came by mid-morning, Cake Lady had visited the stall every week since the scheme began, and at least a dozen others could be relied on to make an appearance.

Midday passed. Some of the regular customers had shown, plus others she didn't recognise. But many had picked disdainfully at the produce without taking anything. After the Alan Garfield interview, she had been expecting more than the usual number of visitors, not less. Something was seriously wrong.

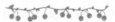

She tried to arrange the goods on the stall more attractively, bringing sweet items closer to the front of the trestle tables. This week there had been a bumper crop of donations from residents of the Wiltons and beyond; it had been difficult to fit them all onto the stall. A supermarket was now delivering sandwiches and fresh items close to their use-by dates, and the ever-growing list of home bakers had produced more loaves and cakes than ever.

At a quarter to one, a middle-aged man arrived in chinos, loafers and small round spectacles. One of those types who read Proust and Tolstoy, probably, she thought. He raised his eyebrows.

'Not doing so well today?'

Tara glared at the man, who clearly had no intention of selecting anything.

'I'm not surprised you haven't got many takers,' he went on, 'given all the rumours.'

'Rumours?' Did he mean the squashed fly someone had supposedly found in a loaf?

'Joy Harris from the bowling club found maggots in a home-made pork pie she took home.' The man eyed her with a deadpan face.

'Maggots?'

She felt her power of speech diminishing. Was he trying to wind her up?

'Rather a lot of them, so I heard. She found them the other day when she served the pie for lunch. Her sister, nieces and nephews were over for the day...'

'How do you know about this?' She didn't bother to keep the suspicion from her voice.

'Everyone in my street was talking about it yesterday.' He spoke with cool amusement.

She stiffened at his tone. Was this only gossip – a fly in a loaf of bread getting inflated into maggots in a pork pie? Or had someone actually donated a pork pie containing maggots – or tampered with a pre-made one, even? Whatever, one thing was clear. Someone was trying to nobble her operation.

With a sly sneer, the man raised his hand. 'See you around.'

As he walked away, fear and outrage fought inside her. She picked up a rye loaf – rather firm and Germanic – and flung it with all her strength at his retreating back. Unfortunately, it didn't reach him.

Several hours later, she was wiping away tears that had sprung into her eyes. More people had turned up, sniffing around the stall with an air of malicious curiosity. Little home-baked produce had been taken, in contrast to the interest in non-food items – especially toilet rolls and disinfecting spray – and pre-made food such as tins of soup and baked beans, and perennially popular items like packets of crisps and bars of chocolate. This was a calamity; there was no other word. She spotted someone plodding towards her – the large frame of Cake Lady. A bulging shopping bag was slung over each of her shoulders.

'Can I interest you in a lemon drizzle cake or a Victoria sponge?' Tara began. 'And we have some delicious loaves, plus these eggs from local free-range chickens.' She indicated the row of egg boxes, filled with the output of Ursula's friend's fowls.

'I'm sorry dear, I won't this time.' The woman looked crest-fallen. 'I've already stocked up at the supermarket.'

She stared. 'You'd rather buy a factory cake than get a perfectly delicious home-made cake for free?' It slipped out before she could stop it.

'I—'

'Sorry, I don't mean to be nasty. I just want to understand what's going on. Did someone tell you there was something wrong with our food?'

Cake Lady's eyes darted about, finally settling on the large Victoria sponge taking pride of place on the baked goods section.

'It's just that... Well, my friend told me about a rather unwholesome find in one of your cakes. Her mother found a...' The woman averted her eyes, her face reddening.

'A what?' Tara's frustration mounted.

'A piece of sh— A stool, I mean.'

'Your friend's mother found a stool in one of our cakes?'

The woman flinched. Tara forced her mouth shut.

'It was a small one, I understand. Not human.'

Tara frowned. What was the woman saying?

'It was more like a dog turd, apparently.'

'A dog turd,' Tara repeated.

'I'm sorry, dear. You've worked so hard at this venture and it's been such a boon to the community. I do hope people come back.' Cake Lady gave an uncertain smile and turned away.

Tara looked around the trestle tables, strewn with home-made cakes, loaves and pies. She felt close to despair. It was three o'clock, the end of the session. What was she going to do with all this unwanted food? The jars, packets and tins would keep till next Saturday, but the fifty-odd cakes and loaves wouldn't, nor the meat pies...

A burst of anger made her heart race. Damn this village of ignorant people who latched onto the first thing they heard! All those put off from taking this delicious, nutritious and totally free food deserved to wallow in their poverty.

'Ha!' A guttural cry emerged from her mouth. She began packing everything into Ursula's roomy Renault estate. As she worked, a plan began to hatch. Those ridiculous people might have turned their noses up at perfectly good food, but there were others who would grab her produce without a qualm. They'd pay good money too – she would bet on it.

She sat down at the wheel and set the satnav for Grimpton Hadlock. The place was perfect for a little entrepreneurial activity: an out-of-the-way village populated with four-wheel-drive-owning people who liked nothing better than to splurge their money on French wine and food from farmers' markets. She wasn't certain if, strictly speaking, one was allowed to drive twenty miles for such a purpose – who could keep up with these constantly changing guidelines? But needs must.

'My pleasure. I hope you enjoy it.'

Smiling broadly, Tara handed over the last item on display – the Victoria sponge that had a few hours earlier been so roundly rejected – to a handsome Panama-hatted gent, sold for £4.99. She transferred the five-pound note to her bulging pocket.

When he'd gone, she had to stop herself from whooping with delight.

After parking in a lay-by opposite the bakery in Grimpton Hadlock's High Street, she'd hastily set up for an impromptu car boot sale behind a banner improvised with a marker pen and several large packs of upturned Pedigree Chum tins: TODAY ONLY! QUALITY HOME-MADE FOOD AT DISCOUNT PRICES!

Now, in less than two hours, everything was gone, sold at a fair price to compensate for her efforts – even the tins of dog food. It had been the perfect time to intercept all the women meeting up for a Saturday afternoon coffee and cake at trendy cafés, or browsing in the overpriced boutique; she'd not even got to the end of her two hours on the meter. Fortunately, no council officers had turned up to tell her she was contravening regulation xyz by flogging food out of a car boot without a licence, and, all the way out here, no one had recognised her. As she'd predicted, no one had quibbled about paying five pounds for a wholesome home-made cake that they would have baked themselves had they not been too busy in Zoom meetings or supervising their children's piano practice.

The size of the crowd gathered around the Renault's boot had surprised her, though. Those who had waited to snap up her goods hadn't been just mums, but also the elderly and a good sprinkling of men. Of the latter, a nice-looking chap had begun to chat her up, complimenting her on her high quality foodstuffs, and other things. She'd been tempted – the frisson of pleasure appearing at the sight of his deepening dimples reminded her it had been too long since any liaison with the opposite sex. But she didn't know him, and didn't want to risk word getting around of her food-selling activities. He'd left without any of her personal details, only a bottle of Spanish olive oil and a jar of haricot beans.

Tara finished stowing the unsold items and closed the boot. It was time to leave. If anyone twigged that she had secretly sold off items donated by the well-off, well-meaning people of Brampton, intended for the village's less fortunate, there'd be hell to pay.

Driving away from Grimpton Hadlock, she couldn't stop smiling at the money she'd amassed. £396! It wasn't a fortune, especially if you factored in the risks she'd taken. But it was a decent amount for a couple of hours' work.

At home, she poured herself a celebratory glass of fizz and took it upstairs. Time for a relaxing soak in the bath. Peeling off her jeans and blouse, she met her mother's eyes in the framed photo on the dressing table. The fluffy whirl of caramel hair around Ivy's small, thin face reminded her of a stick of candy floss. It was one of the better pictures of Ivy, taken before she'd been claimed by ill health. Ivy's direct gaze felt uncomfortable today, though. Tara turned the photo around so it faced the wall.

It was such a pity her mother had become so unwell, scarcely out of middle-age. But at least she'd had a quick end. With her constant pain, breathlessness, difficulty moving and many other afflictions, Ivy wouldn't have wanted to go on living for very much longer, would she?

A chill in the room now. Tara shivered and draped a towel around her shoulders. More than once recently, she had sensed her dead mother's presence. Mouth dry, she hurried out of the room and started running her bath. She didn't believe in ghosts, she reminded herself.

Chapter 21
Elspeth
7 June

Elspeth replaced her mug of tea on the patio table and stretched out with a luxuriant yawn. Her skin, exposed more than usual in shorts and a skimpy top, felt warm in the morning sunshine.

A brooding sense these past weeks that she was becoming more isolated and vulnerable had vanished after the memorial gathering. It had been worth risking infection with a deadly disease to see Mira and Alice again. Also, she was thankful that the tinnitus had abated, as had the foot pain.

She started the CD in the portable music player, a compilation of her favourite ballet music, keeping the volume low so as not to alert Tara; Tara might feel slighted that Elspeth hadn't invited her to join her workout. After another glance over the fence – still no sign of Tara in her garden or on her terrace – she risked a few arabesques and some modest jetés on the lawn.

That felt good. Her legs were springy and strong today. She'd become a dancer again. Using the fence as a barre, she began the familiar sequence of ballet exercises, from simple pliés to more challenging movements. Up in the lime tree, a blackbird's silvery notes blended with the violins. A gentle breeze cooled her, wicking away her sweat.

Panting, she turned to face the other way. Through the gaps between the latticed section at the top of the fence, she could see into Tara's garden.

As the last strains of Stravinsky died away, Elspeth stayed where she was. She scanned the flowerbed along the fence. She could see Tara's reclining chair beside the rhododendron bush – and what was just beyond the bush, partly hidden by copious dark green foliage? A climbing rose was making its way up two sticks in the soil. Flowers with pale pink petals were unfurling from the buds.

How odd.

Standing on her toes, she stretched herself as high as she could for a better view of the plant; the pile of bricks used to communicate with her neighbour had been redeployed. Could it be the missing rose?

Elspeth stepped away from the fence and ran into the house to rummage around for the binoculars. Back again, as she strained to read the words on the label behind the plant, her heart began to hammer.

Margaret Meredith. Climbing rose, Blush Pink. SLIGHTLY FRAGRANT.

Through the binoculars, the label was clear. But she didn't need to look at the label to see that this rose was exactly the same type as the four climbers that Tara had bought for her. That conniving, spiteful bizum *had* stolen her rose.

She slumped onto the bench. The effing temerity of it! For a moment she imagined reporting the theft to the local police station, then laughed aloud at herself. The police were far too busy dealing with people flouting Covid rules to worry about an old woman's stolen rose plant. There was only one way to deal with this.

Still in her exercise garb, she headed out of the house and banged the knocker down on Tara's front door. The kitchen window opened and a head thrust through.

'What is it, Elspeth?' Tara looked over the snazzy reading glasses fixed on her nose. 'I'm rather busy at the moment.' Her tone was distinctly unwelcoming and more than a touch condescending. Elspeth was overcome by a blast of heat, hotter than any menopausal flush.

'Would you mind answering the door, if that's not too much to ask?' She rubbed the fabric of her top against her chest to soak up some of the sweat.

A scowl. 'Couldn't it wait till this afternoon?'

'I'd like to talk to you about something – right now.'

Tara withdrew her head and reappeared at the front door.

'Do you want to come through to the garden?'

Elspeth noted Tara's disapproving scan of her bare legs and arms, and followed. At the glass doors leading to the back garden, Tara stopped.

'Would you like a cold drink? You look hot.'

'I'll have a glass of water, thank you.'

'Take a chair, I won't be a moment.'

Elspeth walked to the white-painted table and chairs. She didn't sit down. Tara placed a tall, ice-cube laden glass on the table then sat down.

'So, what can I do for you?' The frown had gone but the frostiness in her voice remained.

'If you'll excuse me for one moment.'

Elspeth went to the flowerbed along the fence between her and Tara's gardens and found the climbing rose, beside a clump of wilting peonies. Going by the uneven soil around it, it had been planted recently.

'What is it?' Tara crossed one leg over the other and hunched forwards. A pair of long earrings swayed as she did – not the ones Elspeth had given her.

'I trusted you,' she began, turning to Tara. 'I thought you were trying to help me, and instead...' She couldn't finish the sentence.

'What are you talking about?'

'That rose.' Elspeth pointed to the plant. 'That's the one that went missing. The one you said the man behind you at the checkout must have taken by mistake. It's the same kind as the others, Margaret Meredith. You must take me for a fool.'

She took a long swig of water from the glass on the table.

'Have you finished?' Tara sounded bemused by Elspeth's meltdown. 'I don't deny it's the same type as the ones I bought for you. But there's a simple explanation. After you accused me of taking your rose, I went back to the garden centre and bought one for myself, along with a bag of potting mix. If it does well, I'm intending to go back and buy some more.'

Elspeth's jaw dropped. This was unbelievable – the woman was a brazen liar.

'Show me the receipt, then.'

'I'm sorry, I threw it away. It would have been collected with the rubbish.' Her tone became icy. 'I didn't expect to be cross-examined by you, I'm afraid.'

'Of course, you threw it away. How convenient.'

Tara got to her feet, crossing her arms in front of her chest.

'Are you insinuating that I'm lying to you?'

'I'm not insinuating, Tara. I know you're lying. All this is...' She reached for an old-lady-like expression and failed. 'Horseshit! And I know you lied to me about a fox causing the damage to Ashley's rose. A fox, ha! It was you who hacked the stems off, wasn't it?'

'Elspeth, you don't know what you're talking about. You must be losing your marbles.'

Elspeth fought to regain her composure.

'Actually,' she said, 'I think you know perfectly well what I'm talking about. And I think you need to speak to someone about your own mental health. You've got a serious problem!'

Tara's lipsticked mouth opened before clamping shut.

'You'll regret that.'

The words were low, just audible. The threat in them couldn't be missed, however.

Elspeth turned towards the safety of home. As she poured herself a Scotch, her hand shook the bottle. She had said too much. She shouldn't have lost control like that with Tara – who knew what might happen now? The woman *did* have a problem, that was beyond doubt.

Suddenly cold, she pulled on a wraparound cardigan. From now on, she needed to keep her wits about her.

Chapter 22
Tara

The front gate clanked shut behind her. She skirted the green, which was quieter than usual, possibly due to the thickening clouds rather than the council's recent signs instructing people to stay two metres apart from each other and not to picnic or put up barbeques.

She reached the footpath that led down to the lake, running between two sets of fences. There was no one in sight. She needed to scream. Instead, she battered the fence closest to her with her fists, imagining she was punching Elspeth's stupid unfeeling body, on and on until the woman lay inert, unable to say anything ever again.

How dare Elspeth tell her that she was unhinged, when she had spent weeks tending to the woman's needs? Tara was the one who had been treated badly, not Elspeth. Hands up, in her anger at being ignored and taken for granted, she had taken a few small items without permission, and had vented her frustration on that hapless plant. Elspeth had been a good friend, so she'd thought – but all the time that Elspeth had been accepting Tara's generosity, the woman had cared only about befriending that pathetic little Ashley creature. And now, just because Tara hadn't been able to resist taking one single measly rose for herself to compensate for the poor treatment she'd received – which anyone else who possessed a garden packed with gorgeous flowers would have over-looked – Elspeth was accusing her of being a mental case!

Tears threatened. She blinked them away and kicked the fence with venom, imagining it was Elspeth's kneecap – no, head, even better.

She stepped away quickly from the fence. There was someone coming from down the hill... a whole bloody family.

A man preceded by two small stick-waving children nodded to her as they passed. She plastered on a pleasant face and continued downhill, catching glimpses of a ramshackle collection of green fields below. She rarely came this way; she'd never been fond of the idea of rambling with groups of old biddies, or the sorts of country-bumpkin pursuits that some enjoyed.

Right now, though, she needed to be well away from home – and Elspeth, in particular – before she did anything hasty. A fresh wave of emotion took over, making her forget her red-raw knuckles. She thumped the handrail with the side of her hand, harder than she'd intended.

'Fuck you, Elspeth!'

Tears spilled down her face. She forged on, not caring who might see her. The entire fucking village could be here; she didn't care. She took off her cardigan and tied it around her waist. Was that a rumble of thunder in the distance? It was getting humid; a storm was brewing but she didn't care about that, either.

Tara peered into the lake's murky water. What might be dumped down there, hidden from view? Before she realised, a cloud of midges had swarmed off the lake and surrounded her. 'Bugger off!'

She batted them away and sat down on a nearby bench. What an inhospitable place!

No one was here, except Bird Woman. As usual, binoculars were tethered to her neck, and a floppy hat partly obscured her face. She was jotting furiously in her little notebook, a crease imprinted on her brow. She didn't look up.

Well, why should Bird Woman care about her plight? No one cared, now she had no friends left. Despite all her attempts to instil a sense of community in this village, not even her doddery neighbour wanted anything to do with her any more.

The first drops of rain fell on her bare arm. A tear slipped down her cheek. Things might have been different if her father hadn't died, leaving her at the mercy of her family... A sob-hiccup burst out. Before Bird Woman could witness the spectacle she was making of herself, she got up and hurried on towards the shelter of the woods.

Another rumble, louder. The rain fell steadily now. Clouds hid the sun.

The path emerged beside the Quaker house on the far side of the village. She looked around, uncertain what to do. The High Street was empty of pedestrians; only an intermittent car sped by. Her trainers splashed into a puddle. She glanced at her watch. Her top was already damp. If she walked any further, she'd get soaked.

She reached the bus stop, hopping up and down under the shelter in an attempt to get warm. It was nearly 7pm, not a great time to wait for a bus in Brampton. Seventeen minutes later, a 383 pulled up. Tara flashed her pass at the driver and made for the only empty seat, behind a large woman brazenly coughing.

God's sake. Maybe she should have walked, after all. But it was too late to change her mind.

Chapter 23
Tara
10 June

Tara stared at the computer screen, trying to take in Brian Green's resumé. Since the radio interview, she had been contacted by dozens of people wanting her help with publicity for their memoirs, cookbooks and whatever. But it was no use. The sentences had stopped making sense. Her brain refused to work, and as for her body... Grotty, that was the only word for it.

She went upstairs, closed her bedroom blinds and lay down on the bed. The room was dark and quiet, but her own cough kept waking her as soon as she started to doze. She took a sip of water. It was just a tickle, surely. Apart from the occasional cold, she wasn't susceptible to viruses; she'd never even caught the flu.

By five o'clock in the afternoon, her limbs were aching and she was sweating profusely. The cough had worsened, too. Tara put another pillow under her head and closed her eyes again. Despite her exhaustion, sleep was impossible. An ache had spread deep into her muscles; her legs felt like they were being gripped by a vice. The bedclothes were soaked with sweat. She'd never felt as bad as this in her life.

That damned bus. Once again, that coughing woman came to mind. She must have given her this dreadful thing, whatever it was. Could it be Covid? She couldn't recall all the symptoms, but a fever and a cough were definitely on the list. And what about temporary mental incapacity, a raging headache and feeling like shit?

The person who answered her 111 call at the NHS helpline advised her to take two paracetamol tablets every four hours, drink plenty of water, get plenty of rest, and order a test. Tara checked her phone for the latest advice for a person who suspected they had Covid. Order a test, stay at home for seven days and sweat it out, seemed to be the main message. No need to phone your GP or an ambulance unless you were about to croak it.

She clicked on the link to order a test and scrolled down the resulting page. There was a form, a long one, requiring all sorts of personal information. After completing the first few boxes, she came to a halt. What the hell was her National Insurance number, anyway? It was filed away; she wasn't going to go rooting around for it now. How did they expect someone in the throes of Covid to complete such a ridiculously complicated form?

She got out of bed and lurched towards the bathroom. Where was the ibuprofen?

The cabinet shelf was devoid of painkillers, not even a single aspirin. Linda's Pharmacy had run out of aspirin the last time she'd tried to get some... She struggled to remember where she might have left a packet of aspirin. In her handbag? In a kitchen drawer? Gripping the banister, she made her way downstairs. Her strength and coordination had gone, along with her faculties. Now she knew what it was like to be old and decrepit.

This was all Elspeth's fault. If she hadn't been so callous and unkind, if she hadn't hurt Tara so much with that uncalled-for comment about her mental health... Because of Elspeth's horrible words, Tara had urgently needed to get out of the house, which had led to her getting caught in the rain without a jacket, getting cold and wet and having to get on that godforsaken bus... She grabbed her phone and dialled Elspeth's number. She would tell the woman exactly what she thought of her – though maybe first, she should ask Elspeth if she had any aspirin.

The phone rang out. Tara left a voice message.

Are you up, Elspeth?

Minutes passed. She picked up her phone. Her fingers typed and retyped, not landing on the right letters. Finally, she managed to send off a message:

I've got a temperature, feeling very unwell. Have you got any spare aspirin or paracetamol?

Half an hour later, a reply came. By then, she was finding it difficult to make out any words on her phone's screen. They flickered and wavered with a life of their own, accompanied by flashes of light from behind her eyes and a rapid pounding from inside her temples.

Sorry Tara I can't look at the moment. Tired after bad night, trying to have a nap

She read the message again, to make sure she'd read it right. The selfish cow! What about all the time Tara had given up to help Elspeth, often when feeling below par herself?

Some time later, another text from Elspeth landed noisily on Tara's phone, rousing her from the huge, menacing frogs leaping with abandon through her semi-conscious state. The fever must be getting worse.

Have put aspirin through your front door

She stared at the message. No sympathy or kind words. Just

that bald, put-upon-sounding reply, as if Tara was a pest fit only to be poisoned. She would pay Elspeth back for this – and for dropping Tara like a stale cake for the wonderful Ashley.

A fitful slumber began. Frightful images twisted through her fevered mind. Finally, waking with a fit of coughing, she climbed off the bed, shrugged on her dressing gown and slippers and went downstairs. There, on the hall floor below the letterbox, a single foil strip of aspirin. She picked it up. It contained just three tablets.

What a pathetically meagre offering! No note. No promise to return ASAP with a full packet. Rage gathered inside her. How many times had she gone to Linda's Pharmacy for Elspeth, and how many hours had she queued outside? How many times had she needed to return when the medication proved to be not quite right? She tossed the packet aside, went next door and pushed on the doorbell, which rang so loudly and shrilly it hurt her ears. She was going to tell Elspeth exactly what she thought of her.

No answer. Tara tried again twice, with the same result. She patted a tissue over her damp face and neck, shuffling from one foot to the other. It was getting on for 6pm; surely Elspeth wasn't still napping? Maybe she hadn't heard the doorbell – or had she been lying about being tired? Was Ashley the reason she didn't want to answer the door?

The thought inflamed her anger. She wasn't going to give up so easily. With slow, determined steps she returned home, removed Elspeth's keys from the hall table drawer and headed next door once again. She had to hold onto to Elspeth's gate for some seconds, breathing heavily, before she could continue. Elspeth's front door opened easily, by means of only the top lock. Carefully, Tara padded along the hall and into each downstairs room in turn. No sign of Elspeth. She peeped out of the kitchen window. No sign of Elspeth in the garden either, or up on the terrace – where was the woman?

She climbed the stairs, sweating like a hog and clinging onto the hand rail for dear life. But she was propelled onward by a burning sense of injustice.

With a knock, she pushed open the bedroom door, left slightly ajar.

'Elspeth? It's me, Tara. I need to talk to...'

But there was no one in the room and the bed was made up. How odd. She went to the terrace door and looked down. The sight gave her a jolt.

Elspeth was sitting with Ashley in Ashley's garden, holding a cup to her lips, at a table laid out for afternoon tea. It was a spread fit for a queen. A teapot, a silver jug of milk, a plate of biscuits, a large sponge cake, a bowl of strawberries...

Tara opened the terrace door. The pair below were talking in earnest, as if all that mattered to them was each other – no consideration whatsoever for the awful state that Tara was in. Elspeth, who had cream smudged around her mouth, bit into a slice of cake with gusto and carried on talking as soon as she could get the words out. Ashley started to laugh, a low, bubbly chuckle that Tara didn't recognise – Ashley never normally laughed, going around with a sad little face and saying the minimum possible. But with Elspeth, Ashley seemed a different woman.

Tara turned away. An endless well of emptiness was trying to swallow her up. Elspeth had deceived her, taken her for an idiot. Her once-dear friend was clearly too self-centred to care about anyone else except herself and her own pleasures – and Ashley. She closed the terrace door and went downstairs, her rage gathering. She wasn't going to let Elspeth get away with this. She would think of something that dear old Elspeth wouldn't forget in a hurry... Tara went into the kitchen; she would help herself to a glass of water before she left. At that moment, a cough erupted from her chest. Before she could locate the tissue in her dressing-gown pocket and clamp it over her mouth, another phlegmy cough issued forth.

Oh, what unfortunate timing. She coughed again, more vigorously, into her tissue this time, drenching it with mucus. Contemplating what she might do next, a tingle of anticipation went through her. Was this how she'd felt all those years ago, just before Zoe came to her untimely end?

She worked quickly; Elspeth might charge through the front door at any moment. Within three or four minutes, despite her laboured breathing and a desperate wish to lie flat and shut her eyes, she had dragged the tissue over all the surfaces that Elspeth was likely to touch – light and kettle switches; door, cupboard and fridge handles; even a vase overflowing with exquisite lemon-tinged roses. Then she flushed the tissue down the toilet.

Whatever happened now was out of her hands. With a final spluttery cough, she dropped her keys on the doormat inside Elspeth's front door and slipped out of the house.

Chapter 24
Ashley
11 June

'Layla! Your eggs are ready!' She went back to stirring the scrambled eggs. 'Sam, will you come and butter your toast?'

Her son looked up from his laptop with a frown.

'Samir, not Sam. Can't you ever remember?'

Oh, God.

'Sorry, it just slipped out.' After nineteen years of calling her first-born *Sam*, it was difficult to simply switch. He was Sam to her, and always would be.

'They're not done enough, Mum.' Sam loped over to the toaster and re-inserted his two slices of toast.

Ashley gave the eggs a final stir and turned off the gas. This morning was going to pass off peacefully for a change, she was determined.

'Samir, call her again, will you?'

'I'm here, no need.'

Layla appeared in the doorway in a dressing gown and fluffy slippers, wiping sleep from her eyes, her long black hair unbrushed. She slumped into a chair at the table opposite Sam.

Sam crunched loudly into his toast, wiped his mouth with a

stained serviette, scooped up his phone and scraped back his chair.

'Got to go, I'm meeting friends later.'

'Which friends? Where are you off to, Sam?' Her son thudded upstairs. Ashley raised her voice. 'Samir, I mean!'

'Did Elspeth enjoy your tea yesterday?' Layla asked after nibbling a piece of toast.

'I'd say so.'

'So you two had a good gossip?' A rare smile appeared on Layla's face.

Ashley put down her eggy fork, recalling Elspeth's news.

'Elspeth thinks Tara might have Covid.'

'Tara has got Covid?' Layla looked up from her plate.

'Might have. Tara texted her yesterday asking if she had any aspirin. She was feeling unwell, apparently. I don't know if she's been tested.'

'Whatever. If she has symptoms, she should be inside, isolating.' Layla straightened her back, face suddenly animated. 'I saw her standing outside Elspeth's front door yesterday in her dressing gown and slippers.'

Oh, God. What was the matter with that woman?

'What time was this?'

'While you and Elspeth were in the garden. Five thirty, six? She looked quite ill, actually. I was going past on my way to Anna's. I don't think she saw me.'

Ashley let out a long breath. She felt uneasy.

'What was she doing?'

Layla shrugged. 'She was just standing there waiting, like you do when you've rung the bell.'

'That's strange that she'd go over there, knowing she might have Covid and Elspeth being so vulnerable.'

'Isn't it? Especially as Tara was meant to be helping *her*. Before you took over, anyway—'

'I didn't take over!'

'Only teasing, Mum.'

'Come on, gremlin, eat up. Your eggs will get cold.'

After a few more mouthfuls, Layla put down her knife and fork.

'Sorry, I'm not that hungry. I'll get a sandwich when I'm out with Anna. I'm meeting her for a walk this afternoon.'

'Sounds like a good idea.' Ashley hesitated. 'What about Dawn? Are you seeing her tomorrow morning?' She and Zac had suggested that their daughter start seeing a counsellor. Surprisingly, Layla had immediately agreed. The sessions, via Zoom, were going reasonably well, it seemed, though Layla said little about them.

'It's in my calendar. See you later, I'm going up to study.'

College was still shut; Layla was doing online lessons. That didn't seem to stop her and her classmates from exchanging Snapchat messages or posting on Instagram, though – quite the reverse.

When Layla had left the kitchen – hopefully to get on with studying for her History and English A levels next year, rather than pouring over Instagram notifications – she phoned Elspeth.

'You didn't ask Tara to come over yesterday, did you?'

'No, of course not. I told you, she texted to say she wasn't well, did I have any aspirin. I dropped the rest of my packet through her letterbox before I came over to you. Why do you ask?'

'Layla saw Tara waiting outside your front door yesterday, while you and I were having tea. I thought it was a bit strange, given she was ill.'

'She probably came to drop my keys over – I found them on the hall mat when I got home from your place.'

'Tara had your front door keys?'

'Yes, she used to come over to water my plants and pick up my post whenever I was away. I did the same for her.' A note of alarm entered Elspeth's voice. 'Do you think she might have let herself in while I was out?'

'I doubt it.' Ashley tried to inject reassurance into her voice. 'Anyway, how are you feeling this morning?'

Putting the phone down, she still felt uneasy. OK, Tara could have gone over to Elspeth's to drop off her keys. But why wait outside first – and why would she have dropped them off when she was so unwell? Maybe she *had* let herself in with them, then left the keys inside Elspeth's to provide an excuse in case she'd been seen... That seemed unlikely. But she had a feeling that Tara had been up to no good.

Chapter 25
Elspeth
12 June

For goodness sake, what was the matter with her today? She had no puff left.

Elspeth sat down on the back step and patted herself down with a towel while she got her breath back. Was seventy-eight too old to be doing strenuous work-outs? Maybe her body was trying to tell her something – you need to grow old, stop trying to resist.

There were plenty of things to be getting on with. She ought to speak to her GP again and to the tree surgeon about cutting back the lime tree, not to mention Tara. She had meant to phone and enquire how her neighbour was, only it was the last thing she felt like doing.

She took out her phone and punched in Tara's number, now removed from her Favourites list.

'Oh Elspeth, it's you.' Tara sounded croaky and less than pleased to hear from Elspeth.

'How are you? You sound awful.'

'Getting better, thank you.'

'I hope the aspirins helped?'

'Aspirins? Yes, of course, they helped get rid of my headache. Thank you, Elspeth, for taking the trouble to bring them.'

The delivery of these words – frosty yet saccharine sweet – was clearly intended to convey another meaning. But she refused to rise to the bait.

'Is it Covid, do you think?'

'Possibly a mild strain.'

'But what about your symptoms? Have you got a continuous cough? A fever?' Was Tara being obtuse on purpose?

'They're fairly minor. I probably caught a chill from being out in the rain the other day.'

'You were out in the rain?'

'I went out without a jacket and it started to pour, then I had to wait for a bus...' Her tone became brisk. 'I'm feeling much better now, Elspeth.'

Tara seemed to be trying to convince her of this, for some reason. She remembered what else she had wanted to ask.

'Oh, Tara – you didn't come into my house yesterday while I was out, did you? I saw my keys on the inside mat.' She'd put them safely away with a surge of relief. There had been no note.

A micro pause.

'No, I put them through your letterbox. I noticed I still had them and thought you might like them back.'

'Why did you wait outside my front door, then?'

'What?'

'Layla saw you standing outside my front door – Ashley's daughter.'

Down the line, a longer pause followed by a tut of irritation.

'I just rang on the doorbell to let you know it was me. It seemed rude to just drop them off. But you were obviously out – or asleep.'

'I see. I'll let you have yours back too. Well, I'd better get back to my to do list. I hope you get over it soon, whatever it is.'

'Take care, Elspeth.'

Tara's voice sounded oddly flat – cold, even. Elspeth ended the call.

Chapter 26
Elspeth
13 June

Another shiver went through her, the biggest so far. It momentarily took her breath away, as if suddenly she had been engulfed by an icy wave.

Elspeth hugged herself. This cardigan wasn't nearly thick enough. The heat of the late afternoon, so pleasing an hour ago, was now unnoticeable. She would have to get up from this comfortable chair and fetch a blanket. Or lie down under the bedcovers, even.

The thought of walking anywhere, even the few yards to her bedroom, added to the sense of exhaustion that had arrived on waking that morning. It had taken considerable effort to do the most trivial things like having a shower and getting dressed. Even making a cup of tea had been fraught – she'd knocked over the mug and spilled boiling water all over the worktop. All the while, her brain seemed to have switched off and her throat was starting to ache as if a bad cold was coming on.

Could it be a cold, or the flu? But people weren't catching colds and flu at the moment – they were catching something far worse.

She heaved herself off the chair and took a few uncertain steps towards her bedroom. She felt dizzy, nauseous and far too hot. Worst of all, that breathless sensation was back. She reached the bed and sank onto the mattress. She had to lie down; there was no choice.

Her brain wouldn't let her fall asleep, though. It churned away, sending her into a more and more anxious state. This had to be Covid. She could have caught it from Mira or Alice at the memorial gathering... Or someone at the supermarket, maybe, though she'd worn disposable gloves and a surgical mask...

When at last she fell into a fitful sleep, Tara's jaunty music burst through the opened window. She normally wouldn't mind, but today it sounded like a dreadful wailing.

'For goodness sake,' she muttered. 'Turn it down, woman.'

This was more than she could bear. Five minutes later, the noise unabated, she fetched her mobile phone from the dressing table, tottered back to bed and texted Tara.

Please turn off your music, I'm not feeling well. Thanks VERY much. E.

It was a pity that things had come to this. But whatever warm feelings she'd once held for Tara had been mercilessly quashed. She had reached the end of a very long tether. Maybe it wasn't all Tara's fault; quite possibly Tara had mental health problems alongside her character defects. But whatever was wrong with her neighbour, Elspeth had had enough. She wanted nothing more to do with Tara.

Elspeth set the phone to silent and put it down beside the bed, then lay down and pulled up the duvet. A minute later the phone buzzed. She raised her head from the pillow to read the message on the screen.

So sorry to hear that. Music turned off. Anything else I can do for you?

That was needlessly passive aggressive. She sat up and grabbed the phone.

No thank you very much she tapped out, then switched the phone off and rested her head back on the pillows, considering her neighbour's strange behaviour of late. She played back her puzzling phone conversation with Tara about the return of the keys. Had Tara lied about not coming into the house?

Elspeth stared into the room's shadowy corners. Despite not being the sort of woman who was easily perturbed – quite the opposite, in fact – the thought of Tara prowling around alone in her empty house was more than a little creepy.

Chapter 27
Tara
16 June

T ara stared at the list of last week's new clients on her laptop screen. She ought to start finding out how their life stories might help to snare one of her dwindling network of magazine editors, and radio and TV producers. But those tasks required concentration. She pondered the text Elspeth had sent yesterday.

Please turn off your music, I'm not feeling well.

She closed the laptop and went to the kitchen window. The sky was clear and the early morning sunshine was already warm, dappling the grassy area that stretched out across the road. A bird chirped happily from the tree outside the house. Summer had arrived.

Tara sighed and turned away from the window. She felt like shit, though her fever had gone. Now she was no longer under its influence, she wondered how she could possibly have done the things she had. If anything happened to Elspeth, it would be Tara's fault.

She poured another cup of coffee. The group was supposed to be meeting in two hours and she'd done nothing in preparation.

Well, what did she care? Those people had left her to look after the stall alone, to face the ignominy of a handful of picky customers, and the stall three days ago had had to be cancelled because Ferne and Ursula had seized on Tara's illness as an excuse for taking a week's break. Right now, she wouldn't care if she never laid eyes on any of them again.

She sat down at the table with a crispbread spread with low-fat ricotta and sugar-free jam, and checked her phone again. Still no reply to the five messages she'd sent to her neighbour since Elspeth's text, enquiring what was the matter and whether Tara could do anything to help. She could try to phone again, soon – not too early, Elspeth wasn't an early riser. Although if she was in the throes of Covid...

No, that couldn't be. She hadn't meant to harm Elspeth, of course she hadn't. She had been delirious, seized by strange fancies brought on by fever. Tara picked off the scab beside her fingernail, which had only just healed. What if Elspeth was seriously ill? What if she didn't recover? At her age...

An awful realisation grew inside her: what she had done might not be fixable.

Chapter 28
Ashley
16 June

At five minutes to ten in the morning, Ashley sat down at the laptop in Zac's office for the weekly support group meeting. She had scarcely eaten any breakfast, anxious at the thought of what might lie ahead. Worry about Elspeth's condition – declining rapidly, judging from the three phone calls they'd exchanged yesterday – along with Tara's recent behaviour and whether she ought to share her concerns, had occupied her mind for much of the night. She needed to say something to someone, didn't she?

The Zoom session came up – the usual box showing herself on camera. Ashley neatened her hair and joined four other faces in their squares. The meeting hadn't started yet. Tara was blowing her nose, Greg was yawning, and Ursula and John were discussing the shortcomings of social media.

Tara cleared her throat.

'People, your attention please! If you don't mind, we'll get started. Has anyone heard from Ferne?'

'Her Zumba class should have finished by now,' Greg replied.

'My apologies again for not replying to anyone's emails,' Tara continued. 'I was rather unwell last week.'

Ursula, Greg and John attempted to speak at the same time.

'I'm much better now, thank you.' Tara cut them off with a quick smile, shifting in her chair.

'Was it Covid?' Ursula enquired.

'Possibly. Or a stomach bug.'

'How do you know?' John demanded. 'Did you take a Covid test?'

For a beat, Tara didn't respond.

'Actually, I didn't. It's miles to the nearest testing centre and as you know I've had to let my car go... I didn't feel up to getting on a bus.'

'You could have got a test delivered—'

'I tried, John, believe me. But there was so much information to enter on the form and I wasn't feeling at all well.' Tara made an exasperated noise. 'When I finally got it sent off, I was told that the results wouldn't be valid because it was more than five days since my symptoms started.'

Ursula launched in without raising her hand.

'But we're supposed to be setting an example to the community, Tara – you said so yourself! What if you had Covid and gave it to someone else?'

'I haven't left my house for a week, Ursula, since I started feeling ill. How could I have given it to someone else?'

Ashley had an urge to cry out: *Liar! You were seen outside Elspeth's front door after you fell ill.*

But her heart was beating so fast she couldn't speak. No one else did, either.

Tara coughed.

'Moving on. The Food Initiative. I am most disappointed that everyone's commitment to helping feed Brampton's needy seems to have fallen by the wayside. Not only did several of you decide to cancel last Saturday's stall at the last minute, without informing me, but the Saturday before, due to everyone's important commitments, I was left to man the stall alone.'

John thrust his hand up. Tara ignored him. She straightened her back, her gaze stern – like a teacher dressing down her pupils, Ashley thought.

Ursula jumped in to speak before John.

'I'm sorry, Tara. You've done a great job galvanising us all and making sure no one in the village goes hungry. But I did make it clear that I'm busy with the choir's committee at the moment.'

Ferne's face appeared next to Ashley's.

'Sorry I'm late, everyone, I had a few things to attend to.' The young woman gulped from a bottle of water.

'If I may carry on.' Ursula raised her hand belatedly. Irritation settled on Tara's face.

'Go on, Ursula.'

'Can I ask – what did you do with the leftover food from the stall, Tara? Greg and I can deliver the non-perishables to our housebound people. There's been a drop-off in donations the past fortnight, so it would come in handy.'

'There wasn't any leftover food.'

'None at all? I'm surprised the rumours circulating around the village didn't affect the numbers visiting the stall.'

Tara blinked. 'Rumours?'

'I think we all know about them by now. People have been saying all sorts of things about the food they've received from us. Worms found in a Victoria Sponge, a piece of something unmentionable in a pork pie—'

'Enough.' Tara held up the flat of her hand. 'You're right, there have been nasty rumours going around about the quality of our food, and some regulars have stopped coming to the stall as a result. I heard several of them myself while manning the stall.' She closed her eyes briefly. 'I blame that Bulldog Man for spreading them – and Heather Gale at the Post Office. She gossips with everyone...'

John finally had his chance to speak.

'You don't think the rumours might have something to do with you reporting local people to the police? You alienated lots of people in the village, Tara, with your holier-than-thou attitude, including my near neighbour. Ashley and I had to bear the full force of his ire.'

Ashley nodded. She felt an urge to say something too. To back up John and to finally stand up to Tara... But at the thought of speaking her mind, a knot tightened in her belly.

'Out of interest,' John continued, 'are you saying there was no food whatsoever left over from the 6th of June stall? What happened to it all? Surely it wasn't all taken? That would be unusual at the best of times.'

Tara stared into the screen, crimson staining her cheeks. She didn't reply.

'I know the answer to that.' Ferne leaned forward. 'One of the regulars, the Polish woman, told me the stall was as flat as a pancake that day. No one was interested in the baked goods because of the rumours – someone actually blogged about what they'd found in a pie and put a photo up on their Facebook page. But plenty of people in Grimpton Hadlock took our food home, so I discovered.'

Tara frowned, pursing her crimson lips. 'What on earth are you talking about, Ferne?'

'The Saturday before last I was visiting a friend in Grimpton Hadlock. We were walking up the High Street when I saw Tara standing by the boot of Ursula's car, handing a cake to a woman – then taking her money!' Fearne's voice had risen an octave. 'She was selling off the food from the stall—'

'Total nonsense!' Tara spat.

'I have photos to prove it.' Ferne waved her phone at her webcam.

'Bring it closer – I can't see properly.' Ursula leaned into her screen.

'Sorry, the quality's so rubbish. I snapped them in a hurry, I was so shocked to see Tara selling off our food – cakes, loaves, quiches, jars of marmalade and pickle, even the tins of ham I donated, which I could have eaten myself! People were snapping them up. There was a queue going along the pavement.'

Ashley peered at the photo. It showed an ample woman with faded blonde highlights in a low-cut top and a purple face mask, standing behind a station wagon that looked oddly like Ursula's. On its roof were a row of highlighter-daubed tins, spelling out:

HOME-MADE FOOD AT DIS

The woman's face was indistinct. She was handing a pie or pastry to someone whose face was cut off. Four other people and a small variegated terrier were visible in the background.

'I think you've made a mistake, dear.' Tara spoke calmly. 'That woman wasn't me.'

'Oh yes it was.'

Fearne flicked to the next photograph and thrust the phone at her webcam. It was a close-up of the woman's face – unmistakably, Tara's face. Ferne gave a satisfied smile.

'My God!' Ursula's hand rushed to her mouth. 'Ferne's right. It *is* Tara.'

'Not only did she make money out of the produce people donated in good faith,' John said, 'she was selling food out of a car boot with no licence and she didn't care about the possibility of spreading Covid—'

'God's sake! I wore a mask, didn't I?'

Ferne leapt in. 'Most of your customers weren't. They were huddling in close, trying to snap up a bargain—'

'Ferne, be quiet for a moment.' Ursula pushed her glasses up her nose. 'Tara, are you now admitting that you did what Ferne's accusing you of? You took food from our stall, drove to Grimpton Hadlock and sold it all on the High Street to whoever was passing by?' Shock reverberated through Ursula's voice.

Tara rolled her eyes in the manner of a petulant teenager.

'All right, Ursula, I admit it. But this wasn't the heinous crime you're making it out to be. I had a pile of perfectly good baked goods left over from the stall in the back of your car. I thought, why not see if anyone else wants them? I didn't want the food to go to waste—'

'But you didn't give the food away!' John sounded even more outraged than Ursula. 'You made money out of food that people donated to us in good faith, expecting it to be given to those in need.'

'Exactly!' Greg joined in. 'To give the food away would have been understandable. But to take money for it and then not tell anyone...'

'Beyond the pale, I think we all agree,' Ursula took over. 'And you lied to me, Tara, about why you were late bringing back my car. There was no problem with the battery, it was just that you were twenty-five miles away flogging off food, then you had drive back to Brampton.'

Tara raised her hands. 'It was only a few loaves, people.'

'That's a lie.' Ferne jabbed a finger at the screen. 'My friend and I watched you from the florist for fifteen minutes. You sold at least ten items in that time – and it was all sorts, tins and jars too, that could have been kept over for the next stall.'

'This is ridiculous, I'm being painted as the devil incarnate!' Tara bit her lower lip. 'OK, I confess, the stall didn't do very well that day and there was more than usual left over – by three o'clock, I was at the end of my tether. I'd been listening all day to people bleat on about our food being tampered with... I thought what the hell, I'll give the rest to people who'll appreciate it—'

'But you didn't give it away, you sold it.' John's voice wasn't loud but the anger in it was unmistakeable. 'Somewhere twenty-five miles away. Why did you go all that way to sell it – and why didn't you tell any of us what you'd done?'

Tara stared at John, her cheeks salmon-pink.

'I think it's clear enough why she did that,' Ursula said in a sneering tone. 'She obviously didn't want anyone cottoning on to her money-making scheme. How much did you make from selling our food, Tara?'

'It wasn't much. I was broke, I needed a little extra this month to cover my bills. All this time and effort I've been putting into getting the stall up and running, I've not been able to get on with earning a living—'

'Answer the question!' Ursula's voice boomed through Zac's high-performance speakers.

Tara lowered her eyes. '£396.'

A loud gasp from Ferne. Ashley took in the open-mouthed faces on the laptop screen; everyone looked stunned. But she wasn't surprised. This was exactly the sort of thing she would have expected Tara to do.

John spoke first, an air of incredulity in his voice.

'You secretly sold off last week's donations to the food bank, pocketed £396 in the process and said nothing to anyone? That's stealing, in my book.'

'How dare you?' Tara seethed, a picture of indignation. 'I demand that you take that back. I would have said something.'

Silence. Ursula scratched her head. Greg lowered his eyes, chewing something invisible. Ashley's heart banged against her chest. They weren't going to let Tara get away with this, were they? She had to say something.

'No,' she said, fighting to keep the wobble out of her voice, 'you wouldn't have said anything. You told us earlier that most of the food at the stall got taken, and only when cornered did you admit the truth. You're a liar, Tara.'

She sensed everyone's eyes on her, saw the shock on their faces. Her hands were cold and clammy and her heart was beating too hard, too fast. She reached for the mouse beside the laptop – the first thing that came to hand – and squeezed it hard, as if it might help steady her. She could scarcely believe it was her who had spoken. Words had come out of her mouth without warning – were still coming.

'You stole a rose plant from Elspeth, then lied to her. She told me about it.' Ursula, John, Ferne and Greg were listening intently.

'This is ridiculous, she's got it all wrong.'

She felt a flash of anger.

'You told her you must have accidentally left it behind at the garden centre check-out, but you hadn't. You planted it in your own garden and lied about it. And that wasn't a one off. Elspeth told me you often bought extra items when you went shopping for her, things you kept for yourself—'

'What are you on about? This is all nonsense.'

'—cosmetics, toiletries, small items you didn't think she'd notice. Admit it, Tara. You stole from an elderly, vulnerable woman who you were meant to be helping, then lied about it. Just as you stole from the food stall and lied to us all to try to get away with it.'

She came to a halt. She felt released from a weight she hadn't even known she'd carried.

'Well said, Ashley.' John started to clap. Each smack of his hands resonated briskly through the laptop's speakers.

'Thank you, Ashley.' Greg's voice was thick with emotion. 'Well done for speaking out.'

'Fuck you, Ashley.' Tara's eyes brimmed with tears. 'That is all lies. Elspeth never said anything like that, Ashley's twisting it—'

Ursula intervened. 'Let's keep this civil, shall we?'

The nausea returned. Though she couldn't actually tell where the woman was looking, Ashley felt Tara's eyes on her, regarding her with a cold ferocity. Why had she spoken out so brazenly? Of course Tara had been going to react badly.

Things moved quickly. John, Ursula and Ferne demanded that Tara step down from the group, mentioning 'a serious breach of trust'. Ursula suggested that John take over and Greg seconded this.

'How dare you do this to me?' Tara repeated in an anguished voice, which everyone ignored.

Ashley felt a smidgeon sorry for Tara. The woman lacked the most basic ethical principles, but still... Tara had tried to be a good neighbour to Elspeth, hadn't she?

John's voice cut in on her thoughts. 'All those who agree that Tara should leave the group, raise their hands.'

Ashley took a deep breath and held her arm high, not daring to look at Tara.

'Keep your hands up, I haven't counted.'

'There's no need, John,' Ursula said. 'Everyone has their hand up, apart from Tara.'

Ashley sneaked a glimpse at Tara, who looked about to cry.

'I'm through with you all, anyway,' Tara muttered, swiping at the corners of her eyes. 'After all I've done for this group, you turn on me like this.'

Ferne clapped her hands briskly, an unapologetic smile on her face.

'Good riddance,' she said, 'you self-important old crone.'

'And by the way,' Tara said, leaning forward, 'you can host your own bloody Zoom meetings in future. Fuck off, the lot of you!'

The Zoom screen disappeared, replaced by a small box containing the message: *Meeting ended by host*

Chapter 29
Elspeth
17 June

T he kettle was almost impossible to lift, so she put it back down. Damn, she'd have to boil some water in a saucepan instead. Elspeth rooted around in the cupboard for the small one.

While waiting for the water to boil, she wondered if she ought to pack a few things to take to hospital, just in case; Ashley had insisted that Elspeth call 999 if she felt any worse. A paperback, maybe, and some paper to write on. Oh yes, and her phone. Would such items be allowed in hospital? Her thoughts darkened. What if she got seriously ill? What if she ended up in intensive care, hooked up to a machine and struggling to stay alive? She wasn't ready to die yet. She had a good ten years left, surely.

For goodness sake, woman.

She'd been a professional dancer for most of her life, active and strong. She was going to get through this – wasn't she? With difficulty, she poured the saucepan's contents onto a bag of green tea. When the mug was nearly full, she jerked the saucepan away and dropped it onto the hob with a clatter. What a blunderpuss! Her arms were useless. All that coughing in the early hours of this morning had taken her last reserves of energy. It was hard to do anything now except lie in bed.

Elspeth grasped the mug. The sun had come out again; the garden would be lovely now, if she could manage to get there... At a sudden craving to be outside, she made her way slowly onto the patio, leaving the French doors well ajar in case the house phone should ring – she'd left her mobile upstairs. Someone was bound to call while she was outside.

The garden was quiet, with no sign of either Tara or her neighbours on the other side, a middle-aged couple who argued all the time. She scanned the border along the fence. Apart from Ashley's vandalised rose, which still hadn't recovered, the new climbers were shooting up, now showing off delicate cups of pink petals. She approached the large flowerbed where her beloved rose bushes grew. Their blooms were magnificent. Rich crimsons, luscious shades of apricot and lemon...

She reached out to a petal and stroked its velvet softness, then bent down and breathed in the flower's perfume, closing her eyes. Could she keep all this with her, somehow – these roses, this garden, this midsummer afternoon?

A shiver ran through her. She coughed – a raspy, weak little sound. The accompanying movement hurt her chest. Even breathing was an effort now, even standing...

Her legs gave out. She collapsed across the patio wall, arms crashing into a rose bush, hips aloft, legs in a sprawl. Air whooshed out of her lungs like a deflating bicycle tyre.

Panic lurched through her. She tried to push herself up but she didn't have enough strength in her arms. Her lower leg wouldn't move, seemed to be trapped underneath her body. If only she had her mobile phone with her... What if she couldn't get up again? With an effort, Elspeth raised her head and scanned Tara's back windows. Sod's law, now that she really did need Tara there was no sign of the woman. She tried to call out for help but her voice fluttered away, too frail to be heard.

Chapter 30
Ashley

S he checked her neighbour's front door again to make sure Tara wasn't about to rush out, and hurried down the path towards the gate. Early evening sunshine gleamed on window panes along Wilton Close and turned the central area of grass an intense, almost unnatural shade of green. As quickly as she could without running, she passed Tara's house, pushed on Elspeth's gate and rang the doorbell.

Despite the warmth of the evening, her hands were cold. She could still hear the venom of Tara's words.

Fuck you, Ashley.

The profanity was unusual, coming from Tara. The words felt like a curse.

Since yesterday's Zoom meeting, she had hardly eaten. Her concern about Tara had combined with concerns over Elspeth's state of health. Thank God, Elspeth had sounded slightly better at lunchtime on the phone. The alarming wheeziness had gone, as had the long pauses between phrases. But it was getting on for 7pm now and Elspeth hadn't replied to Ashley's texts for several hours, nor was she picking up her mobile phone or landline.

Ashley rang Elspeth's doorbell a second time, then lifted the knocker; Elspeth was probably asleep or dozing and hadn't heard the bell.

A minute later there was still no reply, though her knocking had been loud enough to wake the dead. She pushed aside the ominous thought, removed the keys once possessed by Tara from her jeans pocket and inserted the Yale into the top lock.

Chapter 31
Tara

Tara poured a large whisky and drained half, then took the white leather diary from the shoe box and sat down. With grim resignation she opened the diary and scanned for the next entry about Evie.

It was now or never. She would read the rest, and know the truth of what had happened to her eldest sister.

July 13th 1982

Evie said she knows I cut the rope. She saw me take a knife out of the kitchen drawer and go into the garden with it two days before Zoe's birthday.

That's crazy, I told her. I said I was using the knife to scrape bird shit off the garden chairs so people could sit on them.
Evie screwed up her eyes, said I was lying.

I shook my head and asked why she only mentioned it now. She said she forgot all about it and only remembered when they talked about how the rope snapped in two at Zoe's inquest last week. Evie was allowed to go to the inquest. Mum said I was too young to go but she told me what happened. They decided Zoe's death was an accident. An expert told everyone that the rope she climbed on had snapped due to it fraying over time from rubbing against the pear tree. One day it got so thin it was ready to snap when someone put their weight on it. An accident waiting to happen, in other words.

Evie said she's going to tell Mum that she saw me go into the garden with a knife. Then Mum will go to the police and tell them it was me who killed Zoe.

If you tell anyone I'll kill you too, I said.

The words just came out. Evie made a choking noise and hopped back like I might do it right then. I wasn't even thinking about killing her.

I am now, though.

There were several more entries in the diary that had nothing to do with Evie. She skipped past them impatiently. Then a longer one. Her throat tightened and her heart began to bang in her chest.

August 2nd 1982
I've worked out how to do it. I just need Evie to say yes to going swimming with me.

I haven't got long. Evie's still scared of me but I think she's going to tell Mum what she saw soon, the two of them are getting so chummy. Who knows what Mum might do? I could be locked away for years with a bunch of killer kids. On the other hand, I don't want Evie to die too soon, in case it looks suspicious. More than it will look in any case, that is. I mean, what are the chances that both your sisters die in freak accidents?

Could I really be a murderer, like someone on those true crime documentaries? One of them said people who kill repeatedly have no conscience and are the worst of all. A shiver went through me when I heard that. I didn't mean to kill Zoe, just to send her to hospital for a long time. I put up with her horribleness for so long without once thinking of hurting her. Then something inside me broke.

I'm going to kill Evie for a good reason too, though the police and the people who make documentaries might not think so – or Mum. But that doesn't matter, because no one is going to find out it was me who killed her.

It's not fair that I should have to be locked up for what I did to Zoe, not after all the years of suffering I had to put up with. Evie always went along with Zoe, she had no backbone. She joined in with everything, laughing at me and playing tricks on me and calling me names. She deserves what's coming to her.

Perspiring, her body cold, Tara turned the page to the next entry.

It was written the day she'd gone to the beach with Evie, and Evie hadn't returned. Tara had poured out everything. How she had lured Evie onto the coastal path to Black's Beach by running on ahead, knowing it was dangerous because of the rising tide, due to be higher than usual. She had hoped that Evie would feel obliged to chase after Tara because Evie was supposed to be looking after her. How Evie had indeed followed Tara and Tara had ignored Evie's shouts and pleas to come back, instead watching the incoming tide nibble away the path and, at the last minute, climbing the cliff to safety. Standing on the cliff edge looking down, waiting for her sister to disappear under the waves before she ran for help...

Noiselessly, tears slipped down her cheeks onto the diary's pages. She had done the worst possible thing to her sisters.

However much Zoe and Evie had tormented her all those years ago, they hadn't deserved to die.

Oh, dear God. She must have known all along that she had let Evie die, mustn't she? Just as she had always known, deep down, that she had caused Zoe's death... *The mind forgets what it can't assimilate.* How conveniently the mind allowed you to forget the unpalatable. The therapist had been right, beyond his wildest imaginings.

Tara sipped her whisky, struggling to regain her composure. She had done bad things, yes. But she wasn't all bad, was she? She had to pull herself together now and get on with life. All that business with her sisters had happened so long ago. Was it really worth tormenting herself over?

Things had worked out OK, in the end. Her sisters weren't laughing at her any more, were they? Despite the whiffs of suspicion from her mother, no one had ever found out what Tara had done to her sisters.

She needed to make sure it stayed that way. What if her violent impulses became impossible to resist? If she was to lose control again...

With the assistance of another large whisky, Tara felt her sense of perspective returning. She had survived her miserable childhood and she would withstand this setback, too. Onwards and upwards! No more unhealthy obsessing over the past. She'd have a relaxing evening catching up with *The Crown*. First of all, though... Tara placed the diary in the kitchen sink, fetched a lighter and depressed the lever. Flames licked around the diary, buckling the cover and blackening the pages within. Bit by bit, the diary disappeared, leaving just a pile of ash.

Part Two

Part Two

Chapter 32
Bird Woman
20 June

10.15am

Since dawn broke, I've been sitting on my usual spot on the bench in the cul-de-sac at the top of the hill. So far, I have spotted few birds but plenty of humans – the green is unusually popular this morning. Fortunately for my bladder, I managed to visit the clump of silver birches before anyone arrived.

Here come three more young people looking for a spot to settle in. All are wearing pale blue paper masks over their mouths and noses. One young woman has her hair dyed pink on one side and blue on the other. The other female has the letters 'BLM' marked on her forehead. In one hand she's holding a box blasting out music and in the other a placard. I can't read what it says. The young man holds a refrigerator bag.

They sit down around one of the chalk crosses on the grass and proceed to remove paper cups and plates and a wine bottle. The placard is plonked into the grass behind. I can read it now:
BLACK LIVES MATTER

11am

The green is almost full and no more chalk marks showing where to sit are visible on the ground. But people keep on coming, trying to squeeze into the gaps between the bodies. Some wear face masks, or have them lodged under their chins. Many are young adults or adolescents, often with unusually brightly coloured hair and studs or metal rings through their lips and noses. Most of them are holding placards or larger banners, such as:

RESPECT US ALL
LESBIANS ARE HUMAN TOO
SILENCE IS COMPLIANCE
ENOUGH IS ENOUGH
BLACK LIVES MATTER

This is a protest about that man knelt on by the police in America, I belatedly realise. Even I have heard of Mr Floyd; there was a long article in a newspaper left behind on the bench last week. Humans treat each other even worse over there than they do on this little island, it seems. That is why I do my best to avoid them. Birds are better company and far easier to understand.

The humans on this patch of grass are interesting to watch but rather noisy. Clusters of them occasionally start chanting the same words, over and over, apparently spontaneously. 'We are stronger together' and 'Fight for racial justice'.

A male in jeans with matted hair has started banging a drum. Some females in the centre of the green have taken off their sandals and are dancing.

I have resisted the temptation to observe them through my binoculars. Already I have heard whispered, none too quietly, 'There goes Bird Woman'.

12.40pm

Two women have sat down beside me, one dark-haired and thin, the other grey-haired and overweight. They look a little older than me, in their sixties. As both are wearing face masks, I put mine on too.

The thinner woman, who wears a disconcerting mask resembling a tiger's open jaw, asks if I would mind them joining me. I say not at all. Actually, it is a relief to have company. The overweight woman, wearing a plain black mask, introduces herself. Her name is Hazel and her tiger-masked friend is Stella. I tell them that everyone calls me 'Bird Woman', or occasionally 'that mad bitch' or 'the witch'. Stella laughs. Hazel says 'that's dreadful' and insists on knowing my real name.

I enquire about what is happening. Stella tells me that this gathering is 'a sit-down protest about racial injustice in the UK and the treatment of minority groups in Brampton'.

'No, it's not,' Hazel says. She says it is 'a picnic to celebrate diversity', according to the council.

1.30pm

The pair have taken their masks off to eat. Like me, neither wears make-up. Stella has a piercing on her nose and long earrings like dragonflies.

Hazel shares their lunch with me – two green apples, two huge egg-and-cress sandwiches and two packets of salt and vinegar crisps. She says she would have offered me some of her flask of tea but there isn't another cup. I tell her I have my water bottle and I will have a cup of tea at home – if I have a cup now, I will want to pee and unfortunately there are no public toilets nearby. Stella starts to laugh but stops when she sees Hazel's stern expression.

2.15pm

A large group has arrived, mostly male. Some have close-cropped hair. None have black or brown skin. They are marching up and down along the road, shouting and jeering at the people sitting on the grass.

Stella says they are protesting about the picnic being allowed to take place. She says the village has many bigoted people who don't support diversity and hate people of colour, along with gays, lesbians and transsexuals.

It is hot in the sunshine. Some of the anti-protest group are standing close to us, drinking from cans of beer when they are not yelling insults to the picnickers. Many have taken off clothing, exposing sun-reddened shoulders, backs and chests, and unsightly bellies. Meanwhile, on the grass, young women are dancing in bikinis or half-tops and shorts. I think about rolling up my trousers but am reluctant for anyone to see my hairy legs.

2.30pm

One of the group of men loitering near the bench has just spat at Hazel. The spit landed on her cheek. Stella shouts, 'Go away, you Nazi prick!' The man responds with a derogatory remark and a rude gesture. Hazel gets her tissue out of her rucksack and Stella puts her arm around her. A jeer goes up from the group of men behind us, who are becoming louder and are getting through many beer cans, which, when empty, they scrunch up and toss to the ground.

Stella says, 'Look after yourself, lovely lady,' to me and gets up from the bench, holding her hand out for Hazel to take. Hazel gives me a wave and says she hopes she'll see me again.

The woman from number 33 is intently watching the protesters from the pavement. No part of her has moved for at least two minutes. She wears a straw hat and sunglasses, and is standing two or three metres from a group of older men and women, fellow residents of the cul-de-sac. Sometimes I see her pruning plants in her front garden with a sad expression, that of someone alone in the world. I know that feeling.

Her neighbour, the dancing lady at number 34, has disappeared. I haven't seen her for over a month. Maybe she too has died from Covid, like the butcher who used to save me free scraps of meat to feed the birds. I do hope not.

3pm

The spitting man and another from the anti-protest group have plonked themselves down on the bench beside me. They shouted 'bloody lezzies' after Hazel and Stella, then started calling out things to the protestors. 'This place has gone to the dogs', 'Piss off back where you belong' and other demeaning language full of the f and c words. Both are white, between twenty-five and thirty-five years old and wear trainers with casual shirts, not tucked in, over their jeans. To my ear, they sound uneducated. Neither wears a mask. The spitting man is tanned and has a buzz cut, with a distinctive dragon tattoo on his forearm. His breath stinks of beer. He goes by the name of 'Marksy'. The other has a short neck, protruding belly, red hair and a rapidly reddening nose. His moniker is 'J-J'. On his cheek is what appears to be a birthmark.

'Whadya looking at, lady?' the spitting man has just asked.

J-J peers at my notebook and says, 'Are you writing 'bout us?'

I think it is time I left, too.

4.30pm

Back home, I have a long wee, a big mug of PG Tips and four Hobnobs, then get out my sketch book. There is plenty to draw, while the images are still in my head.

I am pleased I stayed to observe the diversity picnic, and met

Hazel and Stella. Knowing I probably shall not see them again, I feel oddly lost and a touch melancholy. Perhaps I am not as independent as I like to think.

Chapter 33
Tara

Tara checked her reflection one last time. With this hat on, extra-large sunglasses hiding her eyes, a mask covering a good part of her face and this boring old denim jacket and jeans, she was – hopefully – unrecognisable. Still, a tremor of trepidation began, mingling unpleasantly with her breakfast. She felt decidedly icky.

It was the thought of going outside – she hadn't ventured beyond her front door in the four days since that dreadful Zoom meeting – as much as the fact of having drunk the remains of her wine, gin and tonic water the night before, and having to eat her cereal with UHT milk. Unfortunately, her first Ocado delivery wasn't booked until next week.

Taking two shopping bags from the cupboard, she walked determinedly to the front door. She refused to cower indoors any more, afraid of the childish reactions from those who should know better. With care, she pulled the door open an inch. Noise rushed through the gap: a murmur of voices, rising and falling in volume like a wavy sea. Behind it, a distant drumbeat. She made her way to the front gate.

Wilton Close was thronged with young people heading for the green, already crowded. The protest picnic, or whatever it was meant to be called now, had attracted a good crowd. Brampton's pro-diversity lobby, along with every minority group and eco-activist for miles, had descended on the small patch of grass intended for the enjoyment of the surrounding residents.

But she couldn't get worked up about people hogging the green for their own agendas, or chanting and singing without any pretence of social distancing. What did she care about such matters now she had become a *persona non grata*, now the admiration and acclaim that she had worked so hard for had been put through the shredder? They could all get Covid and die, what did she care? Anyway, the more people out here, the emptier Waitrose would be.

She spotted many residents of the Wiltons in their front gardens or clustered on the pavement, observing the activity on the green with curiosity. Four women stood outside Sandy's house – and was that Ashley's slight figure among them?

She approached, wondering whether any of them would notice if she carried on past. Too late. Four heads turned towards Tara; Ashley's eyes widened, as if she had spotted a hungry tiger. Sandy, the tall, fragrant woman who ran the village flower shop, stopped talking abruptly, flushing red. The droopy-shouldered woman beside her – Sandy's live-in mother – stared openly at Tara. The fourth woman smiled, revealing the big teeth crowding her gums. It was that Welsh woman, Rhianna, who'd moved into number 28 three years ago, who everyone used to gossip about.

'Hello, Tara,' Rhianna began in an overly jaunty tone. 'It is you, isn't it? Off out to sell some more cakes, are we?'

Sandy smiled and exchanged glances with her mother. A malicious expression slid over Rhianna's face.

'We heard you've had a bit of trouble with your baking venture,' Rhianna continued.

A titter from Sandy's mother. 'Half baked, by the sound of it.'

'And they don't want you in that group of yours any more.'

Ashley stood looking at the pavement, shuffling her feet and making no attempt to defend Tara. So, it had come to this. Tara jerked her head away from them and hurried on.

By now, she thought, Ashley had probably told everyone in the street all about what had happened at that dreadful meeting – and all about Tara's supposed mistreatment of Elspeth, come to that. She tried to ignore the sudden squeezing of her throat and the pathetic press of tears behind her eyes. She mustn't let those women get to her. They were intolerant, ignorant busybodies. Maybe she should have put off this trip until late at night when no one was about. But her food situation was now critical. Another day and evening without even a glass of beer to quench her thirst...

She hurried on downhill, past the church, towards the main road, mercifully reaching Waitrose on the High Street without encountering anyone else who wanted to harangue her. Even better, no queue – everyone must be out protesting.

Tara took a deep breath, pulled her shoulders back and walked towards the entrance. The glass doors slid open. She squeezed out a blob of hand sanitiser, distributed it over her hands, tore off a piece of rough paper from the roll and dabbed that with sanitiser too, then collected a trolley and wiped the push-bar clean with it. You couldn't be too careful, these days.

She progressed along the aisles, focusing on taking the items she needed as quickly as possible. There were more people here than she would have liked, but no one paid her any attention. For once, she was grateful. Scooping up a handful of easy-cook dinners for two – it was cheaper that way and she didn't want anyone to think that she only ate alone – she noticed a familiar face approaching from the other direction. Anja, her yoga teacher before lockdown.

Smiling from behind her mask, Tara raised a hand in greeting.

The woman's eyes flickered in recognition before she averted her face and walked on.

'Fuck you too.' Tara rounded the corner of the aisle and headed towards the third aisle.

The cheese section had been denuded of continental cheeses. There was no Parmesan or Ricotta, Brie or Camembert. Only Stilton, Wensleydale and other British cheeses she'd never heard of. Britain really was becoming smaller, by the minute... She sighed and reached for a hunk of Stilton. She'd better get to the alcohol section quickly, before they ran out of Sauvignon Blanc and Prosecco.

'Shame on you, Tara Sanderson.' It was a low-pitched woman's voice, clearly enunciated and loud enough for people around to hear. 'Stealing from the people who supported you.'

A plain, pudgy person in nondescript clothes blocked the way with her trolley. Tara let go of the Stilton and gripped her own trolley. For a moment, she was tempted to abandon her shopping and flee the supermarket. But then this whole awful trip would have been for nothing. With as much haste and dignity as she could manage, she shoved her trolley past the woman, collected the remaining essentials and headed to the shortest checkout queue.

The mature woman behind the till gave Tara a look devoid of pleasantness and didn't say hello. Maybe she was at the end of her shift. Tara sped up her unloading. Three sourdough loaves, two cellophane-wrapped packs of four apples, seven TV dinners...

From the queue behind her, voices were plainly audible.

'Isn't she that two-faced do-gooder who was thrown out of that residents' group? The one who sold off all their cakes?'

She turned to glance at the speaker, a middle-aged man about her own age in baggy shorts. He was talking to a younger woman beside him in a long cotton skirt and tie-died top. Tara turned back to the conveyor belt and unloaded the rest of her items, faster. Two packets of roasted almonds, a packet of pistachios...

'Yeah, you could be right. She was spouting all that guff on the radio about the community rallying together.'

'Silly cow, what was she thinking?'

She fumbled and nearly dropped the tub of chocolate ice-cream, managing to rescue it just in time. Her cheeks were hot and her hands as cold as ice. The check-out woman stopped scanning items and glared at Tara from hooded eyes. Tara glanced at the long queue for the self-service checkouts, the instinct to flee almost overpowering. A woman with a sleek coil of hair and pale blue nails unloading at the next checkout glanced towards her, curiosity on her face.

She was trapped. She couldn't leave this spot unless she abandoned all her shopping – and if she did, the village gossips would have something else to feed on. With utmost care, she transferred the remains of her shopping onto the conveyor belt. Three bottles of New Zealand Sauvingnon Blanc, two bottles of Gordon's, four bottles of Schweppes Slimline Tonic...

She unloaded the last item, a bottle of pomegranate and rose-flavoured Edinburgh Gin liqueur, silently pleading with the checkout woman to hurry up. The voices from behind re-started, louder and more contemptuous in tone. '...turning to drink now...' Fortunately, her thumping heart was drumming in her ears, blocking out the rest of their words.

She ran, stopped to pant and ran again. Her bags were heavy and kept banging into her side, and people kept barging into her. Then she was down, stumbling on an uneven paving stone and nearly spraining her ankle. Heads turned towards her as she got back to her feet. The only thing she could think about was getting behind her own front door again, before anyone else had a chance to humiliate her.

Entering Wilton Close, Tara slowed to a brisk walk. Some picnickers on the green were in the process of leaving, their faces worried. A group of about twelve men stood in the road, hurling insults at them.

She stood outside the gate, her oesophagus burning, not to mention her calf and thigh muscles. She needed a long drink of water and a lie down but couldn't stop watching. Was there going to be a fight outside her house? She watched as one of the group, a man in jeans and a T-shirt with a pinkish bald patch at the top of his head, pumped his raised fist and shouted with the others.

'Blacks and queers, we don't want you here! Get out of Brampton, Muslim scum!'

A shower of droplets rushed from his mouth, catching the afternoon sun. Most of her near-neighbours had retreated to their gardens or were watching the scene from behind their windows. Tara went inside.

After she'd unpacked the shopping, poured a large gin and tonic, taken a long bath then sat down to watch a re-run of series ten of *The Great British Bake Off*, she felt her humiliation in Waitrose just as keenly. The searing pain of those endless moments of public ridicule would not go away. If anything, it grew worse, fusing with the humiliation of being ejected from her own group as a liar and a thief, and all the subsequent back turning, finger pointing and name calling she had suffered since.

She thought back to when her life had begun to unravel. Ferne had started it all with her devious attack on her – spying on her and taking sneaky photographs, indeed. Clearly Ferne still resented Tara for the incident six years ago when Tara had had to leave the café in a hurry to be home for a delivery, and Ferne had been left to pay for Tara's cup of tea and slice of cake... It was all so childish.

John, of course, had backed up Ferne. He'd always resented not being picked to run the group – he saw himself as a natural leader and resented a woman being in charge. He had been waiting for his chance to get Tara out. Unsurprisingly, Ursula had sided with John and Ferne. The woman looked down on Tara for being more conservative than she was and not enjoying classical music.

The Bad Neighbour

They all hated her and wanted to undermine her. But Ashley was the worst of them all. For Ashley to have turned on Tara like that, after accepting her overtures of friendship... Ashley had revealed a private matter between Tara and Elspeth, twisting everything to suit her own purposes and branding Tara a liar. Not only that, going by the little gathering she'd witnessed earlier, Ashley was getting chummy with quite a few residents of Wilton Close. By now, the woman had probably passed on her vile tittle-tattle to everyone in the Wiltons.

Tara punched the arm of the sofa. No wonder the whole street knew what had been going on at a supposedly private meeting attended by six people. No wonder everyone knew about the sodding cake sell-off and Tara's expulsion from the group. No wonder Tara was being gossiped about and laughed at by the whole of the Wiltons, and a good part of the rest of Brampton.

She punched the sofa again, as hard as she could. The action brought only a small, momentary relief. How she wished it was Ashley's head she was punching instead of inert leather. She felt her hand clench into a tight fist and her nails dig into her palm.

It was unforgiveable. Ashley was a two-faced bitch. Had she forgotten how Tara had gone out of her way to make Ashley and her family feel welcome when they moved here – amid all the xenophobic locals who despised the woman for being white and having children with a brown-skinned Muslim? Well, Tara hated Ashley too, now – along with Ashley's unhelpful, up-himself husband, their fuzz-faced son and crybaby daughter.

She drank a glass of water then lay on the living room floor and went through the muscle relaxation sequence that the therapist had taught her. Halfway through, an idea came. Going by the ire of people protesting against the George Floyd picnic today, there were plenty in Brampton who wouldn't shed any tears if the fortunes of the family next door were to rapidly dwindle. Plenty of people from the more conservative section of the village would enjoy seeing the Khans face certain... difficulties.

Thoughts of practical action were a welcome distraction from her misery. She got up and paced the living room, not noticing the fading light beyond the windows. Slowly, she started to feel better. She would get her own back on Ashley, and she would enjoy every minute of it.

Chapter 34
Elspeth
1 July

The blanket lay heavy on her. She was way too hot... Elspeth tried to push it off but her brain couldn't coordinate her body, resulting in only a small, ineffective movement. She felt like an upturned turtle left out in the sun.

Not only was she too hot, her whole body ached with a violence she'd never before experienced – her arms, legs, feet, neck, head, abdomen, lungs and other places she'd scarcely noticed before. It was a creeping, darting, eternally shifting pain that would reappear in another part of the body whenever she started to think it might have gone away – the root of her tongue or behind her eyes or big toe, sometimes sharpening into a savage stab that made her cry out. Right now, the pain was concentrated in the front of her head, accompanied by vague, shimmering blobs like giant toadstools.

She felt her nose twitch. The whiff of food, or...? She couldn't tell the difference between chicken soup and disinfectant any more. She'd eaten something from the trolley once when she had first been admitted. It had smelt bad and tasted even worse. How long ago? A week? Two? The usual markers of time had disappeared. Day and night, she was in a permanent semi-doze filled with strange visions and delirious imaginings.

Another deep, anguished moan from the curtained-off bed next door, now with a guttural, animal-like inflexion. Impossible to tell if it came from a man or a woman... Did they separate the sexes of Covid patients? Perhaps it was a pig being slaughtered, or a donkey giving birth...

This place was full of noises. Sudden crashes and clutters and echoey footsteps that never seemed to end, as if the doctors and nurses were walking around an endless loop. Strangely, that infernal buzzing and whining in her ears had gone since the infection began; her hearing was almost back to normal.

Her brain was sluggish, though. They'd taken her to the big hospital in town, not the local hospital, and had told her she had Covid and was 'quite poorly'. No one had been in to see her, as Covid patients weren't allowed to have visitors.

She touched her forearm. A tube still led out of it, into a machine... The wires from her body to monitors were still there. Her nostrils felt uncomfortable... She raised a hand to her nose. There were tubes coming out of her nostrils, too. She glanced upwards, following the tubes. Was that an oxygen machine it was going to?

A panicky sensation grew, making her breathing more laboured. She couldn't move, not with all these tubes and wires attached. What if she needed to go somewhere? Her lungs struggled to work; she couldn't take in enough air. How long had she lain here, in this bed – and what were they doing to her? How long was she going to be here? A terrifying thought crashed past the others. Was she going to die here?

She felt herself pulled back under into a demi-world, where dreams were more real than reality.

A female figure was moving around indoors. She watched it pass a fridge and a sink, stretching out an arm as it did so.

Elspeth's kitchen? The figure was female, rounded, dressed in bright colours...

Tara. The face twisted with a malevolent expression. On a table behind, a vase of dying roses. A rectangular glass vase much like Elspeth's own. Suddenly, the woman coughed hard three times without covering her mouth. Elspeth's heart jolted. Tara was in Elspeth's house, walking about.

Next, Elspeth was back in hospital, lying in bed with all those tubes and wires attached. A female figure was looming over her, her large hands ready, her large blue eyes suffused with malicious intent.

Elspeth screamed and threw off the blanket. Her breath came in shallow pants as she took in her surroundings. She was safe; it was only that dream again... What did it mean? Was it a premonition, or...?

Someone else was standing over her now – a woman in white. Above the beakish mask over her nose and mouth, pale eyes glistened. It was impossible to read her expression.

'Let's get you back under the covers, love.'

Elspeth looked down at the hospital bed. Her pale thighs were exposed beneath the hem of her gown. The nurse pulled up the blanket.

'Did you have a fright, dear?'

'Bad...' *Bad dream*, she tried to say, only she couldn't get enough air in.

Another nurse arrived, also masked. Her voice was weary.

'You've been calling out in your sleep, Elspeth.'

Elspeth tried again to speak, wanting to ask for a glass of water. But a stream of raspy coughs came out instead.

'Her breathing is worse than yesterday, don't you think?' the first nurse asked the second. Their voices were low but Elspeth could hear, just about.

'She might need to be intubated. Dr Gleeson should take a look.'

No! She didn't want them to put a hole in her throat and her body to be taken over by one of those horrible breathing machines. She knew what would happen if she was attached to one of those things – she'd never come back. Elspeth tried to move her hand to pull on the nurse's arm to convey the force of her disagreement. A limp wave resulted. She summoned all her energy.

'Don't put me on a ventilator.' It came out in a barely audible croak.

'We're doing all we can to look after you,' the second nurse said, and turned away. The first nurse leaned over and spoke more gently.

'Don't worry, lovely. The doctor will only put you on if she needs to.'

For a long time after that she stayed awake, her mind racing. Was this the beginning of the end? She was seventy-eight – old enough, many would think. But she wasn't ready to die, not yet. She loved life. She wanted to talk to her friends again, drink wine and go to the theatre. She wanted to dance again, once they'd operated on her foot.

Had the bad dream been a premonition? Was Tara inside Elspeth's home right now, or planning to be? Or maybe Tara had already gone into Elspeth's home... She gasped. Tara *had* been inside Elspeth's home. Had Tara given her Covid – on purpose? Had Tara wanted Elspeth to become very ill – to die, even?

She struggled to sit upright. The truth burned inside her, banishing any doubts. That heinous woman had tried to kill her.

A spark of anger ignited. I'll show her, she thought. She wasn't going to die... If it was the last thing she did, she was going to get better and get out of this hospital.

Chapter 35
Ashley
5 July

I t had been on her mind much of the day before and most of the night, as per usual. But now that what meagre news about Elspeth could be wrung from the hospital staff had taken on an ominous note, it had acquired an added urgency. What if Tara had given Elspeth Covid?

Tara and Elspeth had not seen each other since they rowed, so Elspeth had said – the day before Tara fell ill. But the following day Tara had been spotted by Layla standing outside Elspeth's front door. Two days after that, Elspeth had come down with Covid. What if Tara had secretly gone inside and paved the way for Elspeth to catch this vile disease?

The first time, she'd nearly laughed aloud at the notion. It was preposterous, wasn't it? Now, the idea seemed less wacky. Even if she was right, though, what could she do about it?

Ashley turned over, glanced at the alarm clock and groaned. 8am, time to get the breakfast ready for everyone... No, it was a Sunday; there was no rush to get up. Zac had gone away for the weekend with friends from the angling club. The kids could get their own breakfasts, anyway. Was her purpose in life to cook and clean for a family who much of the time barely noticed her?

Elspeth's body, slumped over her rose-bed, popped into her mind. The poor woman had been deathly pale and too weak to move. Thank goodness, Ashley had found her in time. If she had gone next door only half an hour later...

Once again, as she had been countless times since Elspeth had been taken to hospital, Ashley was consumed by a sense of helplessness. She hadn't been allowed to visit Elspeth once, owing to Elspeth being a Covid patient. Ashley wasn't a family member, so she wouldn't have been allowed to visit, even if Elspeth was at death's door. The way things were going, that might not be too much longer.

There *was* something she could do, though. Whether it proved to be easy or not, it was something that, as Elspeth's friend, she ought to do. She would find out whether Tara really was to blame for Elspeth's infection with Covid.

At the start of the 5pm news, Ashley switched off the radio, opened her front door and stepped up to the gate. She checked up and down Wilton Close. Several small groups of people stood by their gates, clapping self-consciously. From an opened upper window several houses up the road came a series of whoops from Sandy's two teenagers.

She forced herself to join in the 'NHS 72nd birthday clap'. It seemed a bit pointless, making a gesture that probably no one would be aware she was doing, including her own family. Zac was still driving home from Wiltshire, Sam had gone to visit his earnest Muslim friend again and Layla was up in her room with Anna, probably watching an illegal download. Anyway, Layla didn't agree with clapping for doctors and nurses, who should be paid properly for putting their lives at risk.

As the clapping subsided, she walked the short distance to Tara's gate and peered past the profusion of untended shrubs towards the house. Tara had joined in the 'Clap for Carers' on Thursday evenings, but lately she'd become a virtual recluse. To Ashley's surprise, her neighbour was standing on her porch, attired in leggings and a sweatshirt, her hair clipped up messily.

'Ashley.' Tara raised her eyebrows. 'How nice to see you.'

'Hello, Tara. You were clapping too?'

'You needn't sound so surprised. Why shouldn't I be? Especially now my dear neighbour is in hospital in the hands of the NHS.'

My dear neighbour! She bit back a caustic chortle. Tara frowned.

'I'm sorry, Ashley, I've got things to do. Did you want something in particular?'

'Yes. I– I'd like to ask you something.'

'I'm all ears.'

'It's about Elspeth. You went over to her house, I understand, a week before she was taken to hospital?' She came to a halt. Tara flicked a glance sideways towards Elspeth's now-empty house.

'What are you talking about?'

'Layla told me she saw you standing outside her front door, when Elspeth was having tea with me. Then Elspeth found her keys on the doormat when she came home.'

'So?' Tara shifted her weight onto the other foot, her face oddly vacant.

'Elspeth said you had texted her earlier that day saying you were unwell, you had a fever,' Ashley went on, her courage dwindling. It was now or never. 'So why did you go over to her house, knowing you could be infectious? I don't understand why you would want to put an elderly person at risk of catching Covid. Unless you let yourself into Elspeth's house and spread your infection around on purpose?'

No no no. What had she done? She felt her cheeks burning.

She'd meant to build up to this question coherently and reasonably, not blurt it out like that.

'I have to say, that's the funniest thing I've heard in a long time.' Tara looked down at her with a condescending expression. 'How dare you come over here and accuse me of something so vile? I didn't set foot inside the house. All I did was drop the keys through the letterbox, to save Elspeth having to ask for them back. And, just so you know, Elspeth went to see her friends shortly before she got ill. More than likely, she picked up the virus there.'

Ashley stared back at Tara. She was a timid ten-year-old again. As much as she longed to retaliate, to explain herself properly, she couldn't think of a thing to say.

Tara had no such problem.

'I can't believe the cheek of you!' Tara's face had reddened alarmingly. 'First, you rat on me to the group simply for trying to earn a few extra pounds so I can get through these difficult times. Next, you mouth off to all the neighbours about what I did and the group kicking me out. Then, to top it all, you come over here accusing me of trying to deliberately harm Elspeth.' All but growling, Tara bared her teeth. 'Now fuck off and leave me alone.'

Chapter 36
Ashley
6 July

'I'm so glad to see you, John. Sorry to come over at such short notice.'

Ashley entered the large, light-filled kitchen. This was the first time she'd been inside John's home.

'No need to apologise. I was just pottering in the garden, keeping the snails off my tomatoes.' John steered his electric vehicle towards her. A smile lurked at the corners of his mouth. Above his shorts he wore a crinkled T-shirt showing the well-developed muscles of his shoulders and upper arms, more than she'd expected. Just the sight of him eased the gut-churning anxiety that hadn't let up since her confrontation with Tara.

'How do you take your tea, and what sort?'

'Ordinary is fine. A drop of milk, no sugar.' A tray was set out with mugs, spoons and a plate of biscuits. John put a tea bag into a mug beside another, already set up, and poured boiling water into each. He nodded to the tray.

'Would you mind?'

She carried the tray to a table beside opened glass doors giving onto a landscaped garden.

'No need to keep that on.' He indicated her face mask. 'It'll be easier to drink our tea without it. I'll try to keep my distance.'

'Your garden is lovely,' she said, as he manoeuvred the vehicle into position, across the table from her.

'Bryony made it what it is. I'm taking up where she left off.'

She wondered how he managed, living alone.

'A chap comes every week to do jobs around the house,' he said, as if reading her thoughts. 'And I have an excellent cleaner.' He brought his mug carefully to his lips. 'So, what's happened with Tara? You sounded upset on the phone.'

While John crunched into a custard cream, she described the incident on her neighbour's doorstep.

'I thought it would be the right thing to confront her,' she added, 'but her reaction took me by surprise... Now I'm wondering if I'm getting paranoid. Maybe what she says is true – Elspeth caught Covid from her friends.'

'Or maybe she's a good actress.' John raised an eyebrow. 'Do you still think Tara had a hand in infecting Elspeth?'

She took a deep breath. 'Yes I do.. I don't know how deliberate it was, if she went from room to room coughing away, or if she went there for another reason then couldn't help coughing. But I believe she went into Elspeth's house when she was sick, knowing Elspeth was vulnerable...'

He looked at her without speaking.

'Maybe we should go to the police,' he said at last. 'This is serious. We can't know for sure how Elspeth caught Covid. But if there's a possibility Tara was to blame...'

'But there's no evidence that she did anything. I don't want to blacken Tara's name any further, if she wasn't involved. For all her faults, she has a good heart.'

A snort. 'I wonder if the woman even has one!'

'She's done a lot of good in the village, you must admit. Helping people struggling to feed themselves...'

'...and Project Tara.' A flicker of a grin.

She couldn't help smiling. The knot in her stomach was easing; John's tinder-dry humour was the best medicine.

'I'll come with you to the police station, if you want.' John's expression turned serious again.

'What if she finds out we've talked to the police? We don't know what she might do.'

'It sounds like you're scared of her.'

Was she scared of Tara? Yes, she was.

'You should have seen how she angry she got,' she replied.

'I can believe it.' John rubbed his neck, his brow furrowing. 'Have you told your husband what you've told me?'

'He doesn't believe Tara could have harmed Elspeth on purpose.' She recalled Zac's reaction to Ashley's visit yesterday with a swoosh of indignation.

Given what your daughter's going through, I would have thought you'd have better things to do than stoking the outrage of Mrs Holier Than Thou next door. I don't like the woman, I don't trust her and I'm fed up with her constant angling for favours. But no way did she deliberately infect Elspeth with Covid.

John reached over and placed his hand on hers. It was larger and rougher than Zac's, and the fingernails needed a trim. The warmth was comforting, though.

'I should think getting an earful from Tara would be quite a frightening experience. You were brave to confront her.'

She smiled weakly, blinking back tears. 'More foolish than brave.'

John withdrew his hand. They drank their tea in silence. Despite his disability, he had an outdoorsiness about him, she thought. He certainly didn't look like her idea of a retired deputy headteacher. His tanned face showed signs of too much exposure to the sun. There was clearly no one to warn him not to spend too long in the sun, or to remind him to cut his nails.

'Here, take a biscuit.'

She took a chocolate one from the plate.

'Did you enjoy being a teacher?'

'I loved my job. Teaching was my life... I've been lucky. What about you? Did you work, before?'

She paused.

'I was a graphic designer. After I had Sam I tried to carry on part time, but that was too difficult... Sam had bad asthma, there were so many hospital appointments... In the end I gave up my job.' She had looked for another job in graphic design when the children were older, but had struggled to get interviews and given up. Besides, in those days Zac's career had been steamrollering ahead.

'That's a shame. If it was something you enjoyed, and were good at...'

'I know.' Without meaning to, she'd given up the chance of a fulfilling career. She stood, turning her attention to the table. 'Let me take these inside.' She gathered up the leftover crockery.

'Shall we get it over with?' John looked directly at her, expression grave. 'Our visit to the police station?'

'I suppose.' Part of her didn't want to go at all.

'Then it'll be on record if anything else happens.'

'If anything else happens? Like what?'

'I don't know. I've always thought Tara might have an unstable personality – she certainly has' – he made quote marks with his fingers – 'anger issues.' He saw the alarm on her face. 'Don't worry, I doubt she'll actually do anything.'

She didn't reply. John's belated attempt to reassure her had the opposite effect.

It took them ten minutes to reach the old school building, where a skeletal police team had somehow escaped the funding cuts. When the man ahead of them finished talking to a woman in uniform at the counter, they went up.

'Good afternoon,' John said. 'We've come because we suspect that someone we know might be involved in a crime.'

The officer looked weary.

'Right oh.' She raised her eyebrows. 'Are you partners?'

'No,' John replied. 'We live on the same street.'

'We have concerns about my next-door neighbour,' Ashley began. She swallowed to wet her throat, glancing around the small reception area covered in posters about crime prevention and missing people. She felt a smidgeon of paranoia. What if someone from Wilton Close came in and overheard her? 'Could we go somewhere private?'

In a small room behind the reception area, they explained why they thought Tara might be involved in Elspeth's illness. John let Ashley do most of the talking, adding information when necessary. When they had finished explaining, the police officer looked at them in turn.

'You think that Tara Sanderson deliberately tried to infect Elspeth Chambers with Covid-19 by visiting her house when she had the disease?'

'I know it sounds far-fetched—'

'Yes, that's what we believe,' John said firmly.

'I don't even know what category of crime that would come under.'

'GBH?' John replied. 'Attempted murder?'

'Elspeth is seriously ill in hospital as we speak. She might die.' Ashley heard the frustration in her voice.

Several more questions followed, accompanied by the officer's tapping at a keyboard.

'The matter will be looked into,' the officer said without looking up. 'Thanks for coming in.'

'That went well,' Ashley said as they exited via the ramp. 'She obviously thought we were wasting her time.'

'I agree.' John sounded despondent. 'I wonder if they'll do anything to follow up.'

Maybe it was just as well if they didn't, she thought, the uneasy feeling returning.

John insisted on coming home with her. On the way, neither spoke.

'Goodnight, Ashley.' He stopped the vehicle a few feet away from her. 'If you're ever concerned about anything, don't hesitate to come straight over.'

Chapter 37
Tara
7 July

The day started badly.

Tara awoke early, tired and irritable from her sleep being interrupted by the shouting of bin men and the clanking of dustbins. She'd been awake for much of the night, mentally going over Ashley's allegations concerning Elspeth. What if Ashley decided to broadcast her suspicions around the village – or went to the police? She slipped on a shirt and sandals and ran downstairs into the kitchen. Something was stinking in here... God's sake, she'd forgotten to put out the food waste bag.

'Hello!' She called out to a yellow-vested man wheeling a bin to the waste-collection vehicle. He turned. 'You couldn't take this, could you?' She hurried along the pavement after him, holding out the hastily tied green bag.

'Sorry, darling, we're running late.'

'Thanks a lot,' she muttered, aware of Rhianna's curious stare from a few houses along; the woman was picking up detritus from the pavement before setting her bins back in position. Tara glared back. The waste bag would have to wait out here until next week, if the foxes didn't get to it first – or if she didn't nip over to Rhianna's after dark and dump the bag's contents across the woman's front garden.

She made a coffee, ate a piece of toast and tried to get on with the morning's work. She needed to speak to some journos before her new clients deserted her. For the next few hours she left messages on voicemails or, if she managed to speak to someone, was fobbed off with platitudes and excuses. They either had just had Covid or were worried about getting it.

'A bit busy now, I'm afraid,' her former colleague Tina responded to Tara's lunch invitation. 'Maybe we can do something next month – or the one after.'

'All right, speak soon.' She forced an upbeat note into her voice. Tina had always been forthcoming in the past and usually agreed to lunch and a chat, which had often led to coverage for Tara's clients.

'Thanks for nothing,' she muttered, putting the phone down.

At lunchtime, thoroughly dejected, she got out a pot of ready-made salad from the fridge. Was it only the pandemic making people so wary about meeting her? Or had the local gossip spread further afield? Anxiety fluttered in her stomach. Had word spread on social media about her misdemeanours?

As if in answer, her phone buzzed. The white on blue Twitter symbol flashed onto the screen. Damn Twitter! It knew how to get your attention. Ignoring the phone as best she could, Tara took a mouthful from her tub of feta, beetroot and walnut salad, then placed the tub back on the worktop. Her appetite had gone.

At the tenth buzz of her phone, she gave up and swiped in. Some ignorant person had tweeted something judgmental about her moment of madness, no doubt, in the typical manner of Twitter folk with nothing better to do than denounce others. She'd have a quick check, then switch off the phone and stop fretting.

In disbelief, she stared at a long list of Twitter notifications. At the top was a tweet from @bramptonhandyman, whoever he was.

The Bad Neighbour

Just desserts @tarasanderson you meddling hypocritical piece of shit.
You got what you deserved

The tweet had forty-seven likes and had been retweeted fifty-nine times. Her stomach lurched. Fifty-nine! Those horrible words were being viewed right now by total strangers, far from Brampton. She clicked onto his profile picture, wondering if she knew him, but she couldn't see his face clearly under his hat. She'd received a few unkind, sarcastic or dismissive tweets over the years but nothing as nasty as this. This was vindictive and hateful, revelling in her disgrace – and @bramptonhandyman had nearly five thousand followers. Many of them were probably yet to see that tweet, but once they did...

Was this why her old journo friends were avoiding her? Had they seen the tweet but not wanted to say anything? Loads of people in Brampton were on Twitter, too. They would read it soon, if they hadn't already...

A wave of nausea hit her. She tossed the phone away. It crashed against the sink cupboard and skidded across the floor. She ran into the garden and stood in the shade of the house, hands on knees, ready to vomit up her lunch.

'Oh God, I'm sorry,' she said, closing her eyes. 'I didn't want her to die, you know I didn't. It was a moment of madness.'

Tara glanced up at Elspeth's house. The windows were all dark, the curtains shut. No sign that Elspeth had returned from hospital.

'Please God, don't let her die. And I'm sorry about the cakes.'

From inside the kitchen, her phone rang. The shrill, old-fashioned ring-tone sent her heart leaping. Who was that? No one phoned her any more. Had someone got hold of her number to hound her over the phone, too?

She let it ring out to the answer service. In no time at all, the ringing re-started.

Please, stop. Whoever it was, she didn't want to talk to them.

On the third ring, she went indoors and picked up. The number was withheld.

'Who is it?'

'Hello Tara, it's Brenda Lark from the *Elven Herald*. There's been a lot of interest in what you did recently, selling off produce that people had donated. We're running a story on the incident and how it led to you being dismissed from the community group you were running. Would you like to comment? Some people are very angry about your actions. This is a chance for you to give readers your side of the story.'

For a moment her heart stopped, along with her brain.

'Tara, are you there?'

'My side of the story – what are you talking about? Who have you been talking to?'

'I'm afraid I can't tell you anything else. Look, there's no need to worry. This is a chance for you to give us your side of things. Some people are saying you stole from them by pocketing money for the food they donated in good faith.'

'They're wrong!' she blurted out. How dare people say such things! And how dare this Lark creature try to bait her? 'I was the one who set up the food project in the first place. The Brampton Food Initiative it's called, by the way. How could I steal from my own food bank?'

She unscrunched her face. All this stress would do no good for her appearance.

'Thank you, Tara. Can I check, are you a Miss or a Mrs? And could I get your age?'

'Fuck off and leave me alone!'

'I'll email you when—'

Tara ended the call, strode into the living room and tossed the phone into a pile of cushions on the sofa. The cheek of the woman! She raided the fridge for a bottle of wine and necked a generous glass, fighting the urge to scream. Who knew what lies would get into that newspaper now?

Her thoughts raced. This was beyond bad. Who had been talking to this woman, stirring everything up? John, Ursula and Greg wouldn't, would they? Ashley? Unlikely she would have the nous to go to the paper, or the stomach for it. Ferne might, though. The sneaky creep would spill her guts to the media in a heartbeat. But it could easily have been Brampton Handyman or Bulldog Man, or someone who'd found a hair in their Victoria sponge... There was no shortage of envious, disgruntled people in the village who bore a grudge against her. Any of them could be plotting her downfall.

The *Elven Herald* didn't come out till Thursday. In the meantime, she would prepare herself. She eyed the wine bottle. It still had a glass left.

No. She would stay strong. She put on her trainers and sunglasses, hiding as much of her face and hair as possible under a hat. Since the food bank fiasco, a host of fine wrinkles and grey hairs had appeared. If she didn't get away from the house and that damned phone for a while, she was going to go mental.

She crossed the road to the green – empty, fortunately – and began to run around the wooded copse at its centre. After a few minutes, the effort of breathing and a bout of nausea forced her to stop. She sank onto the bench, a panting, sticky mess.

After a long shower, she felt recovered enough to pull on a top and leggings and run a comb through her hair. An urge to check her phone again overcame her. God knows what was happening on social media... She retrieved the phone from the sofa and stood reading the stream of notifications.

Oh, Christ. That vile tweet... It was going viral. It now had 214 likes and had been retweeted 137 times. She scrolled down and read some of the replies, most of which were as foul as the original or worse, seeped in misogynistic language, mockery and condemnation.

She turned off the phone and lay down on the sofa.

On waking from a restless doze, Tara sat upright with a jerk. Her first thought was Twitter. How many more total strangers knew about her selling off that food? She wished she'd never set foot in Grimpton sodding Hadlock. Her life was being torn apart for a measly £396.

She would look at Twitter later. First, she'd see if there was any good news from her friends – former friends in most cases. She tapped into her WhatsApp and text messages. No one had replied to her suggestions for a catch-up coffee. Plenty weren't on Twitter, so that couldn't be the reason. Had they heard the gossip about her – or were they too preoccupied with their children/careers/fitness regimes to spend an hour in her company?

She turned to her emails. There was one from the earnest horsey woman who was expecting a clamour of interest in her debut historical novel. What did she want this time?

Subject: Termination of Services

Dear Tara

While I have valued your recent guidance through the shark-infested waters of book publishing, I'm afraid I cannot overlook the latest revelations about you.

The Bad Neighbour

I was prepared to overlook the Tweets – people can be so cruel, can't they? – but the article about your deceit in the Elven Herald Online has shocked and troubled me deeply. Given that I am paying you to give me good publicity, I feel it no longer makes sense for me to be associated with you. I am sorry but I no longer wish to proceed with the publicity that we had planned.

Kind Regards,

Joyce Crighton-Smedley

Tara let go of her phone and sank her head into her hands. The bloody *Herald* had put up the online article already...

Kind regards, indeed. Wishing you a double dose of Covid, Jug Ears Joyce. Dry mouthed, her heart banging alarmingly, she retrieved the online version of the *Herald* from her phone and began to read.

Woman Shamed For Selling Off Donated Food

Brampton residents are let down and angry after discovering that Miss Tara Sanderson, an unmarried woman of 51, sold off produce that they had donated to the Brampton Food Initiative intended for families struggling during the coronavirus pandemic.

Miss Sanderson, who headed the local community group that started Brampton's food bank this April, admitted during a recent group meeting to selling off an array of items including home-baked bread, cakes and top-end grocery items from the back of a station wagon in Grimpton Hadlock then pocketing the proceeds, totalling £396.

According to a spokesperson for the group who talked to the *Elven Herald*, photographic evidence was provided at the meeting and an admission of guilt swiftly followed. It was decided not to involve the police in the matter, but owing to the serious breach of trust Miss Sanderson was asked to step down as the group's leader.

Many local people have expressed outrage to the Herald at Miss Sanderson's actions.

Nigel Vesper, a butcher based on Brampton High Street for the past 22 years, said: "I am appalled at the blatant hypocrisy of this woman. I regularly donated sausages and pies for her food stall. I hoped they would make a difference to folk who have less than most of us. When I found out what she got up to, I felt a total chump."

Several others were quoted too, including a 'Brampton decorator and handyman'.

'It beggars belief that someone who was seen as an upstanding figure in our community took it upon herself to con us in this way. I listened to her on the radio talking about community spirit and was moved to donate a pile of tins from my food cupboard. There may not be thousands of pounds involved but it's the principle, isn't it? She's taken us all in and she deserves whatever is coming to her.'

She snatched a breath and scanned to the end of the article.

'I was the one who set it up in the first place,' Miss Sanderson said when we asked for her side of the story. 'How could I steal from my own food bank?'

We would all like to know the answer to that, Miss Sanderson.

Tara gripped the arm of the sofa. She wanted to hurl something heavy at the reporter's head and watch Brenda Lark's brains dribble out. This was a hatchet job. That evil reporter hadn't even been able to get Tara's age right, deciding to add on another two years for good measure. And what was that 'unmarried woman' crap – was the *Elven Herald* still in 1950s?

She tried to calm her breathing, which sounded like a steam train going uphill.

Everyone in that so-called support group would be chuckling when they read this. *Spokesperson for the group*, indeed! None of them had had the courage to give their names. But that was hardly unexpected from that bleating, sanctimonious lot.

Not only the group – everyone in the village would know about this soon, even people who'd never heard her name before. So would all her detractors for miles around. They would read these hateful, mocking remarks and her name would be mud. And what of all her new clients who'd flocked to her after her chat on the radio? They would desert her, *en masse*.

After three mouthfuls of supper – the food would not stay down – she consumed the rest of the wine bottle instead. She kept her phone switched off and tried to watch another episode of *The Crown*. But she couldn't take anything in, not even salacious goings-on at the Palace. Only a short time ago, her troubles seemed to be over. She'd been feted, given air time, practically pronounced Queen of Brampton. Her business had been given a new lease of life.

Now, all that had been snatched away. She was the village pariah.

By the time she went to bed, five more emails from clients old and new had arrived in her in-box, all variations of the same message: Sorry, I don't want your help any more. The rest of them would respond similarly soon enough, she thought, with a sinking heart. Whoever came up with that stupid adage, there is no such thing as bad publicity? Soon, her business would be toast.

She climbed into bed and checked her phone for one last time. Amanda or Justine might have replied by now, agreeing to meet up for coffee. They weren't into social media and wouldn't have read the online article.

No messages from them, or anyone else. However, there was a text from Ursula.

You might want to look at the local FB group. There's something about you in it.

Oh no... The first post she saw on the Brampton Appreciation Society Facebook group had been posted by Barry, the group's admin.

Some of you might be interested in this.

There was a link to the *Elven Herald* article. Barry hadn't bothered to tag Tara. In just one hour, the post already had eighty-one reactions – all tearful, open-mouthed or red-faced emojis – and fifty-five comments. Tara read the first one.

Disgusting! How could she do a thing like that?

The phone slipped out of her hand. She wanted to howl. How could Barry have done this to her? He liked her, so she'd thought. He bantered lightheartedly with her on Messenger whenever she submitted posts for approval in the group. Now, practically everyone was destined to know about the little mistake she'd made. Her downfall was complete.

Outside, a barking dog interrupted her rumination. Tara retrieved the phone and tapped out a reply to Ursula.

Was it you who spoke to Brenda at the Herald?

The reply came thirty seconds later. *No it wasn't.*
So who was it? she typed. I know one of you did.

The reporter got in touch with several of us, asking for information. We

212

had an urgent meeting and decided to give her a statement from us all.
I'm sorry for what you must be going through but sad to say you have
brought this on yourself

Go to hell, Ursula. I don't need a lecture from you. How dare you all
betray me like that. Now the entire village is baying for my blood

Sorry Tara I'm not able to discuss this any more

For several minutes she could barely contain her anger at
Ursula and the rest of the group. Not only anger – a searing sense
of loss. The people she had trusted – had even started to become
fond of, in some cases – had turned against her. They had all got
together and decided to pay her back for 'stealing' from the food
bank by making her life hell. What better way to do that than by
spilling the beans to the gossip-hungry local rag?

And Ashley, that two-faced bitch... She had started all this,
persuading the group that Tara was a thief. If Ashley hadn't intervened after Ferne's dramatic entrance flourishing those damning
photographs, they might have forgiven her. What's more, if
Ashley hadn't gossiped to half of Wilton Close, by the time
anyone outside the group had found out it would have been old
news.

She picked up the paring knife, left on a side plate on the
coffee table, and launched the blade into the arm of the sofa. The
fabric ripped easily, exposing foam innards. She stabbed again,
deeper, imagining Ashley's body underneath the blade, then put
the knife down and picked up her notebook and pencil. To hell
with the lot of them – she would give 'her side of the story' in here.
Now no one wanted to have anything to do with her, at least her
journal was her friend.

An hour of fevered jotting later, Tara put the notebook aside
and got ready for bed. Switching off the bedside lamp, a thought
came. What if Ashley *had* gone to the police with her accusations

about Tara trying to kill Elspeth? After that character assassination in the newspaper... Her heart beat uncomfortably hard. Ashley Afraid Of Her Own Shadow Khan would never have the guts to do such a thing. Ferne, Ursula or John might, though. But no one from the police had contacted her; that must mean they hadn't received any untoward reports – or were they too busy with all the people actually seen breaking Covid rules?

Despite the warmth of the summer night, she shivered. What would be next? A denouncement of Tara Sanderson on the front page of *The Times*? An item slagging her off on ITV's *News at Ten*?

Get a grip, she urged herself. She'd survived years of Zoe's and Evie's taunts and mockery, as well as her mother's heartlessness. Ivy had never taken any interest in how Tara's sisters had treated her... Ivy's final moments came back, the images as fresh as ever. Tara would never be able to forget them, even if she'd wanted to.

A woman, not much older than Tara was now, sprawled on the kitchen floor, a strand of saliva wetting her chin. Her eyelids closed, weakly fluttering, her moans seeping into the silent house, each quieter than the one before.

Then the aftermath. Pacing the living room floor until there could be no doubt that her mother was dead. Leaving Ivy's gardening shoe on the wonky, ill-lit step from the hall into the kitchen – a place from where it was all too easy to trip and fall.

Tara stared into the darkness.

Twenty years ago, she had tried to do the right thing for Ivy. When her mother's condition had deteriorated so much she could no longer manage to live alone, Tara had moved in to care for her. Her mother had been cold to her for years before, not encouraging any contact. Ironically, Ivy had ended up housebound and having to depend on Tara.

But Ivy hadn't appreciated all the unstinting work Tara had performed every single day, washing, cleaning, cooking and generally putting her own needs last. Not one bit. What's more, her mother had started questioning her about how Zoe and Evie had 'really' died, as if Tara might have done something to cause their deaths. One day, it had become unbearable.

Traces of long-ago emotions surfaced and subsided. What had transpired that night had been awful, yet at the same time a relief.

I told her not to leave her shoes on that step, she'd told the police, in a suitably bereft voice. No one had questioned Tara's version of events, possibly due to her outpouring of grief, which had not all been faked. The inquest had been cursory, its finding of Ivy Sanderson's accidental death little more than a formality.

Chapter 38
Elspeth
8 July

E lspeth craned her neck from the seat in the patient pick-up area. How much longer? For the past forty-five minutes she'd sat here in her ancient cheesecloth blouse and badly mended linen skirt – the clothes she'd been wearing when she'd collapsed – checking her phone every five minutes for Ashley's call, with the patience of a small child awaiting her birthday presents.

Ashley approached in a fast walk and gave Elspeth an elbow tap instead of a hug. She seemed wary of standing too close.

'Elspeth. It's good to see you again.' Ashley's eyes were damp.

'Hello, dear.' Elspeth swallowed the lump in her throat. 'Thank you for coming all this way.'

'Don't be silly.'

On the twenty-minute drive to Brampton, they listened to the car radio. The day was cloudy with occasional bursts of sunshine, much cooler than it had been before her internment. Elspeth cradled the tote bag containing assorted items from the hospital: her purse and key-ring, a few toiletries she'd bought from the hospital shop, a packet of dried mango pieces and several packets of assorted nuts – far preferable to the hospital food – and the flowering cactus that one of the nurses had placed by her bed after

Elspeth had revealed how sad she felt not to be allowed any visitors.

'I thought you might not make it,' Ashley said suddenly.

'I wondered that too,' Elspeth replied. 'I think it was touch and go at one time. Everyone looked so serious. I wondered if I should ask for a vicar or something.'

Ashley changed gear and glanced at her, but didn't speak.

'Thank God they didn't put me on a bloody ventilator,' Elspeth continued. 'That would have finished me off.' She couldn't wait to start living again. Being cocooned in a ward of Covid patients, some of whom had passed away while she was there, had made her realise how lucky she was to have escaped death. How much she wanted to make the most of whatever time she had left.

Ashley smiled. 'How was it in there?'

'The food was pretty ghastly, and the noise... I'm looking forward to spending the night in my own bed. I was asleep for most of it, thankfully.'

'Alseep, or out of it?'

'I don't know – I felt as if I'd been transplanted into a surreal film. The nurse said my temperature was all over the place, that's why I had such strange dreams.' Her dream of Tara being the strangest, by far.

Ashley, concentrating on the traffic ahead, didn't reply. Elspeth lowered the window. A breeze flounced her cropped blonde hair, longer than she liked it. Brampton and everything in it looked different, as if she had been away for three years not three weeks. She spotted Bird Woman walking downhill along Wilton Close and waved belatedly.

They pulled up outside Elspeth's house. Her front garden needed attention – the hedge had grown, shooting out a brace of straggly arms. With Ashley's help, she hauled herself out of the car. Thank goodness, no sign of Tara.

Ashley insisted on coming inside and helping Elspeth to

'settle in' – picking up envelopes on the doormat, putting crockery away, wiping surfaces in the kitchen with disinfectant and opening windows.

'So,' Elspeth said, when they were sitting in the conservatory with two mugs of tea. The elephant in the room needed addressing. 'What's the latest on Tara?'

Clearly, much had happened while she'd been away. Ashley started talking non-stop about a viral tweet, an *Elven Herald* article shared to the local Facebook group, and Tara coming off social media.

'She hardly sets foot outside her house any more – and now she has a disguise.'

'A disguise?'

'A blonde wig. She wears dark glasses with it.' Ashley's face became serious. 'I know it sounds funny, but it must be awful for her. She's been the butt of horrible jokes... There are some really nasty comments on the Brampton Facebook group.'

Elspeth nodded. She couldn't dredge up any sympathy for Tara.

'I dreamt about Tara in the hospital,' she admitted, taking off her slip-ons and giving her feet a rub. The pins and needles were coming on again, a legacy of this dreadful illness. But at least her toes weren't numb any more.

'She was in my house, looking around. Then suddenly I was in my bed and she was standing over me, about to smother me. It felt so real... What's the matter?'

Ashley was staring at her.

'It just that... Well, I'm worried about Tara, too. She can be so... excessive. Though I don't know if she'd really do anything to hurt us—'

'Us? Has she threatened to hurt you?'

Ashley chewed her lower lip, looking cagey. 'I don't want to alarm you for nothing.'

'Tell me, Ash, for goodness sake.'

Ashley rubbed the back of her neck nervously.

'After you were taken to hospital, I was frightened that you might... not come back out. I was thinking how odd it was for Tara to have been standing outside your house, when she may have had Covid. I decided to ask her directly if she'd gone into your house while you were out, and if she deliberately tried to spread her virus to you.'

'Bloody hell, that was brave! What did she say?'

'She denied it, of course. But she got so, so angry with me. She told me to fuck off, would you believe.'

'That takes the bloody biscuit! I wish I'd been there to see it.' She was overcome by a torrent of laughter. 'Sorry, I don't mean to be unsympathetic.'

Ashely smiled. 'It was quite upsetting at the time.'

'I can imagine – it must have been bloody scary. You must have hit a nerve for her to react like that.'

Through the open window, familiar summer sounds: wood pigeons calling, robins twittering, the screams of small children playing. The couple must have friends or relatives over. Nothing obviously from Tara's side. Then the chug-chug of their petrol lawnmower, obliterating the screams. The restrictions on people's lives were indeed lifting... It was odd to hear normal sounds again. Slowly, the implications of Ashley's words began to dawn.

'Do you really think she could have given me Covid?'

Her rational side had dismissed the dream; she must have caught it at Lou's memorial service; Alice or Mira might have passed Covid on to her. Neither had tested positive, though.

Ashley's brow puckered. 'I honestly don't know. I suppose it's possible that she let herself in with your key while we were having tea, then started sneezing or something. You could have caught it when you came back. If it was Covid she had... The virus hangs around for a while, doesn't it? Maybe she was so upset with you she spread her virus around the house on purpose.'

'She lost her rag with me,' Elspeth admitted. 'After I told her she should see a therapist – not long before she became ill. Then she texted me about getting her aspirin...' Elspeth felt her heart pound alarmingly. 'She might have seen us having tea together and got jealous.'

'God knows what she's capable of,' Ashley replied. 'But to deliberately infect you with Covid, knowing it might kill you...'

She stared at Ashley, a chill going down her spine. Tara wasn't anyone, that was the problem. To say the least, she could be a spiteful so-and-so.

For a while, neither woman spoke. In the distance, shouts of small children.

'I'd better leave you to it, then.' Ashley got up and walked around Elspeth's kitchen, assessing the state of the sink and work-tops. 'Will you be OK here on your own?'

'I'll be fine. If I see the smallest sign of anything suspicious...'

'Text me straight away, or knock on my door. Are Alice and Mira coming over?'

'Alice has gone to Florida to be with her daughter – she's expecting her first baby. Mira is being extra careful after what happened to me. She's not venturing outside unless absolutely necessary.'

Apart from brief text messages, they hadn't had any communication since Elspeth had been struck down with the virus.

Ashley stood near Elspeth's chair, looking uncertain. Her large hazel eyes were intense in her small, delicate face.

'It's all right, we can hug.' Elspeth said, getting to her feet. 'I'll be immune to this thing for a while.'

At first, they hugged keeping a slight distance between them. Elspeth inhaled the fading vanilla and honeysuckle notes of Ashley's perfume, aware of their bodies breathing, alive. Suddenly she felt herself clinging to Ashley, her eyes filling with tears.

After Ashley left, Elspeth wandered from room to room, reac-quainting herself with her house. Upstairs, the rooms were untidy and dusty. Before getting ill, she'd intended to give them a thorough clean.

Tiredness overcame her as she began to unpack her things. She lay down on the bed and quickly fell asleep.

A noise intruded on her dream, regular and insistent. Was someone knocking?

Elspeth opened her eyes, looked around the room. Where was she? Butter-yellow walls, stripes of light across the familiar, rose-patterned bedcover... Of course. She was at home now.

Another series of knocks began, resonating loudly.

Flaming Nora! Was the house on fire? Her hearing had definitely improved. She lowered herself carefully from the bed to the floor, slightly dizzy and still half asleep.

'I'm coming!'

'Elspeth?' Tara's voice through the letterbox. 'Are you there?'

Elspeth stopped a few feet behind the front door. The sound of Tara's voice put her on high alert. Every hair on her body seemed to be taut, listening.

'What do you want?'

'I've got something for you. Are you going to let me in?'

She hesitated. 'I've just woken up, Tara. What is it?'

'A gift.'

Oh, for goodness sake. She didn't want to speak to the woman but she couldn't refuse to let her in, could she? Cautiously, she opened the door a fraction.

Tara shifted from one foot to the other on the porch. She looked different from before. Her make-up emphasised the dark shading around her eyes. Her earrings didn't quite match and her otherwise pretty top bore a faint but noticeable stain.

'I brought you this. It's all fresh.'

Elspeth gazed at the large glass bowl that Tara was holding. Inside was an array of fruit – pears, apples, oranges and a box of strawberries.

'I wanted to say sorry for my... poor behaviour when we last spoke.'

Elspeth stood blinking at Tara. How to respond? Could she take a gift from a woman who had, very possibly, tried to kill her?

Her neighbour thrust the bowl towards Elspeth. She took the offering – how could she not?

'Thank you. That was very thoughtful. I'll have some later.'

'I wanted to welcome you back. I would have come to visit but that wasn't allowed.'

She wondered what to do. The bowl was heavy and she didn't want to stand here with it for long. Nor did she want to invite her neighbour inside.

'How did you get back from the hospital?' Tara continued in a brighter, more assured manner.

'Ashley collected me.'

Tara smiled. 'Of course. Good old Ashley.'

What a bitch! Well, Elspeth's inner bitch was demanding to come out too.

'You've been having a tough time, I hear,' she replied. 'It must be hard, no-one wanting to talk to you and everyone saying horrible things.' Although you totally deserve it. She placed the bowl of fruit on the floor.

'It's not been very pleasant.' A scowl twisted Tara's mouth. 'Some people have nothing better to do than open their mouths and let their tongues wag – Ashley would know all about that.' Tara raised her eyebrows pointedly. 'Well, I won't keep you. You're looking marvellous, considering what you've been through. How do you think you caught it? The coronavirus?'

'I've no idea.' Elspeth blinked at her neighbour. Was Tara

fishing for information, or trying to psych her out? 'Maybe you do?'

'I'd imagine you caught it from visiting your friends, just before you came down with it. I did think it was a bit risky, love, at your age, but I didn't like to say.'

'I wondered that myself,' she replied when her power of speech had returned. 'But there were only three of us and we were outside the whole time. Besides, neither of my friends tested positive afterwards.'

'Maybe you were just unlucky.' Tara hastily withdrew from the porch. 'At least now you'll be protected from the virus.'

Elspeth gave the smallest of nods. But not from people like you.

'Look after yourself.' Tara waved from the gate. 'And could I please have the bowl back when you've finished with it?'

Elspeth closed the door, carried the bowl to the worktop and considered the colourful mound. Suddenly hungry, she took out a shiny red apple. Her teeth were about to crunch into its flesh when a thought struck. Abruptly, she put the apple down. What if Tara had injected something into the fruit? It would have been funny, if it wasn't so damned serious. What a bizum that woman was! Pretending to be so concerned about Elspeth then bitching about Ashley like that, all the while trying to whitewash herself.

She opened the fridge. Inside were the many patently healthy items Ashley had purchased from The Green Goddess. Nothing particularly appealing, though. She closed the fridge.

Sod it, you only live once... She picked up the apple again, examined it carefully for untoward marks then took a bite.

Chapter 39
Tara
17 July

She woke feeling almost normal. Then blackness crashed down as what had happened yesterday came rushing back. Her old life, as flawed as it had been, was beyond reach. What she would give to have just one day of it. The only periods of relief from this torment were the increasingly sparse patches of sleep she managed each night. Even in her dreams she was tormented by ridicule and abandonment. Every morning her jaws ached from her grinding teeth, as badly as they had when she was a teenager.

She went into the bathroom to relieve her bladder, stopping to look at herself in the mirror.

The sight of her face was hard to bear. In one fell swoop it had aged several years, providing a startling premonition of herself as an old woman. Not only that, her grey roots were horribly obvious. She should have bought some hair colour at the pharmacy yesterday... or could she risk a trip to Curl Up and Dye, now that hairdressers were open again? But, by now, Sue at the salon would have heard all about Tara's humiliation. Who was going to notice her hair, anyway? Now she spent her days hiding away inside, what did it matter if she looked like a worn-out, distinctly down-on-her-luck old hag?

Still in a t-shirt and leggings, she went downstairs. What was the point of getting dressed? She pottered in the kitchen, tending to the coffee machine and half-heartedly wiping surfaces free of alcohol smears. No need to have her home spick and span any more; no one would want to do a photoshoot now... She opened the fridge. All the ready meals had gone and there wasn't much else, but she couldn't be bothered to place another order at Ocado. Her appetite had gone, anyway. She couldn't even manage a slice of toast.

Beyond the window, people moved about on the green. Bulldog Man went past with his dog. Her pulse quickened, queasiness returning. Someone might see her... She pulled the blinds cord until the slats were almost shut and sank onto a stool at the island. She couldn't bear the thought of people seeing her in this state and sniggering.

Her downfall had come quickly. In the space of just a few weeks, she had become a nonentity on social media. Three quarters of her four thousand Twitter followers had unfollowed her within a week, and thousands of tweets containing any reference to her had been deleted. Soon after, the number of her 'friends' on Facebook had gone into free-fall. She'd had no choice but to remove her profiles from both platforms. Thanks to her castigation on social media, her career was over. No one wanted to use her for their PR, or have anything to do with her. *I'm so sorry, Tara, but in the current circumstances I don't think I can continue to use your services* was the typical response.

In Brampton, too, she had become a nonentity. Hoping for forgiveness and re-integration into village life, she'd tried to make new friends and rekindle old acquaintances, attempting to explain herself and how foolish she had been to sell off food intended for others. She'd even joined the old biddies' walking group.

Everyone had given her the cold shoulder. No one gave a toss about the reason she had resorted to selling the food in the first place: mounting unpaid bills, such as the £600 she still owed to that scurrilous dentist for implants she probably hadn't even needed. Then, worse than all of that, worse than any of the humiliations that had come before, the incident yesterday.

Almost home from her trip to the chemist, pleased at not having been recognised and the newly prescribed Zopiclone snug in her handbag, a man had accosted her from the corner of Wilton Way.

The video in her head kept on playing.

She'd registered first the anger and contempt on his face. Then she saw he held something in his hand. His mouth opened wide.

'You thievin' Neanderthal!' A yell loud enough to be heard throughout Wilton Close.

The crack of the egg as it smashed onto her collar bone resounded in her ears. The jolt of the impact had made her gasp. Across the road two boys in school uniform had stopped to watch in disbelieving glee.

Tara closed her eyes. An unfamiliar sensation seeped through her core, spreading outwards, warming her cheeks. She had been cast out of society. Everyone hated her, everyone was laughing at her. No one cared about her plight – no one wanted anything to do with her. Even Elspeth, her only true friend left, had spurned her.

The day stretched ahead like a featureless desert, without respite. She imagined eating dinner alone once again with only the TV and her dwindling drinks supply for company. She couldn't face another solitary evening.

She went to the Nespresso machine and inserted a capsule. Standing, she brought the cup to her nose and inhaled the thick earthy fragrance. She took a sip and felt slightly better.

Maybe, in time, Brampton would forget about her transgressions. If she stayed out of sight for long enough, people might start speaking to her again...

No, she couldn't live like this any more. She had to do something now to get out of this hole. Could she re-invent herself once again, go somewhere far away where no-one knew her? But she didn't want to move to a strange place where she'd know no one. For all its faults, she had grown fond of Brampton. Whatever she did, it would not involve running away.

Nine hours later, birds tweeted encouragingly as Tara made her way out of the cul-de-sac. Amber light suffused everything, adding golden highlights to hair and faces. She glanced from side to side as she walked, but no one seemed to recognise her in this vampy new wig. It had arrived this afternoon: a crown of shiny straight black hair down to the end of her shoulder blades, complete with an eyebrow-tickling fringe – perfect with her extra-large Chanel sunglasses.

Outside The Anglers, she stopped. A young couple were walking towards the pub. As usual the old building – white-washed walls, low eaves, lead-light windows flung open – exuded a welcoming charm.

She pulled her mask from her pocket, put it on and forced herself to follow the couple. Voices reached her from inside the pub. At the old wooden entrance she paused, her heart starting to thud. Would someone spot who she was and say something horrible? But she needed to be with others, however fleetingly. She pushed on the door handle and went in.

The smell of beer and antiseptic spray greeted her. Nearly all of the tables in the large dining room were taken. People were eating or waiting for their meals to arrive. She hadn't been in here for years, not since that Christmas meal with the WI.

A man in a black face mask and matching shirt looked at her with an appraising expression.

'I've booked a table,' she said. 'By the window. Avril Appleby.'

The man checked his laptop and looked up with a smile.

'Ah yes. Follow me.'

The table had a pleasant view of the river. She sat down and took off her mask and sunglasses. A waiter came to take her drinks order. Behind her, in the corner, were the couple she'd seen arrive. On the other side of her were three middle-aged men at the end of their meals, by the looks of it. She didn't recognise any of them – and with any luck, with this wig and the glittery green eye shadow, no one would recognise her.

She took out her phone and pretended to study the screen with interest. After much swiping – two former friends had messaged her but weren't available to hook up – she opened her Kindle app.

It felt strange to be eating in a pub without a companion. In this wig though, she felt younger, daring, the sort of empowered modern woman who didn't give a shit about convention. She ate her slightly overcooked fillet of hake slowly, with frequent forays into her lovely large Sauvignon Blanc. Her fellow diners were close enough for her to hear snatches of their conversation – nothing of interest. In between stretches of reading, she gazed through the window at gold glints of late sunshine on the river.

Finally, she pushed her chair aside and headed towards the toilets. This place had been a welcome interlude from her troubles, but she couldn't stay here forever.

'Don't forget your mask, love.'

Tara looked at the speaker in momentary confusion. He was sitting alone at the table beside hers; his two companions had left. His voice held no trace of reprimand.

'Oh, thank you. I wasn't thinking.' She gave him a smile and picked up the mask from the table.

'It's crazy, if you ask me,' the man continued in a Thames estuary accent, 'people having to put those things on everywhere they go.'

'It does seem ridiculous that we have to wear masks just to go a few yards,' she replied, 'when we've been sitting here without them, all this time.'

He nodded effusively. 'Absolutely.'

She attached her mask and set off again.

When she got back, the man was idly scrolling on his phone. He was casually dressed in a shirt, jeans and tan brogues. The items looked expensive, as did his watch.

'Lovely evening, isn't it?' he said after she had paid her bill. 'We could do with a spot of summer weather to take our minds off all this Covid nonsense.'

'Yes, it's been a difficult few months.' It was a relief to talk to someone, no matter what beliefs they might hold. These days, people seemed to believe anything they liked.

The man frowned and touched his ear. She took off her mask.

'Sorry, I forgot I had this on.'

'I hate them, myself.' The man looked indignant. 'The government is treating us like little kids, in my view, forcing us to wear masks whether we want to or not. And forcing us all to work at home, when it's bloody impossible with kids under your feet all day. My work is on the verge of going under... I'm sorry, I'm going off on one.'

'Not at all, I'm with you. Suddenly, everything we took for granted has disappeared.' It was true, though for reasons other than what he might think. 'When you're isolated at home for weeks on end, it can be so miserable. You feel life is passing you by.'

'You've been working from home too, then?' He raised his eyebrows.

'At the moment, yes. I'm in P... personal coaching.' She stopped herself saying "PR" just in time. If he knew that, he might realise who she was. 'Motivational training, setting goals, that sort of thing. It was going well before Covid started. But lately I've lost most of my clients.'

'That's really tough – and you're not alone in feeling lonely.' The man stood, took a couple of steps towards her and offered his hand with a vaguely apologetic smile. 'I'm Rob, by the way. Me and my mates have been coming here for years.'

'Pleased to meet you, Rob.' She hesitated before putting out her own hand. Had he washed his hands recently? But next to the ignominy of becoming a social outcast overnight, the consideration of whether she might catch Covid again seemed minor. 'I'm Avril.'

'Good to meet you, Avril.' He gestured towards an empty chair, adjacent to his own. 'Join me, will you? Can I order you something? My treat.'

She sat down without hesitation. Rob had inviting blue eyes and he wanted to talk to her – why not enjoy the evening while she had the chance? She ordered a chocolate mousse and a glass of Muscat.

Rob ordered a Cognac for himself. He lived seven miles from Brampton, he told her; he was a senior manager in a company that made fibre-optic cable assemblies, whatever they were. He was married and had two children, ten and fourteen. He didn't say anything about his wife, she noted.

'Do you have a family, Avril?'

'No, I've never wanted children.' Rob was peering at her ring finger, she noticed. 'I'm not married – I nearly was, years ago, but my fiancé got cold feet.' She thought of the man who had walked out on her two weeks before the ceremony, accusing her of being an 'evil bitch' only interested in his money.

'You can tell me about it, if you want to. It won't go any further.'

'Actually, Rob, things haven't been great for me lately. It's nice to have the chance to talk to someone so understanding.' He leaned closer, his face softening. Going by his lack of wrinkles, she thought, he must be a few years younger than herself. 'You see, a little while ago, I made a mistake – I did something I shouldn't have and now I'm in an awful mess.'

The wine was making her say things she wouldn't normally – or perhaps it was down to this sudden rescue from social exclusion. Although there was a chance he might recognise her from the newspaper report, or the tittle tattle on social media, this man didn't seem the type who'd follow gossip.

'I won't go into the details. Suffice to say, in a moment of madness I did something foolish, and now I've lost all of my friends – and my livelihood.' Thank God, his face showed no trace of recognition. 'I've apologised and asked for forgiveness, but no one wants to know.'

'I know what it's like to be shunned, looked down on, called names.' He glanced away, his eyes sad. 'It's a terrible thing when you're on the receiving end. But it's human instinct to attack someone who's down, you know. It's a survival thing from when we all used to roam in packs.'

This sounded dubious. But she could have hugged him for understanding how she felt, and being on her side.

'I'm in this group,' he carried on. 'It's really taken off since Covid started. A lot of our members would understand where you're coming from. Some have been ostracised for daring to speak their minds, for questioning the mainstream view of what's going on.'

'You mean, the restriction to our freedom as a result of Covid?'

'Much more than that. We're worried for our country. You can't say or do anything these days without the political correctness warriors pouncing, and denouncing you. People using the' – he made air quotes – '"wrong" word, or someone being offended when you state the bleedin' obvious. Pardon my language – this is something I feel strongly about.'

He was one of those far-right types, then. He looked probingly at her.

'We all have strong views about certain things,' she replied, draining her wine. 'I'm worried myself that things have gone too far. We're a small island, aren't we?' She wasn't sure that she actually believed this – or what, exactly, she believed in. Politics had always bored her.

Rob smiled warmly. Her words seemed to meet with his approval. He took a business card from his wallet and placed it on the table. *Robert Walsh*, she read.

'That is my personal number. I'd like to tell you more about the group, if you're interested.'

'Yes – of course. I would be very interested to know more.'

'We have more men than women at the moment,' Rob went on, his caution dissolving. 'But everyone is welcome, and we're always open to new members. We don't judge – you can say whatever you want without worrying. Many of the members aren't all that political, they just want things to go back to how they used to be, or they're fed up with all the Covid hysteria.' He gave her a meaningful look. 'We're quite careful who we let in. You have to know someone, if you know what I mean.'

'I see, exactly. I'm sure I'll be in touch.' Something occurred to her. 'Actually, I have a few concerns myself. About my neighbours.'

'Really?'

She lowered her voice and looked around. All those close by were engaged in conversation.

'It's a Pakistani family – half white, half Pakistani to be precise.' The corner of Rob's upper lip twitched, just enough to notice. 'The son is at uni – or was before all the students were told to go home. He's let his beard grow. He still wears normal clothes but he's starting to look like one of those traditional Muslims.'

She paused, not wanting to overplay her hand. Rob was nodding encouragingly.

'As for the daughter... She seems to be going off the rails. I saw her on her bedroom terrace late at night, back when people weren't supposed to be visiting each other, knocking back a bottle of wine with her friend. The mother seems to have no control over her kids whatsoever.'

'It's a concern, isn't it? The fabric of our country is changing. These people will be in every town and village soon, bringing with them God knows what.'

His eyes lingered on her breasts for a few moments too long. It must be the wig... No man had paid her this much attention in an age.

Rob glanced at his watch and started putting on his leather jacket. 'Avril, it was lovely to meet you. I have to be going. My wife will be wondering where I am.'

'Lovely to meet you too. Thanks for listening to my troubles.'

'No worries. If you ever need someone to listen... You have my number.'

On his way out, he leaned over and kissed her cheek. It was unexpected and rather sweet.

Later, she picked up the business card and put it in her handbag, then sat for a few minutes looking out of the window. The daylight had almost gone and the river was invisible.

Chapter 40
Ashley
18 July

With all her strength she propelled the spade into the soil, not caring how many worms she might dissect. A creeper with rounded, knotweed-like leaves had taken over near the fence. The repetitive actions and warm sunshine were making her feel better. As always, the outdoors provided a sanctuary when her life seemed in danger of being eclipsed by worries about her husband and children. This morning's family breakfast – a tradition she'd rekindled since the first days of their confinement to home – had been horrendous.

It had escalated from nowhere.

First, Layla had complained about the breakfasts that Ashley went out of the way to prepare – eggs were boring, avocado was unecological and 'pancakes aren't very healthy'.

'Or very Islamic,' Sam added.

'What's an Islamic breakfast anyway, muffin-head?' Layla thrust down her scrambled egg-laden fork. 'Muslims can eat anything other people do, as long as it's Halal.'

'I told you not to use that word, Layla,' Ashley replied.

Layla sniffed. 'I'm not using it.'

'Well please don't use this one, either.' Arguably, 'muffin-head' was better than 'raghead'.

'You're the expert on Islam now, are you?' Sam turned to his sister. 'Is that why you drink so much alcohol?'

'Why should I follow traditions I don't believe in? I'm not a Muslim, nor is Mum!'

'Please don't bring your mother into this,' Zac growled.

'Stop fighting, you two,' Ashley said, as she had a thousand times before. She wondered why she bothered. In all these years, the fights between their children hadn't stopped. Whether low-level bickering, or full-on histrionics, their conflict had existed from when both were capable of speech.

'And look where it's got you.' Sam continued at Layla. 'First you get kicked out of school for being a dope-head, now you're turning into a piss-head. No one likes you, apart from that slutty girl you hang out with—'

Layla got to her feet, her eyes glistening.

'How dare you! I'm not those things and Anna isn't slutty – and they hate me because of you, don't you get it?' Her voice trembled. 'Because you're turning into some sort of fundamentalist, they think I'm one too. After all, we're half Paki—'

Zac's palm thudded on the table.

'Layla, go to your room! I won't have you use that language in my house.' But Layla had already fled the kitchen. Zac, his eyes narrowed, turned to Sam. 'You two will speak to each other properly, not like a pair of street kids.'

'But she started it.'

'You goad her, Samir,' Ashley intervened.

'Ashley, let me handle this.'

'I've a right to speak, I'm their mother!'

'I'm out of here.' Sam scraped his chair away from the table. 'This is a madhouse.'

'Show some respect or you *will* be out of here,' Zac yelled after him, 'fending for yourself!'

'Cooking your own breakfast!' Ashley threw in for good measure.

She was tempted to storm off too, somewhere far away, where they would never find her, where she wouldn't have to witness her family's slow falling apart. She put the remains of her breakfast aside.

What had happened to them all? The children had never been angels, but this... Was it the fault of lockdown, the four of them being forced to live under one roof, twenty-four/seven? It wasn't just the children. With the long summer days and further easing of restrictions, Zac was often away from the house on fishing trips. Even when home, he was often silent and distracted. Like Sam and Layla, he seemed to be struggling with the changes wrought by the pandemic.

With a grim expression, Zac pierced his last tomato, shoved it into his mouth then dropped his knife and fork with a clatter.

'It's our fault,' he said. 'The kids are confused about their identity. We haven't been clear enough.'

'And that's my fault?' The familiar argument threatened.

'I didn't say that. But we've given them mixed messages. They don't know if they're Muslims or atheists, or what.'

'They're not little kids any more. Layla is seventeen, old enough to decide for herself who she wants to be. You have to accept that.'

'But she's still a child in so many ways, following the other girls like a sheep.'

A wave of frustration rolled through her. 'She wants to fit in, that's all!'

'That's the problem. She has a perfectly good brain, far better than most of her classmates. Why does she think she has to fit in? Why does she have to abandon her religion?' Zac took several deep breaths, his nostrils flaring. 'Sam is right. She drinks too much, she's not making friends and she isn't doing well at college. She'd have been better off staying where she was.'

236

'You know that wasn't possible.'

The last school had made it clear that they didn't want their daughter to return, after twice catching Layla smoking marijuana on the premises. After much searching, they'd found the ideal college, not far from the perfect village, or so they'd thought.

'Anyway,' Ashley added, 'she told me she's not going to drink any more until she's eighteen.' Layla had tearfully admitted consuming too much alcohol on occasion, after Ashley discovered an empty wine bottle in her daughter's room.

'So we trust her to do the right thing, like we did before.'

'It's those bullies at college you should be getting upset with, not our daughter.' She fought to keep her voice level. In her view as well as the counsellor's, Layla's issues with depression and substance abuse were down to the death of her friend and the intermittent bullying she'd suffered at both schools. Thankfully, in the past few weeks, the bullying seemed to have stopped and their daughter had been noticeably brighter.

Zac sighed heavily. 'All I'm saying is, we need to instil some values in her while we still have the chance. Then she'd be more resilient, less affected by the other kids at college.'

'I don't agree.'

Zac stared at her. She focused on a pale mauve orchid on the window-sill.

'When you proposed, you said you didn't care that I'm not a Muslim.' That was the nub of it, really.

'I haven't changed,' Zac replied. 'I just don't want my daughter turning into an alcoholic and getting pregnant because she's lost all sense of who she is. What are we going to do if she gets pissed one night and gets knocked up by some boy? What will you say then?'

Her frustration mounted.

'Why do you always focus on Layla? What about Sam? He's been ruder than ever lately – and I don't think he's being honest with us about where he goes every day. Khalid's mother says he and Khalid weren't in her garden yesterday.'

'They could have gone for a walk or something.'

'Since when has Sam ever gone for a walk?'

'He's nineteen, old enough to be able to go out without us interrogating his every move!'

She'd had enough.

'I'm going to do some work in the garden. Elspeth is coming over for tea later, by the way.'

'Take that, you horrible thing!'

Ashley pulled out the last creepery, whatever-it-was invader from Tara's side of the fence and looked at the pile of plucked-out plants with a sense of achievement. There had been far more of the blighters than she'd been aware of, sneaking their tough little tendrils around the flowers she'd inherited and had done her best to look after.

The outpouring of emotion over breakfast had left her with indigestion and a churning stomach. But sometimes it was necessary to stand up for what one believed... Too often, she didn't, in case it upset or offended someone. A thought struck her. Had she made a mistake, marrying someone from a religion that she didn't share? Zac had never been overtly religious, beyond expressing a desire for their children to 'learn about their heritage'. She had willingly supported him, organising visits to Pakistan and celebrating Eid. But maybe religion meant more to Zac than he'd admitted. For all her efforts to accept his faith, she knew in her heart that she would always be an atheist.

'Ashley! Long time no see.'

Tara's head appeared on the other side of the fence. She

looked dreadful, her face unusually pale and her eyes sunk into dark hollows. Startled, Ashley had no idea what to say. Instinctively she ducked down and darted behind the dense curtain of honeysuckle and ivy hugging the fence. Since their last confrontation she had studiously avoided Tara, not going into the garden if her neighbour happened to be in hers.

'Ashley?' More of Tara appeared; her neck stretched over the fence like a goose's. 'I know you're there.'

She held her breath. Tara wouldn't see her, fingers crossed... She glanced up at the back windows – Layla's bedroom and Zac's office. No sign of either daughter or husband.

'God's sake, this is ridiculous!' Tara's tone became petulant. 'Why are you hiding from me?'

She stayed where she was, not daring to move half a centimetre. Eventually, hearing the creak of Tara's back door, she bolted indoors.

By 4pm, when Elspeth was due to arrive for a cup of tea, she had the house to herself. Zac was in his office on a series of Zoom meetings, Sam was on his daily pilgrimage to see his friend Khalid and Layla was at Anna's.

At the doorbell's ring, Ashley dashed on lipstick, ran a comb through her hair and rushed downstairs.

'Hello—' she stopped herself. It wasn't Elspeth.

Tara wore black leggings and a T-shirt and smelt of dried sweat. Her hair looked unbrushed and in much need of a wash, not to mention a root touch-up. Ashley tried not to gawp. Sympathy vied with pity, and finally a swell of frustration.

'Please, Tara, leave me alone. I've already told you, I don't want to talk to you.'

Quickly, Tara stepped closer, as if afraid the door might be shut in her face.

'I only wanted to ask if you could lend me some butter! I'm completely out. My delivery isn't due till the day after tomorrow.'

'Can't you go to the shops and get some yourself?'

Tara's eyes widened and her complexion took on a rosy hue.

'I don't go to the shops any more – everyone whispers about me behind my back. I only go out wearing my wig – and it's too hot for that today.'

This was so pathetic that Ashley relented. She was about to ask what sort of butter Tara wanted when her neighbour tapped her tongue against her teeth with a loud cluck.

'Never mind, Ashley, I'm sorry I asked! Keep your measly butter, I'll get by somehow.'

Ashley watched Tara, turning to leave, nearly collide with Elspeth, who had just come through the front gate. Elspeth carried a large, pale mauve leather bag over her shoulder and wore a plum shade of lipstick with a dash of eyeshadow, a long, large-stoned amethyst necklace over a shirt in a berry smoothie-shade of silk, and a heather-toned linen skirt. Plum-coloured toenails peeped out of her sandals.

'Hello, Tara.' Elspeth frowned. 'What's the matter?'

'No need to bother yourself about me.' Tara's scowl deepened. 'You two go ahead and enjoy yourselves – and have a good old gossip about me, why don't you?'

Tara pushed past Elspeth and strode to the front gate.

'Excuse me?' Elspeth turned to Tara. 'What exactly are you trying to say? I've come to have a cup of tea with my friend. Is that a problem?'

'Leave her, Elspeth,' Ashley said. 'It's not worth quarrelling about.'

Tara stood on the path looking from Elspeth to Ashley and back, her face flushed and her eyes suffused with anger.

'You two are as bad as my sisters were, always ganging up

240

against me. You'd better watch yourselves! I put up with it for years, but in the end I got fed up with them.'

With that, Tara yanked the gate behind her. It closed with a resonant clank.

'Flaming Nora,' Elspeth said after a few seconds. 'What's up with her?'

'Come inside.' Ashley waited until her front door was safely shut before replying. 'It's totally nuts – she came over to borrow some butter. I said why can't you get some yourself and she turned on me. Then you appeared.'

'It's unbelievable.' Elspeth let out a theatrical sigh. 'How could anyone be so childish?'

Ashley ushered Elspeth into the kitchen. Suddenly, the humour of the situation struck her. She started giggling, and so did Elspeth. Ashley clenched her pelvic floor as Elspeth chortled, dabbing at her eyes.

'She's upset because she thinks I've taken you away from her. You were her friend, then I came along.'

'But she stole my bloody rose! Did she really think I was going to stay her friend after that?'

'Keep your voice down, she might be listening. The window's open.' She angled her head to the window giving onto the back garden.

'You're being paranoid now. Unless she has the hearing of a wolf, or she's listening through the wall with a stethoscope, she's not going to hear us from next door.'

'I wouldn't put it past her.' She closed the window, just in case.

Elspeth raised her eyebrows.

'Seriously though,' Ashley continued, 'she could be dangerous. Did you hear what she said? "You'd better watch yourselves." That was a definite threat.'

Elspeth put her bag down on a chair. 'I need a drink. Fancy a G and T?

'Good idea.'

Ashley prepared the drinks, though she didn't usually drink alcohol during the daytime. But she was fed up with setting a good example to the kids. The exchange with Tara had left her with butterflies in her stomach and sweaty palms. She tried to remember exactly what Tara had said about her sisters. They had been 'ganging up' on her, that was it.

You'd better watch yourselves.

I put up with it for years, but in the end I got fed up with them.

'Do you know what happened to Tara's sisters?' She handed a gin and tonic to Elspeth, considerably stronger than her own. 'How they died, I mean.'

'One had an accident in the garden.' Elspeth frowned. 'The other died soon afterwards. Tara said she drowned.'

'She didn't say anything else?' Ashley stared at Elspeth.

'No, she didn't seem to want to talk about it, and I didn't want to pry. It seemed so tragic. It's strange, but she only told me about her sisters a few months ago... Until then I'd always thought she was an only child – she'd not once mentioned them.'

The back of Ashley's neck prickled.

'How old were her parents when they died?'

'Her father died when she was a small child, I think, of a stroke or heart attack... She said they were quite well off – he'd invented some device and got a patent for it. They lived by the sea somewhere.' Elspeth looked thoughtful.

'Not around here, then.'

'No, in Devon or Cornwall.' Elspeth put her glass down and stood gazing out of the window.

'What about her mother?'

'She died when Tara was twenty-nine – she can't have been that old. I think Tara said she had pulmonary fibrosis and died of pneumonia. Apparently she was ill for some time. Tara was at home looking after her towards the end. She said there was no one else around to help – she did it all.'

242

Ashley shivered. She hardly dared voice her thoughts.

'Do you think she inherited her mother's estate?'

Elspeth's eyes widened. Her hand flew to her open mouth.

'You don't think she got rid of her mother and her sisters, do you?'

'I don't know,' she said at last. The implications of Elspeth's question made her dizzy. Her head seemed to have detached from her body and was performing cartwheels. 'But her sisters dying so young and so close in time... That's suspicious, isn't it? What if she got so "fed up" with them that she killed them both, each time making it look like an accident?'

Elspeth drew in a sharp breath. 'Then when her mother got ill, she was perfectly placed to inherit the family estate.'

'Maybe she decided to give her a little nudge to hasten things,' Ashley suggested.

'Bloody hell, Ash, this is serious.' Elspeth folded her arms tightly across her chest. 'Shall we go outside and sit in the sun?'

'Can't we stay here?' She didn't want to risk Tara overhearing them.

'Here is fine.' Elspeth lowered herself into a chair and drained her gin and tonic.

'It's possible we're totally wrong. But all the same... I'm worried about her. What if she tries to hurt us?'

Elspeth pursed her lips. 'Have you said anything to Zac about Tara?'

'He thinks she's harmless. He told me not to go to the police about her, but I did anyway.'

'You went to the police about Tara?'

Ashley explained how she and John had gone to the police station while Elspeth was in hospital. 'He thought it would be a good idea, in case she ever... does something. I wasn't so sure.'

Elspeth tilted her head, frowning. 'Why didn't you tell me?'

'I should have done, I'm sorry. But I didn't want to frighten you.'

'You're the one who's frightened, Ash! I'm old enough not to care about the silly bizum.' Elspeth leaned back in her chair and tapped her fingers on the tabletop. 'So, what do you think we should do now?'

'I think we should find out exactly what happened to Tara's sisters.'

After Elspeth left, Ashley did some sorting out in the kitchen. Pieces of the puzzle that was Tara were jiggling about in her mind, not yet fitting together. But she resolved to get to the bottom of whatever there was to get to the bottom of. She wasn't going to let this unsettling woman defeat her.

At bed-time, while Zac was undressing, she asked him the question that had been on her mind all evening.

'Did Tara ever mention anything to you about her sisters?'

'No. Why?'

'She said something odd when she came over this afternoon—'

'She came over? You didn't tell me. I thought you two weren't speaking any more.'

'I spoke to her on the doorstep, only for a minute. She came to borrow some butter... She got irked with me for suggesting she could get some at the shops—'

'You didn't let her have any?' Zac stood over the bed, undoing his shirt. 'Ashley, you surprise me sometimes. The woman is clearly going through some kind of crisis.'

'There's no need to attack me. I was about to tell her she could have some, when she got the hump and turned to go – then Elspeth appeared.'

'That would have gone down well.'

'Tara got so angry. She implied that she'd done something to harm her sisters, and we should watch out. According to Elspeth they both died young, within a short time of each other.'

Zac rolled his eyes. 'Tara didn't actually admit to killing them, I take it?'

'Of course she bloody didn't! Don't take the piss, this is serious. We don't know what she might have done to them—'

'Nothing, I'm sure. You've got a wonderful imagination, sweetheart. I just wish you had as much common sense.'

'Oh, piss off, will you?' She turned out her bedside light.

The memory came in the middle of the night. She had been trying to recall anything Tara might have mentioned about her now-deceased family.

She'd said something, ages ago... Yes, it had been that day last September, when Tara invited them all over for a welcome cup of tea and home-made brownies.

'Do you have any family?' Ashley had asked Tara, after talking about her own one.

'Not any more,' Tara had replied in a brisk tone that didn't encourage further questions. An oddly inappropriate expression had appeared on her face, verging on a smile. Almost as if Tara was glad to have no family left.

Hours later, Ashley still hadn't managed to sleep. She couldn't shake off a certainty that something terrible was going to happen.

Chapter 41
Tara
19 July

As usual, on these warm July evenings, people were enjoying themselves on the green – walking hand in hand, exercising, sitting on the grass... As usual, Tara sat on a stool at her kitchen island, watching.

Occasionally, something interesting would happen. The local nutcase would warn everyone of impending doom. There'd be a lovers' quarrel, a punch-up between youths or an illicit gathering. Sometimes there was naked sunbathing. You never knew what you might spot or who might be doing it.

Tonight, she had hit the jackpot.

Most people had already left the green; it was past dusk and the air was getting cool. A trio of young people was still there, sitting by the group of spindly trees; a pair of teenage girls and a long-limbed youth. A bottle of wine was being passed between them. It was hard to be certain from this distance, but the girls looked very much like Ashley's daughter, Layla, and the tattooed blonde who'd spent the night with Layla on her bedroom terrace a couple of months earlier, at the height of lockdown. Once again, they were drinking.

Tara watched with increasing interest, sipping her vodka

tonic. She'd already eaten dinner – a Pad Thai chicken noodle meal, zapped in the microwave for three minutes, washed down with a few glasses of red – and there was nothing much on TV. Anyway, this made a change from the TV. It was her own personal reality TV show.

The blonde and the youth started kissing. Layla swigged from the bottle.

The moon came out from behind a cloud, illuminating all three. Her heart pumped harder. Yes, it was definitely Layla. The black hair was distinctive, and Tara could almost make out her thick, arched eyebrows and pouty lips. The other girl was definitely Layla's friend – she had a cute fringe. Then the youth pulled off the blonde's top and the pair got up and vanished into the copse of trees. Layla carried on necking the wine, no doubt with her characteristic sulky expression.

Tara waited patiently, nursing her diminishing vodka tonic. She didn't want to get up for a refill in case she missed something.

After about ten minutes, Layla got to her feet and disappeared into the copse too. After another fifteen minutes or so, all three reappeared and began walking slowly across the green. The blonde's top showed more of her cleavage than before and her hair was messy. Had she and the youth been shagging? Might Layla have watched?

Tara kept watching, as the youth and the blonde waved goodbye to Layla, who headed through next door's gate. One effect of being in solitude for so long, she mused, was that the smallest of events in the outside world took on an extra meaning. Maybe she was kidding herself, but this event seemed to be dripping with significance. In fact, it promised to change everything.

For the first time in a long while, she felt excited and optimistic. There were so many ways to exploit the information she now possessed. Ashley was going to have her life slowly ripped apart.

Chapter 42
Tara
20 July

S he woke with the alarm at 8am and set to work on her plan. At 8.45am, showered, scented and wigged, she found a Laura Ashley knock-off floral print dress she hadn't worn since the nineties. The demure young woman look knocked at least ten years off her, she thought, studying herself in the bedroom's full-length mirror.

The wig didn't quite fit the image, though. She tied back its luxuriant tresses with a ribbon and grabbed a prim white handbag languishing at the back of her wardrobe. Low-heeled sandals, a straw hat and sunglasses completed the outfit. No one would recognise her like this.

At 9.30am, with small, ladylike steps, she headed down Wilton Close towards the centre of Brampton. On the way she discreetly rehearsed the somewhat affected, higher-pitched voice she intended to deploy for her escapade, which would fool any locals observant enough to see through her disguise.

Several hours later, walking up the hill towards home, Tara reflected on the morning's activities. She had begun, or forced her way, into at least a dozen conversations with various villagers, carefully picked for their potential to spread the salacious news with which she entrusted them. The salaciousness of her news would, of course, have decreased considerably if it was known to have come from Tara Sanderson, disgraced former community figurehead. She was well aware of this. But no one would think to question the assertion coming from the lips of a softly spoken woman of uncertain years, that she had witnessed the girl from number 32 getting it on with two young males on the green. The news would fuel Brampton's gossip rocket for weeks.

Several times, she'd had to think on her feet. During a conversation outside the dog grooming parlour, where several women were waiting to collect their animals, she had been asked where she lived, how long she'd been a resident and what breed of dog she owned.

'I'm thinking of getting a poodle,' she'd replied, caught off guard. 'Now I don't have to commute any more.'

Fortunately, she had prepared the rest of her responses better. Avril Appleby had been a Brampton resident for a year and lived in Wilton Park Road – close enough to the green to be strolling past it yesterday evening. Her job in finance had entailed long hours before lockdown, which explained why no one had seen her around.

The beauty salon receptionist had peered at Tara for a second or so before opening her mouth, as if she couldn't quite place her face. But by the end of Avril's spiel about the shocking scene she had witnessed, while strolling on the green to take the evening air, Chantal had been fully on board.

Sandy, at the flower shop, had been taken in from the off, even enquiring if Avril might like to come to a morning coffee networking session for professional women. Tara had felt obliged to purchase a small bouquet of flowers – the cheapest one she could spot. Mrs Hale at the post office had been particularly interested in Avril's news, going off on a rant at the outrageousness of young people today. Tara had also informed the bakery assistant who'd served her coffee and a sandwich, and a gaggle of women outside the library. All in all, the first stage of her scheme had gone with aplomb.

As she approached number 33, she spotted Ashley's son hurry out of the Khans' front gate and stride off down the hill. Facial hair, not quite a beard, dominated his face. Something about his downward glance and intense gaze stirred her curiosity. Where was Fuzz Face off to?

She dumped her shopping bag in the porch and hurried after him. The young man turned into the footpath off Wilton Close, turning right at the fork into the lane leading to the allotments. He was walking fast and purposefully; she had to jog to keep up and held onto her hat, which was on the large side. No one else was around so she didn't need to be ladylike Avril any more, thank goodness.

Minutes later, they reached the allotments. Fuzz Face removed a key from his pocket, inserted it into the entrance gate and strode through. It was the only way into the allotments, she realised as the gate began to close behind him. She rushed forward and caught the gate just before it slammed shut, without him seeing her. Her heart pattered with excitement. Whatever was this young man going to do here, of all places? Surely, he wasn't a devoted gardener at his age?

Inside the large area, rectangular plots stretched out into the distance. She scanned them for the young man. He had disappeared, damn him. She hurried along the main path and saw him heading down one of the smaller paths criss-crossing the allotments.

She followed him from a safe distance, until he produced a key and opened the door of a shed beside an allotment backing onto the far corner. Feeling exposed and a little ridiculous, Tara looked for somewhere to shelter. She was hardly dressed for gardening. What would she say if he spoke to her?

She stood behind another shed nearby, which kept her out of sight but was close enough for her to see Fuzz Face clearly. He was setting out three camping chairs in a circle. There was going to be a meeting! She looked around the allotments. The place was virtually empty, just a lone figure in the far distance and, closer by, an elderly man digging. This was the ideal spot for an illicit gathering if you lived with your parents and had secrets to keep.

Fuzz Face sat down, got out his phone and started sipping from a can of Coke. She felt a sudden thirst. She ought to have taken something to drink... This had been a stupid idea. What if the old man spotted her – or Fuzz Face did?

Minutes later, two young men approached Fuzz Face, who was obviously put out to be kept waiting. One Asian-looking and slim, one black, stockier. They looked like many local youths, she thought – scruffy, jeans hanging low on the waist. Both had an excess of facial hair.

The black youth said something she couldn't hear.

Fuzz Face stood and hugged each of them without awkwardness, as if they were best buds. Coke cans were distributed from the ice bucket and the meeting began. Tara took her notepad and a pen out of her handbag, ready to jot anything down. Frustratingly, for much of the time they talked in low voices with pronounced accents, using slang terms she didn't understand. But whenever their words were unclear, her imagination was sufficient to plug the gaps.

Soon, she was so engrossed in the proceedings she forgot the sweat sticking her dress to her skin and her longing for a cool glass of chardonnay. The first word she wrote down was 'anti-Islam', followed by 'racists'. Then she heard, quite distinctly, 'fightback'. After more indistinct muttering, the young men became animated and began to argue with each other. About six or seven times she heard 'mosque'.

'There's one in Elven,' Fuzz Face said.

'It's eighteen miles away,' the Asian replied. 'It takes fuckin' hours to get there by public transport!'

'We need one here in Brampton,' the black youth said. 'It's shameful that we Muslims have nowhere where we can pray together.'

'Absolutely bro, you're dead right. The churches in the village are open again. We've got nothing.'

There was further discussion she couldn't hear properly, then a Thermos was produced and its contents poured into cups.

So, this ragtag group wanted a mosque in the heart of Brampton. Lots of people would be interested in that... One person, in particular. Of course, she didn't go along with the mindless Islamophobia, xenophobia and so on, that some in Brampton espoused. But now wasn't the time to stand on principle. Rob would be most interested in the exploits of Fuzz Face and his friends.

Someone opened a packet of biscuits. At the sight, her stomach rumbled loudly. She returned the notebook to her handbag. Time to go home, get off this hot, itchy wig and change into shorts...

'Oi, you! What are you doing?'

She spun around. Christ, the old man. He stood a few feet from her, his face red and damp, his eyes screwed up with suspicion.

Tara produced her most beguiling smile, fluttered her eyelashes and put on Avril's demure little lady voice.

'Oh, hello there. I just popped in on my way home to visit my...' Asparagus? No, they would be over. Marrows? No, they needed a greenhouse. '...strawberries, to check they're doing OK.' She gestured vaguely into the distance. 'Then I had a dizzy spell and had to rest.'

'The heat can do that.' He gave her a wink and wiped his sweaty brow with his forearm. 'I don't think I've seen you here before. I'm Danny, by the way.'

'Avril. Pleased to meet you, Danny. Gosh, is that the time?'

She extracted herself before the chap could get too friendly. Thank God, the young men hadn't spotted her; they were busy putting their chairs away.

'I'll look out for you!' Danny called, as she hurried away.

Tara put down her hand weights and turned off her workout music. The shouting from next door had intensified, eclipsing *I Will Survive* – it sounded like the Khan children were about to come to blows.

'Stop lying!' Fuzz Face yelled. 'Tell me what you were doing.'

'It's none of your business!' Layla yelled back.

'Yes it is! You're my sister. Everything you do here affects me.'

'I was with Anna! We were on the green talking, that's all.'

'Really? Someone has told me another version.'

'What have they told you?'

She strained to hear but heard only Layla's reply.

'That's mad. I'd never do anything like that!'

More frantic shouting between the siblings. After a minute or so she heard Zac's voice intervening, asking what was going on. Then everything went quiet. No doubt Ashley had rushed to shut any open windows in case the woman next door was listening – which, of course, she was.

Tara smiled and removed a bottle of Prosecco from the fridge. Her scheme to make Ashley pay had got off to a fine start. Before long, she'd know if it had been successful. In the meantime, wasn't a small celebration in order?

Chapter 43
Tara
21 July

'It's good to see you again, Avril. You're looking lovely, I must say.'

'Thank you.' Tara flashed a smile, making sure he saw her generous breasts as she sat down. 'It's good to see you too, Rob. How have you been?'

'Not bad. There's an issue at work that's causing me grief, but apart from that...'

A pleasant aroma drifted off the man. He was stubble-free and simply, but stylishly dressed, in a cornflower shirt over black jeans. It was nice to be sitting with a smart-looking man, for a change – to be sitting with anyone at all, in fact.

She'd phoned Rob yesterday saying she had something to tell him that was a little sensitive, and she'd rather discuss it face to face than on the phone. The table he'd booked in The Anglers' garden had no view of the river but was nicely secluded. They would be able to talk without worrying about being overheard.

Their drinks arrived while Rob was telling Tara about a 'new bloke at work who's causing trouble', who had accused Rob of being a racist. She sipped her wine, impatient for him to finish his story so she could tell him hers.

'Sorry, Avril, I've taken over. Your concerns about your neighbours... What's happened? I'm all ears.'

Now she had his attention, paranoia hit her. Was he genuine in his nationalist fervour, or could he be faking? What if he was actually an undercover reporter for *Panorama* or *Dispatches*, with a hidden camera and microphone recording her every word?

'Before I launch in... The group you're in – what did you say it was called?'

'I didn't, actually.' He spoke somewhat sharply.

'Oh, is it hush hush?'

'We don't like to give out too many details. Everyone's security conscious; these days.'

'I see. I don't want to intrude, of course.' The hurt in her voice wasn't put on. She had never taken rejection well. Even slights that others didn't notice could rankle for days.

'I think I can make an exception in your case, though.' Rob scooped up a handful of nuts, the corners of his eyes crinkling. He glanced at the nearest tables – a family at one busy eating and a young couple busy arguing at the other – and said in a near whisper, 'We're the Patriotic Alliance.'

It sounded familiar, sort of. Or was she thinking of the Countryside Alliance?

'Excellent name, very catchy.'

'It was my idea, mostly.' His voice had swelled with pride. 'I started the group.'

'I'm impressed. Do you have many members?'

'A few hundred at the moment. Every week we have more joining.' He glanced around again. 'The antics of Cummings and those other government goons have helped recruitment no end.'

'Ah yes, the Barnard Castle affair.' The 'sight test' and the outrage surrounding it was one of the few recent political events she'd taken on board; it had provided a mildly amusing diversion from her troubles. 'What a...' She withdrew the c-word hastily; Avril would never use such a vulgar term. 'What a so-and-so that

Dominic Cummings is. And all the rest of them. No wonder people are turning to groups like yours.' Tara took a slug of wine. 'By the way Rob, I forgot to ask. Are you on Facebook or Twitter, by any chance? Personally, I mean.'

If he was active on social media, he might find out about her public shaming and revise his opinion of her. Then her plan would wither on the vine.

'Facebook, once in a while. As for Twitter – I've never touched it and I don't intend to start now. I try to avoid social media wherever possible.'

'Very sensible. It's an evil place, trust me.'

He smiled back, his dimples showing. 'Now, those issues with your neighbours...' Rob raised his eyebrows.

'Quite a lot has happened in the last few days... Where do I even start?' She sighed with gusto and leaned forwards flirtily, her boobs and her shiny black locks swinging towards him. The man was salivating already – she was going to enjoy this.

'You remember I told you about my neighbour's son looking like he was pursuing a more... traditional path, shall we say? Well, my fears proved to be true.'

She told him what she had seen and heard at the allotment meeting, plus a few things she could imagine being said if only she'd been able to hear. By the end of her account, Rob was spluttering with horror and very red in the face. It might be better for his health, she thought, to keep quiet for now about the unwholesome threesome on the green.

'Thanks for passing this on,' he said. 'This band of extremists has to be stopped.'

'I thought you should know. I'm not totally against mosques, in their rightful place – in other countries, of course,' she added quickly. 'Certainly not a cathedral-sized one in the sacred space of Brampton.'

'Absolutely! The very idea of it. It's an affront to everything we hold dear.'

'Are you all right?' She conjured a suitably sombre face. This was going even better than she'd hoped. Rob had gone pale.

'A chill just came over me, thinking about this band of jihadis in our midst.' He reached for his jacket. 'Can you text me the address of this family? I'll see if my boys can give them a gentle nudge in the right direction.'

'Of course. I'll get that over to you.'

On the way home – she'd insisted on walking, for the exercise – she wondered what was in store for Ashley and her clan.

Chapter 44
Elspeth
22 July

With renewed determination, Elspeth set off towards Tara's front door for the second time in twenty minutes. The first time, she'd given up at Tara's gate, certain that her neighbour would see through her lame excuse for visiting.

She rang the bell and waited, wishing she'd had a wee first. The fluttering in her stomach was worse, as if she was about to dance on the opening night of a new show, but with none of the pleasant anticipation.

Come on girl, get a grip. She was getting as bad as Ashley, turning into a nervous old hen.

'Hello?' Tara sounded startled. Her face wasn't made up and there was a dark smudge on her cheek. 'Oh, Elspeth, it's you. Is something the matter?'

'Not at all.' She plunged in. 'Everything's fine. I just wanted to have a quick chat about the back fence – is now a good time?' The fence, which belonged to Tara, was now uneven in places and needed re-building. She attributed this to Tara's hacking down much of the greenery on Elspeth's side of the fence.

'It's as good as any, I suppose. I'd invite you in but my place is a mess. I've not kept up with the housework lately.' Tara smiled awkwardly, combing her fingers through her hair. 'So am I, probably.'

'That's OK. I mean, you've had a lot to deal with lately. I was hoping I'd see you in the garden, but I haven't.'

'I've been indoors mostly, keeping my head low – I get most of my shopping online now, you know.' Tara's jaw tensed. She looked sternly at Elspeth. 'It's better than getting dissed by people I thought were my friends and getting eggs thrown at me in the street.'

'That must have been awful.' She'd heard about the egg throwing from Rhianna, but didn't like to mention this to Tara.

Tara didn't reply. Elspeth felt a faint stirring of sympathy. This woman was self-obsessed to an alarming degree – but could she really be a danger to herself and Ashley?

'I'm sorry you're having a difficult time,' she said. 'Maybe you should get away from here for a while, until all this hoo-hah blows over. Go and visit a friend, or—'

'I don't have any friends left.' A whining note entered Tara's voice. 'Since that article in the paper and all the frenzy on social media, no one wants to know me. I've been left to rot.' At the word 'rot' a fleck of spittle shot onto Elspeth's cheek.

Casually, Elspeth rubbed it off. This was awful. She couldn't stay talking to this woman – but her mission wasn't yet accomplished.

'What about people you used to know from where you grew up? Whereabouts did you say it was?'

Tara shrugged. 'A small place by the sea, in the west country. But I don't know anyone there now.'

'Oh, I love the west country. The coast around there is fabulous. What's it called?'

If they had a name, Ashley had said, it would be easier to search for articles about Tara's sisters' deaths in the local papers. Only Tara's mouth remained shut, a crease deepening between her eyebrows.

Elspeth waited, on tenterhooks. What a blunderpuss she was! Tara must have guessed what she was up to.

'Dove Cross.' The reply came at last.

'Where's that?'

'Devon,' Tara replied flatly.

'It must have been a fantastic place to grow up in,' Elspeth carried on valiantly, injecting enthusiasm into her voice. 'So close to the sea.'

'I suppose it was all right. I can't remember many happy times, to be honest. My father died of a stroke when I was eight, and after that my mother was hardly ever around.' Tara looked up into the porch and batted at a strand of cobweb. 'And, as I said, my sisters spoilt things for me.'

'You didn't get on with them?'

A sarcastic laugh. 'You don't have any brothers or sisters, Elspeth, do you?'

'No, I'm an only child.' An involuntary sigh escaped her. 'I always longed for a sister, but alas...' She girded herself, trying to sound casual. 'You must miss your sisters very much.'

'Of course.' That sharp note again. Something was wrong.

She took a deep breath.

'What happened to them, exactly?' Evie had drowned, she remembered, and Zoe had had some sort of accident in the garden. But Tara had provided no details.

Tara turned slightly away from Elspeth, then spoke in a low voice.

'Zoe fell out of a tree in our garden. She'd been climbing up a rope attached to a branch – somehow it snapped in two.' A muscle at the corner of Tara's eye began to twitch.

'Tara, I'm so sorry. How old was she?'

'It was the day of her thirteenth birthday party. I was eleven.'

Tara moved her head to and fro quickly several times, as if trying to shake off something.

'She was your younger sister?'

'No, I was the youngest. Zoe was in the middle.'

Elspeth gathered her resolve. She was almost too afraid to ask.

'What about your other sister?'

'Evie drowned six months later. We were on our way towards a beach further along from our usual one. It was Evie's idea to go there, she knew it was dangerous – I didn't want to. The tide came up and the beach path got cut off.' Tara looked at the ground. 'I ran to get help – there were no mobile phones then, of course – but it was too late by the time they came. She was never much of a swimmer.'

'How awful.' She wished she hadn't asked. There was something disconcerting, rehearsed-sounding about Tara's reply.

Tara seemed to read her thoughts.

'It was a long time ago. I've had to deal with it, get on with my life.'

Something was wrong with this story. 'How did you manage to escape, but not your sister?'

Tara frowned. 'I found a path going up the cliff. I thought Evie was following me, but she wasn't.' Her eye muscle twitched again. Tara was lying, Elspeth knew in her gut.

'What about your mother? She must have struggled.'

'I suppose. She certainly resented me for being the one to survive.' A trace of venom entered Tara's voice. 'She did her best not to look at me and wanted me gone from the house as soon as I could find somewhere. The irony was, I was the one who looked after my mother when she got ill. She and her second husband were divorced by then. There was no one else.'

Tara looked straight at Elspeth, her forehead wrinkling.

'But I'm sure you don't want to hear my entire life story. Didn't you want to talk about the fence?'

'Yes, yes, of course.'

Oh God, she'd asked too much. Tara was suspicious. In a moment of panic, Elspeth took a quick step backwards. Her foot caught on a stone. She wobbled and lurched towards the fence, grabbing a handful of brittle twigs.

'Oh shit!'

Thank God, she recovered her balance just before her ankle turned over. Belatedly, Tara took hold of her arm.

'Watch yourself, Elspeth. You don't want to be falling over at your age.' Tara's voice was devoid of sympathy. It could have been Elspeth's imagination, but she could have sworn that a smile had flickered on Tara's lips. Elspeth shivered. Images raced through her mind. A girl toppling from a branch, another struggling to keep her head above the waves...

'Since I came down with Covid my balance has been up the spout,' she said. She was flustered, words were spilling out. 'I must do more yoga. The tree pose is a good one, they say.' But Tara clearly wasn't interested in either the tree pose or Elspeth's deteriorating balance. 'Your fence...' Elspeth pushed her thoughts back to the subject she was meant to be addressing. 'It's got rather wonky – ever since you cut back the ivy. I was thinking it might be a good idea to replace the section at the end...'

Aware of Tara's increasingly stony expression, she juddered to a halt. Waves of animosity were emanating from her neighbour.

'You might not be aware, Elspeth, but I'm a little short of money at the moment. Practically all my clients have ditched me in the wake of the horrible gossip going around – didn't Ashley tell you? I'm afraid I'm not in the position to spend money tinkering with that fence.'

Elspeth felt blood rush to her face. Her mouth opened but she couldn't get any words out. No wonder her sisters had hated her! The woman was insufferable.

'If you'd like to arrange for someone to put up another fence yourself, and pay for it of course, be my guest.' Tara went on, not waiting for an answer. 'And those things I told you about my sisters – please keep them to yourself. I'm sure Ashley would be interested to know, but I'd rather not have her spreading any more lies about me. Now, if you don't mind, I'm going to make myself a cup of tea.'

With a resounding slam of her front door, Tara disappeared.

Back at home, Elspeth poured herself a large glass of wine and sat down. Her breaths were laboured and she couldn't get in quite enough air – as if a huge wave had just come along and rolled her over and over.

Chapter 45
Ashley

'**M**um! Are you listening?'

Layla looked hurt. Ashley marshalled her thoughts back to the here and now. Much as she wanted to leave it behind, her conversation with Elspeth, just before her family had sat down for dinner, kept intruding.

'Sorry, love. What did you say?'

'A man spat at me as I walked past him.'

'A man spat at you? Where was this?'

'She's already said.' Zac frowned at her. 'Weren't you listening to any of it?'

Layla sighed theatrically.

'On the corner, as I was coming into Wilton Close. It was just now, on my way back from the pool.'

'What man? Did you know him?'

'I think he lives in the Wiltons but I've never talked to him. He sometimes walks past our house. He's got greasy skin and horrible bulging eyes.'

Sam, about to take a mouthful of chicken, lowered his fork.

'Are you sure it wasn't one of your ex-boyfriends?'

'Shut up, muffin-head!'

'Ow! Stop, you're hurting! Get off!'

In an instant, time slipped back to when her offspring would regularly engage in physical combat.

'Stop it, you two,' she ordered. 'You're behaving like ten-year-olds.'

'You two, behave yourselves!' Zac thundered. 'I've got a stinking headache. I'm not in the mood for this.'

The four of them carried on eating in silence. Ashley tried to process what Layla had just said, along with Elspeth's news.

'Did it get you?'

'What?' Layla pulled a face at her brother's question.

'The gob, did it get you?'

'No, it landed on the pavement.' Layla glared at Sam.

'What did you do?' Sam asked.

'What do you think, I karate chopped him in the nuts?' Layla rolled her eyes. 'I just carried on walking, obviously.'

Another silence. Ashley's thoughts slipped back to Elspeth's update on her exploratory visit to Tara that afternoon. In one fell swoop – in her anxiety, she'd actually fallen – Elspeth had gone from being sceptical about the possibility that Tara had caused her sisters' deaths to wholeheartedly agreeing with Ashley.

You should have seen her face – she didn't care one iota! Her voice was so... emotionless. It gave me the heeby-jeebies, I tell you. She might not have deliberately set out to kill her family, but I bet you anything you like that she had a hand in their deaths.

From a distance, she heard her family talking. They were trying to uncover the spitter's identity.

'Was it the guy who has a union jack in his window?' Sam asked.

Zac tore his naan in two. 'He's got a Range Rover.'

'I've no idea what car he drives.' Layla pursed her lips.

'I wouldn't be surprised if it's him,' Zac said. 'He's a nasty piece of work.'

'He always looks at me like he wants to stick me with a blade,' Sam added.

'We should all keep an eye out.' Zac's frown deepened. 'People can surprise you. They might laugh and joke with you sometimes and pretend to like you, but underneath...'

Sam looked at his father.

'The union jack guy is part of that bunch of Nazis, do you reckon?'

'What bunch of Nazis?' Ashley asked, catching the look between father and son.

'It's just some local idiots,' Zac replied. 'The Patriotic Alliance. They think Trump walks on water and Covid was invented by the Chinese so they can take over the world.'

'They hate everyone except white-skinned Brits,' Sam added. 'Especially people of different races and religions who get together and have kids.'

'Yeah,' Layla said quietly. 'People like us.'

Ashley put her knife and fork down. She didn't feel hungry any more.

Wearily, Ashley clicked onto the next screen of articles from the *West Skelton and Dove Cross Herald*.

She now had a greater-than-wanted knowledge of the area in which Tara had spent her childhood, during 1982 in particular. It was the year in which Tara's sisters had probably died, she and Elspeth had worked out. This knowledge ranged from the size of hailstones that fell during a particularly severe thunderstorm to the weight of the prizewinning marrow in the 1982 Home Growers Competition. Fortunately for their quest, the paper also clearly relished the reporting of all manner of violent or unusual incidents, especially when they resulted in death or serious injury. Unfortunately, the search feature of the newspaper's archives didn't work for articles created back then, so she couldn't search for 'inquest', 'tragic accident' and the like.

There was plenty of space devoted to inquests, she had discovered, especially when they involved freakish events – a woman squashed by a falling tree, a boy electrocuted when his kite flew onto a power line, a vicar who'd attacked his neighbour with a spade in a dispute over the height of a Leylandii... So far, she had found three drownings in the relevant period, but they involved either pre-teen children or adults. No one had been killed after falling from a tree.

This was a waste of time, she thought, clicking onto yet another screen of the articles from September 1982. Even if she found one that shed any light on the deaths of the sisters, what difference would it make?

She jolted upright as her eye caught a headline:

Tragic death of girl trapped below cliffs by tide

Evie Sanderson, 14, drowned yesterday after she was trapped by the rising tide at the bottom of cliffs while walking from Myers Beach towards Black's Bay.

We understand from Evie's mother, Ivy Sanderson, that Evie had been trying to catch up with her younger sister, Tara, 11, who had become separated from Evie after the pair set off together from Myers Beach shortly before 3pm.

Tara managed to climb the rocks onto the safety of a cliff path as the sea was about to submerge the shoreline path. Tara, hearing Evie's calls for help, peered down from the cliff edge and saw Evie in the sea, surrounded by crashing waves. She ran up the cliff path to Bella's Café and raised the alarm.

Frantic efforts were made to save Evie by the café's manager, Peter Inglis, and several of his customers, to no avail. Evie was pronounced dead when emergency services arrived at the scene.

The section of coastline between Myers Beach and Black's Bay is known to be dangerous due to its frequent fast-rising tides. A fifty-nine-year-old man drowned there in 1978.

The article was dated September 5 1982.

Ashley sat back in Zac's office chair. Seeing the incident reported in black and white made Evie's death seem horribly real.

She clicked quickly through further screens. A few minutes later she found a short report on the inquest, held a few months after Evie's death, baldly stating the inquest's conclusion: Evie Sanderson had died from 'misadventure'.

So, Tara's sister Evie really had drowned at sea – Tara hadn't lied about that. There was nothing to indicate that Tara had been anything other than a bystander in a tragic accident. But something didn't feel right. If there were no other witnesses, which the article didn't mention, the information must have originally come from Tara herself. What facts might Tara have not mentioned, or distorted, to make her actions more palatable? Why had the sisters taken that path in the first place, knowing it to be dangerous? Had it been Tara's idea? How had Tara and Evie become separated – and why had Tara managed to find her way to safety but not Evie? Had Tara really done all she could have to help her sister?

Ashley ran into the en-suite bathroom, closed the door and phoned Elspeth. Trepidation and excitement surged through her. It was nearly 11pm but she had to tell Elspeth, right now.

'I've found out what happened to Evie! The eldest sister, the second to die. It's all in the local newspaper. How she got trapped by the tide, how Tara saw her drowning and raised the alarm... Hold on, I'll read it to you.' She read out the article and the inquest's conclusion.

Silence.

'Elspeth? Are you still there?'

'Oh my God,' Elspeth said in a near whisper. 'What made Tara go on ahead without Evie, when she could see the tide was coming in? And why on earth did she start going up that path without her sister? I asked her about it and she said she thought Evie was following her. But why would she have thought that? Bloody hell, Ash. It makes no sense.'

'It looks odd, doesn't it? And if it was just the two of them on that path... She could have lied to you about how Evie died – and to the police, and everyone else.'

'Exactly. No one would have known the truth. She could have set off from Myers Beach deliberately, hoping Evie would realise the danger and come after her. Maybe she had an escape route planned in advance. She could have let Evie drown before she went to tell anyone, who knows...'

A rap on the door interrupted Elspeth. Zac.

'Going to be long?'

'Sorry,' she said to Elspeth. 'I've got to go. Let's talk again tomorrow.'

'Ashley, wake up.'

Zac was tugging the duvet near her head.

'Go away, I need to sleep,' she murmured without opening her eyes, an intense irritation coming over her at this brusque interruption to her sleep. Disturbed by thoughts of Tara and the mysterious deaths of her sisters, she'd finally got off around 4am.

'Ashley, wake up!' Zac started tugging at her shoulder. 'There's something outside you need to see.'

She opened her eyes. 'What is it?'

'Someone's sprayed the garage doors with graffiti. Come and see for yourself.'

She shrugged on her dressing gown and followed Zac downstairs.

'What the hell?'

They stood side by side in the driveway, staring at the words sprayed in white over the metallic grey garage door. At first, she couldn't make sense of them. Then she did, and wanted to throw up.

FILTHY PAKI RAGHEADS
FUCK OFF THE LOT OF YOU

She stared at the horrible message. It occupied a large part of the door, and would be visible to anyone passing.

'Who would do this to us?'

'Some facist zealot? Maybe the same one who spat at our daughter yesterday.'

'I'll go and get dressed. I want a cup of tea.'

'No, I want to do this now. The sooner we start, the sooner it'll be gone.'

'We should report this to the police,' she said. 'This is vandalism.'

Zac laughed. 'The police will probably be on the side of those Nazis who did this.'

It took nearly an hour to get rid of the graffiti. Later that morning, after drinking a mug of strong tea, Ashley phoned Elspeth and explained what had happened. Elspeth's reply was typically forthright.

'What a shitty thing to do. I hope whoever did it falls over and breaks both their legs – and their arms too! You have no idea who it might be?'

'Not really. Zac thinks it's someone in a far-right group. There's one close by, apparently.'

The Bad Neighbour

After a brief chat to Elspeth, Ashley sat on a chair in the kitchen. She still felt stunned. The words were a violation, puncturing the illusion of a safe, mostly benign world. Who had left such an odious message, and why? It was horrible to think that someone could hate her family enough to disfigure their property.

Chapter 46
Tara
23 July

P en poised above her notebook, Tara sat in a garden chair in the shade. Once again, despite Ashley's heroic attempts to shut windows, she could hear the family next door quarrelling.

This time it was the two teenagers. They were in the girl's terrace bedroom with the door open, by the sound of it, and seemed to have no idea how far their voices travelled.

'It's not true! Do you really think I'd bonk three boys at once in front of the whole street?'

'Why is everyone saying it then? I'm getting it from my friends now.'

'Someone's spreading lies about me! I don't know how you could believe that crap. I thought you were my brother, why don't you act like one?'

Tara couldn't hear the reply. In a rush of excitement, she started to scribble down the latest installment of this unfolding drama. The Asian family provided better entertainment than Netflix.

All was quiet, apart from the clacking of Elspeth's shears on the other side of the garden. Tara put down her pen.

To her delight, the rumour she'd started had spread quicker

than she'd imagined it might, and seemed to have gathered moss along the way. Likewise, the small group of passionate young men planning to build a mosque in the village had swollen into far more. According to snippets of conversation she'd overheard, Brampton was in the grip of a 'foreign takeover'. The council was supposedly considering a planning application for a mosque to be built beside the Quaker meeting house.

No doubt fuelled by the rumours she'd started and the panic whipped up by Rob and his cronies, a backlash had begun against various groups, from East Europeans to people of colour. Shops and restaurants deemed 'foreign' had been sprayed with graffiti, notes had gone through doors. Posters saying *No Mosque in Brampton* and *Foreigners Out!* had been stuck up on fences, lamp-posts and community noticeboards. Where would it all end?

Tara yawned, stretched out her legs and sipped her cocktail.

It was a lovely day. She would have a relaxing afternoon in the sunshine. The sense of agency she had felt of late was most pleasant. But the very best thing was knowing that Ashley and her family were sinking ever deeper into the shit. Not only that – as she'd hoped, Tara herself was being rehabilitated. A welcome side effect of this spate of local gossip was that everyone seemed to have forgotten their animosity towards her, or they couldn't be bothered with it any more. Whatever the reason, she had been out and about without the wig three times now and nothing untoward had happened. There had been a few frowns and nudges but nothing that she couldn't handle. Several acquaintances had nodded to her when they passed. She had even risked replenishing her supplies of alcohol in Waitrose, which Ocado invariably got wrong. Things were definitely on the up.

Chapter 47
Ashley
24 July

A shley drove home, her mind occupied with the trip she'd just made to the supermarket. It wasn't just her imagination, as she'd thought at first. People had stopped talking and stared at her when she approached. In Waitrose, a woman she didn't know whispered something behind her back that sounded like *Muslim Lover*. In the queue outside the bakery, she distinctly heard someone behind her say, 'We don't want your sort here.'

She had taken the last shopping bag out of the boot and placed it on the driveway when she saw the flower shop owner stop on the pavement.

'Sorry if I'm speaking out of turn,' Sandy said with an unconvincing smile. She was easy to spot, being a tall, large-framed lady with very bright orange hair and a penchant for equally bold dresses. Today, she wore footless tights and trainers under a dress decorated with pink roses on a green background. 'The last thing I want to do is intrude into your affairs. But you've always seemed like a lovely lady. I thought you should know what people are saying, if you don't already.'

'What are people saying?' she repeated, too startled to try to be polite.

A distinct pause.

'Word is going around that your daughter Layla has been... getting up to mischief with some local boys. On the green.' Sandy tilted her head in the general direction of the grassy space on the other side of the road.

'Getting up to mischief? You mean...' she repeated, incomprehension replaced by horror.

Sandy put her hand on Ashley's forearm and lowered her voice.

'She's been seen having sex with some local lads. I'm sure it's only a vicious lie, but I thought you should know. The other thing... There's a rumour going round that your son – Samir, is it? – is part of a radical Islamic group that's planning to build a mosque in our village.'

Ashley blinked at Sandy. She couldn't stay here, listening to this.

'Thanks for letting me know. Sorry, I have to go.'

'I'm sorry, I didn't mean to cause any trouble.' Sandy stepped back.

Ashley hauled the collection of shopping bags into the porch. Inside, she dumped them on the kitchen floor and stood, tears welling. She wanted to weep. How could anyone say those things about her children? She wanted to snuggle into Zac's body and cry, and for him to comfort her like he used to.

He'd gone out to 'see some mates', she remembered.

Upstairs, the sound of voices. Layla and Sam were fighting again. The animosity in their voices startled her. She hurried upstairs, stopping outside Sam's room.

'What do you think it's like, having a slut for a sister?'

'Shut up, raghead! I told you, it's not true. Anyway, what about you? They say you and your band of brothers are planning to build a mosque right here in the village. That's why they wrote that stuff on our garage. No one wants a fucking mosque in a little place like this, do they?'

Taking a deep breath, Ashley opened the door. Sam was sitting on his bed. He jumped to his feet when he saw her. Layla was standing by the window, her phone in her hand.

'Stop fighting, you two! I don't want you to speak to each other like this ever again, do you hear me?' The anger in her own voice sounded alien to her ears. 'What is the matter with you both? You are brother and sister, or have you forgotten?'

Silence.

'I'm sorry, Mum.' Sam's head stayed lowered.

'Now apologise to your sister.'

'Sorry, Layla. I didn't mean it.'

'Layla, apologise to your brother.'

Layla looked at her brother for several seconds then spoke softly. 'I'm sorry.'

Ashley let out a long breath and addressed both of them.

'Now, I want you to tell me what's going on.'

'They're spreading lies about us,' Sam began. 'They're saying Layla's a slut and I've been having secret meetings in the allotments with a radical Islamic group.'

'Who is saying this?'

'Everyone. Kids from college, their parents...'

'They say that someone saw me bonking three boys on the green.' Layla flushed crimson. 'It's total rubbish.'

'I know it is, Layla.'

'I went there with Anna and her boyfriend, that's all. They went behind the trees and started kissing. I was fed up with waiting so I went to tell them to hurry up. Someone passing by must have seen us and decided to make trouble – or maybe it was someone watching from one of the houses.'

Someone watching from one of the houses. The top of her scalp prickled.

Layla tapped at something on her phone and hurried out of the room. Ashley turned to her son.

'What about you, Samir? Is there any truth in the story about you?' *Please, tell me there isn't.*

'You think I've turned into a raghead, too?'

'Of course I don't. But you haven't been honest with me. You've been out of the house for hours every day since lockdown started, not telling me where you're going or who you're seeing. What have you been doing? I'm asking you to tell me the truth.' Looking at the dark patch of sweat forming on his T-shirt, she uttered a silent prayer.

'It was a study group, that's all. It was Khalid's idea for a few of us to read and discuss the Koran together. A friend of Khalid's wanted to join us. We were all getting a bit lonely and miserable... His dad didn't like the three of us meeting in his garden, so we started going to the allotments instead. Isa's parents have a shed there.' Sam huffed out a breath. 'We had to stop meeting, after the rumours started.'

She went closer to him. 'Is that all you do, study the Koran?'

'We talk about stuff too.' Sam's chin jutted upward. He looked at her defiantly.

'What sort of stuff?'

'Just normal stuff between friends.'

Her heart thudded. 'Did you ever talk about setting up a mosque in Brampton?'

'Khalid likes to talk about political stuff. He's always saying we must stand up to Muslim haters. At one meeting he said we ought to have a mosque nearby, cos it takes so long to get to the one in Elven if you haven't got a car.'

It made sense. She had overheard Khalid talking to Sam when the two were chatting on WhatsApp. He had seemed a serious young man.

'That isn't a crime, is it?' Sam looked directly at her, his chest rising and falling. 'And I don't go along with everything he says, either. But I think if people say bad things about you, you should stand up to them.'

'What do you mean, stand up to them?' Her heart thudded harder, creating a drumming inside her head.

He shrugged. 'Talk to them, confront them. Not bomb them or kill them, I'd never do anything like that. I hate violence, you know I do.'

'I believe you. I just wish you had talked to me before. I got so worried...' Ashley wiped away her tears. She loved her son more than she knew how to say. He had only tried to do what she had encouraged him to do, yet found so hard to do herself.

'I'm sorry, Mum. But around here, most people see me as an outsider, and they think if you're interested in Islam you must be a fanatic who goes around planting bombs.' He rubbed his damp brow. 'Khalid challenged me to explore my religion, decide what I believe and what I don't.' He slapped the window-frame with the heel of his hand. 'But now everyone thinks I'm into crazy shit and Layla is... It's madness. It's like someone has been watching us and now they're twisting everything we did into whatever they think will stir people up the most.'

On tenterhooks, she waited for Zac to come home. She would have to tell him about this conversation, and what the residents of Brampton had been saying about them and their children. Layla had shown her a Facebook post from a Mark Smith that had been shared by a girl at college along with many others. It showed photos of Ashley, Zac, Sam and Layla embellished with lies and innuendo, ending with: 'Do we really want people like this in our midst?'

It's not just us, Zac had told her the other day; the hateful message, left on their house was part of a wider campaign of intimidation against 'outsiders'. Apparently, the Turkish restaurant had also been daubed with hateful messages and other business owners had received flyers through their letterboxes telling them to leave Brampton. But no-one else's family had been hounded. Someone was targeting her family in particular. Someone who had it in for herself or her family.

Tara. She was involved in this, somehow. Could she be spreading rumours about the kids to get back at Ashley for her own disgrace? Zac would probably laugh, if she told him. All the same, the thought wouldn't go away.

Chapter 48
Elspeth
25 July

'Thank Christ,' Elspeth said aloud, as the article appeared on her computer screen. Religion, of the organised variety at least, had never been top of her priority list. Cursing, however, was on her dwindling list of pleasures. 'Thank bloody Christ,' she repeated with relish.

The article began with a photograph of a young girl with striking looks. Dark blonde hair framed a tanned, freckled face. Her widely spaced hazel eyes had a piercing, melancholy gaze, seeming to reach out across the years. Elspeth felt an ache at her throat. She tugged her eyes away from the girl and began to read the article, from the end of March, 1982.

Zoe Sanderson died in tragic circumstances, last Saturday afternoon, during a party to celebrate her thirteenth birthday two days earlier.

Witnesses reported that Zoe fell to her death after the rope she was playing on snapped in two.

It is understood that the rope had been attached to a branch of a tree in her family's back garden, as it had been for many years. Children were playing on the rope shortly before the incident, taking it in turns to swing across the lawn.

Zoe was seen to climb up and hold herself upside down moments before the rope snapped. She is believed to have hit the ground head first and was pronounced dead when an ambulance arrived at the scene.

Elspeth took a screenshot of the article. Ashley would be pleased that she had managed to find a report about the first death. It could wait a little, though; she didn't want to bother Ashley while she was so preoccupied with her family.

Scrolling through the endless stories of village life – unlike Brampton, Dove Cross was small enough to be a proper village – she had a yearning for a cup of tea. But first she had to find what she was looking for.

An hour later, below a long article on the summer crime upsurge in Dove Cross that was hitting the area's beaches, she spotted a short article on the inquest into Zoe's death. Elspeth scanned the first paragraph. The inquest, which had taken place that July, had resulted in an open verdict. In other words, the paper explained, the coroner's jury had come to the conclusion that there wasn't enough evidence to decide whether the death was deliberately caused or accidental. She read on, her heart beating faster.

Evidence was presented that the rope had been tampered with. However, it was not clear when this act may have occurred or who carried it out.

Elspeth stared at the screen, the hairs on the back of her neck rising. So, she and Ashley had been right to have suspicions about Tara's role in her sisters' deaths. Maybe others had too, all those years ago.

She clicked back to the first article. Zoe's gaze seemed even sadder. Deep within her, something stirred. She could feel the connection between the two of them, young girl and old woman. She smiled at her whimsical thoughts – it was sentimental foolishness, borne of too much wishing for her own child, surely. She didn't believe in life after death or anything like that. Still...

Elspeth closed her eyes, resolve forming. Maybe, in a manner of speaking, she could offer Zoe something of value. She could find out the truth of how Zoe had died and obtain some kind of reparation for the dead girl, couldn't she?

Chapter 49
Ashley
28 July

'Going out now!' Ashley put her head around Zac's office door. 'Won't be long.'

'Where did you say you're going?' Zac tapped into his computer, not looking up.

'Just up the road, to John's. The group is meeting there.'

He raised his eyebrows. 'I thought you said it wasn't going any more, with the food bank imploding and people no longer shielding?'

'We've decided to meet occasionally, in case the situation gets worse again.' That wasn't untrue, but it wasn't the only reason they were meeting. 'And Elspeth and I are worried about Tara.'

Zac groaned. 'Not that again. Honestly, I think you're both letting your imaginations get the better of you.'

'I'm running late, I haven't got time to discuss it now.'

Ashley closed the front door behind her with relief; the atmosphere at home had been claustrophobic of late. She had resolved to pay as little attention as possible to the smear campaign, doing her best to ignore occasional hostile glances in her direction. There had been no new accusations or Facebook posts as far as she could tell, and she dared hope that, in time, things would settle down. In the meantime, the lies hadn't only affected the relationship between brother and sister, but that between father and son, and herself and Zac.

Zac had reacted angrily to Sam's admission that he'd been meeting his friends in the allotment and accused Sam of lying to him. He questioned Sam about his beliefs and whether his group of friends did something other than study Islam. Ashley had tried to smooth things over between the two, to no avail. Zac had attacked her for her 'woolly stance' on his religion, saying it had caused their daughter to reject Islam completely and start 'going off the rails' and their son to mix with young men who wanted to 'infect his mind with all sorts of nonsense'. It hurt deeply, the accusation that she was somehow responsible for damaging their children. He had never asked her to share his faith, and she had done her best to understand it. What more could she have done?

She stopped outside the gate to John's bungalow.

'It's this one, isn't it?' It was Ursula, coming along the pavement from the opposite direction, in a summer dress and sandals. She was hurrying and frowning at her phone. With a flustered smile, Ursula came to a halt beside Ashley. 'I hear you've been having problems with Tara... What bad luck to be living next door to her.'

'Things have been difficult lately,' she admitted. 'But I'm looking forward to seeing everyone again. It's been such a long time.'

'It certainly has. Tuesday mornings don't seem the same without our Zoom meetings.'

John buzzed them in, waving as they approached the conservatory. The doors to the garden were wide open, admitting warm, humid air.

'Hello, and welcome. I hope you're both hungry.'

Ursula gestured to the table, decked with plates of biscuits, cheese and fruit.

'Oh, what a spread! My mouth is watering.' She helped herself to a grape. 'You've pulled out all the stops for us, John.'

'It's my pleasure, Ursula. I'll get the coffee going.' John gave Ashley a smile before turning his electric vehicle towards the kitchen. 'I don't think we'll need to be wearing masks with the doors open, do you?'

A minute later, a suntanned Ferne arrived in a T-shirt and leggings. Greg was with her, dapper with a Panama hat and cherry-red silk scarf.

'Hiya, hun. Good to see you again.' Ferne leaned across and gave her a light squeeze.

'Hey, you,' Greg drawled to Ashley. 'Long time, no see.' He winked and they elbowed.

Seated around the table, the five eagerly shared their news. Ashley said little, thinking how much she'd missed them all. In the weeks since Tara had been ejected from the Zoom meeting, they had kept in touch by email. This group, for all its spats and dramas, had become more to her than she'd realised.

'OK, everyone...' John addressed them all. 'We're here to discuss whether we want to keep our group going – can it still serve a purpose and if so, what should we focus on?'

'Before we go on, excuse me, everyone, for pigging out on this wonderful food.' Greg helped himself to a croissant. 'Tony and I slept in this morning and I didn't get a chance to eat breakfast.'

Ferne lifted a flyer. 'Can I just say, if anyone is interested in a Zumba class, they're on at the community centre all through the summer holidays – only seven pounds for an hour's workout.'

'Worth every penny, I'm sure,' Ursula added. 'I'll come along now the choir is having a break.'

After some discussion, they agreed to carry on meeting to do whatever might help local residents through the pandemic, given 'the virus' was likely to have an impact during the winter months. They would meet as before on the first Tuesday of the month, in person or by Zoom, if that became necessary. Everyone immediately agreed to Ursula's proposal that John should chair the meetings.

Greg took another croissant and Ferne refilled cups from a pot of coffee, while John waited for everyone's attention.

'Now, if no one minds, there have been some worrying developments concerning our old friend Tara. I'll let Ashley tell you about them herself.'

Ashley nodded appreciatively at John. She took a deep breath, glancing around the table.

'I wanted to ask for advice about what I should do. I'm not sure where to start. For a while now, Tara has seemed put out about me and Elspeth becoming friends – Elspeth lives two houses along from me, on the other side of Tara. She blamed me for her having to leave the group. Then I began to wonder if she might have had anything to do with Elspeth catching Covid. I asked her about it and she got very upset...' Remembering, her stomach churned.

'Ashley thinks Tara may have deliberately infected Elspeth,' John explained, while she got herself together.

Ferne gasped. Ursula's biscuit stopped halfway to her mouth.

'It was something my daughter said.' Ashley described Layla's sighting of Tara on Elspeth's doorstep. 'Elspeth was seriously ill in hospital, I was afraid I wouldn't see her again. I told John about my suspicions and we decided to go to the police. They said they'd look into it – but we don't know if they've done anything.'

'I doubt it. They thought we were wasting their time, that was obvious.'

Ashley took a sip of water and continued.

'Anyway, after Elspeth left hospital we started looking into Tara's past. She told us both her sisters had died in accidents in their teens. We found reports in the local paper about the deaths – they were thought to be accidental. But there were little things that worried us. Tara got very angry with Elspeth once, when Elspeth asked about her sisters. Another time, she said something to us about how she'd got her own back on them. It felt like a threat, somehow.'

Silence. No one moved.

'My husband thinks we're reading too much into things,' she went on. 'But Elspeth is convinced that Tara's sisters didn't die in accidents – Tara killed them. I'm starting to think the same.'

A collective intake of breath.

'There's something else.' She hesitated. It was a risk, telling everyone. But it seemed the right thing to do. 'My family has been targeted.' She described the graffiti left on the garage door.

'Oh no, that's horrible!' Ferne's hand shot up to her mouth.

Greg moved his head from side to side. 'I'm sorry to hear that. People can be so foul.'

'There's been vile talk going around about so-called 'outsiders' taking over the village,' Ursula said. 'I think we all know who they are – the Brexit mob and rabid right-wingers doing their best to stir things up.'

'That's not all. Someone is spreading lies about my children.' Ashley took another sip of water. The glass trembled in her hand so much she had to put it down. 'They're on Facebook too, with photos of my family.'

'What are they saying, Ashley?' Greg spoke gently.

'They say my son is part of a radical Islamic group that is planning to build a mosque in the village, and my daughter has...' She came to a halt. John saved her.

'I don't think there's any need to repeat the smears. It's clear to me that someone with a particularly foul mind has made Ashley the target of the most abominable lies. And it isn't hard to guess who that person might be.'

Greg looked down at his plate. Ursula pursed her lips.

'Who?' Ferne asked, frowning.

John angled his head towards Ashley, indicating that she should answer. Ferne turned to her. 'You think it's Tara?'

A flood of emotion swirled inside her – fear of Tara finding out and retaliating, alongside a desperate need to tell what she believed.

'I don't know for sure,' she replied, voice trembling. 'But I think Tara is behind it all, yes.' An ache of tears behind her eyes. She scraped her chair back, scarcely aware of Ferne's 'Oh fuck' or Ursula's once-more gaping mouth.

Ashley peered into the rockery, laden with tiny silk-bright flowers. Tears dribbled out of her eyes, slid down her cheeks and dripped onto the grass.

'Sorry you're going through this, Ash.' Ferne's voice, behind her. The hesitant touch of a hand on her back. 'If there's anything I can do?'

'Thank you.' She blew her nose and smiled gratefully at Ferne.

Back inside, a chorus of concern.

'I'm all right now.' Ashley reassured them. 'To get to the point of all this. Elspeth thinks she and I should do something. But I've no idea what. So if anyone has any ideas...'

'We could all go over and confront Tara,' Ferne said. 'Make her tell us the truth.'

Greg pulled a face. 'What, take some pliers with us and threaten to pull out her fingernails?'

Ferne laughed. Ursula put down her cup.

'You're frightened of her, aren't you?'

'I suppose I am.' Ashley explained how she went out of her way to avoid Tara, even when the fence separated them, and hurried inside whenever Tara came into the garden. 'Also, this will sound paranoid, but I'm sure she eavesdrops on our conversations.' She repeated what Elspeth had told her several days ago: while tending plants on her terrace, she'd spotted Tara standing beside the back fence between Tara's and Ashley's gardens, jotting in a notebook.

'I can believe it,' Ferne said. 'She always was a nosey biddy.'

'Being nosey isn't a crime though, is it? Or half of this town would be in prison.' John picked at a piece of cheese on his plate. 'I've given it some thought but I can't think of much more Ashley can do. Confronting Tara directly is a no-no, as far as I'm concerned, given the possible repercussions for her and Elspeth.'

'It would only put Tara on her guard,' Greg added. 'I hate to say this, guys, but I agree with John. I don't think there's anything we can do except watch and wait to see if she actually does anything.'

Ursula nodded. 'However suspicious things might look, we still have no proof that she's done anything illegal. I mean, what sort of person would go to such lengths as killing their siblings and making it look like an accident? It's possible that someone else is behind the rumours about Ashley's children, and Tara had nothing to do with Elspeth getting ill. She could be completely innocent.'

'Hah, I doubt it.' Ferne rotated her shoulder one way then the other. 'That woman has more cunning than everyone in Brampton put together. Fancy driving all the way out to Grimpton Hadlock to sell off our produce. She must have thought she'd be safe setting up there.'

Ursula frowned. 'Yes, but does that make her a murderer?'

'She's devious enough,' Ferne replied. 'And she can get so jealous. A few years ago when we were friendly, I met her for coffee sometimes. One day a woman from my yoga class came up to us and said she loved my class, I was inspirational – Tara came over like a storm cloud. She practically told the woman to shove off.'

'She wasn't all bad though, was she?' Ursula looked at Greg, who smiled.

'She laughed at some of my jokes when no one else did.'

'She was only trying to butter you up, Greg.'

'And she was generous with baking cakes, wasn't she?' Ursula went on. 'At first, anyhow. She did have a good side...'

Ashley said nothing. Strange, she thought, how they were all talking about Tara in the past tense.

After the others left she said goodbye to John. He was slumped forward on his scooter, looking into the garden. She perched on the table, near him.

'Thank you for this morning.'

'I don't think we were much help.' He sighed, not moving. 'But we're here for you, remember that. Your husband may not take your concerns seriously, but we do. I do.'

She nodded and didn't reply. It was comfort to know she had his support, along with the others. But what if Tara got angry again? One never knew what she might do next.

'I know, it's all very well for me to say that. You have to live next door to her.'

'That's just it. I can't get away from her.'

John turned towards her.

'Be careful, Ashley, won't you? Don't be alone with Tara, even when you're with Elspeth.' His voice changed, huskiness breaking through. 'I wouldn't want anything bad to happen to you.'

Chapter 50
Ashley
29 July

'You're very quiet, sweetheart. Are you all right?'

Ashley stopped chopping chilli peppers and looked up in surprise. Zac stood in the corner of the kitchen, tapping into emails on his phone. His voice was tender, not distracted or irritated as it was so often lately.

'I'm worried, that's all. About the kids, and...'

'That woman next door?'

'I hardly go into the garden any more in case she's watching me from her bedroom window. Or standing behind the back fence listening. I spotted her again yesterday.'

Zac nodded, his face serious. This time he didn't suggest she was blowing things out of proportion.

The thud of the front door closing. It was Sam, judging by the clump of his footsteps. No hello, as usual.

'Sam?' She looked up at her son, already at the top of the stairs. 'Dinner will be in half an hour—'

She gasped as he turned to her. The area around his left eye was red and swollen, the eye almost closed up. There was a mass of dried blood under his nose and a long cut across his cheek.

'Oh God. What happened to you?'

'I got into a fight. Me and some bloke I've seen around. Then his friends came along. They all piled in.'

'Come into the kitchen and let me look at your face.'

'I'll be OK.'

'Samir, listen to your mother.' Zac was standing at her side.

Reluctantly, Sam let her clean his face and hands with anti-septic in warm water, flinching every so often.

'Take off your T-shirt and let me look at your back.' The skin on parts of his lower back and one side was reddened and starting to bruise. She touched it as gently as she could. 'They kicked you,' she said, aware of Zac close by.

'What was the fight about?' Zac demanded.

'The usual.'

'Tell us, Samir', Ashley said. 'We need to know.'

'They said they don't want me here any more. They think my friends and I are plotting to take over the village.' He pulled away from her, his face distorting with anger. 'It's mad.'

Zac kneaded the tabletop. 'Tell me who they are.'

'This is my business, Dad. Keep out of it, will you?' Sam helped himself to a glass of water, and drained it. 'I'm going to my room. I'll eat later.'

Layla arrived home twenty minutes later, in time for dinner at seven. She dumped her tote bag on the worktop.

'Hello, love. How was the picnic?' Layla and Anna had left for a picnic by the lake earlier in the afternoon.

'Did you go swimming?' she added when there was no reply.

'Where's Sam?'

'In his room. Wait, do you know what happened?'

Layla went upstairs without replying and came down as Ashley was serving dinner. She ate little and said even less.

'What's the matter, love?' Ashley asked.

'Nothing,' Layla said in a flat voice.

Ashley met Zac's eyes. It would be best to wait for Layla to volunteer information, she knew.

'I'm going for a walk,' Layla said after they'd finished eating.

'Where are you going?' Zac demanded.

'I don't know. Around the block?'

'I don't want you out on your own after dark, it's not safe.'

'It's not dark for another hour or so, Dad. What do you think's going to happen?' Layla's voice rose unsteadily in pitch. 'You think I'm going to be out screwing boys on the green or something?' She scraped back her chair and ran out of the kitchen. They heard the thud of her bedroom door.

'What's the matter with that girl? I told her I believed her.' Anger and frustration spilled out of Zac's voice.

Ashley lowered her head to her arms. Had those kids been saying things again on Layla's social media? When would it all end? Whoever had started these vile rumours, she thought, was responsible for the suffering of her children.

After a cursory clear-up in the kitchen, she went into the garden to distract herself from her circling thoughts. She worked until past dusk, chopping the stems of ivy clogging the fence between her and Tara's back gardens. As the light faded, it was hard to see clearly. Eventually, leaving a pile of tangled plant matter on the patio, she returned to the house.

Before going to bed, she knocked on Layla's door.

'Can I come in?'

No reply. Ashley opened the door a fraction.

'Are you all right, love?'

The room was dark. The outline of Layla's body was visible on the bed, silhouetted against cold moonlight streaming through the window.

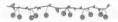

Ashley opened her eyes and pulled back the duvet. A noise had woken her from a light, troubled sleep. Layla? Something was wrong.

She pulled on her shorts and singlet, opened Layla's bedroom door and switched on the light. A wine bottle on the bedside table, empty. No glass in sight. The terrace door ajar.

She went outside. On the table, a stub of hand-rolled cigarette, burnt at its tip. She made herself go to the metal railing at the end of the terrace and look over. Her daughter lay on the ground below, not moving.

No!

Ashley screamed.

Let her not be dead. Please, let her not be dead.

She ran downstairs and yanked open the door into the garden. Night air, warm on her bare arms and legs. When she saw the body, she stopped. Layla was lying on her side, her head surrounded by a dark crown, her legs and arms bent as though she was sleeping.

She kneeled beside Layla. The dark crown turned into a pile of thorny stems. As she reached over, one caught the top of her hand. It ripped the skin, drawing blood. Ashley held her hand close to Layla's mouth. Breath, warm against her palm. She put an ear to her daughter's chest, felt the heart, still beating.

She touched Layla's cheek, the skin soft under her fingers. A moan. Layla's eyelids fluttered. Nothing else moved.

'Mum.' The word almost inaudible. 'It hurts...'

Ashley jumped to her feet.

'Zac! Sam! Call an ambulance!'

The silence grew, each small noise serving to amplify it.

A frustrated noise from Zac, sitting beside her in the small room. The volley of taps into Zac's phone as her husband Whats-Apped their son. The squeak and trundle of passing trolleys in the corridor outside. The thud of her heart.

Still no news of their daughter, beyond the fact that her injuries were being assessed by doctors, and she was in a stable condition.

At last, a doctor entered the room. Layla had a minor head injury and concussion, he explained. But her brain was functioning normally and there was no injury to the spinal cord or any spinal column compression fractures. It appeared that she'd landed on her feet, fortunately with bent legs, and quickly rolled onto her side, which had distributed the impact. Her right heel and right elbow were fractured, however, and she had several broken ribs.

'She's very lucky she escaped without more serious injuries, given the height of the fall.' The doctor touched his balding head. He sounded drained of energy. 'She jumped from a first-floor balcony onto concrete, is that right?'

'Yes,' she replied. 'But when I found her, her head and most of her back were on top of a pile of stems from my gardening last night. I'd been going to bag it all up and bring it in, but it was too dark.'

The doctor pushed his specs higher up his nose.

'That may well have saved her life. If her head had struck the concrete as she landed, she might have had a fatal brain injury.'

Ashley dug a nail into her palm as hard as she could.

'Is she going to be all right, doctor?'

'I expect her to recover fully – physically, at least. She'll need an operation for the heel fractures – she'll probably need to be in hospital for two or three weeks.'

'Thank you, thank you.' Zac put his palms together in the prayer position and lowered his head. Tears ran down his cheeks, merging into his stubble.

'There may be a lasting mental health impact, though. Substantial amounts of alcohol were found in her blood and she had a strong positive test for cannabis in her urine,' the doctor explained. 'It's likely that the combination may have affected her state of mind.' He paused. 'She wasn't a regular cannabis user, to your knowledge?'

Zac moved his head a fraction. 'Not any more. She took it before we moved here.'

'There was a roll-up on the table,' Ashley said. 'She must have started again.'

'Given the circumstances, a psychiatrist will assess Layla as soon as she's well enough.' The doctor looked from Zac to Ashley. 'Has she tried to take her own life before, as far as you know?'

Take her own life. The words struck her with force. Zac frowned.

'She didn't necessarily intend to kill herself when she jumped, did she? If she was out of it...'

'Most females of Layla's age who attempt suicide don't actually want to kill themselves,' the doctor explained. 'They want to let people know they need help.'

A whorl of horror and sadness engulfed her.

'Can we see her?' she asked eventually.

On the way home, Zac said little. Twice he made a fist and rapped his knuckles on the top of his head.

Ashley stared through the windscreen. Instead of the road, she saw Layla's bandaged head and her beautiful face with her eyelids closed as if she was having a rest.

They arrived home at 4am. That night she scarcely slept, replaying all that she knew and imagining all she didn't. Topmost was the agony of having been physically close to her daughter and yet utterly unable to prevent her actions. Over and over, she wondered at Layla's thoughts in the moments before her fall – or jump, if that was what it was. Had the bullying got too much to bear? Had her daughter wanted to leave everything behind, forever?

Each new imagining grew worse. Guilt surged past the feeble barriers she'd tried to erect. Why hadn't Layla turned to Ashley in her distress – or to Zac or Sam? Why hadn't they done something to stop this terrible thing – why hadn't she? She was Layla's mother. Why, oh why hadn't she seen this coming and done something to stop it?

Chapter 51
Ashley
31 July

L ayla was sitting up in bed, now curtained off from the rest of the ward. Her surgeon had inserted screws in her heel bones. He'd told them the operation had been successful, though she would have limited mobility for two or three months, and full recovery might take up to a year.

'Why did you do it, sweetheart?'

Ashley spoke first. They had debated endlessly what to say and what to ask their daughter. But in the end, neither could follow the outline they'd prepared.

'You could have killed yourself,' Zac said. A sob caught in his throat. 'Or ended up in a fucking wheelchair for the rest of your life.'

She put a hand on his arm. That morning they had also spoken to the psychiatrist, who had told them they could talk to their daughter but to be careful as Layla was extremely vulnerable.

'What happened, love? We aren't angry with you, but we need to know what happened. I know you were upset when you came home.'

'I – I couldn't stop thinking of what they were saying about me.' Layla looked at her hand, resting on the blanket. 'Just after Sam got beaten up, I saw loads of horrible comments on my Instagram post. It was just a picture of flowers I took while Anna and I were having a picnic. Then, when I went up to my room, there were even worse comments from some boys in my class. I felt so sad, like I wasn't worth anything any more... I just wanted to block it all out, try to feel better.' Layla met Ashley's eyes. 'That's why I drank the wine. I was only going to have a glass or two but it wasn't helping. Then I found some of the weed Anna gave me—'

'Anna gave you cannabis?'

'She had a bit over after we smoked some together, a few weeks ago. I went out to the terrace so it wouldn't stink out my room. I was sitting there in the dark and I started to feel strange. Suddenly this idea came to me – it would be a good idea to climb over the rail, it would end all my problems. I was scared, I tried to resist. But I couldn't stop thinking that's what I should do.' Layla swallowed. A tear emerged from the corner of her eye and rolled down her cheek. 'I'm so sorry, Mum. And you, Dad. I'll never do anything like this again, I promise.'

Tentatively, Ashley took Layla's hand and squeezed. She wanted to pull her daughter close and never let go.

Zac held Layla's other hand, blinking back tears.

'You've nothing to be sorry for, darling.'

'We're the ones who are sorry,' Ashley said. 'We didn't realise how far this had gone. We weren't there for you.'

After they said goodbye, Zac spoke to the nurse who'd met them earlier and asked if they could see their daughter's phone. Layla had told them that the messages were still on the phone. Forty minutes later the nurse hurried towards them, out of breath, and handed Zac a phone, encased in pale blue plastic decorated with silver stars. Zac punched in the passcode; they had bought the phone for Layla on the condition that they would be able to access it at any time, if needed. Ashley watched the screen as Zac scrolled through Layla's Instagram notifications.

Have you heard about your big bro? He was in a mess when they finished with him, haha.

they've flattened your raghead brother, saddo. it's you next

Hey Lally are you up for a 3some

Zac heaved out a breath. 'This is depraved.'

Ashley didn't reply. Deep inside her, something seemed to wither. How could this be? How could anyone do this?

'Those kids deserve to be punished for this,' Zac said, as they left the hospital.

With permission, the ward sister had contacted the police, who were investigating the bullying. It was important to Zac but right now was of no significance to Ashley. She said nothing, relieved to be outside, away from the over-bright lighting that allowed nothing to be hidden.

They walked to the hospital car park. It was dusk already. As she belted up and Zac drove off, she felt a weird sense of nothingness, as if she was incapable of further emotion. It was only when they approached the house that she felt a shudder pass down her spine into her fingertips. Her heart was a huge, useless lump, containing all of the anger dredged up from the depths of her system, where it had lain in silted-up tributaries. For so long, she had tried to bury her anger, to keep it within the bounds of reason, modifying it into an emotion acceptable to Zac, their children and the people around her. A blaze of fury had been channelled into tolerance and quiet resentment.

But no longer.

Zac pushed open the front door. Ashley stood on the drive looking up at their house and Tara's, beside it. Whoever had caused her daughter to attempt to take her own life would face the consequences, she knew with absolute certainty: someone would have to pay for what they had done.

Chapter 52
Elspeth
12 August

Elspeth tried to make herself get out of bed. She was due to go over to Ashley's in an hour; before then, she needed to shower and make herself presentable. But lying here under the cool smoothness of the cotton sheet, her head sinking into the pillow, felt so nice. Thoughts came and went, leaving a wash of contentment. Dozing was such an under-rated pleasure.

Come on, old girl.

She pulled off the sheet and swung herself into a sitting position, her feet resting on the floor. Getting out of bed was more difficult than it used to be, whether down to ageing, the weather or the after-effects of Covid – which had been surprisingly few, considering the force with which the illness had invaded her. The August air was too damp and too hot, making her skin soggy and her brain lethargic. She'd not yet re-started her morning workouts, and was always short of breath after climbing the stairs. With an effort, she pushed herself onto her feet.

Elspeth went outside and sat listening to sleepy tweets. Even the birds were affected by the weather. There were no other sounds – no children playing in gardens, no dogs barking.

What sort of mood would Ashley be in today? Since that

terrible incident with Layla, her friend had been different every time they'd met, veering from depressed and guilt-ridden to a grim cheeriness. Sometimes there were hints of something else, a side of Ashley she hadn't known before, something steely and resolved.

They sat in Ashley's kitchen while the coffee machine churned. The kitchen had more gadgets and equipment than Elspeth's and was far tidier, with things put away rather than assorted objects and plants cluttering every possible square inch. It was quite a bit cleaner too, she had to admit; the windows gleamed rather than reluctantly admitting light. Imperfect as it was, Elspeth felt a sudden appreciation for her own messy house. Life was short – who had time for all that sorting and cleaning?

'It's good to see you.' Ashley managed to smile, just. She looked as tired as she sounded and seemed indefinably older, or perhaps it was the lack of make-up. She hadn't made any effort with her appearance – just jeans and a T-shirt, no jewellery. Elspeth felt overdressed, though she'd dressed simply enough, in a raw silk top over long linen shorts.

'That's yours.' Ashley gestured to a mug on the worktop. 'Biscuit?'

Elspeth took a digestive from the packet and looked longingly at the garden. A smell of fresh cut grass wafted in through the open window. Although it was hot already, and Ashley would hate the thought of Tara overhearing their conversation, it would be lovely to chat among the scattering of late-blooming flowers.

'Do you want to stay inside?' she asked.

Ashley shrugged. 'I don't mind going outside. I'm beyond caring if she hears us.'

That's one good thing, Elspeth thought. Bollocks to the bizum next door.

They arranged themselves at the low table on the grass.

'How's Sam?' Elspeth asked. She hoped nothing else had happened to him since he was attacked.

'He's camping in north Wales.'

'With his Muslim friends?'

'No, two boys from his old school in north London. They used to be close.'

'That's good.'

'I hope he can rekindle some of his old friendships. He's seemed more like his old self the last few days, thank God.'

Elspeth crunched into her biscuit. 'How's it going with you and Zac?'

'It feels like we're both making an effort. But since Layla...' A deep sigh. Ashley stroked the curve of her mug. 'It's been a shock for us both. We already have issues we haven't dealt with. Now we're being forced to face them.' She met Elspeth's eyes. 'I really don't know if we're going to stay together.'

'Do you want to stay with him?'

'I still love him. Is that enough?'

Elspeth squeezed Ashley's hand.

'Things will work out for the best, I'm sure.'

She was aware of how inadequate this sounded. Marriage advice wasn't her forte, though. A relationship lasted as long as it lasted, in her view. She'd had plenty over the years, from passionate flings to sedate, companionable friendships, and everything in between. Never had she felt inclined to marry any of her partners. She hadn't wanted any of that patriarchal nonsense.

'How's Layla getting on at the hospital?' Ashley's daughter had been placed in a 'mental health unit' or some such thing, where they could keep an eye on her. It was temporary, Ashley had said.

'She's doing well. The routine is good for her, I think – she says it's a bit like being at school, but with all sorts of fun activities instead of lessons.'

'Really?'

'They have yoga, baking, gardening, plus group therapy, one-to-one counselling... Art therapy is her favourite – though possibly more the guy in charge, reading between the lines.'

'It must be hard, not seeing her.'

Ashley nodded, her gaze far away.

'It is. But I have to let go, trust that she's going to be OK. I can't stand guard over her twenty-four/seven.'

'No, you can't. And remember, you're not to blame for what happened.' *That cunt next door is*, Elspeth stopped herself from adding. 'We both know who is, though. I'd like to throttle that woman with my bare hands.' She glanced over to Tara's garden beyond the fence. There was no sign of her, though that meant nothing.

'No, that's too good for her.' Ashley's face broke into a huge smile. 'I'd prefer slow torture and an agonising death.' She picked up her mug and drank heartily.

Elspeth subsided into a fit of giggles. The prospect of Tara listening in had brought on a girlish excitement. By now, Tara's surveillance systems would be fully deployed. Ashley joined in with her full-bodied laugh, bigger than you'd think could come from such a small-framed woman.

'That's cheered me up,' Ashley said as her laughter abated, dabbing her eyes. 'Thank you.'

'There's nothing like a dose of laughter to make one feel better, is there?' Especially at your enemy's expense, Elspeth thought.

Ashley stood, picking up their mugs. 'Another cup?'

They went back indoors and talked more. Ashley carried out tasks in the kitchen, until Zac came in with half a dozen bulging shopping bags.

'You'll have to come to mine next time,' Elspeth said. 'We can have lunch – inside, if you like.'

'I'd love to.'

She didn't usually invite people inside her place, unless she'd known them for years. The house was always bursting at the seams with bits and bobs, from time immemorial. But she wasn't going to be bothered with that, any more.

'Oh, by the way.' Ashley angled her head towards next door. Her eyes held a peculiar intensity. 'That notebook she's always writing in. I've been wondering if we should try to get hold of it. See if she's been saying anything about us.'

'It would be interesting to have a look, sure. But how would we get it from her?' The thought of nosing around Tara's house filled her with alarm.

'I don't know. I'll have to think of a way.'

Ashley sounded resolute and somehow calmer, as if something in her had been restored.

Chapter 53
Tara

She could hear Ashley and Elspeth from here, though this time she wasn't even trying. Their voices were too quiet to make out more than occasional words. Tara yawned and turned onto her other side. The sun-lounger was comfortable and this heat was making her languid. She didn't want to stir from her doze, and there was no need to move from this spot; she was hidden from view by the overhanging curtain of Ashley's wayward honeysuckle.

Close by, a bee hummed with a queenly overtone. Ribbons of her dreams floated serenely past. Herself, suffused in a golden aura, high up on a stage behind a podium surrounded by rapt faces, a scarlet robe adorning her shoulders. At last, restored to the heart of the community...

The vision frayed, snagging on the real world. Something about Layla having therapy. Frustratingly, she couldn't make out the details. There was more of Elspeth's soppy, balm-over-troubled-waters voice, no doubt trying to soothe Ashley. Then Elspeth's tone changed.

'I'd like to throttle that woman with my bare hands.'

What?

306

Ashley's reply came clear as a bell.

'No, that's too good for her. I'd prefer slow torture and an agonising death.'

Tara jerked upright. This malice-filled ridicule sliced deeper than the sharpest knife. She pressed her hands over her ears to block out the laughter now erupting from the pair. Their mutual mirth, a wild cackling and bellowing, made her think of two hysterical cows. She was thrust back to childhood, to the days and nights in that house, exposed to her sisters' merciless teasing. She tried to imagine a calm blue sea, suffused with the smell of salt air and pines, as the therapist had suggested, to no avail. Laughter past and present merged, taunting her.

Oh, you silly, silly girl. What were you thinking? We don't want you – we never did.

Stifling her sobs, Tara took slow, deep breaths to calm herself. No one liked cry-babies, did they?

She went indoors, prepared a tall glass of strong mojito and carried it back to the sun-lounger. She picked up her journal. Now she knew what she had to do.

Ways to get rid of them

Fall from a high place (Railway bridge? Bridge over a fast section of the river?)

Fall in front of fast-moving traffic

Poisoning – separately with a decent interval between, to defuse suspicion? Or the two of them in one fell swoop?

Wolfsbane. While wolfsbane seems to be a most effective poison, getting hold of it without detection is a pain, as I found with dear Ivy.

Hemlock. Symptoms can be delayed up to three hours. Leaves resemble chervil, though the pee smell could be a problem. Chop up with other herbs, add ginger to disguise the taste, as in Waitrose's peppermint, nettle and ginger infusion? Or offer as a herbal tea with age-defying properties, great for skin and hair, rich in collagen/ab-sorbable amino acids or some such pseudo-scientific nonsense. Perfect for Elspeth! She spends a fortune on her herbal remedies.

<u>Death cap mushrooms</u>. Easy to find and you don't need much, less than half a cap. Small ones are easily mistaken for button mushrooms – maybe disguise with some shop mushrooms. But could either be enticed to eat mushrooms? I know – I could put the caps in the food processor and bake them into a cake. Ashley loves chocolate cake. She won't be able to resist a brownie with her afternoon tea

Her pencil paused less and less as ideas began to flow. Thinking about what she'd like to do to those two, in between sips of *mojito*, she started to feel better. There was nothing like journaling to free the mind, was there? It also purged emotional baggage and any misplaced foolishness. For a while – hard to believe now – she had actually felt bad about the girl's dramatic plunge over the balcony. She'd even wondered if she'd gone too far in her campaign against the family and if it had been a mistake getting that racist Islamophobe Rob involved.

Since the Khan girl had been taken away to hospital, the three Khans left had been unusually quiet, aside from periods of weeping and moaning in the middle of the night. Several times Tara had been on the verge of going over to express her sympathies to her neighbour but had stopped herself, knowing Ashley was likely to rebuff her.

Then yesterday morning, an opportunity had presented itself. Ashley was tidying up on the terrace on the other side of the fence, bending down to pick up small items from the gutter. Their eyes met for a moment. Instinctively Tara had rushed outside to her own terrace, despite being dressed only in an exercise bra and lycra shorts.

308

'I'm so sorry about what happened to Layla,' she'd called out, while Ashley stared as if Tara was a body in the morgue that had just got to its feet. 'It must be terrible—' She hadn't got halfway through her sentence when the woman hurtled indoors. That had hurt – rather more than she could have expected.

Tara put down her journal. A spot of mushroom hunting was in order; there was no time to waste. The nearest woods, by the lake, were a haven for mushrooms. Surely, among them she'd come across one or two death caps.

She put her mojito aside. All was quiet now, except for the faint buzzing of a bee about to be drowned.

Carefully, Tara unscrewed the jar, took out a teaspoonful of pale grey sludge and stirred it into the saucer of freshly warmed milk. She disposed of the teaspoon in a ziplock bag, re-sealed the jar and put it back in the fridge. Then she tossed in a few croutons and sprinkled nutmeg on top. What would tonight's visitor make of that?

She switched on the outside light and hurried into the back garden. A brownish lump was cautiously nosing around the border, beside the lavender. There wasn't much to see – why did people get so soppy about hedgehogs? She placed the saucer near the animal's snout. The thing promptly turned into a small, spiky bundle.

She tried to coax the creature.

'Here, hedgy-hog, don't be afraid. Here's a lovely drink for you.'

It didn't react.

Oh, balls! She curbed her impulse to give it a good kick. Maybe hedgehogs preferred to eat in the dark – or didn't they like to eat while being watched? Or had this one just eaten? If it was the same creature that kept sneaking through from the gap in Elspeth's fence, it had probably been copiously fed already. She went back inside, turned off the outside light and waited.

If the hedgehog actually drank her concoction, how long would be needed for the poison to kill it? An hour or two maybe? Although she'd read somewhere that squirrels and rabbits weren't affected by death cap mushrooms – perhaps hedgehogs weren't, either.

The information provided by her ancient *Encylopedia of Plants and Flowers* had been most helpful in deciding the best poison to use; there had been no need to take the risk of digging around the internet, activity that the police would no doubt attempt to discover should her plan come to fruition. Death cap mushrooms, aka *Amanita phalloides*, seemed perfect for her needs. The poison they contained, amatoxin, destroyed the liver and kidneys over several days. The first symptoms weren't supposed to appear for between six and twenty-four hours after ingestion, so by the time Ashley was vomiting copiously she would be mystified as to what had caused her malaise. Of course, by then all evidence of Tara's involvement would have long since vanished – meaning there'd be nothing except wagging tongues for the police to link her to the heinous crime.

All going well, within a few days her neighbour would be writhing in agony, wishing she was already dead. Unfortunately for Ashley, unlike the relatively kind state of paralysis induced by hemlock, victims of poisoning by death cap mushrooms remained conscious and in 'excruciating' pain until they fell into a coma and expired.

However, finding the right poison and a way to make the stuff palatable was one thing, and creating an opportunity to administer it was quite another. Even if she managed to create a suitably lethal concoction that could be slipped into brownie mix or a cup of herbal tea, there was no guarantee that the victim would be enticed to imbibe. And how was she going to get either Ashley or Elspeth to step inside her house again, let alone accept her hospitality? Her unconscious would have to find an answer, sooner or later.

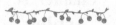

There it was, on the path, about eight feet from the saucer of milk – now a saucer minus milk. Only one soggy crouton remained.

Tara blinked at the scene. A whoosh of adrenalin swept through her. It hadn't even been an hour! She bent over the creature. It lay on its side, inert, paws curled up – dead, surely? She grabbed a stick and poked the quills to make sure. Then she returned to the kitchen, safely disposed of the body (wrapped within two Waitrose bags) in the non-recycle dustbin and drank a celebratory Prosecco.

Thank God, all those hours this afternoon scurrying around woodland, searching under trees for those supposedly common mushrooms, then risking life and limb to process the buggers hadn't been for nothing. A hedgehog had lapped up the poison without batting an eyelid – and so would Ashley!

Next task, to bake a small batch of poisoned brownies. A little death cap sludge among such a rich dark chocolate goo wasn't going to be noticeable, was it? It might add a little texture and flavour, even. Mary Berry would be impressed. Another, normal batch might be useful too – carefully labelled, of course. She'd put some by, to be ready in case an opportunity presented itself, and freeze the rest.

Tara turned on the TV and sat down to watch another episode of *Bake Off*.

Chapter 54
Ashley
13 August

The day began normally enough, or what had become normal since her son had got beaten up and her daughter had almost succeeded in killing herself. Layla's fall – or jump, Ashley believed to be more likely – had felt like a bomb going off inside her family.

There was still only the three of them, which felt wrong. Her daughter's absence made it easy to imagine what might have been, had Ashley not left that pile of ivy on the ground. But the staff of the mental health unit were pleased with Layla's response to treatment. All going well, the leader of her care team said, Layla would be home in another two weeks.

After a subdued breakfast of scrambled eggs and tomatoes – her husband had prepared it, for a change – Zac had left on a fishing trip with three of his angling friends. It was a three-hour drive from Brampton; he wouldn't be back until late that evening. Sam was still away camping. On the phone, he'd sounded excited about a planned expedition to a mountain lake. He'd told them he was giving up Islamic studies 'for a while'. She hoped this would mark the start of a new phase in his life.

The Bad Neighbour

'Call me when you get there,' Ashley said, as Zac took his gear to the car.

She was looking forward to a day at home, alone. There had been precious few opportunities to enjoy her own company since lockdown began. Also, being with her husband for long periods was often difficult. She and Zac were talking and laughing more, thankfully. Sometimes, though, she felt as if she was wading through a river thick with invisible weeds. The surge of hate towards her family, and the near-disaster that had beset their daughter, seemed ever present.

After a quick recce of the fridge and cupboards, Ashley set off for the High Street, her backpack snuggled under her arm. She wasn't a fan of shopping, especially the boring, everyday kind, but they had run out of fruit, green vegetables and – most importantly – chocolate.

The sky was still clear and there wasn't a breath of wind. Some leaves were yellowing already. But to her mind, the tints of orange, soft browns and gold in the trees only added to the beauty of the scene. It was the perfect day for a walk. She'd been walking more than ever lately, much further than normal. Somehow the physical action of moving her body from one place to another calmed her, allowing her to carry on.

From here, on the cul-de-sac at the top of the hill, you could see for miles, past the confines of Brampton into the surrounding countryside. Once again, she felt a sense of wonder, even though she must have walked this way hundreds of times. Objectively speaking, this was a fabulous place to live. But did she belong here? Would her family be better off somewhere else – back inside a city perhaps – away from the xenophobes and racists and all the other small-minded, small-town people? As she descended towards the main road into the village the view disappeared and she felt a familiar qualm. Since the assault on the family home, she preferred to walk on quiet footpaths and out-of-the way lanes, away from others. When someone she didn't know looked at her, she couldn't help wondering if they were one of those who wanted her and her family gone.

The High Street was busy. The Big Issue woman was installed outside Waitrose, a homeless man and his dog sat beside the cash machine, teens talked into invisible phones, women clung on to shopping or the arms of small children.

She went into the greengrocer. It wouldn't be as crowded as the supermarket.

'Hello, Ashley?'

The speaker was a tall, slim woman with sleek auburn hair standing just ahead of her, gathering satsumas into a paper bag. The voice was friendly, but Ashley didn't recognise the face.

'I'm so sorry.' The woman deposited the bag of satsumas into her shopping basket and gave an embarrassed smile. 'I'm Brie, my daughter is in the same class as yours at St Hilda's.'

She tried to place the woman. There weren't many other parents at Layla's sixth-form college that she had actually spoken to.

'We've never actually met, don't worry.' Brie tucked a strand of hair behind an ear and stepped closer to Ashley. 'I've heard you've been through the mill lately, with your daughter and... everything else.'

Ashley felt herself staring at a large freckle on Brie's chin. Was this how celebrities felt when people who they'd never met came up to them and talked as though they were friends?

'I just wanted to say,' Brie continued, 'I hope things get better for you and your family. There are plenty of people in this village who are on your side, you know.'

She nodded, still stupidly tongue-tied.

'Well, I won't keep you.'

'Thank you, that's...'

'Have a lovely day.' Brie smiled broadly before raising her arm with a final flourish and disappearing into the next aisle.

Ashley pondered the fruit display. So many to choose from.

Apple, kiwi, passionfruit... After far too long she approached the till with a bunch of bananas, four large figs to bake for Zac, a bottle of apple juice and a bar of raspberry-flavoured dark chocolate. Of course, Brie had only been trying to be kind. But the encounter had unsettled her.

Outside, a dog raised a leg and peed against a parking meter.

'Hello, Ashley. Is that you?' The voice, with its precise enunciation and accent verging on plummy, sounded like Ursula's.

A woman in a blue facemask emerged from the shade of a slender tree, marooned on a rectangular island in the pavement. It *was* Ursula, she saw with a cascade of relief. One lens of her glasses was smudged. A bright orange shopping bag hung from each shoulder.

'Are you all right, dear? You look a bit pale.'

'I'm OK,' Ashley lied. 'It's good to see you.'

It was, surprisingly so. Ursula removed her facemask and lowered her shopping to the pavement.

'How have you been keeping?'

'It's been...' Awful? Unimaginable?

'John told me about Layla – he told us all. I'm so sorry, Ashley.'

She nodded. Since Layla's admission to hospital everyone in the group had sent her supportive emails, wishing her and her family well and offering practical help, should it be needed. She had been touched by their concern.

'It must be a nightmare,' Ursula went on, 'having to deal with all this, on top of the situation with Tara.'

'I'm over the worst, fingers crossed.' Was she? She didn't have a clue, not really.

Ursula glanced around, lowering her voice.

'You know, I feel that, in a way, we're all partly responsible. Brampton, I mean. Many of us had our suspicions about Tara – but we didn't do anything.' Ursula raised her eyebrows pointedly. 'It *was* her, wasn't it? She started the rumours about your children – everyone in the village is saying it now.' Before Ashley could reply, Ursula glanced at her watch. 'Sorry, I've just remembered. I've got a singing lesson coming up, I have to be going.'

'See you, Ursula.'

Ashley set off along the high street. She longed to be alone, and anywhere but here. No one had tried to stop this hatred that had been festering, poked and prodded at until it had risen up and engulfed her family. But nearly everyone in the village, so it seemed, believed Tara to be responsible.

The day was getting hot and humid. Instead of taking the direct route home, she found herself continuing past the Quaker meeting house then turning off towards the lake. As she walked, her mind became a stew of restless, half formed thoughts. Then one emerged, stark and complete. Was Brampton going to let Tara get away with what she'd done? She thought again of how Tara had tried to speak to Ashley the other day and offer her sympathy. After the horrible things Tara had said... How could anyone be such a hypocrite? It was mystifying.

The lake glistened under a now partly cloudy sky, a blue-and-grey-flecked oval like a bird's egg. Ashley emerged from the woods at the water's edge. About ten metres away, a woman sat on the bench holding a small bag, a large floppy hat hiding her face and the long sleeves of her blouse hiding her arms. She was hefty in build and tall – Bird Woman. Around her neck hung a pair of binoculars. She was crunching on something.

Bird Woman studied her with a slightly disarming frankness. The woman had a tooth missing on the top row and an earthy smell. But the skin on her face was smooth and unblemished, and her eyes tanzanite blue.

'There's room for two, despite my large bottom.' Bird Woman moved herself along the seat.

Ashley removed her backpack and perched on the end of the bench, though she had been intending to walk on.

'Thanks, I might sit down for a minute. I could do with a rest before going up the hill.'

'It's going to be another hot day. Best not to over-extend oneself.' The woman held the small bag towards Ashley. 'Have some nuts. They're very good.'

'Thank you.' She scooped a few peanuts from the bag and put them in her mouth.

She watched a line of young Egyptian geese cross the lake. No one else was about. It was such a tranquil scene, far removed from the human turmoil surrounding her. She let out a long breath.

'I've seen you before,' Bird Woman said abruptly. 'You live up at the top of the cul-de-sac, don't you? Next door but one to the dancing lady.'

'That's right. I've seen you, too. You often sit on the bench on the green.'

'It's a good spot for watching the birds – people, too.'

'I'm sure.' She wondered what the woman's name was, feeling bad for not knowing. 'I'm Ashley, by the way.' Awkwardly, she held out her hand. Although Covid had deterred handshaking in general, it seemed the appropriate thing do.

'Clare. Pleased to meet you.' The woman took her hand firmly.

A young Egyptian goose climbed onto the bank from the water. Clare leaned forward, watching intently as a larger Canada goose approached, full of bluster.

'Do you like it here?' Clare had turned to Ashley.

Living in Brampton, presumably. Did she?

'There are some things I like very much,' she replied, 'and some things I don't like at all.'

'Same here. I often wish all the people would just disappear and leave this place to me and the birds.'

Ashley laughed, surprised yet delighted that someone would say such a thing. Just now, she agreed wholeheartedly with the sentiment. Except for her family and Elspeth, of course.

'They don't seem to like me much. I'm too different, I suppose.' Clare's voice was wistful, a touch defiant.

'I like you.' She met Clare's eyes, alive with light and sky and water. 'People here don't like me much, either. Some think I don't belong here. But I'm not going to let it worry me, any more.'

'You're a wise woman.' Clare scrunched up the empty nut bag and gulped from a plastic bottle labelled 'apple juice', then turned back to the lake. Ashley got to her feet.

'It was good to talk to you, Clare.'

Going next door to see what I can find out, she texted Elspeth when she'd put away the shopping.

Be careful! Elspeth texted back. She's dangerous.

Deciding not to reply, Ashley slipped her phone into her bag and set off. What she might find out, she wasn't sure. Tara might decide to tell her the truth, or maybe Ashley would find the truth in the notebook Tara was always writing in. Somehow, she had to find out what Tara had done, or not done, even though she was afraid of Tara. Her fear wasn't eased by Elspeth's conviction – and her own increasing one, it had to be said – that Tara had murdered both her sisters and quite possibly her mother, too.

She pushed the doorbell.

Eventually, Tara appeared in the doorway – fully dressed this time, in jeans, a puffed-sleeve top and flip-flops. The clothes and minimal make-up gave her a girlish air.

'Ashley.' Tara's eyes widened. 'Is something wrong? I didn't expect to see you, after the other day.' Tara's face looked on the red side, as if she'd been lying too long in the sun or drinking excessively, or perhaps both.

'Nothing's wrong.' She girded herself. 'I'm sorry about that,

Tara. I was... insensitive. You were being neighbourly and I brushed you off.'

'Don't worry, that's water under the bridge.' Tara gave a strangled-sounding laugh. 'Do you want to come in?'

Ashley paused for longer than she intended. 'No' would have been the right answer. No, she had no desire whatsoever to step over the threshold and spend time in the company of this hypocritical, manipulative narcissist. But she had a mission to accomplish.

'Thanks, that would be lovely.' With feigned lightness, she followed Tara through to the kitchen area, ignoring the uncomfortable beating of her heart.

'Take a seat.' Tara gestured at the island worktop, surrounded by stools. 'Sorry, the place isn't tidy. I'll put the kettle on... unless you'd prefer something stronger?' Something played on Tara's face – a dark, unreadable expression.

'Tea's fine, thanks.' She needed her wits about her.

'I must say, I didn't expect to see you here again. But now you're here – well, it's good to see you.' Tara sounded genuine, also oddly excited. Ashley could sense waves of relief coming off the woman. Had Tara been lonely? Or was something else going on? 'You're in luck,' Tara gushed. 'I've just made a batch of brownies... I'll get us some. I know you can't resist them.'

Before she could answer, Tara busied herself removing cling-film-covered plates from the fridge. Ashley slipped away to scan the living area. Assorted objects lay on various chairs and surfaces: a pair of neoprene hand weights, a Pilates band, a large unwashed wine glass, a paperback, a pair of shorts with a sewing needle stuck into the pocket, thread dangling... No sign of any notebook. She wasn't sure now what it looked like. A5-ish? A pinkish or orange sheen on the cover, maybe.

Without warning, Tara approached holding a tray. On it was a teapot and matching jug of milk, two cups, two side plates and a plate bearing four brownies.

'Let's go outside, shall we?' Tara opened the French doors that gave onto the back garden, set everything out on a table underneath an open sunshade and pulled up another chair. When Ashley sat down, Tara held out the plate of brownies. 'Go on, take one.'

Obediently she lifted a brown cube, one of two closest to her, and placed it on her plate. Unusually, she didn't feel like eating anything containing chocolate. Tara plucked up one of the other two brownies and took a large bite.

'Not bad, if I do say so myself.'

Ashley took a sip of tea. The air was getting more humid as the afternoon progressed; it would be uncomfortable, soon. She was glad of her shorts and short-sleeved top, which she'd changed into after returning from the lake. Her muscles had tensed and her heart banged in her chest. She rubbed perspiration off the back of her neck, trying to appear relaxed.

The conversation had wilted. Tara had finished her cup and was observing her intently, along with Ashley's untouched brownie. Ashley shifted in her chair. Something wasn't right.

'Are you having someone over?' she asked. 'I mean, did you make these for a reason?'

Tara began to cough, taking several seconds to regain her composure.

'My nephew is coming over tomorrow.'

'Your nephew? I didn't know you had one. Didn't your sisters both die years ago?'

A scowl crossed Tara's face and a terse tone entered her voice.

'Not a nephew exactly. A cousin once removed, on my father's side. He's younger than me so I think of him as a nephew.'

'Right.' She didn't believe Tara, but no matter. 'Why do you never talk about your sisters?'

'I do talk about them.' Tara held her gaze. 'I remember mentioning them to you before. And to Elspeth.'

Ashley glanced at the flowerbeds, noting three roses climbing the trellis of the border alongside Elspeth's fence. Nearby, a sun-lounger and an occasional table bearing a cocktail glass with a slice of lime wedged onto the rim, and... the notebook! It lay opened, cover up, on the grass beside the sun-lounger. Her adrenalin surged.

Tara, still watching her, took another bite of brownie. Ashley looked down at the one on her own plate and sighed. It would be rude not to eat it... She picked up the brownie and took a bite. The cake tasted moist on her tongue, the perfect mixture of crumbliness and silkiness.

That moment, her phone buzzed. Chewing, she pulled the device to the top of her bag without letting Tara see, and read the messages on the screen. Both were from Elspeth. The first had been sent twenty minutes ago.

What are you doing over there? You've been gone ages. Are you all right?

Then another:

DON'T EAT OR DRINK ANYTHING! she might put something in your tea!!!

Ashley let go of her phone and spat out the piece of brownie. 'What is it?'

'Something went down the wrong way, that's all.' She retrieved the phone from beside her foot, her heart pounding. That had been a close shave. Thank God, she'd not swallowed any of that brownie. She'd already drunk nearly half of her cup of tea, though. If Tara had put anything in it... No, no, she couldn't have – the tea had been poured from a pot.

Tara gave her a reproachful look.

'There's nothing wrong with it, you know. Do you think I'd try to poison you?' Contempt threaded her voice.

Ashley stared at the bitten-into brownie on her plate. A chill went through her. What might Tara have put inside it? Why had Ashley been foolish enough to risk visiting and accepting her hospitality? She had to get away from Tara, somewhere safe... But she couldn't leave yet. She had to wait a little longer and keep on pretending everything was OK, until she had a chance to grab the notebook.

'Aren't you going to eat any?'

Tara's voice was sharp, as if Ashley was a naughty child.

'I'm sorry. It must be the heat. I've lost my appetite.'

'Poor you.' Her neighbour seemed unconcerned. 'I shouldn't blow my own trumpet, but these really are delicious.' Tara popped the remains of her own brownie into her mouth.

Ashley tried not to laugh. This situation would be ridiculous, if it wasn't so fraught. Surely, Tara hadn't resorted to poisoning the brownies? Or the two brownies that she'd arranged on the plate for Ashley to take, perhaps... It was crazy, wasn't it?

She wiped her brow. Tara would have to get up for something soon, surely.

'Back in a mo.' Finally, Tara got to her feet.

She waited for Tara to disappear inside the house then tipped the remains of her tea onto the grass. Then she hurried to the border, dropped her brownie beside a rose and trod it into the soil with her trainer. Fortunately, the brownie's dark brown shade almost matched the soil. Once she'd ground the brownie into invisibility, she hurried to the sun-lounger, scooped up the notebook and thrust it into her bag. She hurried back to the table and chairs, pretending to be admiring the roses in the border. From the corner of her eye, she saw Tara standing at the French doors, a watchful expression on her face.

Her heart pounded furiously, as if having one final burst before it expired. Had Tara seen her destroy the brownie?

'I'd better go, Tara,' she said as her neighbour approached.

'I've a few things to do and I'm feeling a bit... frazzled. Thanks for your hospitality.'

Tara's lips stretched in a weird impression of a smile.

'Oh, don't mention it. Pop over again soon, won't you? And I hope you feel better soon.'

Safely at home, Ashley retrieved her phone from her bag. A stream of texts from Elspeth.

Have you found the notebook yet?

Are you back home? Please call I'm worried

She tapped the disk containing Elspeth's face.

'I got it! The notebook.'

'You took your time. Are you all right? I nearly called but I didn't want to interrupt anything.'

'I felt a little off, before... But it was probably the stress of being with Tara for so long, not the tea I drank.'

'You drank her tea?'

'Half a cup, that's all—'

'Oh my God, Ashley! She could have put something inside it.'

'No, she poured the tea from a pot – and she drank all of her cup. I'd just taken a bite of her home-made brownie when I saw your text. I spat it out before I'd swallowed. So I won't come to any harm, not unless she put polonium in them.'

'Don't joke, we've no idea what that woman might be capable of. If she killed both her sisters... So, what does the notebook say?'

'I haven't looked at it yet, give me a chance. I'll call you when I've gone through it.'

'Don't be too long. She might realise you've taken it and come over to get it back.'

'I won't answer the door, don't worry.'

Ashley ended the call and settled on the sofa with the notebook. She flipped through the pages. Roughly two thirds had been written on. It was obviously a journal of sorts. Most entries were short, underneath the day or date or some other heading. The words, in pencil, were laid heavily onto the lined paper, not terribly neat but legible. Doodles and human figures adorned the margins.

She started reading. The entries were about Tara's daily life and her efforts to become someone of note. Later entries mentioned her grievances with Ashley, Elspeth and members of the support group. After many gasps of disbelief, indignant huffs and some stronger language, she started giggling and phoned Elspeth.

'Are you ready for the first installment of Tara's journal? This is priceless. There's a lot about you in this thing, I think you're entitled to know what she's written.'

'Hold on, let me get my tea... Right, I'm ready.'

'You'll like this one.' Ashley started to read the entry aloud.

'Ashley next door has come to my attention lately. She recently moved to the area, has no local friends and obv wants to be part of the local community. Trying hard to be friendly to her. She's a bit shabby looking and could do with more regular trips to the hairdresser. She likes her food too – she wolfed down several brownies at the afternoon tea I put on to welcome TAF.'

Ashley paused. 'I've no idea what TAF is. It's in caps.'

She read on 'The husband is well off, a fund manager who invests in businesses. Quite fit, tbh. I wonder if he might want to invest in my PR business. That could use a shot in the arm.'

'Bloody hell, what a bitch!' Elspeth put on an exaggerated version of Tara's carefully honed upper-crust voice. '*She's a bit shabby looking and could do with more regular trips to the hair-*

dresser... I'm wiping away my tears. I haven't heard anything so funny for ages.'

'She has a way with words, that's for sure.'

'But she mentions you liking her brownies – and today she baked some for you. That could mean...' Elspeth trailed off.

'I know.' She shivered, imagining again what Tara might have done to that brownie.

'You're not feeling any ill effects from this afternoon?'

'I'm a bit shaky, that's all. It's probably just stress.'

'You don't have any symptoms of poisoning? Headache, blurry vision, stomach pains, nausea? I looked it up on the computer.'

'No, nothing like that. Isn't it too early to get symptoms?'

'It depends on the poison. Some act faster than others.'

They fell silent.

'What's TAF, do you think?' Elspeth asked.

'The Asian Family?'

'Oh, how rude! What a bizum she is.' She pictured Elspeth leaning forward, hands on thighs. 'Making out she was your friend when she really wanted to get her hands on your husband's money – and his you-know-what!' Smothered laugher down the line. '*Quite fit*, indeed.'

'I know.' Long ago, she'd guessed that Tara would have an ulterior motive for practically everything she did.

Ashley turned the pages. 'Ah, here's something about you.'

She read out an entry concerning the rose-stealing incident, after Tara described how she had taken a rose plant home.

They were too beautiful to all go to E. Anyway, I deserve some reward for my efforts.

In a later entry, Tara's fury was apparent.

That old crone has accused me of stealing from her!

325

'Oh no, can you believe it?' Elspeth's voice came shrilly down the line. She sounded livid. 'She's so cross with me for daring to suggest that she might have walked off with my sodding rose – but just before, she admits to taking it.'

'It's like there's two of her.'

'That's it! There's two people in one body – outraged cow and cunning vixen.'

'And hard-done-by victim, don't forget.' Ashley flipped through further pages. 'Ah, here's another one about you.' She read the entry aloud.

am
———
Feeling like shit. What a bitch this virus is.

pm
———
Went over to have it out with E, who was supposed to be napping. No answer, which seemed suspicious, so I used my keys to get in. Went upstairs but her bed empty – then saw her with A, eating cake in A's garden!!!

Could not believe my eyes. I wanted to go next door and choke the pair of them. Sense intervened. Unfortunately, my distress at E's betrayal must have triggered a fit of coughing when I returned to the kitchen.

'Unbelievable!' Elspeth's voice boomed into Ashley's ear. 'She lets herself into my house for no good reason then she gives me her vile illness. How could anyone do that? What a git she is! What an insufferable... trollop!'

The last words were delivered so loudly, Ashley had to move the phone away from her ear. Never before had she so heard Elspeth so angry.

'Does she say anything about trying to poison you?'

'I don't know, I'm looking now. Oh, here's something.' She had started reading another, more recent entry, which was unusually explicit.

'Ashley! Read it out, will you? Don't leave me in suspense.'

'It starts off *Ways to get rid of them*.'

'Oh, my giddy aunt.'

'Then there's a long list of things... *Poisoning*.' Ashley turned the page. She took a sharp in-breath. '*While wolfsbane seems to be a most effective poison, getting hold of it is a pain, as I found with dear Ivy*.'

'Ivy? Who's she?'

'A sister?'

'No, there were only two, Evie and Zoe. Ivy must be her mother.'

'You're right. I remember seeing her name in that news report.' Elspeth's voice lowered. 'If she killed her mother too, that would make her a serial killer.'

Ashley read on.

Death cap mushrooms. Easy to find and you don't need much, less than half a cap ... Ashley loves chocolate cake. She won't be able to resist a chocolate brownie...

What? A shudder went through her.

'I think Tara really did poison the brownies she offered me,' she said. 'With death cap mushrooms.'

'Oh my God, Ashley! I'll call an ambulance – and the police.'

'No, not yet. I want to read the rest of this.'

'What if you get ill?'

'I'll be OK, Elspeth. I told you, I didn't swallow any of the brownie.'

'If you're sure.' Elspeth sounded doubtful. 'They could pump your stomach, just in case. And I really don't think you should be on your own reading that poisonous diatribe. No pun intended.'

'Don't worry. I'll call you later.'

She drank two glasses of water and swirled mouthwash around her mouth before checking her phone. There was a text from Zac saying he had found a brilliant fishing spot and he hoped she was enjoying her day, whatever she was up to.

Guilt settled inside her. What would he say if he knew what that was? Her thoughts rushed on. More urgently, what if Tara realised the notebook was missing and came to the house, suspecting Ashley had taken it? Tara would be upset, to say the least, that her private thoughts about her neighbours were being read – including a description of how she'd planned to kill the two of them...

She would go over to John's – she'd be safe there. But first, she had to find out if there was anything in here about Layla or Sam. She flicked back through the pages, scanning the words carefully. An entry from July caught her eye.

Just as it was getting dark I spotted the Asian girl from next door sitting on the green with her friend and a strapping young chap. Mr Muscles started kissing the friend then disappeared behind a tree. A few minutes later so did L. One wonders what the three of them might have been doing. How brazen young people are these days, no respect for community values. I bet everyone in the Wiltons would love to know what Little Miss gets up to when she's not pretending to be a good Muslim girl.

Ashley put the notebook down. She felt queasy suddenly, not from any poison except that in Tara's words. She'd begun to suspect the sort of things that Tara might have written and how unpleasant they might be, yet couldn't quite believe that the woman could have written something so vile. She steeled herself to read more. So, the woman had crouched behind a shed in the allotments to eavesdrop on Sam and his friends. It was there, in black and white... She turned the page. Desperate as she was to have a break from the notebook, she was equally desperate to know what else was inside.

Met with Brampton's Nigel Farage in The Anglers again then we had another chat on the phone. His eyes practically came out on stalks when I mentioned the scene in the allotment. They will be on TAF's case, he promised. Not just Ashley and her lot, but all the other 'undesirables'. Trust me, we'll leave no stone unturned to get the roaches out, he said.

Very nice to be out and about showing my face again, tbh. Tara has risen from the ashes!! The wig went down well too.

It all made sense now. Tara was behind the campaign to try to drive her family from this village. She had come up with the stories about Sam and Layla then paraded them in front of a man she knew would respond to them as she wished. Tara was the reason that Layla had tried to kill herself.

Ashley pulled on her trainers and placed the notebook inside her backpack.

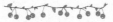

'Sorry to descend on you without notice,' she said, as John scooted towards her. 'But I had to see you urgently.' She took out the notebook and placed it on the table. 'It's Tara's journal.'

'You took it from her?'

'I needed to know the truth.' She pulled out a chair. 'It's all in there. How she deliberately tried to infect Elspeth with Covid and what she did to my family. How she hounded my children and spread her vile stories around to everyone who would listen.'

John looked at her, slowly shaking his head.

'I'm sorry, Ashley.' He reached over and touched the top of her hand. 'I'm here for you. We all are.'

'Thank you.' She swallowed to relieve the tightness in her throat.

'I'll call the others.'

She leaned over the table with her eyes shut while John phoned Greg, Ursula and Ferne in turn. There was an urgent situation involving Tara, he said, could they come quickly. She jolted at the ring of her phone – Elspeth.

'Where are you? Tara just turned up at my front door! She asked about her notebook, where it's gone and where you were. I said I had no idea about either and told her to piss off.'

'Thanks for fending her off. Sorry, I forgot to call you. I'm at John's, a few minutes down the road.'

'Are you all right?'

'I'm fine. A bit shaky, that's all.' Hopefully with just shock and anxiety, not something sinister.

Within minutes, Greg, Ferne and Ursula had arrived. They crowded around the opened notebook as though it was an oracle.

'Oh no! You have to read this, guys.' Ferne placed a finger on the page. 'It's classic Tara.'

'I can't read that writing,' Greg said. He wore shorts and a loose, paint-stained T-shirt. 'Even with my glasses on.'

'Here, let me.' Ursula picked up the notebook and read aloud. 'I know what they're doing. The group is trying to undermine me. Ferne still resents me for an imagined slight years ago. Ursula pretends to keep me on side but looks down her nose at me because I don't like classical music. Greg goes along with anything as long as it'll make him popular. John misses his glory days as head of academy and can't wait to take over...' She looked up. 'The woman spares no one, does she? For the record, I couldn't give a damn what music she likes.'

'Also, for the record, I was never a headteacher nor did I teach at an academy.'

'There's more.' Ursula turned the pages. 'John trying to take over as usual. He was insufferable today. Bit my tongue but sorely tempted to shove him and his damned chair into the bushes...'

'And I'm sorely tempted to go over there and ram that book into that woman's insufferable mouth!' John's face had darkened to a reddish purple. 'How dare she?'

Ursula continued as if mesmerised.

'This one looks like it's about our last meeting... Got the heave ho today. In a state of shock, can hardly find words. Frugal Ferne burst into the Zoom—'

'Frugal Ferne!' squealed Ferne, wiping her hands on her leggings.

'—talking over me, burbling like some souped-up Bette Davis that she'd seen me secretly selling off goods from the stall. The others gave her the floor, lapping it all up. They were all totally on her side. They voted me out, it was humiliating. I've never been treated like that in my life.'

Greg blinked, meeting the eyes of the others.

'Jeez, that takes the biscuit.'

John looked at Ashley. 'Are you all right?'

'You're looking pale, dear.' Ursula pursed her lips.

'I think Tara tried to poison me this afternoon,' she replied.

Ursula stared, her mouth an 'O'.

'What?' John sat upright abruptly, his elbow sending his mug crashing to the floor.

'I went over to Tara's a few hours ago to look for her notebook. She offered me a brownie... I didn't eat any, don't worry.' She gestured to the notebook. 'It's in there. There's a list of ways she could kill me and Elspeth – one is poisoning.'

'Show me.'

She found the entry for him. He read in silence. The only sounds were of their breathing and the ticking clock.

'I'm calling 999 right now,' John said in a grim voice, looking up. 'We need the police to deal with this.'

'Not yet.' Her reply was equally firm. 'I'm going over to speak to Tara.'

'Wait.' John's brow puckered. He laid his hand on her forearm. 'You can't go there by yourself, it's too dangerous.'

She pushed her chair back. Her body seemed to be responding not to her own will, but to some external force – her anger, perhaps, finally set free.

'Is anyone coming with me?'

Chapter 55
Tara

S he closed the front door, hurried into the garden and examined Ashley's plate. It was empty except for a sprinkling of dark brown crumbs. Ashley had eaten the brownie, after all!

Remorse momentarily dampened her excitement, swiftly followed by a stab of fear. The police mustn't find out it was Tara who'd poisoned Ashley. They might find out that Ashley had been to visit, and get suspicious... No doubt there was some kind of high-tech forensic analysis that would detect traces of poison.

Tara placed the plate in a washing-up bowl of hot water liberally dosed with bleach, scrubbed it for a few minutes with a scouring pad then loaded the plate into the dishwasher, programmed for a full wash, as she had already cleaned the utensils and kitchenware that she had used to process the death cap mushrooms and concoct the brownies. Her kitchen would be rid of any last remaining death cap molecules. She was safe, now.

Tara sat down on the sofa, fingers and feet tapping restlessly. There was something she'd forgotten... Her journal – where was it?

She ran into the garden. Inexplicably, the notebook was no

longer under the sun-lounger. She stared at the empty space underneath. She could have sworn...

With a sickening lurch in her gut, she knew what had happened. Ashley had taken it. The calculating bitch had found it – that was why she'd come here, not to apologise and make up. She would be devouring it, this very second!!

Her mind rushed ahead. Was there anything that could be incriminating inside the notebook? She'd been so careful for so long, just in case someone got their hands on it. But she'd slipped up here and there. People might imagine that Tara had tried to harm Ashley and her family. And what about her observations of Layla and Jihadi John, and her chats with Rob? The page with its stark heading *Ways to get rid of them* appeared in her mind's eye. Those two laughing at her had made her drop her guard. She had let out too much.

Shitty, shitty shit! How would she be able to explain what she'd written? What if Ashley took the notebook to the police before she expired? What if Elspeth found Ashley dead, sprawled over Tara's words? This wasn't part of the plan.

She collapsed into the sun-lounger. What the hell was she going to do now? Sweat beaded on her brow and upper lip. Shadows lengthened across the lawn and birds tittered with *schadenfreude*.

Chapter 56
Ashley

Tara held the door open, blinking at Ashley, her mouth in a tight line.

'Where's my journal? I know you took it.'

Her eyelids looked puffy and red. Had she been crying? A loose cardigan was draped over a puffed-sleeve top.

'I need to talk to you,' Ashley said. John and Elspeth stepped forward, in line with her. A beat later, Ursula, Greg and Ferne appeared at her other side.

Noticing the others, Tara's eyes widened.

'What are you lot doing here?'

'We're here to support our friend.' John's voice trembled with anger.

'If you've hurt Ashley...' Elspeth sounded fierce, tigerish.

'Excuse me?' Tara squinted at Elspeth then Ferne, her face a picture of puzzlement. 'Why would I want to hurt Ashley?'

Elspeth rolled her eyes. 'Do I need really to tell you?'

'Aren't you going to let us in?' Greg said, half smiling, his voice steely below the amicable veneer.

'If she gives me back my journal,' came the petulant reply.

'For heaven's sake.' Ursula moved into Tara's face. 'Can we come inside? I'm not standing out here all evening.'

Scowling, Tara stood aside to let them enter, closed the door then flip-flopped ahead into the kitchen and stood with her back to the sink. They followed her, forming a loose clump around the island breakfast bar. Tara didn't invite them to sit.

Ashley glanced around. The kitchen was neater than when she'd visited earlier, and cleaner. An odour of lemony bleach lingered. Through the tilted blinds covering the window she could see the cul-de-sac and the green. Light was slowly draining from the sky. No one was about, as far as she could see.

'So.' Tara glared at Ashley, thrusting out her lower lip. 'What did you want to say to me?'

Ashley's body tensed. She heard the rushing of her blood through her veins and arteries, sensed the frantic squeezing of her heart.

'I know it was you, Tara,' she said.

'What are you talking about?' Puzzlement suffused Tara's face.

'I know it was you who started the rumours about my children. That my daughter is a slut and my son is a Muslim fanatic who's trying to build a mosque in the centre of Brampton. Admit it. You intimidated my family and tried to drive us out of our home.'

'I did no such thing, love.' Tara's mouth twisted. She tapped her forehead. 'You've been out in the sun too long.'

'I also know that you killed your sisters.'

Tara closed her eyes, then moments later, re-opened them. 'You've totally lost the plot.'

'Elspeth and I read the articles in the local paper. Your sisters Zoe and Evie died within six months of each other. You were jealous of them, weren't you? They laughed at you and you couldn't handle it. So you killed them and made their deaths look like accidents.'

'That's utterly preposterous. This is slander!'

'And a few years later you killed your own mother. Ivy. Did you want her out of the way so you could get your hands on her money?'

Tara's gaze shifted from Ashley to John and the others, assembled around the island. Her eyes were wide. Everyone stood rock still, watching her.

'Then you tried to kill me and Elspeth,' Ashley continued. She had no fear of this woman now. 'You were jealous of our friendship, weren't you? We reminded you of your sisters. You passed your Covid on to Elspeth, deliberately, landing Elspeth in hospital, fighting for her life. When that didn't work, you decided to finish us both off. This afternoon you tried to kill me with poisoned brownies—'

'She's gone crazy. Don't listen to her!' Tara's pupils were huge in her irises, now dilated with fear.

Ashley stepped closer to her adversary.

'I have proof. Right here, in your own words.' She took out the notebook from her backpack. Tara's face had blanched, she noted with satisfaction. 'Where do you want me to start?'

Tara didn't respond.

'Here we go. Does this sound familiar? Ways to get rid of them... Fall from a high place. Fall in front of fast-moving traffic... Poisoning is number 3 on your list.'

A moan escaped from Tara. Ashley glanced at the others. Their expressions showed varying degrees of shock and horror.

'You list some poisons you might use. Wolfsbane – good, you say, but difficult to find. While wolfsbane seems to be a most effective poison, getting hold of it is a pain, as I found with dear Ivy. Hemlock – you could add ginger to disguise the taste and offer it as a herbal tea with age-defying properties... Perfect for Elspeth!'

'Oh my God. Tara, you're a witch! How could you?' Ferne looked stricken. She received no reply.

'There's more,' Ashley said. 'Death cap mushrooms. Easy to find, and you don't need much, less than half a cap.' She looked up; her hands were starting to shake. John sat on his scooter with his back rigid, his face grim. Ferne was running her fingers repeatedly through the length of her hair. Both Ursula and Greg stood motionless. Elspeth, behind the pair, stood in her floaty green top over turquoise trousers, a hand covering her mouth, her gaze fixed on Ashley. 'You wonder how someone could be enticed to eat them – bake them into a cake? Ashley likes chocolate cake...' Her voice shook. 'She won't be able to resist a chocolate brownie with her afternoon tea.'

Something inside her seemed to give way, unleashing fury. She ripped out the page she had read out from the notebook, then several more pages, screwed them into a ball of paper and tossed it at Tara, who ducked and backed towards the fridge.

Ashley looked to the island behind. A large glass bowl sat on top of the worktop near John, crammed with fruit. She picked up a plum. Its mottled mauve flesh dented under her fingers as she tightened her grip and took aim. The fruit made a small thud as it made contact with Tara's breastbone. Then it slithered an inch or two down her cleavage and dropped to the floor.

Greg smiled, reached into the bowl and picked out an orange. He tossed the fruit at Tara. It made contact with her right shoulder.

'Fuck off and leave me alone!' Tara rubbed her shoulder, her eyes wet and face twisted in pain. She had the look of a wounded, trapped animal.

'Good shot!' Ursula clapped and turned to the fruit bowl.

'Stop, this is madness!' Tara's hands juddered about in front of her body. Her eyes wild. 'Please, Ashley. Stop them.'

She had no desire to stop this; the phrase *Just desserts* came to mind. Ashley glanced through the half-open blinds. There was someone standing on the pavement on the far side of the road. It was nearly dark; she couldn't see the features clearly. The sturdy frame and the slight hunch of the shoulders were familiar, though... Whoever it was, they were looking straight into Tara's kitchen.

'Ashley, please. I beg you!'

She turned her attention back to the scene inside the kitchen. With a loud squelch, another plum landed on Tara's body, this time on her neck. Tara yelped, shut her eyes and began to talk in a loud, hysterical voice, her eyes fixed on Ashley.

'You're right, I did kill my sisters! I was only a child, I didn't know what I was doing. And my mother – she was in pain and losing her memory. She was dying anyway, I just hastened things. I did it to be kind—'

'What about Ashley?' John's face had gone the colour of the plum in his hand. 'Did you poison her to be kind?'

'I didn't poison her, I swear.'

'Liar!' Elspeth pushed between Ferne and Ursula to get to the fruit bowl. She held up a large tomato. 'If it was anyone else, I'd have some sympathy for them right now. But not you. Take that, bizum!'

The tomato landed on Tara's cheek, depositing a sticky red mess.

'You... ungrateful shrew!' Tara wiped her face with her hands, glaring at Elspeth. 'After all I did for you. Yes, it was me who gave you Covid. I should have finished you off properly!'

Elspeth gasped. Tara turned to Ashley.

'And you... I'm afraid you haven't got long left, lovely. There was enough poison in the brownie you ate to kill a herd of cows.' Tara's face contorted into a smile. 'Your end won't be pleasant. Apparently poisoning from death cap mushrooms is one of the worst ways to go.'

'Bitch.' Ferne reached into the bowl. Tara shielded her face with her forearms. With a grunt Ferne propelled a grapefruit through the air, which hit her target in the stomach. Tara belched and fell onto her hands and knees.

'Pigs! How dare you do this to me?' Her voice shook.

Moments later another orange followed, hitting Tara's ribs and bouncing off. Between hiccups, Tara tried to speak.

'Please, all of you,' she whimpered. 'Leave me alone. You'll hurt me if you don't stop.'

Ashley glanced again at the window. The figure had gone.

'That's right.' John spoke in a quiet voice, but the anger it contained cut through the pitiful sounds Tara was making. 'You deserve to be hurt.' He picked up a rounded, blackish object from the bowl and moved his scooter into position. Tara scrabbled to her feet, turned and took a step away, towards the fridge. Ashley turned back to John.

His eyes narrowed as he took aim. With his right arm he brought back the object like a fast bowler about to execute the perfect delivery. It spun through the air and struck Tara in the temple.

A collective gasp. Tara stood, swaying slightly.

'Fuck you, John. Fuck the lot of you! I hope you all rot in hell!'

Ashley felt her whole body trembling. Heat surged through her. She couldn't bear to listen to any more of Tara's foul words. She knew she should try to stop what was happening and help this pathetic woman. But she wanted to hurt Tara more.

She reached into the fruit bowl and brought out a green apple. She drew back her arm, despite its unsteadiness, aiming for Tara's chest, only Tara ducked. As if watching a film in slow motion, she noted the jerk of Tara's upper body as the apple made contact with her eyebrow, followed by a squeal of surprise as Tara's foot, on making contact with a purplish stain, skidded along the floor. A moment later, with a loud crack, Tara's head struck the corner of the worktop, her legs buckled and Tara collapsed.

Ashley blinked at the prone figure on the floor. A chill went through her. They were all staring at Tara. No one spoke, no one moved.

Tara lay on her right side, the hips and knees bent. Her upper foot twitched a few times, then she was completely still, except for the blood that was oozing from a wound at her temple. Around her, a colourful mess of fruit and fruit stains, not unlike a Jackson Pollock painting.

With an effort, Ashley walked towards to the prone figure. But it was like walking through treacle. Her leg muscles suddenly gave way, landing her onto her knees with a bump.

'I'm calling an ambulance.' John took out his phone.

'Wait!' Ursula was bending over Tara's body. 'Don't call yet. I can't find a pulse or a heartbeat. She's dead.'

'What?' John was shaking his head. 'She can't be.'

'John.' It was a command. 'Put the phone down.'

Greg squatted beside the body. 'Ursula's right. There's no vital signs.'

Ferne blinked at Ursula. 'How can she be dead?'

Ursula reached across to a dark green avocado lying beside Tara's body and held it up.

'It's hard as a brick.'

Silence, except for the hum of the fridge. Greg returned to the island and slumped onto a stool.

'We killed her,' he said.

'We didn't mean to,' Ferne wailed. She leaned over the work-top, propped on her elbows, her head in her hands. 'It was an accident!'

'That's right, it was an accident.' Ursula stepped away from the body. 'We were only throwing fruit, not hand grenades. We didn't know she was going to slip over and bash her head.'

'No, it wasn't an accident.' John's head moved slowly from side to side. 'I killed her. I didn't intend to kill her, but that isn't the point. I wanted to hurt her. My arms are strong, stronger than most people's... I'm the one responsible for her death.'

Ashley got to her feet and turned to John. She couldn't bear this. Whatever happened, he mustn't take the blame.

'No, you're not,' she said. 'I was the one who started this. It was my idea to come over here. I was first to throw something –

and the last. If I hadn't thrown that apple, Tara wouldn't have slipped and banged her head. She would still be alive.' It was true, as much as John's version was true.

Greg clenched and unclenched his fists.

'This is nuts. This is all our faults, isn't it?' He looked around the others, his eyes beseeching.

'The police will work out what happened and they'll charge us all with murder.' Ferne's voice climbed in pitch, ending in a wail. 'We need to get away, before anyone sees us here!'

'We can't just leave her.' John's voice was loud and unsteady. Red blotches stained his cheeks.

'If we did,' Ursula replied, 'would anyone know it was us who killed her?'

'They'll find our fingerprints on the fruit, won't they?' Greg looked at John.

'No, they won't.' Ferne gestured at the fruit missiles scattered around Tara's body. 'Not if we take this lot home with us and throw it away into our food waste bins – or we could cook it and eat it.'

'You're suggesting we eat the fruit that we threw at her?' Greg sounded aghast.

'Good idea, Ferne.' Ursula bent down and picked up the squished plum. 'I'll put some of this fruit in a crumble. It would be fitting, don't you think?' She smiled. 'Tara wouldn't want it to go to waste.'

'There will be marks from the fruit on her skin,' John countered, tilting his head towards Tara's body. 'Even if we take the fruit away, the pathologist who examines her will find signs of it, probably. The police will be able to work out how she died, or at least take a guess. There's not much left in that fruit bowl—'

Ferne lifted her head. Her face was damp with sweat.

'We could take the bowl, too.'

No-one replied.

Ashley turned away from the others. Tara's head was mercifully angled away from her, so she couldn't see Tara's face. She could see the blood from her wound, though. It had formed a red pool on the floor.

She looked away. The dim glow from the kitchen's up-lighters picked out the others' faces, making them unfamiliar. Outside, the last of the daylight had gone.

'We can't let ourselves be blamed for this.' Elspeth spoke for the first time in a firm, clear voice. 'It's not fair, not after what that woman put us through.' She went to the sink, picked up a wiper and rinsed it under the tap. 'I'll clean the fruit stains off her. Then it might not look as if a pack of crazy people attacked her.'

'We shouldn't touch her.' Ferne sounded frightened.

Elspeth ignored this.

'Put some gloves on first,' Ursula instructed. 'We mustn't leave fingerprints. And be careful, try not to disturb the blood on the floor.' She headed to the window. 'I'll close the blinds. Someone needs to clean the fruit stains off the floor.'

'What are we doing?' Greg protested. 'Do you really think we can get away with this? Someone might have seen us. On the way here, or when we were outside her door—'

'Who would have seen us?' Ferne frowned at Greg.

'The neighbours? Someone with CCTV?'

'It's four minutes' walk from my house,' John said finally in a low voice, looking down at his knees. 'I didn't see anyone on the way here.'

Ursula and Ferne said they hadn't, either.

'There isn't anyone between my house and here with CCTV, as far as I know.'

Ashley said nothing. This conversation was surreal. How could they be standing here with Tara's dead body lying on the floor just a few feet away, discussing matter-of-factly whether or not they should admit to killing her?

Greg frowned. 'What about people on the green?'

'I doubt there would have been many people on the green at

7.45 in the evening,' Ursula pointed out, picking fruit off the floor and dropping it into her shopping bag.

'You never know.' Greg wasn't convinced. 'Someone might have seen us walking here. And someone might see us when we leave.'

Ashley closed her eyes. She remembered, now. The woman.

'I saw someone outside earlier,' she said. 'A woman looking in when we were throwing the fruit. Bird Woman, I think.'

'Do you think she saw anything?' Ferne wiped sweat off her brow. 'Given the light was going and the blinds were half shut.'

'It's possible.' Ashley tried to picture the woman's face. 'Maybe not enough to understand what was going on.'

'She might tell the police what she saw,' Ursula said.

'I don't think she would,' she replied. 'Not unless they asked her directly.'

'What about your husband?' Ursula was studying Ashley intently. 'And your children? They might have heard something from next door.' She tilted her head towards Ashley's house.

'No one's at home. Sam's away camping and Zac is on his way back from Lincolnshire. He won't be home for another few hours.'

'What about the neighbour on the other side?'

Elspeth spoke up. 'That's me – and I'm right here. I live on my own. I haven't got anyone to tell.'

Ursula looked back to Ashley. 'Are you going to tell Zac what happened?'

'I don't know.' She couldn't hide anything from him for long, she knew.

'None of us need tell anyone,' Ferne insisted.

'Exactly,' Ursula agreed. 'If we all keep this to ourselves, no-one will know we had anything to do with Tara's death.'

'You're saying we should all lie to the police?' Greg glared at Ursula. 'To cover up what really happened? That's conspiring to pervert the course of justice. They'll work out she was pelted with something or another, which caused her to hit her head. They won't believe she just toppled over for no reason.'

'What's the alternative?' Ursula growled back at Greg. 'We risk all of us being blamed for killing her. We could go to prison.'

'Unless I say that it was me who killed her.' John's eyes flicked from face to face. 'I'll say I was the one who threw the fruit.'

'Woah, steady on.' Greg turned to John. 'Do you know what you're saying?'

John rubbed the stubble on his jaw.

'It's like this. For most of my life I used to be active – I played two sports at a decent level and ran five miles a day. Since my accident I've been confined to this chair, and now Bryony isn't around to cheer me up...' His voice became rough with emotion. He dipped his head. 'So I may as well spend my last years in prison as alone at home moping.' A wry smile spread over his lips. 'Hopefully they'll treat me well, given I'm disabled.'

'No, you're not doing that.' Ashley felt surprise at the force of her voice. 'I'm not going to let you take the blame. We need to tell the police that we all did this together. We all threw the fruit. We didn't intend to hurt her, not badly, only she slipped and banged her head.' It sounded lame, she thought. But truth was always the best option, wasn't it?

Lines raked John's brow. He looked at her, then down at his hands, which gripped the arm rests of his scooter.

'All those who agree we should keep quiet about this,' John said in a low voice, 'hands up.'

All except Ashley and Greg raised their hands.

'That's settled then,' Ursula said. 'We don't say anything to anyone. If anyone asks, we say we were at home.'

Ashley lowered herself onto a stool. She was desperate to wee. But she wasn't going to in a dead woman's house.

After Ferne had mopped the fruit stains off the floor and Ursula had wiped the work surfaces and checked that Tara's body bore no tell-tale signs, they all discussed when they should leave

Tara's house. They agreed it would be best to wait until it was properly dark outside, another fifteen or twenty minutes.

Ashley said nothing. She still couldn't take in that Tara was dead, and half expected to hear Tara's voice telling them to stop this at once, this was absolutely preposterous.

'Let's get going,' John said, once the fifteen minutes was up. 'Before someone finds us here with a dead body on the floor.'

They left the house in ones and twos – everyone agreed this was less likely to attract attention than them all leaving *en masse* – making sure no one was in sight before stepping onto the pavement. Of course, this wouldn't preclude anyone seeing them from an upstairs window, as Greg had pointed out.

Ashley was the last to leave. She retrieved the ball of screwed-up paper from the kitchen floor and dropped it inside her backpack, taking care not to look at the lifeless body, especially not the eyes, rolled back into their sockets, or the face, open mouthed and etched with shock. Then she clicked the front door shut behind her and walked to the house next door.

Chapter 57
Elspeth
15 August

E lspeth tapped three times on Ashley's front door and waited.

She would have phoned, given it wasn't yet nine in the morning. Only yesterday, Ursula had visited everyone present during Tara's final hours, to instruct them not to phone each other in case the police should obtain records of their phone calls or some such thing. 'Better safe than sorry', Ursula had told her. Even Zoom chats were potentially risky. All future communication was to be done the old-fashioned way, through in-person meetings.

'What is it?' Ashley opened the door. She sounded tense. She was still in her dressing gown and looked as if she'd just tumbled out of bed, her eyelids encrusted with sleep and purplish half-moon hollows under her eyes.

'I've just called the police, they're on their way,' Elspeth replied. 'They might ring on your door, too, so be prepared.'

'Oh God,' Ashley replied in a stricken tone. 'I'm not ready! And I haven't got rid of the journal yet.'

'Don't worry, just keep it out of sight for now.' Elspeth lowered her voice. 'They're not going to search your house for it, are they? They probably don't even know she had one.' If Ashley carried on like this, they would all be in trouble. 'We're concerned neighbours remember, not murder suspects. Take a few deep breaths and you'll be fine.'

Back at home, Elspeth carried on with her tidy-up and declutter, vacuuming in between throwing away various bits and pieces. If the police wanted to come inside to talk to her, she didn't want them thinking she was a slob.

The activity distracted her from her nerves, too. The correct answers to all the questions that the police might ask were tangling up in her brain. It was doing well for its eighth decade but occasionally made little slips. What programmes had she watched the night before last during her quiet night in? Oh yes... At 7.30pm she'd watched *EastEnders* as usual followed by a documentary about cosmetic procedures gone wrong. At 9pm she'd had a bath while listening to Radio 3 – that last part, at least, was perfectly true.

The doorbell went while she was checking her face in the downstairs toilet mirror. Two uniformed officers stood on the porch.

'Hello, are you Elspeth Chambers?'

'That's right.'

One introduced himself as Police Sergeant Mills and the young, bright-eyed man beside him as PC Lovecock. Elspeth smothered her inappropriate response. She must have misheard the PC's name, surely.

'You're worried about your neighbour, I understand? A Mrs Tara Sanderson?'

She explained again that her next-door neighbour had not answered her door or picked up her phone all day, and the last time she'd gone over a foul stench had come through the letterbox.

The officers gave each other a meaningful look.

'We'll be back shortly, Mrs Chambers,' the PC said.

'*Miss* Chambers,' she corrected. 'And Tara is a Miss too, I believe. She's never married, I mean.'

Without further ado, the pair strode over to number 33. Elspeth lingered on her doorstep, curiosity mingling with occasional twinges of anxiety. She had reluctantly volunteered to report Tara's conspicuous absence – or presence, to be accurate – to the police. Everyone had agreed that this would be in keeping with the actions of a friendly neighbour, though she should wait until the body had started to smell.

Elspeth went back inside. She didn't want to appear excessively curious, or anything else that might suggest she was a killer returning to the scene of the crime.

'We have some news, I'm afraid,' the PC said, some time later, on the pair's eventual return. 'Mrs – Miss Sanderson is dead. We found her body inside her home.'

'Oh my goodness!' Elspeth did her best to appear shocked, though anyone with eyes in their head would have noticed the police cordon that had gone up outside the house, now guarded by a uniformed officer, and the figures in head-to-foot protective clothing who had entered Tara's house. 'I did start to wonder though, given the smell. How did she die?'

'We don't know that just yet,' the PC replied. 'Could we come in and ask you a few questions?'

'Of course.' Her pulse began to race. You'll be fine, she told herself. Just breathe.

She showed them into the freshly cleaned, tidied and decluttered living room. They sat down in the two armchairs, leaving her to take the sofa, and launched straight into their questions.

'When did you last see or speak to your neighbour?'

'Um... three days ago, I think.' Her heart thumped harder.

Why couldn't she remember the answer that she had planned to this most obvious question?

'So that would be the 12th of August?'

'Oh yes, I remember. It was a bin day, Wednesday. I saw her just after nine in the morning, when she came out to put her bins back into position. That would make it the 12th, yes.' This was, in fact, the time before the last time that Elspeth had seen Tara, the afternoon that she and Ashley had drunk tea – and Ashley had jokingly wished Tara dead. She wrenched her attention to the next question Sergeant Mills was asking.

'Did you notice anything unusual about her? Her manner or her appearance?'

She pressed her lips together, frowning in concentration.

'I don't think so. She was in her leggings as usual and wasn't wearing make-up. Her hair was tied back – she didn't have the wig on—'

'The wig?'

'She started wearing a wig a month or so ago, on and off... I didn't like to ask why.'

It wasn't strictly untrue. The PC scribbled industriously in his notebook while the sergeant carried on with the questions.

'Have you noticed anything unusual from next door in recent days?'

She shook her head. 'No, I can't say I have.'

'Did you happen to notice anyone entering or leaving Miss Sanderson's property?'

'I didn't, I'm afraid.'

'You've been staying here at home for the past few days, have you?'

'Yes, most of the time.' She frowned. Did they suspect her of being involved in Tara's death, or did they ask everyone this?

The PC nodded.

'Excellent. Thank you for your cooperation, Miss Chambers. We may need to come back with more questions later. In the meantime, if you think of anything else that might have a bearing, please get in touch.'

They stood in unison. Elspeth followed them to her front door.

'This is such a shock,' she said, channelling her inner old lady. 'Tara was so very much alive the last time I saw her.'

Watching as they closed her gate behind them and headed to Ashley's front door, she couldn't shake the sense that something awful was about to unfold.

Please, let Ashley not panic and say anything silly, or stray too far from what they'd agreed. And please let the police not suspect that both Elspeth and Ashley were lying through their teeth.

Chapter 58
Ashley

'Y ou think I lied to the police? You think it was me who killed Tara?'

Ashley heard the wobble in her own voice. She and Zac were standing in the living room, awash with early morning sunshine. Ever since the police left, her husband had been peppering her with questions.

Why had she gone over to see Tara the day before yesterday – simply to have a neighbourly chat, as she'd told the police, or to try to smooth things over, as she'd told Zac – or for something else altogether? What had she and Tara – her avowed enemy, so Zac had believed – really spoken about? On the evening of the 13th of August, after they parted at roughly 5.15pm, as she'd told both him and the police, had Ashley really been at home the whole time, apart from a brief visit to John's for a meeting, and neither seen nor spoken to Tara?

Zac removed his hand, which he'd placed on her shoulder.

'It just seems strange to me. First, you and Elspeth have all these wacky notions about Tara killing all her family years ago. Next, you're convinced she's trying to kill the two of you. Then the police find her dead.' His nostrils flared as his voice rose in volume. 'And it seems that you were quite possibly the last person to see her alive.'

'I see what you mean. It does seem a little weird—'

'—a little weird! It's more than a little weird. It's as strange as hell!'

She exhaled to a count of five, trying to quell the flurries of panic. Her heart was fluttering oddly. Thank God, Zac hadn't mentioned anything to the police about her and Elspeth's 'wacky notions' and had left Ashley to do most of the talking. She had told them as little as she could get away with, hoping to convey the impression that her relationship with Tara had been cordial though not especially close.

'It might be best,' she said, 'if we didn't mention any of that to the police, should they ask in future. Or anything about Tara falling out with me and Elspeth, and the trouble she's caused our family.'

He rolled his eyes, motioning with his hands.

'I'm your husband! Of course I'm not going to tell the police anything that might get you arrested for murder. Whatever nefarious things you and Elspeth have been getting up to.'

She opened her mouth to protest, then closed it. It had been wrong to lie to Zac, very wrong. But because of the decision that had been taken the night before last, she had been forced to lie to both the police and her husband. She needed to tell Zac the truth about everything, right now. If he knew what she'd done to Tara though, would he be able to forgive her? And what about the others, and her promise to go along with their decision?

Ashley picked up her backpack, feeling through the material to double-check that the notebook was still inside. She had hidden it in her underwear drawer at first, then, unable to stop worrying, moved it to a shelf in the garden shed. But that wouldn't be safe, would it? She had to destroy the journal in case the police found it and realised what a strong motive she'd had to kill Tara.

She went to the bedroom window again. Light was draining from the sky. A pair of uniformed police officers was still going house to house along Wilton Close. An hour before, a white van had pulled up outside next door, taken receipt of a covered, body-shaped object and driven away, presumably to the mortuary.

When the officers were safely inside, she went downstairs, quietly closed the front door behind her and hurried across the road to the green.

Someone was sitting on the bench. Their outline and posture were familiar. A woman, broad-backed, shoulders hunched, in a cardigan over a simple cotton dress. Thank God.

She had spent hours scouring Brampton's birdwatching spots, in between knocking on the door of Clare's rickety cottage, thanks to the group's insistence that Ashley should speak to Bird Woman before she had a chance to tell the police what she'd seen. And now here she was, practically on Ashley's doorstep.

Clare looked as if she was dozing. Her eyes were shut, her lips were parted and her head sloped forwards at an awkward angle. Beneath one hand, a pair of binoculars rested on her lap.

Tentatively, Ashley sat down beside her, scanning the grassy oval and its spinney of silver birches. No sign of anyone. She glanced back at the house, hoping that neither the police nor Zac would notice her sitting here and wonder why she was talking to this woman. Remembering the packet of roasted cashew nuts in her backpack, she brought it out and opened it. At the crackle of packaging, the woman's eyes opened.

'Hello, Clare.'

Forehead creasing, the woman looked at Ashley and yawned.

'Hello... Ashley, isn't it?'

'That's right.' Ashley smiled. 'Um, fancy a nut?' She thrust the packet towards the woman. She felt awkward, not to mention manipulative. 'How are you?'

Clare looked at her as if Ashley had spoken in a foreign language. Ashley pressed on.

'I haven't seen you around much lately. I've been looking for you.'

The woman didn't reply, but dipped her hand into the packet and withdrew a handful of cashew nuts. Ashley ploughed on.

'About the other day... I thought I saw you standing opposite my neighbour's house, looking in through the window.' She turned and pointed towards it. 'Number 33, over there.'

Clare moved her head a fraction.

'Did you... see anything?'

'What if I did?'

Ashley swallowed to relieve the dryness of her throat.

'What exactly did you see?'

The woman cocked her head and looked into Ashley's eyes. Her lips stretched into a broad smile, revealing a missing top incisor.

'It looked like the woman from number 33 was being set upon by a group of people who didn't like her. They were pelting her with apples and oranges, that's what it looked like. And you were one of them.'

Ashley closed her eyes for a moment. She felt sick. What if Clare went to the police? Their plan would be scuppered – if it wasn't already. Once again, she silently cursed Ursula and Ferne for their haste to hide the truth about the night before last.

'But it was nearly dark – can you be sure what you saw?'

Clare fingered the binoculars on her lap.

'The light wasn't good, that's true. But I had my binoculars with me, didn't I?'

'You looked through the window with your binoculars?'

'I usually use them for watching birds, as you know. But humans are far more interesting.'

Ashley shivered. 'Have you told anyone what you saw?'

The woman's eyebrow raised a notch.

'Are you going to tell anyone?'

A slight movement of the head, which might have indicated 'no'.

'I doubt that I would want to tell anyone,' Clare said eventually, reaching into the cashew nut packet. 'Unless, of course, they had a good reason to know.'

'What if the police ask if you saw anything unusual at Tara's house?'

'Are you asking me to keep quiet about what I saw?' Clare popped a nut into her mouth and crunched into it.

'Would you?'

Clare looked at Ashley without speaking then pushed herself off the bench, momentarily grimacing.

'I'll think about it. I have to get home to feed my birds.'

Ashley watched the woman walk, somewhat clumsily, down the hill, one foot dragging slightly. She wasn't sure whether she felt relief or foreboding. Minutes later, after checking that no one was in sight, she walked slowly towards the copse of silver birches.

It was as good a place as any. Darkness had fallen; the meagre sprinkle of lampposts around the loop of Wilton Close added little light to the scene. The trees were close together, enhancing the darkness at the heart of this small green island. No one who happened to be looking out from any of the houses would spot anything untoward. Also, given its significance within a certain scene described in Tara's journal, the spot seemed particularly apt.

She took the empty PG Tips tin and the notebook from her backpack. She placed the tin on the leafy earth then tore out the notebook's remaining pages. Some she tore up into smaller pieces, others she screwed into loose balls. She dropped the resulting paper into the tin. Then she carefully placed the notebook's skeleton inside, took the box of matches from her backpack, struck one of them and lowered the flame to the paper. The paper blackened and curled, then the cover slowly disintegrated, until there was nothing left of the notebook except a thin trail of smoke, ash and dozens of small black flakes fluttering down.

Tara's secrets were safe.

Chapter 59
Bird Woman
16 August

5pm

I take another peek through my binoculars. From my vantage point at the centre of the oval, I can see much of what's happening without anyone noticing I'm not looking at the birds.

The police are still doing the rounds of the Wiltons. Today, they are only calling at certain houses and, when they are let inside, staying for longer. The pair in their smart hats has just emerged from the yellow-curtained house with the NHS rainbow in the window, where the exercising woman lives. A pair without uniform has been calling on certain houses, too. They seem to know they are on the trail of something important.

The investigation into the meddling woman's death seems to be gathering pace. It is certainly dominating the thoughts of Brampton's inhabitants, judging from their careless speculation on 'who did it'. In the snippets of conversations I've overheard, there has been mention of 'her neighbours' and 'the new woman'.

I put down the binoculars as the red polo-shirted American comes into view. He slows his pace as he passes the police officers and looks casually in their direction. He was another one of those in number 33's kitchen the other day, I'd be willing to swear.

What if I told the police what I saw? It's been on my mind much of the time lately. I'm sure they would be interested to know how six local residents gathered in the kitchen of the meddling woman and threw a variety of fruit at her until she staggered to the floor, shielding her face with her arms. Thanks to my honed observation skills, and meticulous note-taking after the event, I could describe all of the participants in detail – and sketch them too.

It's a shame that the dancing lady was one of the throwers. I don't want her to get into trouble, nor her friend Ashley. But someone should be brought to justice.

My intervention might well lead to an arrest, possibly several. I would no longer be ignored and invisible, taken for an eccentric, past-her-best woman who cares only for birds. Although why caring for birds should be considered a bad thing, I don't know. Why wouldn't anyone seek solace from their company – those small, innocent beings that don't store up hate as humans do, and enrich humankind with their colourful displays and exquisite songs?

Perhaps it's selfish of me, but I'm going to savour the unusual experience of having significance in this village. Whatever I decide to do, it will almost certainly have consequences.

Chapter 60
Elspeth
17 August

T he knock on the door came as she was preparing an early
   dinner, nibbling on seaweed crackers washed down with
alcohol-free beer.

For a blissful two hours, she'd been able to tend to the garden
and put Thursday's horrible events out of her mind. The police
hadn't returned, though uniformed officers had been buzzing
around the Wiltons ever since Tara's body was found. She hoped
against hope that they wouldn't find the death suspicious. It was
possible that Tara had collapsed after having a heart attack, stroke
or brain haemorrhage, wasn't it, or she'd had some underlying
condition that made her liable to keel over without warning? Any
marks on her head might have been obtained from her fall against
the kitchen cabinet, mightn't they? Even if they did find unex-
plained bruises and whatever else on her body, and suspected
something untoward had happened, surely the police would have
no reason to direct any suspicions towards Elspeth, a vulnerable
woman approaching eighty?

'Elspeth Chambers?'

'That's right.'

A middle-aged chap in dark trousers and a red-and-white

checked shirt stood on the doorstep. He had sideburns, an unevenly shaven chin and a twinkle in his eye. A velvety voice too, rather actorly. Beside him, a younger woman in a grey skirt suit jiggled from foot to foot. She had an unhealthy, unbecoming look; bags under her eyes and greasy hair tickling her shoulders, along with several white flecks. Both wore masks over their mouths and noses. They could have been canvassing for the Lib Dems.

'I'm Detective Constable Renn and this is Detective Sergeant Lister. We're investigating the death of Tara Sanderson.'

'Oh goodness.' She blinked at them, her heart racing.

'We have a few questions we'd like to ask – can we come in?' DS Lister spoke in a cold voice.

Crossing her fingers under her sleeve, Elspeth showed them to the armchairs, offered refreshments, which were refused, and hurried to get her face mask.

'What would you like to know?' She put on a bright smile, aimed mostly at the detective constable. The corners of his eyes crinkled in return.

'First, could please you tell us about your movements on Thursday 13th of August?' the sergeant asked, maintaining her immobile expression.

Oh dear, this wasn't good. It was what the police said to suspects, wasn't it?

'We ask as a matter of routine, Miss Chambers,' the constable interjected. 'There's nothing to worry about.'

'You can call me Elspeth,' she replied. 'Miss Chambers sounds like a woman from the Victorian era.'

The ghost of a smile from DC Renn, who started jotting in his notebook. DS Lister raised her eyebrows as if to chivvy Elspeth on.

'I was at home,' Elspeth said. 'I did a few chores in the morning and some gardening in the afternoon... For most of the evening I watched the television. There was a documentary on about cosmetic surgery mistakes. Then I had a bath and went to bed.'

'Apart from going into the garden, did you leave your house for any period of time during the 13th of August?'

'No, I didn't.'

'Did you speak with anyone, or see anyone?'

'Only my near-neighbour, Ashley. We had a brief conversation on the phone.'

'What time was this?'

'I'm a bit hazy, I'm afraid. Six o'clock, maybe.'

'What was it concerning?'

'Oh, this and that. I think I mentioned a cosmetic procedure I'm thinking about having and asked what she thought. Ashley isn't keen on anything like that.'

'Did you discuss anything else?' Oh, God. She had to get this right.

'She told me she'd been having tea with Tara. She mentioned Tara seemed much brighter, more like her old self.'

A long look from DS Lister.

'How long did you know Tara Sanderson, Elspeth?'

'I moved here in June 2003. Tara had moved in the year before, I believe... I must have known her for seventeen years.'

'What was your relationship like?'

Elspeth's eye muscle twitched. She tried to sit without moving any other body part. Did DS Lister suspect something was amiss – or was that rigid back and downturned mouth her usual look?

'We got on very well, mostly. We became quite friendly over the years. We were both home a fair bit – she had a PR business that she ran from home after she had to leave her office.'

'You were friends as well as neighbours, would you say?'

'Yes, I'd say so. We used to chat over the fence quite often...'
She painted a picture of two neighbours who were friendly with each other, mentioning Tara's propensity to do kind and generous things – for example, the time Tara had come over with a casserole

and a bouquet of flowers one year, when Elspeth had come down with flu, and helping Elspeth declutter the house and tame her wild garden. 'Back when the over-seventies were advised to stay home, Tara helped me out with shopping, collecting my prescriptions and so on.'

A cautious nod in return. Elspeth fished in her pocket for tissue and dabbed at the corner of her eyes. She longed to also dig out an annoying piece of apple skin that had got lodged between two lower teeth, but that had better wait.

'Did she have any other friends, to your knowledge?'

'There were local women she had coffee with sometimes... But I couldn't give you their names. Women she did yoga with, old colleagues from her journalism days, people in the village... There was an ex-boyfriend or two, a while back. No one special, as far as I could tell.'

Again, the constable wrote in his notebook. He was clearly the junior member of the team.

'What about relatives?'

'She mentioned two sisters who died a long time ago... Her mother is also dead, I believe. As far as I know she doesn't have any other relatives. None she was in contact with, anyway.'

She wasn't going to mention what Elspeth and Ashley had found out – that Tara had probably been responsible for the deaths of her mother and sisters – in case the police construed this as a motive for Tara's murder. It seemed a shame though, not to be able to reveal this nugget of detective work. For weeks she'd been picturing the moment of revealing everything to the police, then Tara being led away and charged with the murders of her family. Now Elspeth was the one in danger of being led away and charged with murder.

The sergeant frowned and crossed one leg over the other.

'Do you happen to know who is Tara's next of kin?'

'No, I'm afraid not. She might not have had one.'

Suddenly, she felt intensely sad. Tara had left this world

alone, with no one special in her life, hated by many... But the woman had brought it on herself, hadn't she?

'Miss Chambers... Elspeth?'

'I'm sorry, what did you say?'

DS Lister moved her head a fraction, as if irritated.

'What about enemies? Did you know anyone who didn't like Tara, or who might have wished her harm?'

Oh God. What should she reply? If the police talked to others in the village, they would soon find out the truth. Practically everyone had disliked Tara, with the possible exception of a few fervent right-wingers.

'I'm not sure.' She felt her face grow warm. The woman's eyes seemed to be boring through Elspeth's skull. Both officers were waiting for her to continue. 'I mean, quite a few people in Brampton didn't like her much. There was a bit of a scandal recently involving the food bank thingie she started, and she got into trouble on Twitter. Plus she did tend to rub people up the wrong way. She could be...' She grasped for the right words. '... rather annoying at times.'

'In what way?'

'She could be rather sharp with people, and quick to judge. Everyone but herself, that is.'

An appraising look.

'Oh, I was used to it,' Elspeth added quickly. 'It didn't bother me.'

A disconcerting smile hovered over DS Lister's face.

'You've been most helpful. One last thing – could we grab your fingerprints and a DNA sample for elimination purposes? We're asking other nearby residents to do the same. That way if we should find anything at the scene, it'll speed up the processing.'

'Yes, of course.' Clearly, she had no real choice in this. She let the DC swab her mouth and pressed her fingers into his finger-print kit.

'I think that's all for now.' The sergeant sprang to her feet. DC Renn got up more sedately, wincing as he did so and pressing his hands onto his thighs.

'Thank you, Elspeth.' He sounded apologetic. It must be difficult having a boss like DS Lister, she thought.

After they had gone, DS Lister's phrase 'for now' struck her. Did the pair expect to return with further questions? And why had they asked her for her movements on the 13th? The police had obviously worked out that Tara died on that day – and that someone or some people had killed her. Was Elspeth now a suspect in Tara's murder?

She drank the rest of her beer, picked up another seaweed cracker and crunched down on it, scarcely noticing what was in her mouth.

Chapter 61
Elspeth
19 August

E lspeth made herself a second coffee. Normally she wouldn't have two in one day, as caffeine kept her from sleeping at night, but these were unusual times. She needed to keep her brain alert in case Detective Sergeant Lister phoned again with 'something we forgot to ask'.

The police were combing the village, talking to anyone who had known Tara or ever had a brief conversation with her, by the looks of it, including everyone in the support group. Brampton was full of gossip about Tara's unexpected death, and the latest issue of the *Elven Herald* had carried a statement from the police, saying they believed that Tara had been murdered. They had launched an investigation and were appealing for information.

She fervently hoped that the police wouldn't find any witnesses to their arrival or departure from Tara's house that evening, or any other crucial information. The village wasn't chomping at the bit to get justice for Tara, as far as she could see. Many of Brampton's inhabitants had disliked the woman for being an attention-seeking hypocrite.

Elspeth swigged the rest of her coffee and tucked into a pancake smothered in maple syrup. Since the detectives' visit, her healthy diet had started to lose its appeal. Another lovely day lay ahead, she thought, ideal for a spot of gardening. Through the opened window, the glorious cups of petals beckoned.

Without warning, a memory arrived of Tara and Elspeth laughing together after that impromptu dance session on their back terraces. Before she knew it, she was wiping away tears.

Silly. That woman didn't deserve them.

Her landline rang, making her jump. Since the doctor had removed surprising amounts of wax from her ears, her hearing had improved no end. Ashley, perhaps. These days, scarcely anyone else called on the old-fashioned phone. Alice only phoned on Sundays, Mira always WhatsApped and Oliver, in New Zealand, hadn't rung since that disastrous conversation. Everyone else texted, emailed or rang on her mobile.

But it wasn't Ashley.

'Elspeth Chambers? I'm Adam Peters, a solicitor based in Brampton High Street.' He coughed. 'You are aware that Tara Sanderson has died, I presume?'

'Yes, of course.' How could anyone not be?

'Did she tell you that she had appointed you as executor of her will?'

She nearly dropped the phone.

'No, she didn't.' Why would Tara have done that and not told her? She and Tara had long ago had a conversation about wills, after a near-neighbour in his nineties had died, she dimly recalled. They had touched on issues that could arise when someone didn't leave one; Elspeth had mentioned that she'd made a will, and most of her estate would go to her godson. There had been nothing whatsoever about Elspeth acting as executor for Tara's will. 'Is there another executor apart from me?' She didn't fancy the job much, to be honest.

'No, you're the only one. You're not obliged to accept. There are quite a few tasks you would need to do as the executor, and there's usually a fair bit of paperwork involved to get probate, deal with the estate and so on. But given the circumstances, I'd advise you to consider taking on the executorship.'

'The circumstances?' Something in his voice made her sit up straight. 'Tara left me something of hers?'

'I'd think it would be better for us to talk in person, if that's convenient. Would you like to make an appointment to come to my office?'

She arranged to visit the solicitor that afternoon.

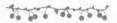

'You are the main beneficiary of Tara Sanderson's will, Elspeth. Which means that the majority of her estate will pass to you.'

Mr Peters waited for a response. She tried to grasp the meaning of his words, how this could possibly be. It seemed far-fetched indeed that the woman would have left anything to her.

The solicitor looked worried. His tone changed to that infuri-ating one certain people use when they think they're dealing with a dotty old woman.

'Are you all right? I imagine this is quite a shock.'

She peered at the youngish man in over-large spectacles in front of her. His nose and mouth were hidden by a throw-away paper face mask, which dominated his small face. But he was solid, an anchor to reality. She wasn't dreaming or hallucinating.

'Stay there, I'll get you some water.'

Mr Peters laid a paper cup on the table in front of her. The table was fairly ordinary looking and bore signs of wear, much like the rest of his office.

'I'll leave you to browse through that,' he said, placing the *Will of Tara Sanderson* beside the cup.

It was true, she saw, turning the pages. Tara had left Elspeth almost everything. Her entire estate – essentially the house and its contents – excluding her workout bicycle, hand weights and Pilates books, which went to Ferne, and her garden gnome, which went to John.

Ten minutes later, the solicitor returned.

'It all looks bona fide to me,' she said with a smile.

'Of course.' He sounded uncertain as to whether she was serious.

'When was this drawn up?'

Mr Peters indicated the cover of the will. It was dated July 2017 – three years ago.

No wonder. They had been on good terms, back then. But why hadn't Tara removed Elspeth from it since? Had she forgotten about her will, or not wanted to spend the money getting it changed – or had there been some other reason?

'This has certainly been a surprise.' She got up from her chair. 'Thank you, Mr Peters. I'll be in touch if I need any help with anything.'

He coughed and indicated she should sit back down.

'There's one more thing – it's not so pleasant, I'm afraid.' He gave his glasses an upwards nudge, looking sheepish. 'I should tell you that the police have been in touch, in relation to their inquiry into Miss Sanderson's death. We confirmed that Tara Sanderson's will was prepared by us in July 2017, and informed them that you are named as both the executor of the will and the main beneficiary.'

'I see.' Her heart began to beat faster.

'I expect they'll contact you in due course. I'm sure there's nothing to worry about.'

Which, for several hours after the meeting with the solicitor, was all she did. The police would think she had murdered Tara now, wouldn't they, because Tara had left Elspeth nearly everything in her will? Even she had to admit, it seemed a tiny bit suspicious.

Chapter 62
Elspeth
20 August

The detectives arrived fifteen minutes earlier than Elspeth had expected, while she was waiting for the toast to pop up. She was only halfway through her coffee.

'Hello there, Elspeth.'

It was the affable DC Renn. He had emailed to ask if they could return for a 'voluntary interview'. Beside him stood DS Lister.

'Morning, Miss Chambers,' DS Lister said stiffly. 'We have received some new information that might have a bearing on Tara Sanderson's death.'

New information? They must mean the will. Why couldn't they just say?

'We'd like to discuss it with you, if you don't mind – and it's an opportunity for you tell us anything else you may have remembered that might have a bearing on what happened to Tara.'

Her tone was neutral, though hinted that this was definitely one of those offers that one shouldn't refuse.

'Of course. I'm sorry, I'm not quite ready – I'm often a bit slow getting up in the morning. Would you mind if I waited for my toast?' Elspeth gestured to the toaster. 'I start feeling light-headed if I go without my breakfast.'

DS Lister gave a miniscule smile. 'Of course.'

'Go and take a seat in the living room, if you like.'

Obviously, they didn't want to leave her alone; they shuffled towards the hall, murmuring to each other. Elspeth managed to butter and marmalade a piece of toast and crunch through half before abandoning it, self-conscious at the thought of two pairs of eyes scrutinising every detail of her breakfast. She made sure to pick up her mug of coffee, though. No way was she going to do without that.

'Would either of you like a tea or coffee?'

The DC glanced at his boss.

'No thanks, Miss Chambers.' He pointed to his mask. 'We're supposed to keep these on. Er... could you put yours on too?'

'Of course, how silly of me.'

Oh dear, this wasn't a good start. They both seemed up-tight, as if on a mission. She wasn't a God fan. But if he or she happened to be listening in... Please, don't let her slip up, or say something she shouldn't. She was too old to go to prison. She wanted to enjoy her last years at home, tending her lovely garden.

Elspeth hurried upstairs and found her nicest mask, made of a green silky material. When she returned, the pair of detectives were waiting for her in the two armchairs. She lowered herself onto the sofa with the remains of her lukewarm coffee. At least the room was still clean and more or less tidy.

'There are a few things I need to explain,' DS Lister began. 'First, you are entitled to have a legal representative present, if you wish. Do you have a solicitor you wish to contact?'

'I'll go ahead without one.' DC Renn had mentioned this in his email and she'd decided not to. Apart from the hassle of finding one and the cost it would entail, engaging a solicitor might make her seem guilty.

'My colleague will be recording the interview.' DS Lister

pointed to a small sound-recording device sitting on her coffee table.

'It's standard procedure, nothing to worry about,' DC Renn said. 'We want to make sure we accurately record what you say.'

All this seemed dreadfully serious. She should have found a solicitor, after all, perhaps. But if she asked for one now it would delay proceedings, and they'd think she was messing them about.

DS Lister crossed one leg over the other and pulled her skirt down a fraction.

'To remind you, you're not under arrest. This is a voluntary interview, which means you can ask us to leave at any time. However, I need to caution you.' She continued in a chill monotone. 'You do not have to say anything. But it may harm your defence if you do not mention when questioned something which you later rely on in court. Anything you do say may be given in evidence.'

Elspeth's head felt light.

'Do you understand, Miss Chambers?'

'Yes, I do. You're not arresting me, though?'

'We'll let you know if we do, don't worry,' DC Renn said.

She wondered if he was trying to put her at her ease, or trying to psych her out.

'Someone in your situation would normally be brought into the station for questioning,' the sergeant snapped, frowning at DC Renn. 'But in view of your age and your recent stay in hospital, we decided that wouldn't be appropriate.'

For the first time, she felt a little afraid. Not being treated as an addled old woman had been refreshing at first – but not any more.

First, they asked about Tara's will and how Elspeth found out she was the main beneficiary. She told them the date that she had first been aware of this fact, which was when the solicitor informed her yesterday afternoon.

'Would either of you care for a biscuit?' A hunger pang had

interrupted her train of thought. Her bladder was bursting too, but she didn't want to admit that.

'No thanks, we won't.' DC Renn switched off the recorder. 'But you go ahead. I think we can dispense with the masks now too.' The sergeant looked at her watch with an irritated expression.

Elspeth hurried into the toilet, pulled off her mask, and sank onto the seat with relief.

She fished out her lipstick and touched up her lips, gave the tap mixer, toilet seat and flush button a wipe with the disinfectant spray then went to change the hand towel. She didn't want the police to catch anything.

Returning to the detectives with a fresh mug of Lavazza and a digestive biscuit, Elspeth quashed a sense of despondency. DS Lister's eyes shone. The woman was puffed up with a truckload of questions and raring to let them loose. Elspeth was certain that, armed with their new knowledge, sooner or later they would return to the will. But she was helpless to alter the course of their attack.

DC Renn flicked the recorder on. Immediately the sergeant, still masked, sprang into action.

'You've lived beside Tara for a long time, seventeen years... You described to us her frequent acts of kindness and generosity towards you. Before Tara's death, did it ever occur to you that you might benefit from Tara's will?'

She huffed out her indignation.

'For goodness sake! No, I didn't. I'm nearly thirty years older than she is – was. Surprisingly enough, I didn't spend my time dwelling on whether she might leave me anything in her will when she died. Anyway, do you really think I'd murder my neighbour because she was going to leave me her house?'

Elspeth folded her arms across her chest, glaring at both of them. That hadn't come out quite right, she realised belatedly. It sounded as if she *had* considered murdering Tara, but for some other reason.

DC Renn nodded and scribbled profusely in his notebook. The sergeant maintained her unvarying expression, as unmoved as a stone.

'So it was a total surprise when you discovered that you stood to inherit Tara's estate? In particular her property, an asset estimated to be worth in the region of one million pounds?'

This time, she couldn't stop herself from rolling her eyes.

'It was a total surprise, yes. I was utterly flabbergasted when I found out she'd left me practically everything.'

'Why do you think she did leave her estate to you?'

She waited before speaking. Was this a trick question?

'Elspeth?' DC Renn prompted. 'Did you hear the question?'

'Of course, I'm not deaf! I'm considering my answer.' She took a gulp of coffee and crunched into the biscuit. Caffeine and sugar would kickstart her brain into action, with any luck. 'I suppose because she was fond of me. We got on well, most of the time – we became quite good friends, as I said before.'

A trace of a smile appeared on DS Lister's face, though under the mask it wasn't easy to tell. Another question quickly followed.

'You've just told us that you and Tara Sanderson "became quite good friends". So, can you explain how was it that on 6th July 2020, Ashley Khan and John Briars went to Brampton police station and made a statement to the effect that they believed Miss Sanderson had tried to kill you by deliberately passing on the Covid-19 virus that had infected her?'

Sod it, how was she going to explain that? The police hadn't ever contacted her about John and Ashley's visit to the police; she'd hoped that they'd managed to lose the statement in a frenzy of pandemic-related misdemeanors. Clearly, they hadn't.

'It was a misunderstanding, that's all. Ashley and John had their doubts about Tara... They were well meaning, I'm sure, but they acted rather hastily. I was in hospital with Covid at the time – I had no idea they would think to do something like that.'

The sergeant tapped her pen on her knee with a thoughtful expression.

'Did you yourself believe that Tara had tried to kill you?'

'No, I thought she was basically a good person with a kind heart.' So she had, once.

'So why do you think John and Ashley went to the police and said what they did?' The sergeant's voice was sharp with frustration.

Elspeth flinched.

'Ashley's daughter said she'd seen Tara on my doorstep in her dressing-gown, shortly before I came down with Covid. It was all a bit ridiculous, really. I think they put two and two together and made five, if you know what I mean.' She was talking a little too fast, she knew. They would know she was lying.

'Did you ever have any concerns that Tara might try to harm you?'

'I suppose it did cross my mind that Tara might have done something malicious – we had a few words just before I went into hospital.'

'It crossed your mind that Tara might have done something malicious, i.e. infecting you with Covid?'

'Only briefly. I'd been getting hallucinations, my mind was all over the place.'

An eager look showed on DS Lister's face, that of a dog awaiting a bone.

'You said you and Tara "had a few words" before you went into hospital... Could you describe what happened, please?'

'Oh, it was nothing serious. I can't remember exactly what it was about now.'

DS Lister raised her eyebrows and indicated for the DC to let her use the laptop. She took it onto her lap, stroked the touchpad for a while, then indicated for DC Renn to collect the device.

'Could you make an effort to remember, Miss Chambers? It might be important.'

So, it was Miss Chambers now, and no *please*. That was a bad sign.

'She got upset when I said she should consider seeing a therapist. It was while she had Covid. She had been particularly prickly – as people often are when they're sick.'

DS Lister's brow furrowed.

'What happened that led you to suggesting to Tara that she see a therapist?'

She searched her memory. It had been lots of things, hadn't it? Tara's insufferable pettiness and envy. Stealing from Elspeth then having the gall to pretend she hadn't. Destroying the rose from Ashley... But she couldn't admit any of this, could she?

'Tara could be good fun, and was often affectionate and generous,' she said at last. 'But at the same time, she could be a little petty. It seemed to get worse when the pandemic started. I think she was having financial problems. Suddenly, she seemed envious of my clothes, my jewellery... And she thought I didn't appreciate what she was doing for me. Not enough, anyway.' She groaned at the memory, quickly turning it into a cough. 'She even seemed jealous of Ashley—'

She stopped herself abruptly. She was saying too much; she mustn't drag Ashley into this.

DS Lister's eyes narrowed, her brain clearly going into overdrive. She jotted something on her notepad.

'In what way did Tara appear to be jealous?'

'Oh, it was just little things.'

'Did you ever accuse Tara of stealing from you?'

With a jolt, Elspeth met the sergeant's eyes. Where had Stone Face got that from?

'Who told you that?'

'Several people we have spoken to have told us that they understood you and Tara had quarrelled about a week before you

376

were admitted to hospital with Covid. They also understood that you had accused Tara of stealing from you and informed Tara that you didn't want her help any more.' A smug expression hovered on DS Lister's face, before her features froze again. 'Would you please answer my question, Miss Chambers?'

Elspeth studied her hands in her lap, trying to shape an appropriate response.

'There's no rush, Miss Chambers,' DC Renn added with an apologetic smile. 'Take your time.'

'I should have mentioned it before, I suppose. But it wasn't at the forefront of my mind. There were a few issues, yes. I did suspect Tara of stealing a few small items from me, which was rather upsetting at the time. I also found out she'd damaged a climbing rose that Ashley had given me, deliberately. So I told her I didn't want her shopping for me or collecting my medication any more – I suppose our relationship changed a little after that.'

'Your relationship with Tara changed quite a lot over the last few months of her life, is that a fair assessment?'

The sergeant had an air of impending triumph as she waited for Elspeth to answer.

'Is that a "yes", Miss Chambers?'

'Yes, it is.' She felt like she'd done once at school, caught out for lying about skipping double maths.

'What was Tara's reaction when you accused her of stealing from you?'

'She denied it, at first.'

'And how did you react to that?'

'I was quite taken aback, I admit.'

'It must have been painful to discover that she had stolen from you. A betrayal of your friendship—'

'I tried not to let it bother me too much.'

'After you were released from hospital, did you ever ask Tara if she had deliberately attempted to infect you with Covid?'

'No, I didn't.' Frustration welled inside her. Was the sergeant trying to trick her?' 'I didn't want to be on bad terms with her. And she would hardly have admitted it if she had, would she?'

'But you said earlier you had suspicions that Tara may have deliberately infected you. I'm surprised you never mentioned them. I understand the illness resulted in you being admitted to hospital, and nearly killed you.'

Oh, what to say? 'I wondered about it, that's all. Later, when I found out...'

Perhaps it was the memory of that dead girl's face, her eyes seeming to reach out to Elspeth, so serious and so sad. Part of her wanted to tell the sergeant what Tara had done to her sisters and mother, that everyone present had heard Tara confess to their murders, moments before her death, and that the police should be trying to get justice for those slain girls and woman rather than hounding Tara's two long-suffering neighbours, whom Tara had driven to desperation. She stopped herself in time. Telling the truth would risk Elspeth being arrested for manslaughter, even murder – and Ashley too.

'Later when you found out about what?'

'It was something about her past. Nothing important.'

'Could I remind you to be frank with us, Miss Chambers.'

Briefly, she closed her eyes, wishing she could beam herself into a sun-kissed orchard. How she longed for another shot of caffeine. But the detective was mid-performance. DS Lister leaned forward, her face animated.

'If I may summarise what we know so far... We know you are due to benefit significantly from the late Tara Sanderson's will. We know that your friendship with Tara came to an abrupt end after you accused Tara of stealing from you and damaging a plant that Ashley had given you. We also know that – for a time, at least – you suspected Tara of attempting to seriously harm you by infecting you with Covid-19.'

Elspeth's stomach rumbled loudly. DS Lister swept on.

'Did you want to get even with Tara, Elspeth?'

'Of course I didn't.'

'Did you ever want to hurt Tara?' A flake of dandruff fell onto DS Lister's shoulders.

'No. I've never wanted to hurt her.' Another lie.

'Could you speak up please?'

'No,' she repeated at double volume.

'Did you kill Tara, Miss Chambers?'

'No, I didn't kill her.'

'You didn't go to her house on a pretext, then when her back was turned, hit her on the head with a heavy object – a glass fruit bowl, for example?'

'No, of course not!' Her voice trembled. How could they consider such a thing? She wiped her eyes, now filled with real tears.

'Did you perhaps take a piece of fruit from the bowl and throw it at Tara?'

'No, of course I didn't.'

'You didn't throw a piece of fruit at Tara that struck her head and resulted in her falling against a kitchen cabinet and fracturing her skull?'

'What do you think I am, an Olympic athlete? I'm seventy-eight. These days I usually miss when I try to toss something into the wastepaper bin from three feet away.'

'Perhaps, Miss Chambers, you handed the fruit to someone else, who threw it for you? An avocado, or an apple?'

She didn't reply. How did they know about the avocado? And the apple that Ashley had lobbed at Tara, making her lose her footing? Had Ursula missed them when she was picking up the fruit from the floor? Or had someone been telling the police what had happened?

'That's a no, is it?'

'No, I didn't hand any fruit to anyone. Nor did I throw any fruit at Tara.' With a wistful twinge, she pictured the tomato she'd thrown and the mess it had made squishing on Tara's cheek. What a pity she couldn't mention it to counter ageist stereotypes, and gain credit for the force and accuracy of her fruit-throwing.

'Then how do you explain the fact that fruit fibres were found on several places on Tara's head and body – along with bruising, lacerations and marks on the skin that indicate she had been pelted with fruit shortly before her death?'

Elspeth frowned.

'I – I'm not sure why that would be.' They were closing in, she thought. The methods they had these days were much more powerful than any of them had imagined.

The sergeant threw down her ace.

'And how do you explain the fact that your fingerprints were found on the fruit bowl in Tara's kitchen?'

What? How could that be? She hadn't touched the bowl itself, only the fruit inside. She might have forgotten though, in all the drama of that evening. Ursula must have forgotten to wipe down the bowl along with the kitchen surfaces... With a gasp and a huge wave of relief, she remembered.

'Tara came over with some fruit in that bowl when I came out of hospital. I took the bowl from her and put it back on her porch next morning. That's why my fingerprints are on it.'

Both detectives stared at her.

'What date would Tara have visited you?' The sergeant's eyes narrowed. She seemed cross, now. She had clearly been banking on there being no explanation for the prints.

'Last month.' Elspeth coaxed her brain. 'It would have been the 8th of July, the day I came out of hospital.'

'Could anyone confirm that this visit actually happened as you suggest?'

'I doubt it.' There wasn't anyone, was there? No one, to her knowledge, had witnessed the arrival or departure of the fruit bowl.

'I see. Is there anything else you would like to say, Miss Chambers?'

Elspeth shook her head.

'For the tape, Miss Chambers is shaking her head.'

DC Renn stopped the recorder and shut his laptop. With a wince, he pushed himself to his feet. He didn't meet her eye. The sergeant, needless to say, appeared impervious to the impact of her questions.

'Thank you, Miss Chambers. I think we're done here. Do you have any questions for us?'

'I'm a suspect then, I take it?'

Stone Face looked surprised and hesitated, as if deciding whether Elspeth was being sarcastic.

'You certainly are a person of interest to our investigation. I can't say any more than that, I'm afraid.'

There was more relish than fear in the sergeant's utterance, Elspeth noted. When the pair had gone, she went upstairs, lay on her bed and covered herself to the top of her head with the duvet. She didn't want to emerge for a year, at least.

Chapter 63
Ashley

After driving Ashley to the police station, for the interview that the police had requested, a uniformed officer kept her waiting half an hour while he faffed about with 'procedural matters' and fetching her a cup of coffee. Apparently the coffee machine was 'on the blink'.

'The detectives are on their way,' he informed her, once again. Sitting in the small, cool, damp-smelling room devoid of furniture except for a table, four chairs and a camera tucked high in one corner, she wondered how much longer it would take for them to arrive. It couldn't be coincidence, she thought, that they'd been due to start questioning Elspeth at 9am that morning. During a visit to the toilet, she'd phoned Elspeth to find out how her interview had gone. But the call had gone through to voicemail. The detectives must still be with her.

The interview was a voluntary one, the detectives stressed when they finally arrived – clearly the same 'knicker-ruffling' middle-aged male DC that Elspeth had mentioned and his boss, 'Stone Face', the female DS.

She was entitled to have a lawyer present, the DC added in a bored voice, adding that she was allowed to leave at any time and didn't have to say anything. He then said she was being interviewed under caution, and told her anything she said could be used as evidence in court, and something else she couldn't hear for the frantic drumming of her heart in her ears. Pulling her cardigan across her body, she prayed that the police wouldn't have found any forensic evidence that pointed to herself or Elspeth being guilty.

The DS asked most of the questions, leaving the DC to take notes and make occasional interjections. At first, many seemed innocuous. *How would you describe your relationship with Tara? Did you like her? How would you describe your relationship with Elspeth?* She tried to answer as honestly as she could, without mentioning anything that would make either Elspeth or herself look guilty.

Then the questions became more pointed.

'How did Tara react after you accused her of stealing from Elspeth during a Zoom meeting of the local Covid-19 community support group?'

'She was upset, naturally. After I said that, the group voted to exclude her. She got angry and ended the meeting.'

'And after that how did she behave towards you?'

'She was cool with me for a while.'

'Just for a while?'

'Well, from then on, with one or two exceptions.'

At every inconsistency and attempt to obfuscate, the detective homed in with razor-sharp claws. Then she played her ace.

'We've found the statement you made to the police with John Briars on July 6th, containing your concerns that Tara had transmitted Covid-19 to Elspeth, causing her to become seriously ill. Why didn't you mention this to us before, when it was clearly relevant?'

I hoped you wouldn't find it? I was scared, I thought it would make me look bad?

'I don't know. It must have slipped my mind – life has been a little stressful lately.'

'Did you accuse Tara of infecting Elspeth with Covid?'

'Yes, I did.' She could have lied, but Zac already knew. Also, she'd be in danger of tying herself up in knots. DS Lister seemed to possess an inbuilt, laser-guided lie detection system.

'How did she react?'

'She got angry with me. I did my best to avoid her after that.'

'We've talked to several people who say they believed that Tara held you responsible for her expulsion from The Wiltons' Covid-19 support group. Do you agree with their assessment?'

'I don't know for sure what Tara believed. We collectively asked her to leave the group because she had secretly sold off items that people had donated in good faith.'

'I understand. But you facilitated her departure, didn't you, by informing the other group members of Elspeth's accusations of Tara stealing from her?'

Bam. There was no escape.

'I felt I ought to tell them, yes. And yes, Tara seemed to hold that against me.'

'How was she perceived after her expulsion, by the village and people generally, would you say?'

'People were angry with her. She was mocked by some on social media. Someone on Twitter tweeted something about her that went viral. There was an article in the local paper that caused a stir in the village and nasty comments in the local Facebook group.'

'How did Tara react to all this?'

'She came off social media, I believe, and stopped going out of the house.'

'When did you next come into contact with her?'

'She came to borrow some butter, just as Elspeth was coming over for tea. I said I didn't have any and couldn't she get some herself? She said no, she didn't want to leave the house.' She suppressed a smile at the bizarreness of this exchange.

'So Tara reacted strongly to the situation that she found herself in, would you agree?'

'It was hard for her, yes.'

'Can you confirm that, in July, your house was sprayed with racist graffiti and your children were the subjects of malicious rumours and online bullying?'

She closed her eyes, sorely tempted to run out of this room and out of the police station. The detective was building up to something, and there was no stopping her.

'Yes, that's true. It wasn't long after the Black Lives Matter protests – some people in the village were trying to stir up trouble.'

'Why do you think you were targeted in this way, do you think?'

'Some people in Brampton don't like us living here. They see us as outsiders who don't belong. They don't like me being married to a Pakistani man who's a Muslim, or our mixed-race children.'

'Was there any other reason why you and your family were subjected to this anonymous hate campaign, did you suspect?'

'No.' Her voice sounded less certain than before. She had had suspicions aplenty, before Tara's journal had confirmed them.

'Did you ever suspect that you yourself might be the prime target for whoever was responsible?'

'I considered it – I considered just about everything.'

'Did you come to believe anyone in particular to be responsible?'

'There's a group of right-wing types in Brampton called the Patriotic Alliance. I thought one of them might be behind the rumours.'

'Did you consider that Tara might have been responsible for what you went through?'

'I wondered if she might have had something to do with it. But it was only a guess, really. My husband and I probably suspected everyone in the village at one time, you can imagine.'

The detective wrinkled her brow as if she couldn't possibly imagine this. Ashley adjusted her position in the hard plastic chair; her bottom was going numb. When would these questions end? This interview had become an interrogation.

'Was there anything in particular that led you to suspect Tara?'

'It was to do with how she behaved towards me, I suppose, and a few things she'd said.'

'How exactly did she behave towards you?'

'She was upset with me for me telling the group about her stealing from Elspeth, as I said before... and she was put out about me visiting Elspeth.'

'Tara was upset about you visiting Elspeth? Could you elaborate on that?'

'A couple of months after the lockdown started, I got into the habit of going over and chatting to Elspeth – outside, of course, in masks and well distanced. Tara seemed to dislike our friendship.'

'She showed signs of being jealous, would you say?'

'To an extent, yes.'

The sergeant tapped her fingers noisily on the table between them and glanced at her notepad.

'What did Tara say that made you think she might have been responsible for the hate campaign against you?'

Oh, God. This was awful. She scratched her head.

'There were a few things. I'm not sure I can remember them all.'

DS Lister smiled. 'Just one will be fine, to start off.'

'Tara sometimes spoke as if she disliked me – and she said something once that sounded vaguely like a threat.'

'Which was?'

'Something about her sisters – we weren't sure what exactly it meant.'

DS Lister made an annoyed-sounding tongue tap on roof of her mouth and studied her notes at length.

'Is it true that your daughter Layla was admitted to hospital in July after she jumped from the first floor of your house, a matter of hours after she had received abusive text messages and comments on Instagram?'

No, they couldn't go there. They couldn't bring Layla into this. She squeezed her eyes shut. But of course, the police had found out about that terrible night. The nurse at the hospital had said she was going to inform the police...

'That's true, yes. Layla had been struggling with her mental health for a while. I had arranged for her to see a counsellor, which seemed to be going well. But when another spate of bullying started online...' She felt her throat closing up.

'As you've already told us, you guessed that Tara Sanderson might have been ultimately responsible for the gossip and online bullying that led to your daughter's suicide attempt. How did you feel towards Tara after you learned what had happened to Layla?'

'I was...' She bit down on her lower lip. She had fallen into a trap, as a leaf is pulled by swirling rainwater into a drain. Long before, she had sensed it, but had been unable to stop herself falling in. 'I was angry with her.'

'In summary, is it fair to say that your relationship with Miss Sanderson deteriorated significantly in the weeks before her death, to the point that you believed that Tara may have been responsible for your daughter attempting suicide?'

She couldn't reply.

'Mrs Khan?'

'Yes.' Her voice small. 'That is true, yes.'

The sergeant's eyes flicked to DC Renn. *Are you taking notes on how to do it?* they seemed to say.

'Did you ever believe that Tara wanted to kill you?'

'How would I have known that?'

'Let me rephrase my question. Did Miss Sanderson ever give you the impression that she would like to harm you?'

'I wouldn't say so.' Another outright lie.

'But you went to the police because of your belief that Tara had attempted to seriously harm your friend and neighbour, Elspeth?'

Ashley stared at DS Lister. She was finding it difficult to speak. This was unbearable. She didn't believe in lying or misleading anyone, had tried all her life to do the right thing. But now, she was caught up in a web of lies. What sort of example was she setting to her children? Besides, if she was arrested and sent to prison for Tara's murder, how would Sam and Layla cope without her? Layla was still vulnerable; both needed a stable family and a mother they could turn to when in trouble. They needed Zac, too – so did Ashley, more than ever.

'Regarding a motive for Tara Sanderson's murder, it appears you have more than enough reasons to want her dead, would you agree?'

'You're right, I did have a motive. I was angry with her and I disliked her intensely. But I didn't kill her.'

DS Lister turned the pages of her notebook, then looked up.

'You told my colleagues previously that you visited Tara Sanderson on the afternoon of the 13th of August, between approximately 4pm and 5.15pm, is that correct?'

'That's correct, yes.'

'What was the nature of this visit?'

She tried to remember what she had said to the first set of police officers.

'I went over to find out how she was. I was a bit concerned as I hadn't seen her as much as usual. She asked me in for a cup of tea... We sat in the garden. She'd made some chocolate brownies. We ended up chatting for a while.'

'What did you chat about?'

She frowned, as if trying to remember. No one had asked this question before.

'She told me about what she'd been doing lately. She wanted some advice about her wig, if it suited her more than her real hair. She said she'd been thinking about going on a cruise to get away from the village for a while, after all the rumours and the bad publicity. I said I thought it was a good idea.' Where this came from, she didn't know. The detectives seemed satisfied, thank goodness.

'Did she seem to be any different from normal?

'I wouldn't say so, no.'

'Did anything out of the ordinary take place between you?'

'No, I can't remember anything.'

'What did you do after visiting Miss Sanderson?'

'I came straight home.'

'Did you speak to anyone?' A nod of the head, as if to encourage her to speak.

'I spoke to Elspeth on the phone for a few minutes soon after I got back from seeing Tara. She lives on the other side of Tara... Tara's house, I mean.'

'How long did you talk for?'

'Twenty minutes, half an hour.'

'Did you phone Elspeth, or the other way round?'

'I phoned Elspeth.'

'What was the conversation about?'

She looked at the detective blankly. Damn it, she'd forgotten what, if anything, she had agreed with Elspeth to tell police about the conversation.

'It was just a friendly catch-up. I wanted to let her know that Tara was OK – she'd been worried about Tara too.'

'And did you leave your house again that evening?'

'I popped out to John Briar's house for about an hour, about seven. He took over our community group after Tara... We had all agreed to meet up for a drink. We'd had so many Zoom meetings, we thought it would be nice to meet up in person.'

A flurry of questions: who else was at John's house, what was talked about, did anyone mention Miss Sanderson, what time did she leave, how long did it take to walk home... Ashley tried to commit her answers to memory. She had mentioned the group's meeting already, to the first pair of officers; the others had agreed that they ought to mention it to the police in case a neighbour or passer by had noticed any of them entering or leaving John's house, but they would say nothing about Tara or going on to Tara's house.

'After you arrived home from John's house, did you see or talk to anyone?'

'No, just my husband, Zac. He came home about eleven. We talked for a while then went to bed.'

'Did you return to Tara's house at any time after you left at around 5.15pm on the 13th of August?'

'No, I didn't.' Her heart thumped heavily, surely loud enough to be heard by everyone in the room.

'You didn't go into her house for a second time?'

'No.'

'As far as we can ascertain, you were the last person to see Tara alive. You admit that you were alone with Tara Sanderson in her home for between one and two hours on the day we believe she died, and that you had a motive for killing her.' The detective fixed her gaze on Ashley's for an interminable time. 'Marks have been found on the victim's head and upper body, consistent with her being struck repeatedly. Did you kill Tara Sanderson, Ashley?'

'No, I didn't kill her.' Her voice contained a tell-tale waver. She forced herself to stay calm.

'Did you enter Tara's house then attack her with a fruit bowl?'

She inhaled sharply. Blood drained from her head. This couldn't be happening.

390

'No, I didn't do that. Please, you must believe me.'

'Did you throw the contents of the bowl at her? Pieces of fruit, an avocado or an apple, maybe?'

She stared at the detective, forgetting to shut her mouth. Did they know about the apple she'd thrown – the last piece of fruit to hit Tara before she collapsed?

'No. No, I didn't.'

'We found traces of various fruits on her head and body, along with marks suggesting that the victim had been viciously pelted with fruit shortly before her death. Can you enlighten us as to why this might be?'

Oh God, no. She shook her head.

'I'm sorry, I don't know.'

DS Lister wasn't finished.

'We found an apple on Tara Sanderson's kitchen floor within four feet of the body, bearing your fingerprints. It contained a dent where it had struck an object and microscopic traces of the victim's skin. Residues of apple skin were also found on Tara's face. Could you explain to us how this came about?'

The sound of a giant machine roared in her ears, blocking out every other sound. Her own heart thumping? She shook her head again; the DC noted it for the recorder.

'Did you and Elspeth Chambers kill Tara Sanderson together, Ashley?

She felt an urge to scream.

'No,' she said again.

The DC asked the next question, his voice oddly gentle.

'You must have been very angry to find out your neighbour had caused your daughter to act as she did. I can understand how tempting it must have been to lash out without thinking. Did you kill Tara without intending to, Ashley?'

Yes.

It would have been so easy to give in.

'No.' A whisper, barely audible.

Afterwards, someone asked if she would like a lift home. She would rather walk, Ashley told them. It would give her a chance to recover, she thought, and decide what she was going to tell Zac.

She walked briskly along the High Street, not looking left or right. The clouds were low and leaden. The interview had been nothing like the ones in TV police dramas; nothing could have prepared her for it. How strange to think that her actions of that evening, just one week ago, taken with so little forethought yet at the time seeming so necessary, might in law constitute manslaughter, possibly even murder. Whatever charge might be levied at her, if proven it could result in a prison sentence, so she had gathered, from a search on the internet. The maximum penalty for manslaughter was life.

The detectives wanted to pin Tara's killing on herself and Elspeth, that was clear. If anyone had to take responsibility for their crime, though, shouldn't it be her? Ashley had initiated the visit to Tara, and had been the first and last person to attack her... Shouldn't she be the one to pay the price?

After the third knock, Elspeth answered the front door and led her through to the kitchen.

'What did they say? I'm having a G and T, do you want one?'

'Sure.' Ashley slumped into a chair. She didn't know where to start briefing Elspeth. She felt exhausted, mentally and physically.

'Did that DS Lister question you?' Elspeth looked ready to spit.

Ashley nodded. 'She didn't let up. It was gruelling.'

'What a bizum she is! She kept prodding me, pouncing on every tiny thing, all the while with a face that a stone would be proud of. The whole time they were here, I was expecting her to arrest me.'

'I think they might arrest us both, soon.'

Elspeth stopped preparing the gin and tonic and stared at Ashley.

'They know everything, Elspeth.'

'What do they know?'

'About you and Tara falling out, about Tara being jealous of our friendship and blaming me when the support group kicked her out. How we thought she'd tried to give you Covid. They know about her becoming a pariah in the village and that I believed she stirred up the racists to attack me and my family.'

Elspeth shrugged and squeezed lime into a tumbler.

'All that means is that we both have good motives to kill her. They can't have enough evidence that we actually did, or they would have charged us.'

'They know we were involved, though,' Ashley replied. 'They've found marks on her body where the fruit hit. And they've got my fingerprints on the apple I threw. They think the two of us killed Tara together.' The police might not need much more evidence in order to charge them both with murder, she thought.

Elspeth sighed heavily.

'They've found my fingerprints on the fruit bowl. Stone Face asked me if I whacked her on the head with it. I finally remembered that Tara brought me over some fruit when I came out of hospital. She handed me the bowl, so of course my fingerprints were on it.' Elspeth lowered herself into the chair opposite. Her eyes seemed deeper in their sockets than Ashley remembered, and the skin on her face thinner, with a translucent bluish tinge where veins showed through. She looked every one of her seventy-eight years. 'What are we going to do, Ash?'

Ashley didn't reply. She wished she knew the answer. Before arresting anyone, the police needed reasonable suspicion that a crime had been committed. Would their combined attempts to remove the fruit and all signs of their visit prove sufficient? Now, they had Elspeth's fingerprints on that fruit bowl and Ashley's on the apple. Neither of them had an alibi for the evening of August 13th and both had motives for killing Tara... She knew she couldn't resist this onslaught much longer. If it kept up, it would only be a matter of time before she confessed.

Zac barred her way at the foot of the stairs. His back was hunched, his mouth tight-lipped. He slapped his hand on the banister.

'What the hell is going on, Ashley? What are you hiding?'

She recoiled at the loudness of his voice. Rarely did her husband get this angry.

'I can't tell you just yet.'

'When can you tell me?'

'I'll tell you everything soon, I promise.'

Before he could reply, she pushed past him, out of the front door and into Wilton Close. Ten minutes later, she was with Elspeth and the group, gathered around the table in John's house. The meet-up had been called at short notice to discuss the latest developments in the murder investigation and the attempts to get Ashley and Elspeth to confess. This time there were no nibbles at the table, only mugs of over-brewed tea.

'Ashley and Elspeth might be charged with Tara's murder

soon,' John began. 'We can't let them take the blame for something we all took part in.'

'But they're the ones who started this,' retorted Ferne. 'We wouldn't be here now doing this if they hadn't quarrelled with Tara. Why shouldn't they take the blame?'

'Look, this is getting us nowhere.' Ursula looked uncomfortable. 'We don't need to make any hasty decisions. We can wait and see what the police do next. They haven't charged either Ashley or Elspeth yet, so they obviously don't have enough evidence.'

John looked up from the notes he'd taken.

'They've found Elspeth's fingerprints on the fruit bowl and Ashley's on an apple. They could find something else – or someone might come forward.'

Ashley spoke for the first time. She was tired beyond all normal tiredness; speaking was an effort.

'Clare saw us all in Tara's kitchen, remember.'

'Clare?'

'Bird Woman. When I talked to her she hadn't gone to the police. But she wouldn't promise not to report us.'

'If Clare goes to the police,' Ferne said, 'they could charge us all with murder. Or manslaughter, whatever.'

'No, I don't think so,' Greg replied. 'They'd only charge Ashley – and Elspeth, maybe. They're the only ones they have evidence against. The rest of us would only be charged with covering up their crimes... Besides, we'd be treated more leniently if we came clean now, from what I understand of the British legal system.'

Ursula tutted loudly. 'Who thinks we should all go to the police now and confess what we did?'

Greg was the only one of them to raise his hand. Elspeth munched on a carrot.

'I'm certainly not going to confess,' she said. 'I'm as guilty of killing Tara as anyone else here, I'm not denying it – and I would do the same again. She killed her mother and sisters and made their deaths look like accidents. She deserved to be punished, didn't she?'

'And we don't?' Greg's face reddened. 'If we told them the truth, that we were all involved in attacking Tara, the charge might be less serious—'

'Huh?' Ferne wrinkled her nose. 'How d'you reckon that?'

Ursula held up her hands. 'Do we have to do this? We're squabbling like children.'

'If anyone wants to go to police and admit what they did, that's fine with me.' Ferne's eyes were fierce. 'As long as they keep my name out of it.'

'If we confess, we all do it together,' John said, in a low voice, thick with emotion.

No one spoke. Ursula took a sip from her mug and put it down quickly with a look of distaste. The discussion continued without resolution.

Ashley broke a piece off her bar of chocolate and ate it. Maybe, she thought, it would revive her.

'We're going round in circles,' Ursula said again.

'I think I must have dozed off.' Elspeth yawned and lifted her head off her folded arms. 'What have we decided?'

'Nothing new,' Ursula snapped. 'We're going to carry on as normal and not admit to anything.'

'In that case, I'm going home.' Elspeth picked up her bag.

'I'll come with you,' Ashley added, standing up. She had something to do that she couldn't put off any longer. She wasn't sure what the group would make of it, but that wasn't her top concern right now.

'Of course, Ashley.' Ursula sounded conciliatory. 'You've been through an ordeal. Go home and get some rest. Your interview sounded horrific.'

John looked searchingly at Ashley but said nothing. She opened her mouth to ask him a question, then closed it.

'Zac, I have something to tell you.'

Her husband moved away from the set-top box, which he had been trying to reset. She hadn't told him that she had been meeting with the group, letting him think she was going for a walk, and had told him very little about what had happened at her police interview.

'Go on, then. I've been waiting.'

She shut the door behind her and sat down on an armchair. Zac stayed standing in the middle of the room.

'I want to tell you what really happened to Tara. You'd better sit down.'

As he sat, Zac's black hair flopped down over his forehead in the way it had done years ago, when they began dating. It made him seem younger suddenly. She felt a tug of love for him, followed by a ripple of fear. What if she was making a mistake? There were some things that couples shouldn't share, weren't there?

She took a deep breath and told him everything. Getting rid of the brownie Tara had served her, suspecting it was poisoned. Reading Tara's journal and discovering that Tara really had planned to kill her, along with Elspeth, and had orchestrated the smear campaign against Sam and Layla. Going with the others to confront Tara and attacking her with fruit, which caused Tara to slip and crack her skull against the cabinet corner. The collective decision to hide what they had done. Fleeing the scene of the crime with the others, after promising to say nothing to anyone, not even her husband.

Zac blinked, moving his head from side to side. He seemed bewildered, uncomprehending.

'That's all, I think. This morning the police asked if I killed

Tara – or if Elspeth and I killed her together. My fingerprints are on an apple they found on the kitchen floor and Elspeth's fingerprints are on Tara's fruit bowl.'

Breathing heavily, Zac leaned his forearms on his thighs.

'Say something, sweetheart.' After unburdening herself she had felt a surge relief. Now, only gnawing doubt. 'Talk to me.'

'I understand what you've said. I need time to process it.'

'I didn't mean to kill her. I only meant to let her know that she had nearly killed my daughter, and I held her responsible. But it got out of control.'

'What happened to the journal? Do you still have it?'

'I burned it. I was afraid the police would find it and realise the truth, why I was so angry with her...'

He rested his elbows on his thighs with his head on his chin, his hands covering his face, and didn't respond.

'Zac?' she prompted.

He lifted his head, not looking at her.

'I get how upset you must have been, Ashley, finding out what that woman really thought about us and her plans to poison you. She was a fucking nutter.' Anger leaked into his voice. 'I get why you lied to the police. But I don't understand why you've lied to me.'

'I'm sorry, Zac. I shouldn't have lied to you, I know. I was just... overwhelmed by everything. And I promised the others...' She put her hand on his but he pulled his hand away and walked to the door.

'I'm going to bed. Don't say anything yet to Sam or Layla.'

She tried again.

'Please, forgive me. I should have told you before.'

'You should have done, yes.'

He left the room.

It took her hours to fall asleep. She listened to the endless whirr of the electrical sub-station down the road, punctuated by Zac's slow, steady breaths.

Chapter 64
Bird Woman
22 August

Morning

My visit to the police station takes longer than I expect.

After I've waited fifteen minutes in a room with armchairs, a low table and, in one corner, a basket with toys, two detectives come in. They offer me a coffee from a machine and look at me with distaste (female detective) and surprise (male detective), then at each other with raised eyebrows, when I say I have information about the murder of the woman at 33 Wilton Close.

Initially, both seem to treat what I tell them with considerable caution. But, by the time I've told them everything that I observed while standing opposite number 33, on the evening of 13th August, and replied to their many questions, they seem to accept that I am telling the truth.

The female detective refers to me several times as a 'valuable witness' and buys me a hefty sandwich (avocado, goat's cheese and fig chutney).

Afternoon

At first, the dancing lady looks startled to see me.

'Hello... Clare, isn't it? How lovely to see you.'

Elspeth opens the door wider. She wears a stretchy top with thin straps, loose-fitting shorts and slip-ons.

'Hello, Elspeth,' I say. 'I thought you'd be up by now. Shall I come back at a more convenient time?'

'Not at all.' Elspeth smiles, showing off a line of perfect teeth. 'I've been up for a while but I still haven't sorted myself out... So sorry for my dishevelled state.' She asks me to come through and sit down; she'll put the kettle on, and some clothes.

While I wait, I study the view from the other side of the window, one house along. Across the street is the spot from where I observed the woman from number 33 – Tara Sanderson, I now know – being attacked.

Elspeth returns a minute later, this time dressed in a translucent floral-print top, silky grey trousers and wedge-heeled sandals. I am impressed by the rapid transformation of her appearance. If I manage to reach my late seventies, I shall endeavour to have the same sprightliness.

She asks what sort of tea I would like and gives me a long list of flavours. I tell her anything will do, but I drink PG Tips at home.

We settle down with delicate teacups, a matching teapot, a jug of milk and a small plate of individually wrapped biscuits. I study my corduroy trousers (bearing faint stains of dried-in mud) and jumper (bearing a hole in one sleeve and a loose thread in the other). I ought to have dressed more appropriately for a visit to someone's home, I think, not to mention the police station. Elspeth's scent suffuses the room. She reminds me of a beautiful, refusing-to-fade rose.

Elspeth says she wanted to invite me over before, but lately it has been one thing after another.

'First, I nearly died of Covid, then my neighbour from hell was killed and the police think that I have something to do with it.'

'Tara,' I supply.

'You know about Tara's death?'

'I saw it.'

Elspeth blinks.

'From outside, over there.' I point through the kitchen window.

'Have you told anyone what you saw?'

'I told the police this morning,' I say.

Her eyes widen. I crunch into my biscuit, which is crisp and utterly delicious.

'I told them I saw two people in the woman's kitchen throwing objects at the meddling woman,' I elaborate. 'An orange and other fruit-like objects. She brought her arms up to protect herself then appeared to stumble... I couldn't see the rest as it was below my line of sight. The police asked me if I could describe their appearance and I assured them I could.'

She gasps. 'You described me and Ashley?'

'No,' I reply. 'I described the two thugs who plonked themselves down beside me on the bench during the protest picnic.' I tap the pocket of my weatherproof jacket. 'I always carry a notebook for my bird observations. I was able to provide the names that they called each other and several distinguishing marks.'

'But... Why them?'

I tell her that I haven't been able to forget the disturbance they caused to everyone around them that day, and their foul behaviour to me and the two women I met.

'I thought I'd heard it all.' Elspeth stares at me. 'Why did you do it? You'll be in big trouble if the police find out you lied to them.'

I tell her I overheard some people in Wilton Avenue saying they thought the police were going to charge her and Ashley with murder, and I didn't want to see Elspeth or her friend go to prison.

'That wouldn't be right,' I add. 'Not that my solution is perfect, by any means.'

Elspeth isn't listening. She leans her head back against the armchair, a half-smile on her face, her eyes unfocussed.

'I thought we were done for. You don't know how much this means to me.'

I tell her I supplied the police with my sketches of the two men, and helped the police artist to create two 'photofit' images.

'Oh my Lord, Clare, you've saved the day! The police have their sights trained on me and Ashley. This could change everything!'

She springs up from her chair and hugs me vigorously. I cry out at the twinge from my sore arm.

'I'm sorry, my dear! I didn't mean to press quite so hard.'

'No harm done.'

Actually, I enjoyed the hug. I say I am glad to be able to help out.

'You're both more than welcome to visit me in my little shack. It's not the most luxurious but I have everything I need.'

'I'd love to,' Elspeth replies, as if I've invited her to my palace.

Chapter 65
Ashley
29 September

'W ho on earth is that?' Elspeth hissed, craning her neck in her attempt to stare at someone behind them.

Ashley stopped studying the stained glass windows of Brampton's St Mary's church and turned towards the well-groomed woman at the back who was picking up a *Service of Remembrance for Tara Sanderson* leaflet from the pile on the table. The woman, middle-aged, wore a formal black outfit with matching court shoes and mask, and an inquisitive expression.

'I don't recognise her,' Ashley replied. 'Could it be that reporter for the *Herald* who wrote that article about Tara?'

John arrived in a black coat and scooted to a pew at the back of the church. He gave Ashley a nod and an appropriately grave smile, which she returned.

'There's someone with a camera behind her,' Elspeth carried on, more excitedly. 'I think you're right, they're from the local paper... Now he's taking pictures. Are they allowed to, without permission?'

'There's hardly anyone here to object, apart from us, John and the detectives.'

The vicar stepped up to the lectern.

'Good morning,' he began. 'We are here to remember the life of a notable resident of Brampton, Tara Sanderson. Thank you all for coming along in such difficult times.'

'I suppose Tara would enjoy her funeral making the newspaper, though,' Elspeth carried on.

'Shush!' Ashley nudged Elspeth; they were in the front pew and would be conspicuous. Tugging at the tight waistband of her funeral trousers, she tried to devote her attention to the vicar's words. He was adeptly skirting all potentially difficult issues, such as the manner of Tara's death.

It was a shame, she thought, that so few were here to remember Tara – fewer even than the Covid-restricted maximum. Zac had refused to come, as had most residents of the Wiltons and everyone in the group, apart from herself and John. As Tara had had no next of kin, Elspeth had organised the funeral. She'd wanted to give Tara 'a proper send-off'.

'This pew is jolly hard,' Elspeth whispered. 'Could you pass me one of those hassocks?'

'Cassocks, isn't it?'

'Whatever.'

Ashley discreetly passed one to Elspeth, suppressing a giggle; Brenda Lark would be sure to notice if the two initial suspects for Tara's murder were to descend into gales of laughter at the victim's funeral. So would DC Renn and DS Lister. The detectives had turned up half an hour earlier, though the murder investigation seemed to have stalled.

No one had been charged in connection with Tara's death. Police had questioned two men, according to the *Elven Herald*. Someone in Ursula's choir, who knew someone at Brampton police station, said that the two men had been in a pub playing darts in a village twenty miles from Brampton on the evening of Tara's death. The police had wanted to charge the men with murder, only the Crown Prosecution Service doubted whether they would have been able to kill Tara and return to their darts match in time.

She had been relieved that the police had let the men go without charge – they were now pursuing two teenage boys, suspecting them of a prank gone horribly wrong, so Ursula's contact thought. It had been an even bigger relief to learn that the police had released Tara's body for the funeral, after a second post mortem had been carried out. Finally, it seemed that the investigation into Tara's demise was running out of steam, and she and Elspeth were no longer in danger of incarceration.

The organist began to blast out 'All Things Bright and Beautiful'. She wondered why Elspeth had chosen the hymn. No one else appeared to be singing, though Elspeth was making up for that.

She watched sunlight deepen the reds and yellows of the huge window while the vicar talked about the importance of forgiveness and reconciliation. His words struck her. Zac had not totally forgiven her for lying to him, but said he understood that Ashley had been placed in an impossible situation by the others.

Ashley looked at her hands, folded on her lap. The vicar was reciting a prayer, now. Although a committed atheist, for a moment she was tempted to ask that she be offered the job she'd applied for, or at least be shortlisted, and for her family to thrive. They were going in the right direction. Layla was making new friends and set on studying for a psychology degree. Sam Whats-Apped from uni every week. He had taken up boxing and was volunteering at a charity to help the homeless two hours a week.

'Oh God, it's me next!'

Elspeth scrambled for her notes and reading glasses and hurried to the lectern. She walked with a slight limp after her foot operation and took a few seconds to get her breath back. Despite this, she looked as stylish as ever, her black outfit set off by gold jewellery and her hair freshly cut.

'I'd like to say a few words about Tara.'

'Mask!' someone hissed. Elspeth hastily pulled her mask off and carried on.

'She was my neighbour for seventeen years, and my friend for much of that time. Our relationship had its difficulties – she could be abrasive and opinionated, and she wasn't a woman easily ignored.'

A loud titter from John's direction.

'She certainly made some mistakes – her actions have caused much heartache. But she could also be generous and thoughtful to those she cared about. Despite our many issues, I have some fond memories of Tara.' Elspeth glanced pointedly towards the reporter. 'I hope that something good will come from Tara's untimely death, and all of us in Brampton will do our best to put our differences aside.'

Rising from the sparse gathering, the sound of enthusiastic clapping.

When the service ended, Ashley strode along the aisle. She reached John just as he scooted through the wooden entrance door.

'Before you go.'

He turned to her. She checked no one was within earshot.

'Those two sports you played at a "decent" level. What were they?'

'I took up archery when I was in my forties. Before that I played cricket.'

'Were you a bowler?'

'I was indeed. A medium-fast bowler.' A wistful smile passed over John's face. 'I wasn't a bad player once. As a youth, I played for Nottinghamshire.'

'Your secret's safe with me,' she said. Somehow, she wasn't surprised at the revelation.

The two women sat on Elspeth's sunny terrace, dipping into a bottle of champagne left over from the wake. Rather more people had turned up to the wake, held in the function room of The Anglers, than the funeral. Free food and drink had been a factor in the better attendance, both agreed.

'The cupcakes went down a treat, didn't they?' Elspeth sounded chuffed. She had ordered them especially, each one iced with an image of Tara's face.

From here, they could see into the adjacent back garden that used to be Tara's, and on the other side, Ashley's own garden, in need of attention as usual. Stretched out in front of them was Elspeth's garden, splendid with its crop of late-blooming roses. The climbers were doing well, too.

'I wonder who'll move in next door?' she asked. 'It'll be strange to have someone else living there.' A *For Sale* sign had gone up beside Tara's front gate. Ashley couldn't get used to the idea of someone else living next door. Elspeth, not wanting any of Tara's money for herself, had offered to use the house sale proceeds to repair and refurbish Clare's cottage. Clare had gratefully accepted.

'Not another unhinged killer, hopefully.' Elspeth examined her fingernails, painted a dramatic shade of purple. 'I still don't get why Tara left her estate to me. I know the will was made back when we were friends, but even so...' She looked up. 'Maybe after she decided to do away with us, she was devious enough to realise that it would be best not to change her will, in case the police were suspicious.'

'Maybe she just forgot to change it,' Ashley replied. 'I think she loved you, in her own way. That's why she left you everything. When I came along, she thought I was taking you away from her.

That's why she got so angry with me – and with you, for leaving her.'

'...and for having some nice jewellery.'

'I suppose we'll never know what really went on in her head, will we?'

Elspeth huffed. 'I think we found out quite enough in that journal of hers.'

They sipped from their flutes, not talking, looking down at the garden below and its late-blooming roses. Then Elspeth glanced at Ashley.

'Are you still deciding whether to stay?'

'Not any more. I want to stay in Brampton, so do Zac and Layla.'

This village wasn't perfect, by any means; certain people still reacted to her family with a degree of unfriendliness, sometimes hostility. But Brampton would do. The other day, walking back up the hill, she had said hello back to two residents of the Wiltons, waved to John, who was zipping past on his souped-up scooter, and stopped at the bench on the green to chat to Clare. A strange ease and contentment had settled over her. This place was her home now, wasn't it?

'I'm so glad, Ash. I'd miss you if you went away.'

'I meant to say this before.' Ashley put her hand on Elspeth's forearm. 'Thanks for saving my life. If you hadn't messaged me, I'd have eaten all of that chocolate brownie – and I might not be here now.'

'That's quite all right, my dear. Anyway, you saved mine too, don't forget. If I'd been lying unconscious on the flowerbed any longer...' Elspeth poured more champagne and held up her glass. Her earrings glinted in the sunshine, nearly as brightly as her smile. 'To friendship. And triumph over adversity!'

Ashley brought her glass up to Elspeth's. Hopefully, they would both be around for a few years yet. She had a feeling that they were going to become good friends.

Acknowledgments

Thanks to Rebecca Collins and Adrian Hobart at Hobeck Books for their continuing hard work and enthusiasm, and to the Hobeck authors who have offered their support, in particular Linda Huber. Thanks to designer Jane Mapp for creating a brilliant cover for my book, and my diligent copyeditor Sue Davison for weeding out all the errors and inconsistencies in my manuscript, from characters' ages to what they remembered when.

Huge thanks to Graham Bartlett and Kieron Freeburn for their invaluable advice relating to police procedures, and to Brian Price for his advice and suggestions on both the police side and forensics.

Thanks to all *The Bad Neighbour* blog tour participants and thanks to everyone who's shown support for this in any way whatsoever – whether that's shouting about the book on social media, reading an advance copy, or anything else. I'm grateful to everyone who has bought a copy of *The Bad Neighbour*, including some loyal readers who have read every single one of my books. If you enjoyed this one, please do tell a friend or review on Amazon, etc!

A special thank you to authors S.E. Lynes, Leigh Russell, Keri Beevis, Jackie Fraser and Alex Day.

Three cheers to all at my writers group who read sections of the draft novel and told me exactly what they thought! You guys are the best.

Thanks to my friends for their enthusiasm and support over

the years, especially Miranda Hampton, Lumiel Cunin-Tischler, Jacki Hall, Janet McCunn, Runilla Chilton (also for her interviewing skills) and Diana Berriman (also for her ability to bring my characters to life in readings).

Thank you Stuart, for everything.

About the Author

Jennie Ensor is a Londoner with Irish heritage. She lives with her husband and Airedale terrier in London and the mountains of south-west France. She writes dark-themed, daring fiction: mainly crime, psychological suspense and thrillers, sometimes with a thread of dark humour. Her last book, psychological crime thriller, *Silenced*, was a semi-finalist in the 2022 Book Bloggers Novel of the Year competition, and appeared in seven 'best books of the year' lists. Jennie's previous books include *The Girl in His Eyes* and *Blind Side*.

Jennie began her writing career as a freelance journalist, writing investigative pieces on subjects from corporate malpractice to forced marriages before turning to writing fiction. As well as novels she writes short stories and poetry, some of which has been placed in competitions. Her prose poem 'Lost Connection' placed second in the 2020 Fish Lockdown Prize. In her spare time (?) she reads widely, sings in a choir, practices yoga and cycles. When not doing all that she enjoys watching TV drama (*Happy Valley, The Sinner, The Split...*).

Find out more about Jennie (and see photos of her dog, favourite walks, etc) on social media and her website https://jennieensor.com.

Hobeck Books – the home of great stories

We hope you've enjoyed reading Jennie Ensor's novel. Jennie has also written a short story prequel to her last Hobeck novel, *Saviour*.

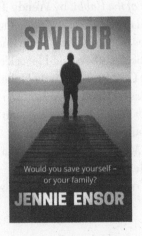

This story, and many other short stories and novellas, is included in the compilation *Crime Bites*. *Crime Bites* is available for free to subscribers of Hobeck Books.

Crime Bites includes:

- *Echo Rock* by Robert Daws
- *Old Dogs, Old Tricks* by AB Morgan
- *The Silence of the Rabbit* by Wendy Turbin
- *Never Mind the Baubles: An Anthology of Twisted Winter Tales* by the Hobeck Team (including all the current Hobeck authors and Hobeck's two publishers)
- *The Clarice Cliff Vase* by Linda Huber
- *Here She Lies* by Kerena Swan
- *The Macnab Principle* by R.D. Nixon
- *Fatal Beginnings* by Brian Price
- *A Defining Moment* by Lin Le Versha
- *Saviour* by Jennie Ensor
- *You Can't Trust Anyone These Days* by Maureen Myant

Also please visit the Hobeck Books website for details of our other superb authors and their books, and if you would like to get in touch, we would love to hear from you.

Hobeck Books also presents a weekly podcast, the Hobcast,

where founders Adrian Hobart and Rebecca Collins discuss all things book related, key issues from each week, including the ups and downs of running a creative business. Each episode includes an interview with one of the people who make Hobeck possible: the editors, the authors, the cover designers. These are the people who help Hobeck bring great stories to life. Without them, Hobeck wouldn't exist. The Hobcast can be listened to from all the usual platforms but it can also be found on the Hobeck website: **www.hobeck.net/hobcast**.

Also by Jennie Ensor

"Sally Rooney meets Lynda La Plant." — Kerensa Jennings, author of literary thriller, *Seas of Snow*

"...storytelling of the highest order..." — Alex Day, author of *The Best of Friends* and *The Missing Twin*

"Crime fiction at its best." — Ian Skewis, author of *A Murder of Crows*

The Girl in His Eyes

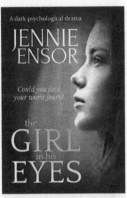

Abused as a child, a woman believes her father is grooming a new victim.

Laura, a young woman struggling to deal with what her father did to her a decade ago, is horrified to realize that the girl he takes swimming might be his next victim. Emma is twelve—the age Laura was when her father took away her innocence.

Intimidated by her father's rages, Laura has never told anyone the truth about her childhood. Now she must decide whether she has the courage to expose him and face the consequences.

Also by Jennie Ensor

Can Laura overcome her fear and save Emma before the worst happens?

"A must read." — James Jansen

"Compulsive." — Sebnem Sanders

"Highly recommended." — H.M. Holten

Blind Side

Can you ever truly know someone? And what if you suspect the unthinkable?

London, 2005.

Despite her friends' warnings, a young Englishwoman can't resist her attraction to a charismatic Russian ex-soldier recently arrived in London. But, realising how deeply war-time incidents have affected him, she starts to suspect that he's hiding a horrifying secret...

Set in the year of London's 7/7 bus and tube terrorism attacks,

Also by Jennie Ensor

Blind Side is a powerful tale of love and friendship, trauma and betrayal, secrets and obsession.

"builds suspense brilliantly" — Gail Cleare, USA Today bestselling author

"An absolutely stunning debut." — The Book Magnet

Not Having It All

Bea Hudson juggles her job at the 'Psycho Lab' with looking after her demanding five-year-old daughter, badly-behaved dog and ex-au pair. When her chief executive husband Kurt is sent overseas and she's left without childcare, Bea turns to best friend Maddie for help.

Kurt, downing whiskies in his overheated hotel room, convinces himself that Bea is having an affair with Maddie. He persuades a neighbour to spy on the pair.

Maddie, meanwhile, longs for a child of her own with a man she can trust – and he must love cats. She meets divorced, risk-averse

Also by Jennie Ensor

Colin in a lift. He's smitten, and resolves to displace Maddie's feline companions. But he starts to fear that Maddie sees him only as a 'handy stud with a fat wallet'...
Can Bea and Kurt find happiness again? Can Maddie and Colin risk falling in love?

"This is something different, and Jennie Ensor has totally cracked it." – bestselling author, Anita Waller

Ingram Content Group UK Ltd.
Milton Keynes UK
UKHW041826080623
423093UK00004B/16

9 781915 817101